Mike

P. G. Wodehouse

Mike

The present edition is a reproduction of previous publication of this classic work. Minor typographical errors may have been corrected without note, however, for an authentic reading experience the spelling, punctuation, and capitalization have been retained from the original text.

ISBN: 978-1-64799-286-6

CONTENTS

CHAPTER I

MIKE

It was a morning in the middle of April, and the Jackson family were consequently breakfasting in comparative silence. The cricket season had not begun, and except during the cricket season they were in the habit of devoting their powerful minds at breakfast almost exclusively to the task of victualling against the labours of the day. In May, June, July, and August the silence was broken. The three grown-up Jacksons played regularly in first-class cricket, and there was always keen competition among their brothers and sisters for the copy of the Sportsman which was to be found on the hall table with the letters. Whoever got it usually gloated over it in silence till urged wrathfully by the multitude to let them know what had happened; when it would appear that Joe had notched his seventh century, or that Reggie had been run out when he was just getting set, or, as sometimes occurred, that that ass Frank had dropped Fry or Hayward in the slips before he had scored, with the result that the spared expert had made a couple of hundred and was still going strong.

In such a case the criticisms of the family circle, particularly of the smaller Jackson sisters, were so breezy and unrestrained that Mrs. Jackson generally felt it necessary to apply the closure. Indeed, Marjory Jackson, aged fourteen, had on three several occasions been fined pudding at lunch for her caustic comments on the batting of her brother Reggie in important fixtures. Cricket was a tradition in the family, and the ladies, unable to their sorrow to play the game themselves, were resolved that it should not be their fault if the standard was not kept up.

On this particular morning silence reigned. A deep gasp from some small Jackson, wrestling with bread-and-milk, and an occasional remark from Mr. Jackson on the letters he was reading, alone broke it.

"Mike's late again," said Mrs. Jackson plaintively, at last.

"He's getting up," said Marjory. "I went in to see what he was doing, and he was asleep. So," she added with a satanic chuckle, "I squeezed a sponge over him. He swallowed an awful lot, and then he woke up, and tried to catch me, so he's certain to be down soon."

"Marjory!"

"Well, he was on his back with his mouth wide open. I had to. He was snoring like anything."

"You might have choked him."

"I did," said Marjory with satisfaction. "Jam, please, Phyllis, you pig."

Mr. Jackson looked up.

"Mike will have to be more punctual when he goes to Wrykyn," he said.

"Oh, father, is Mike going to Wrykyn?" asked Marjory. "When?"

"Next term," said Mr. Jackson. "I've just heard from Mr. Wain," he added across the table to Mrs. Jackson. "The house is full, but he is turning a small room into an extra dormitory, so he can take Mike after all."

The first comment on this momentous piece of news came from Bob Jackson. Bob was eighteen. The following term would be his last at Wrykyn, and, having won through so far without the infliction of a small brother, he disliked the prospect of not being allowed to finish as he had begun.

"I say!" he said. "What?"

"He ought to have gone before," said Mr. Jackson. "He's fifteen. Much too old for that private school. He has had it all his own way there, and it isn't good for him."

"He's got cheek enough for ten," agreed Bob.

"Wrykyn will do him a world of good."

"We aren't in the same house. That's one comfort."

Bob was in Donaldson's. It softened the blow to a certain extent that Mike should be going to Wain's. He had the same feeling for Mike that most boys of eighteen have for their fifteen-year-old brothers. He was fond of him in the abstract, but preferred him at a distance.

Marjory gave tongue again. She had rescued the jam from Phyllis, who had shown signs of finishing it, and was now at liberty to turn her mind to less pressing matters. Mike was her special ally, and anything that affected his fortunes affected her.

"Hooray! Mike's going to Wrykyn. I bet he gets into the first eleven his first term."

"Considering there are eight old colours left," said Bob loftily, "besides heaps of last year's seconds, it's hardly likely that a kid like Mike'll get a look in. He might get his third, if he sweats."

The aspersion stung Marjory.

"I bet he gets in before you, anyway," she said.

Bob disdained to reply. He was among those heaps of last year's seconds to whom he had referred. He was a sound bat, though lacking the brilliance of his elder brothers, and he fancied that his cap was a certainty this season. Last year he had been tried once or twice. This year it should be all right.

Mrs. Jackson intervened.

"Go on with your breakfast, Marjory," she said. "You mustn't say 'I bet' so much."

Marjory bit off a section of her slice of bread-and-jam.

"Anyhow, I bet he does," she muttered truculently through it.

There was a sound of footsteps in the passage outside. The door opened, and the missing member of the family appeared. Mike

2

Jackson was tall for his age. His figure was thin and wiry. His arms and legs looked a shade too long for his body. He was evidently going to be very tall some day. In face, he was curiously like his brother Joe, whose appearance is familiar to every one who takes an interest in first-class cricket. The resemblance was even more marked on the cricket field. Mike had Joe's batting style to the last detail. He was a pocket edition of his century-making brother. "Hullo," he said, "sorry I'm late."

This was mere stereo. He had made the same remark nearly every morning since the beginning of the holidays.

"All right, Marjory, you little beast," was his reference to the sponge incident.

His third remark was of a practical nature.

"I say, what's under that dish?"

"Mike," began Mr. Jackson—this again was stereo—"you really must learn to be more punctual—"

He was interrupted by a chorus.

"Mike, you're going to Wrykyn next term," shouted Marjory.

"Mike, father's just had a letter to say you're going to Wrykyn next term." From Phyllis.

"Mike, you're going to Wrykyn." From Ella.

Gladys Maud Evangeline, aged three, obliged with a solo of her own composition, in six-eight time, as follows: "Mike Wryky. Mike Wryky. Mike Wryke Wryke Wryke Mike Wryke Wryke Mike Wryke Mike Wryke."

"Oh, put a green baize cloth over that kid, somebody," groaned Bob.

Whereat Gladys Maud, having fixed him with a chilly stare for some seconds, suddenly drew a long breath, and squealed deafeningly for more milk.

Mike looked round the table. It was a great moment. He rose to it with the utmost dignity.

"Good," he said. "I say, what's under that dish?"

After breakfast, Mike and Marjory went off together to the meadow at the end of the garden. Saunders, the professional, assisted by the gardener's boy, was engaged in putting up the net. Mr. Jackson believed in private coaching; and every spring since Joe, the eldest of the family, had been able to use a bat a man had come down from the Oval to teach him the best way to do so. Each of the boys in turn had passed from spectators to active participants in the net practice in the meadow. For several years now Saunders had been the chosen man, and his attitude towards the Jacksons was that of the Faithful Old Retainer in melodrama. Mike was his special favourite. He felt that in him he had material of the finest order to work upon. There was nothing the matter with Bob. In Bob he would turn out a good, sound article. Bob would be a Blue in his third or fourth year, and probably a

3

creditable performer among the rank and file of a county team later on. But he was not a cricket genius, like Mike. Saunders would lie awake at night sometimes thinking of the possibilities that were in Mike. The strength could only come with years, but the style was there already. Joe's style, with improvements.

Mike put on his pads; and Marjory walked with the professional to the bowling crease.

"Mike's going to Wrykyn next term, Saunders," she said. "All the boys were there, you know. So was father, ages ago."

"Is he, miss? I was thinking he would be soon."

"Do you think he'll get into the school team?"

"School team, miss! Master Mike get into a school team! He'll be playing for England in another eight years. That's what he'll be playing for."

"Yes, but I meant next term. It would be a record if he did. Even Joe only got in after he'd been at school two years. Don't you think he might, Saunders? He's awfully good, isn't he? He's better than Bob, isn't he? And Bob's almost certain to get in this term."

Saunders looked a little doubtful.

"Next term!" he said. "Well, you see, miss, it's this way. It's all there, in a manner of speaking, with Master Mike. He's got as much style as Mr. Joe's got, every bit. The whole thing is, you see, miss, you get these young gentlemen of eighteen, and nineteen perhaps, and it stands to reason they're stronger. There's a young gentleman, perhaps, doesn't know as much about what I call real playing as Master Mike's forgotten; but then he can hit 'em harder when he does hit 'em, and that's where the runs come in. They aren't going to play Master Mike because he'll be in the England team when he leaves school. They'll give the cap to somebody that can make a few then and there."

"But Mike's jolly strong."

"Ah, I'm not saying it mightn't be, miss. I was only saying don't count on it, so you won't be disappointed if it doesn't happen. It's quite likely that it will, only all I say is don't count on it. I only hope that they won't knock all the style out of him before they're done with him. You know these school professionals, miss."

"No, I don't, Saunders. What are they like?"

"Well, there's too much of the come-right-out-at-everything about 'em for my taste. Seem to think playing forward the alpha and omugger of batting. They'll make him pat balls back to the bowler which he'd cut for twos and threes if he was left to himself. Still, we'll hope for the best, miss. Ready, Master Mike? Play."

As Saunders had said, it was all there. Of Mike's style there could be no doubt. To-day, too, he was playing more strongly than usual. Marjory had to run to the end of the meadow to fetch one straight drive. "He hit that hard enough, didn't he, Saunders?" she asked, as she returned the ball.

4

"If he could keep on doing ones like that, miss," said the professional, "they'd have him in the team before you could say knife."

Marjory sat down again beside the net, and watched more hopefully.

CHAPTER II

THE JOURNEY DOWN

The seeing off of Mike on the last day of the holidays was an imposing spectacle, a sort of pageant. Going to a public school, especially at the beginning of the summer term, is no great hardship, more particularly when the departing hero has a brother on the verge of the school eleven and three other brothers playing for counties; and Mike seemed in no way disturbed by the prospect. Mothers, however, to the end of time will foster a secret fear that their sons will be bullied at a big school, and Mrs. Jackson's anxious look lent a fine solemnity to the proceedings.

And as Marjory, Phyllis, and Ella invariably broke down when the time of separation arrived, and made no exception to their rule on the present occasion, a suitable gloom was the keynote of the gathering. Mr. Jackson seemed to bear the parting with fortitude, as did Mike's Uncle John (providentially roped in at the eleventh hour on his way to Scotland, in time to come down with a handsome tip). To their coarse-fibred minds there was nothing pathetic or tragic about the affair at all. (At the very moment when the train began to glide out of the station Uncle John was heard to remark that, in his opinion, these Bocks weren't a patch on the old shaped Larranaga.) Among others present might have been noticed Saunders, practising late cuts rather coyly with a walking-stick in the background; the village idiot, who had rolled up on the chance of a dole; Gladys Maud Evangeline's nurse, smiling vaguely; and Gladys Maud Evangeline herself, frankly bored with the whole business.

The train gathered speed. The air was full of last messages. Uncle John said on second thoughts he wasn't sure these Bocks weren't half a bad smoke after all. Gladys Maud cried, because she had taken a sudden dislike to the village idiot; and Mike settled himself in the corner and opened a magazine.

He was alone in the carriage. Bob, who had been spending the last week of the holidays with an aunt further down the line, was to

5

board the train at East Wobsley, and the brothers were to make a state entry into Wrykyn together. Meanwhile, Mike was left to his milk chocolate, his magazines, and his reflections.

The latter were not numerous, nor profound. He was excited. He had been petitioning the home authorities for the past year to be allowed to leave his private school and go to Wrykyn, and now the thing had come about. He wondered what sort of a house Wain's was, and whether they had any chance of the cricket cup. According to Bob they had no earthly; but then Bob only recognised one house, Donaldson's. He wondered if Bob would get his first eleven cap this year, and if he himself were likely to do anything at cricket. Marjory had faithfully reported every word Saunders had said on the subject, but Bob had been so careful to point out his insignificance when compared with the humblest Wrykynian that the professional's glowing prophecies had not had much effect. It might be true that some day he would play for England, but just at present he felt he would exchange his place in the team for one in the Wrykyn third eleven. A sort of mist enveloped everything Wrykynian. It seemed almost hopeless to try and compete with these unknown experts. On the other hand, there was Bob. Bob, by all accounts, was on the verge of the first eleven, and he was nothing special.

While he was engaged on these reflections, the train drew up at a small station. Opposite the door of Mike's compartment was standing a boy of about Mike's size, though evidently some years older. He had a sharp face, with rather a prominent nose; and a pair of pince-nez gave him a supercilious look. He wore a bowler hat, and carried a small portmanteau.

He opened the door, and took the seat opposite to Mike, whom he scrutinised for a moment rather after the fashion of a naturalist examining some new and unpleasant variety of beetle. He seemed about to make some remark, but, instead, got up and looked through the open window.

"Where's that porter?" Mike heard him say.

The porter came skimming down the platform at that moment.

"Porter."

"Sir?"

"Are those frightful boxes of mine in all right?"

"Yes, sir."

"Because, you know, there'll be a frightful row if any of them get lost."

"No chance of that, sir."

"Here you are, then."

"Thank you, sir."

The youth drew his head and shoulders in, stared at Mike again, and finally sat down. Mike noticed that he had nothing to read, and wondered if he wanted anything; but he did not feel equal to offering

6

him one of his magazines. He did not like the looks of him particularly. Judging by appearances, he seemed to carry enough side for three. If he wanted a magazine, thought Mike, let him ask for it.

The other made no overtures, and at the next stop got out. That explained his magazineless condition. He was only travelling a short way.

"Good business," said Mike to himself. He had all the Englishman's love of a carriage to himself.

The train was just moving out of the station when his eye was suddenly caught by the stranger's bag, lying snugly in the rack.

And here, I regret to say, Mike acted from the best motives, which is always fatal.

He realised in an instant what had happened. The fellow had forgotten his bag.

Mike had not been greatly fascinated by the stranger's looks; but, after all, the most supercilious person on earth has a right to his own property. Besides, he might have been quite a nice fellow when you got to know him. Anyhow, the bag had better be returned at once. The train was already moving quite fast, and Mike's compartment was nearing the end of the platform.

He snatched the bag from the rack and hurled it out of the window. (Porter Robinson, who happened to be in the line of fire, escaped with a flesh wound.) Then he sat down again with the inward glow of satisfaction which comes to one when one has risen successfully to a sudden emergency.

The glow lasted till the next stoppage, which did not occur for a good many miles. Then it ceased abruptly, for the train had scarcely come to a standstill when the opening above the door was darkened by a head and shoulders. The head was surmounted by a bowler, and a pair of pince-nez gleamed from the shadow.

"Hullo, I say," said the stranger. "Have you changed carriages, or what?"

"No," said Mike.

"Then, dash it, where's my frightful bag?"

Life teems with embarrassing situations. This was one of them.

"The fact is," said Mike, "I chucked it out."

"Chucked it out! what do you mean? When?"

"At the last station."

The guard blew his whistle, and the other jumped into the carriage.

"I thought you'd got out there for good," explained Mike. "I'm awfully sorry."

"Where is the bag?"

"On the platform at the last station. It hit a porter."

Against his will, for he wished to treat the matter with fitting solemnity, Mike grinned at the recollection. The look on Porter

Robinson's face as the bag took him in the small of the back had been funny, though not intentionally so.

The bereaved owner disapproved of this levity; and said as much. "Don't grin, you little beast," he shouted. "There's nothing to laugh at. You go chucking bags that don't belong to you out of the window, and then you have the frightful cheek to grin about it."

"It wasn't that," said Mike hurriedly. "Only the porter looked awfully funny when it hit him."

"Dash the porter! What's going to happen about my bag? I can't get out for half a second to buy a magazine without your flinging my things about the platform. What you want is a frightful kicking."

The situation was becoming difficult. But fortunately at this moment the train stopped once again; and, looking out of the window, Mike saw a board with East Wobsley upon it in large letters. A moment later Bob's head appeared in the doorway.

"Hullo, there you are," said Bob.

His eye fell upon Mike's companion.

"Hullo, Gazeka!" he exclaimed. "Where did you spring from? Do you know my brother? He's coming to Wrykyn this term. By the way, rather lucky you've met. He's in your house. Firby-Smith's head of Wain's, Mike."

Mike gathered that Gazeka and Firby-Smith were one and the same person. He grinned again. Firby-Smith continued to look ruffled, though not aggressive.

"Oh, are you in Wain's?" he said.

"I say, Bob," said Mike, "I've made rather an ass of myself."

"Naturally."

"I mean, what happened was this. I chucked Firby-Smith's portmanteau out of the window, thinking he'd got out, only he hadn't really, and it's at a station miles back."

"You're a bit of a rotter, aren't you? Had it got your name and address on it, Gazeka?"

"Yes."

"Oh, then it's certain to be all right. It's bound to turn up some time. They'll send it on by the next train, and you'll get it either to-night or to-morrow."

"Frightful nuisance, all the same. Lots of things in it I wanted."

"Oh, never mind, it's all right. I say, what have you been doing in the holidays? I didn't know you lived on this line at all."

From this point onwards Mike was out of the conversation altogether. Bob and Firby-Smith talked of Wrykyn, discussing events of the previous term of which Mike had never heard. Names came into their conversation which were entirely new to him. He realised that school politics were being talked, and that contributions from him to the dialogue were not required. He took up his magazine again, listening the while. They were discussing Wain's now. The name

Wyatt cropped up with some frequency. Wyatt was apparently something of a character. Mention was made of rows in which he had played a part in the past.

"It must be pretty rotten for him," said Bob. "He and Wain never get on very well, and yet they have to be together, holidays as well as term. Pretty bad having a step-father at all—I shouldn't care to—and when your house-master and your step-father are the same man, it's a bit thick."

"Frightful," agreed Firby-Smith.

"I swear, if I were in Wyatt's place, I should rot about like anything. It isn't as if he'd anything to look forward to when he leaves. He told me last term that Wain had got a nomination for him in some beastly bank, and that he was going into it directly after the end of this term. Rather rough on a chap like Wyatt. Good cricketer and footballer, I mean, and all that sort of thing. It's just the sort of life he'll hate most. Hullo, here we are."

Mike looked out of the window. It was Wrykyn at last.

CHAPTER III

MIKE FINDS A FRIENDLY NATIVE

Mike was surprised to find, on alighting, that the platform was entirely free from Wrykynians. In all the stories he had read the whole school came back by the same train, and, having smashed in one another's hats and chaffed the porters, made their way to the school buildings in a solid column. But here they were alone.

A remark of Bob's to Firby-Smith explained this. "Can't make out why none of the fellows came back by this train," he said. "Heaps of them must come by this line, and it's the only Christian train they run,"

"Don't want to get here before the last minute they can possibly manage. Silly idea. I suppose they think there'd be nothing to do."

"What shall we do?" said Bob. "Come and have some tea at Cook's?"

"All right."

Bob looked at Mike. There was no disguising the fact that he would be in the way; but how convey this fact delicately to him?

"Look here, Mike," he said, with a happy inspiration, "Firby-Smith and I are just going to get some tea. I think you'd better nip up

9

to the school. Probably Wain will want to see you, and tell you all about things, which is your dorm. and so on. See you later," he concluded airily. "Any one'll tell you the way to the school. Go straight on. They'll send your luggage on later. So long." And his sole prop in this world of strangers departed, leaving him to find his way for himself.

There is no subject on which opinions differ so widely as this matter of finding the way to a place. To the man who knows, it is simplicity itself. Probably he really does imagine that he goes straight on, ignoring the fact that for him the choice of three roads, all more or less straight, has no perplexities. The man who does not know feels as if he were in a maze.

Mike started out boldly, and lost his way. Go in which direction he would, he always seemed to arrive at a square with a fountain and an equestrian statue in its centre. On the fourth repetition of this feat he stopped in a disheartened way, and looked about him. He was beginning to feel bitter towards Bob. The man might at least have shown him where to get some tea.

At this moment a ray of hope shone through the gloom. Crossing the square was a short, thick-set figure clad in grey flannel trousers, a blue blazer, and a straw hat with a coloured band. Plainly a Wrykynian. Mike made for him.

"Can you tell me the way to the school, please," he said.

"Oh, you're going to the school," said the other. He had a pleasant, square-jawed face, reminiscent of a good-tempered bull-dog, and a pair of very deep-set grey eyes which somehow put Mike at his ease. There was something singularly cool and genial about them. He felt that they saw the humour in things, and that their owner was a person who liked most people and whom most people liked.

"You look rather lost," said the stranger. "Been hunting for it long?"

"Yes," said Mike.

"Which house do you want?"

"Wain's."

"Wain's? Then you've come to the right man this time. What I don't know about Wain's isn't worth knowing."

"Are you there, too?"

"Am I not! Term and holidays. There's no close season for me."

"Oh, are you Wyatt, then?" asked Mike.

"Hullo, this is fame. How did you know my name, as the ass in the detective story always says to the detective, who's seen it in the lining of his hat? Who's been talking about me?"

"I heard my brother saying something about you in the train."

"Who's your brother?"

"Jackson. He's in Donaldson's."

"I know. A stout fellow. So you're the newest make of Jackson, latest model, with all the modern improvements? Are there any more of you?"

"Not brothers," said Mike.

"Pity. You can't quite raise a team, then? Are you a sort of young Tyldesley, too?"

"I played a bit at my last school. Only a private school, you know," added Mike modestly.

"Make any runs? What was your best score?"

"Hundred and twenty-three," said Mike awkwardly. "It was only against kids, you know." He was in terror lest he should seem to be bragging.

"That's pretty useful. Any more centuries?"

"Yes," said Mike, shuffling.

"How many?"

"Seven altogether. You know, it was really awfully rotten bowling. And I was a good bit bigger than most of the chaps there. And my pater always has a pro. down in the Easter holidays, which gave me a bit of an advantage."

"All the same, seven centuries isn't so dusty against any bowling. We shall want some batting in the house this term. Look here, I was just going to have some tea. You come along, too."

"Oh, thanks awfully," said Mike. "My brother and Firby-Smith have gone to a place called Cook's."

"The old Gazeka? I didn't know he lived in your part of the world. He's head of Wain's."

"Yes, I know," said Mike. "Why is he called Gazeka?" he asked after a pause.

"Don't you think he looks like one? What did you think of him?"

"I didn't speak to him much," said Mike cautiously. It is always delicate work answering a question like this unless one has some sort of an inkling as to the views of the questioner.

"He's all right," said Wyatt, answering for himself. "He's got a habit of talking to one as if he were a prince of the blood dropping a gracious word to one of the three Small-Heads at the Hippodrome, but that's his misfortune. We all have our troubles. That's his. Let's go in here. It's too far to sweat to Cook's."

It was about a mile from the tea-shop to the school. Mike's first impression on arriving at the school grounds was of his smallness and insignificance. Everything looked so big—the buildings, the grounds, everything. He felt out of the picture. He was glad that he had met Wyatt. To make his entrance into this strange land alone would have been more of an ordeal than he would have cared to face.

"That's Wain's," said Wyatt, pointing to one of half a dozen large houses which lined the road on the south side of the cricket field. Mike followed his finger, and took in the size of his new home.

"I say, it's jolly big," he said. "How many fellows are there in it?"

11

"Thirty-one this term, I believe."

"That's more than there were at King-Hall's."

"What's King-Hall's?"

"The private school I was at. At Emsworth."

Emsworth seemed very remote and unreal to him as he spoke.

They skirted the cricket field, walking along the path that divided the two terraces. The Wrykyn playing-fields were formed of a series of huge steps, cut out of the hill. At the top of the hill came the school. On the first terrace was a sort of informal practice ground, where, though no games were played on it, there was a good deal of punting and drop-kicking in the winter and fielding-practice in the summer. The next terrace was the biggest of all, and formed the first eleven cricket ground, a beautiful piece of turf, a shade too narrow for its length, bounded on the terrace side by a sharply sloping bank, some fifteen feet deep, and on the other by the precipice leading to the next terrace. At the far end of the ground stood the pavilion, and beside it a little ivy-covered rabbit-hutch for the scorers. Old Wrykynians always claimed that it was the prettiest school ground in England. It certainly had the finest view. From the verandah of the pavilion you could look over three counties.

Wain's house wore an empty and desolate appearance. There were signs of activity, however, inside; and a smell of soap and warm water told of preparations recently completed.

Wyatt took Mike into the matron's room, a small room opening out of the main passage.

"This is Jackson," he said. "Which dormitory is he in, Miss Payne?"

The matron consulted a paper.

"He's in yours, Wyatt."

"Good business. Who's in the other bed? There are going to be three of us, aren't there?"

"Fereira was to have slept there, but we have just heard that he is not coming back this term. He has had to go on a sea-voyage for his health."

"Seems queer any one actually taking the trouble to keep Fereira in the world," said Wyatt. "I've often thought of giving him Rough On Rats myself. Come along, Jackson, and I'll show you the room."

They went along the passage, and up a flight of stairs.

"Here you are," said Wyatt.

It was a fair-sized room. The window, heavily barred, looked out over a large garden.

"I used to sleep here alone last term," said Wyatt, "but the house is so full now they've turned it into a dormitory."

"I say, I wish these bars weren't here. It would be rather a rag to get out of the window on to that wall at night, and hop down into the garden and explore," said Mike.

12

Wyatt looked at him curiously, and moved to the window.

"I'm not going to let you do it, of course," he said, "because you'd go getting caught, and dropped on, which isn't good for one in one's first term; but just to amuse you—"

He jerked at the middle bar, and the next moment he was standing with it in his hand, and the way to the garden was clear.

"By Jove!" said Mike.

"That's simply an object-lesson, you know," said Wyatt, replacing the bar, and pushing the screws back into their putty. "I get out at night myself because I think my health needs it. Besides, it's my last term, anyhow, so it doesn't matter what I do. But if I find you trying to cut out in the small hours, there'll be trouble. See?"

"All right," said Mike, reluctantly. "But I wish you'd let me."

"Not if I know it. Promise you won't try it on."

"All right. But, I say, what do you do out there?"

"I shoot at cats with an air-pistol, the beauty of which is that even if you hit them it doesn't hurt—simply keeps them bright and interested in life; and if you miss you've had all the fun anyhow. Have you ever shot at a rocketing cat? Finest mark you can have. Society's latest craze. Buy a pistol and see life."

"I wish you'd let me come."

"I daresay you do. Not much, however. Now, if you like, I'll take you over the rest of the school. You'll have to see it sooner or later, so you may as well get it over at once."

CHAPTER IV

AT THE NETS

There are few better things in life than a public school summer term. The winter term is good, especially towards the end, and there are points, though not many, about the Easter term: but it is in the summer that one really appreciates public school life. The freedom of it, after the restrictions of even the most easy-going private school, is intoxicating. The change is almost as great as that from public school to 'Varsity.

For Mike the path was made particularly easy. The only drawback to going to a big school for the first time is the fact that one is made to feel so very small and inconspicuous. New boys who have been leading lights at their private schools feel it acutely for the first week. At one time it was the custom, if we may believe writers of a generation or so back, for boys to take quite an embarrassing interest in the newcomer. He was asked a rain of questions, and was, generally, in the very centre of the stage. Nowadays an absolute lack of interest is the fashion. A new boy arrives, and there he is, one of a crowd.

Mike was saved this salutary treatment to a large extent, at first by virtue of the greatness of his family, and, later, by his own performances on the cricket field. His three elder brothers were objects of veneration to most Wrykynians, and Mike got a certain amount of reflected glory from them. The brother of first-class cricketers has a dignity of his own. Then Bob was a help. He was on the verge of the cricket team and had been the school full-back for two seasons. Mike found that people came up and spoke to him, anxious to know if he were Jackson's brother; and became friendly when he replied in the affirmative. Influential relations are a help in every stage of life.

It was Wyatt who gave him his first chance at cricket. There were nets on the first afternoon of term for all old colours of the three teams and a dozen or so of those most likely to fill the vacant places. Wyatt was there, of course. He had got his first eleven cap in the previous season as a mighty hitter and a fair slow bowler. Mike met him crossing the field with his cricket bag.

"Hullo, where are you off to?" asked Wyatt. "Coming to watch the nets?"

Mike had no particular programme for the afternoon. Junior cricket had not begun, and it was a little difficult to know how to fill in the time.

"I tell you what," said Wyatt, "nip into the house and shove on some things, and I'll try and get Burgess to let you have a knock later on."

This suited Mike admirably. A quarter of an hour later he was sitting at the back of the first eleven net, watching the practice.

Burgess, the captain of the Wrykyn team, made no pretence of being a bat. He was the school fast bowler and concentrated his energies on that department of the game. He sometimes took ten minutes at the wicket after everybody else had had an innings, but it was to bowl that he came to the nets.

He was bowling now to one of the old colours whose name Mike did not know. Wyatt and one of the professionals were the other two bowlers. Two nets away Firby-Smith, who had changed his pince-nez for a pair of huge spectacles, was performing rather ineffectively against some very bad bowling. Mike fixed his attention on the first eleven man.

He was evidently a good bat. There was style and power in his batting. He had a way of gliding Burgess's fastest to leg which Mike admired greatly. He was succeeded at the end of a quarter of an hour by another eleven man, and then Bob appeared.

14

It was soon made evident that this was not Bob's day. Nobody is at his best on the first day of term; but Bob was worse than he had any right to be. He scratched forward at nearly everything, and when Burgess, who had been resting, took up the ball again, he had each stump uprooted in a regular series in seven balls. Once he skied one of Wyatt's slows over the net behind the wicket; and Mike, jumping up, caught him neatly.

"Thanks," said Bob austerely, as Mike returned the ball to him. He seemed depressed.

Towards the end of the afternoon, Wyatt went up to Burgess.

"Burgess," he said, "see that kid sitting behind the net?"

"With the naked eye," said Burgess. "Why?"

"He's just come to Wain's. He's Bob Jackson's brother, and I've a sort of idea that he's a bit of a bat. I told him I'd ask you if he could have a knock. Why not send him in at the end net? There's nobody there now."

Burgess's amiability off the field equalled his ruthlessness when bowling.

"All right," he said. "Only if you think that I'm going to sweat to bowl to him, you're making a fatal error."

"You needn't do a thing. Just sit and watch. I rather fancy this kid's something special."

Mike put on Wyatt's pads and gloves, borrowed his bat, and walked round into the net.

"Not in a funk, are you?" asked Wyatt, as he passed.

Mike grinned. The fact was that he had far too good an opinion of himself to be nervous. An entirely modest person seldom makes a good batsman. Batting is one of those things which demand first and foremost a thorough belief in oneself. It need not be aggressive, but it must be there.

Wyatt and the professional were the bowlers. Mike had seen enough of Wyatt's bowling to know that it was merely ordinary "slow tosh," and the professional did not look as difficult as Saunders. The first half-dozen balls he played carefully. He was on trial, and he meant to take no risks. Then the professional over-pitched one slightly on the off. Mike jumped out, and got the full face of the bat on to it. The ball hit one of the ropes of the net, and nearly broke it.

"How's that?" said Wyatt, with the smile of an impresario on the first night of a successful piece.

"Not bad," admitted Burgess.

A few moments later he was still more complimentary. He got up and took a ball himself.

Mike braced himself up as Burgess began his run. This time he was more than a trifle nervous. The bowling he had had so far had been tame. This would be the real ordeal.

As the ball left Burgess's hand he began instinctively to shape for

15

a forward stroke. Then suddenly he realised that the thing was going to be a yorker, and banged his bat down in the block just as the ball arrived. An unpleasant sensation as of having been struck by a thunderbolt was succeeded by a feeling of relief that he had kept the ball out of his wicket. There are easier things in the world than stopping a fast yorker.

"Well played," said Burgess.

Mike felt like a successful general receiving the thanks of the nation.

The fact that Burgess's next ball knocked middle and off stumps out of the ground saddened him somewhat; but this was the last tragedy that occurred. He could not do much with the bowling beyond stopping it and feeling repetitions of the thunderbolt experience, but he kept up his end; and a short conversation which he had with Burgess at the end of his innings was full of encouragement to one skilled in reading between the lines.

"Thanks awfully," said Mike, referring to the square manner in which the captain had behaved in letting him bat.

"What school were you at before you came here?" asked Burgess.

"A private school in Hampshire," said Mike. "King-Hall's. At a place called Emsworth."

"Get much cricket there?"

"Yes, a good lot. One of the masters, a chap called Westbrook, was an awfully good slow bowler."

Burgess nodded.

"You don't run away, which is something," he said.

Mike turned purple with pleasure at this stately compliment. Then, having waited for further remarks, but gathering from the captain's silence that the audience was at an end, he proceeded to unbuckle his pads. Wyatt overtook him on his way to the house.

"Well played," he said. "I'd no idea you were such hot stuff. You're a regular pro."

"I say," said Mike gratefully, "it was most awfully decent of you getting Burgess to let me go in. It was simply ripping of you."

"Oh, that's all right. If you don't get pushed a bit here you stay for ages in the hundredth game with the cripples and the kids. Now you've shown them what you can do you ought to get into the Under Sixteen team straight away. Probably into the third, too."

"By Jove, that would be all right."

"I asked Burgess afterwards what he thought of your batting, and he said, 'Not bad.' But he says that about everything. It's his highest form of praise. He says it when he wants to let himself go and simply butter up a thing. If you took him to see N. A. Knox bowl, he'd say he wasn't bad. What he meant was that he was jolly struck with your batting, and is going to play you for the Under Sixteen."

"I hope so," said Mike.

16

The prophecy was fulfilled. On the following Wednesday there was a match between the Under Sixteen and a scratch side. Mike's name was among the Under Sixteen. And on the Saturday he was playing for the third eleven in a trial game.

"This place is ripping," he said to himself, as he saw his name on the list. "Thought I should like it."

And that night he wrote a letter to his father, notifying him of the fact.

CHAPTER V

REVELRY BY NIGHT

A succession of events combined to upset Mike during his first fortnight at school. He was far more successful than he had any right to be at his age. There is nothing more heady than success, and if it comes before we are prepared for it, it is apt to throw us off our balance. As a rule, at school, years of wholesome obscurity make us ready for any small triumphs we may achieve at the end of our time there. Mike had skipped these years. He was older than the average new boy, and his batting was undeniable. He knew quite well that he was regarded as a find by the cricket authorities; and the knowledge was not particularly good for him. It did not make him conceited, for his was not a nature at all addicted to conceit. The effect it had on him was to make him excessively pleased with life. And when Mike was pleased with life he always found a difficulty in obeying Authority and its rules. His state of mind was not improved by an interview with Bob.

Some evil genius put it into Bob's mind that it was his duty to be, if only for one performance, the Heavy Elder Brother to Mike; to give him good advice. It is never the smallest use for an elder brother to attempt to do anything for the good of a younger brother at school, for the latter rebels automatically against such interference in his concerns; but Bob did not know this. He only knew that he had received a letter from home, in which his mother had assumed without evidence that he was leading Mike by the hand round the pitfalls of life at Wrykyn; and his conscience smote him. Beyond asking him occasionally, when they met, how he was getting on (a question to which Mike invariably replied, "Oh, all right"), he was not aware of having done anything brotherly towards the youngster. So he asked Mike to tea in his study one afternoon before going to the nets.

17

Mike arrived, sidling into the study in the half-sheepish, half-defiant manner peculiar to small brothers in the presence of their elders, and stared in silence at the photographs on the walls. Bob was changing into his cricket things. The atmosphere was one of constraint and awkwardness.

The arrival of tea was the cue for conversation.

"Well, how are you getting on?" asked Bob.

"Oh, all right," said Mike.

Silence.

"Sugar?" asked Bob.

"Thanks," said Mike.

"How many lumps?"

"Two, please."

"Cake?"

"Thanks."

Silence.

Bob pulled himself together.

"Like Wain's?"

"Ripping."

"I asked Firby-Smith to keep an eye on you," said Bob.

"What!" said Mike.

The mere idea of a worm like the Gazeka being told to keep an eye on him was degrading.

"He said he'd look after you," added Bob, making things worse.

Look after him! Him!! M. Jackson, of the third eleven!!!

Mike helped himself to another chunk of cake, and spoke crushingly.

"He needn't trouble," he said. "I can look after myself all right, thanks."

Bob saw an opening for the entry of the Heavy Elder Brother.

"Look here, Mike," he said, "I'm only saying it for your good—"

I should like to state here that it was not Bob's habit to go about the world telling people things solely for their good. He was only doing it now to ease his conscience.

"Yes?" said Mike coldly.

"It's only this. You know, I should keep an eye on myself if I were you. There's nothing that gets a chap so barred here as side."

"What do you mean?" said Mike, outraged.

"Oh, I'm not saying anything against you so far," said Bob. "You've been all right up to now. What I mean to say is, you've got on so well at cricket, in the third and so on, there's just a chance you might start to side about a bit soon, if you don't watch yourself. I'm not saying a word against you so far, of course. Only you see what I mean."

Mike's feelings were too deep for words. In sombre silence he reached out for the jam; while Bob, satisfied that he had delivered his message in a pleasant and tactful manner, filled his cup, and cast about him for further words of wisdom.

18

"Seen you about with Wyatt a good deal," he said at length.

"Yes," said Mike.

"Like him?"

"Yes," said Mike cautiously.

"You know," said Bob, "I shouldn't—I mean, I should take care what you're doing with Wyatt."

"What do you mean?"

"Well, he's an awfully good chap, of course, but still—"

"Still what?"

"Well, I mean, he's the sort of chap who'll probably get into some thundering row before he leaves. He doesn't care a hang what he does. He's that sort of chap. He's never been dropped on yet, but if you go on breaking rules you're bound to be sooner or later. Thing is, it doesn't matter much for him, because he's leaving at the end of the term. But don't let him drag you into anything. Not that he would try to. But you might think it was the blood thing to do to imitate him, and the first thing you knew you'd be dropped on by Wain or somebody. See what I mean?"

Bob was well-intentioned, but tact did not enter greatly into his composition.

"What rot!" said Mike.

"All right. But don't you go doing it. I'm going over to the nets. I see Burgess has shoved you down for them. You'd better be going and changing. Stick on here a bit, though, if you want any more tea. I've got to be off myself."

Mike changed for net-practice in a ferment of spiritual injury. It was maddening to be treated as an infant who had to be looked after. He felt very sore against Bob.

A good innings at the third eleven net, followed by some strenuous fielding in the deep, soothed his ruffled feelings to a large extent; and all might have been well but for the intervention of Firby-Smith.

That youth, all spectacles and front teeth, met Mike at the door of Wain's.

"Ah, I wanted to see you, young man," he said. (Mike disliked being called "young man.") "Come up to my study."

Mike followed him in silence to his study, and preserved his silence till Firby-Smith, having deposited his cricket-bag in a corner of the room and examined himself carefully in a looking-glass that hung over the mantelpiece, spoke again.

"I've been hearing all about you, young man." Mike shuffled.

"You're a frightful character from all accounts." Mike could not think of anything to say that was not rude, so said nothing.

"Your brother has asked me to keep an eye on you."

Mike's soul began to tie itself into knots again. He was just at the age when one is most sensitive to patronage and most resentful of it.

19

"I promised I would," said the Gazeka, turning round and examining himself in the mirror again. "You'll get on all right if you behave yourself. Don't make a frightful row in the house. Don't cheek your elders and betters. Wash. That's all. Cut along."

Mike had a vague idea of sacrificing his career to the momentary pleasure of flinging a chair at the head of the house. Overcoming this feeling, he walked out of the room, and up to his dormitory to change.

In the dormitory that night the feeling of revolt, of wanting to do something actively illegal, increased. Like Eric, he burned, not with shame and remorse, but with rage and all that sort of thing. He dropped off to sleep full of half-formed plans for asserting himself. He was awakened from a dream in which he was batting against Firby-Smith's bowling, and hitting it into space every time, by a slight sound. He opened his eyes, and saw a dark figure silhouetted against the light of the window. He sat up in bed.

"Hullo," he said. "Is that you, Wyatt?"

"Are you awake?" said Wyatt. "Sorry if I've spoiled your beauty sleep."

"Are you going out?"

"I am," said Wyatt. "The cats are particularly strong on the wing just now. Mustn't miss a chance like this. Specially as there's a good moon, too. I shall be deadly."

"I say, can't I come too?"

A moonlight prowl, with or without an air-pistol, would just have suited Mike's mood.

"No, you can't," said Wyatt. "When I'm caught, as I'm morally certain to be some day, or night rather, they're bound to ask if you've ever been out as well as me. Then you'll be able to put your hand on your little heart and do a big George Washington act. You'll find that useful when the time comes."

"Do you think you will be caught?"

"Shouldn't be surprised. Anyhow, you stay where you are. Go to sleep and dream that you're playing for the school against Ripton. So long."

And Wyatt, laying the bar he had extracted on the window-sill, wriggled out. Mike saw him disappearing along the wall.

It was all very well for Wyatt to tell him to go to sleep, but it was not so easy to do it. The room was almost light; and Mike always found it difficult to sleep unless it was dark. He turned over on his side and shut his eyes, but he had never felt wider awake. Twice he heard the quarters chime from the school clock; and the second time he gave up the struggle. He got out of bed and went to the window. It was a lovely night, just the sort of night on which, if he had been at home, he would have been out after moths with a lantern.

A sharp yowl from an unseen cat told of Wyatt's presence somewhere in the big garden. He would have given much to be with

20

him, but he realised that he was on parole. He had promised not to leave the house, and there was an end of it.

He turned away from the window and sat down on his bed. Then a beautiful, consoling thought came to him. He had given his word that he would not go into the garden, but nothing had been said about exploring inside the house. It was quite late now. Everybody would be in bed. It would be quite safe. And there must be all sorts of things to interest the visitor in Wain's part of the house. Food, perhaps. Mike felt that he could just do with a biscuit. And there were bound to be biscuits on the sideboard in Wain's dining-room.

He crept quietly out of the dormitory.

He had been long enough in the house to know the way, in spite of the fact that all was darkness. Down the stairs, along the passage to the left, and up a few more stairs at the end. The beauty of the position was that the dining-room had two doors, one leading into Wain's part of the house, the other into the boys' section. Any interruption that there might be would come from the further door.

To make himself more secure he locked that door; then, turning up the incandescent light, he proceeded to look about him.

Mr. Wain's dining-room repaid inspection. There were the remains of supper on the table. Mike cut himself some cheese and took some biscuits from the box, feeling that he was doing himself well. This was Life. There was a little soda-water in the syphon. He finished it. As it swished into the glass, it made a noise that seemed to him like three hundred Niagaras; but nobody else in the house appeared to have noticed it.

He took some more biscuits, and an apple.

After which, feeling a new man, he examined the room.

And this was where the trouble began.

On a table in one corner stood a small gramophone. And gramophones happened to be Mike's particular craze.

All thought of risk left him. The soda-water may have got into his head, or he may have been in a particularly reckless mood, as indeed he was. The fact remains that he inserted the first record that came to hand, wound the machine up, and set it going.

The next moment, very loud and nasal, a voice from the machine announced that Mr. Godfrey Field would sing "The Quaint Old Bird." And, after a few preliminary chords, Mr. Field actually did so.

"Auntie went to Aldershot in a Paris pom-pom hat."

Mike stood and drained it in.

"... Good gracious (sang Mr. Field), what was that?"

It was a rattling at the handle of the door. A rattling that turned almost immediately into a spirited banging. A voice accompanied the banging. "Who is there?" inquired the voice. Mike recognised it as Mr. Wain's. He was not alarmed. The man who holds the ace of trumps has no need to be alarmed. His position was impregnable. The enemy

21

was held in check by the locked door, while the other door offered an admirable and instantaneous way of escape.

Mike crept across the room on tip-toe and opened the window. It had occurred to him, just in time, that if Mr. Wain, on entering the room, found that the occupant had retired by way of the boys' part of the house, he might possibly obtain a clue to his identity. If, on the other hand, he opened the window, suspicion would be diverted. Mike had not read his "Raffles" for nothing.

The handle-rattling was resumed. This was good. So long as the frontal attack was kept up, there was no chance of his being taken in the rear—his only danger.

He stopped the gramophone, which had been pegging away patiently at "The Quaint Old Bird" all the time, and reflected. It seemed a pity to evacuate the position and ring down the curtain on what was, to date, the most exciting episode of his life; but he must not overdo the thing, and get caught. At any moment the noise might bring reinforcements to the besieging force, though it was not likely, for the dining-room was a long way from the dormitories; and it might flash upon their minds that there were two entrances to the room. Or the same bright thought might come to Wain himself.

"Now what," pondered Mike, "would A. J. Raffles have done in a case like this? Suppose he'd been after somebody's jewels, and found that they were after him, and he'd locked one door, and could get away by the other."

The answer was simple.

"He'd clear out," thought Mike.

Two minutes later he was in bed.

He lay there, tingling all over with the consciousness of having played a masterly game, when suddenly a gruesome idea came to him, and he sat up, breathless. Suppose Wain took it into his head to make a tour of the dormitories, to see that all was well! Wyatt was still in the garden somewhere, blissfully unconscious of what was going on indoors. He would be caught for a certainty!

CHAPTER VI

IN WHICH A TIGHT CORNER IS EVADED

For a moment the situation paralysed Mike. Then he began to be equal to it. In times of excitement one thinks rapidly and clearly. The main point, the kernel of the whole thing, was that he must get into the garden somehow, and warn Wyatt. And at the same time, he must keep Mr. Wain from coming to the dormitory. He jumped out of bed, and dashed down the dark stairs.

He had taken care to close the dining-room door after him. It was open now, and he could hear somebody moving inside the room. Evidently his retreat had been made just in time.

He knocked at the door, and went in.

Mr. Wain was standing at the window, looking out. He spun round at the knock, and stared in astonishment at Mike's pyjama-clad figure. Mike, in spite of his anxiety, could barely check a laugh. Mr. Wain was a tall, thin man, with a serious face partially obscured by a grizzled beard. He wore spectacles, through which he peered owlishly at Mike. His body was wrapped in a brown dressing-gown. His hair was ruffled. He looked like some weird bird.

"Please, sir, I thought I heard a noise," said Mike.

Mr. Wain continued to stare.

"What are you doing here?" said he at last.

"Thought I heard a noise, please, sir."

"A noise?"

"Please, sir, a row."

"You thought you heard—!"

The thing seemed to be worrying Mr. Wain.

"So I came down, sir," said Mike.

The house-master's giant brain still appeared to be somewhat clouded. He looked about him, and, catching sight of the gramophone, drew inspiration from it.

"Did you turn on the gramophone?" he asked.

"Me, sir!" said Mike, with the air of a bishop accused of contributing to the Police News.

"Of course not, of course not," said Mr. Wain hurriedly. "Of course not. I don't know why I asked. All this is very unsettling. What are you doing here?"

"Thought I heard a noise, please, sir."

"A noise?"

"A row, sir."

If it was Mr. Wain's wish that he should spend the night playing Massa Tambo to his Massa Bones, it was not for him to baulk the house-master's innocent pleasure. He was prepared to continue the snappy dialogue till breakfast time.

"I think there must have been a burglar in here, Jackson."

"Looks like it, sir."

"I found the window open."

"He's probably in the garden, sir."

Mr. Wain looked out into the garden with an annoyed expression, as if its behaviour in letting burglars be in it struck him as unworthy of a respectable garden.

23

"He might be still in the house," said Mr. Wain, ruminatively.

"Not likely, sir."

"You think not?"

"Wouldn't be such a fool, sir. I mean, such an ass, sir."

"Perhaps you are right, Jackson."

"I shouldn't wonder if he was hiding in the shrubbery, sir."

Mr. Wain looked at the shrubbery, as who should say, "Et tu, Brute!"

"By Jove! I think I see him," cried Mike. He ran to the window, and vaulted through it on to the lawn. An inarticulate protest from Mr. Wain, rendered speechless by this move just as he had been beginning to recover his faculties, and he was running across the lawn into the shrubbery. He felt that all was well. There might be a bit of a row on his return, but he could always plead overwhelming excitement.

Wyatt was round at the back somewhere, and the problem was how to get back without being seen from the dining-room window. Fortunately a belt of evergreens ran along the path right up to the house. Mike worked his way cautiously through these till he was out of sight, then tore for the regions at the back.

The moon had gone behind the clouds, and it was not easy to find a way through the bushes. Twice branches sprang out from nowhere, and hit Mike smartly over the shins, eliciting sharp howls of pain.

On the second of these occasions a low voice spoke from somewhere on his right.

"Who on earth's that?" it said.

Mike stopped.

"Is that you, Wyatt? I say—"

"Jackson!"

The moon came out again, and Mike saw Wyatt clearly. His knees were covered with mould. He had evidently been crouching in the bushes on all fours.

"You young ass," said Wyatt. "You promised me that you wouldn't get out."

"Yes, I know, but—"

"I heard you crashing through the shrubbery like a hundred elephants. If you must get out at night and chance being sacked, you might at least have the sense to walk quietly."

"Yes, but you don't understand."

And Mike rapidly explained the situation.

"But how the dickens did he hear you, if you were in the dining-room?" asked Wyatt. "It's miles from his bedroom. You must tread like a policeman."

"It wasn't that. The thing was, you see, it was rather a rotten thing to do, I suppose, but I turned on the gramophone."

"You—what?"

24

"The gramophone. It started playing 'The Quaint Old Bird.' Ripping it was, till Wain came along."

Wyatt doubled up with noiseless laughter.

"You're a genius," he said. "I never saw such a man. Well, what's the game now? What's the idea?"

"I think you'd better nip back along the wall and in through the window, and I'll go back to the dining-room. Then it'll be all right if Wain comes and looks into the dorm. Or, if you like, you might come down too, as if you'd just woke up and thought you'd heard a row."

"That's not a bad idea. All right. You dash along then. I'll get back."

Mr. Wain was still in the dining-room, drinking in the beauties of the summer night through the open window. He gibbered slightly when Mike reappeared.

"Jackson! What do you mean by running about outside the house in this way! I shall punish you very heavily. I shall certainly report the matter to the headmaster. I will not have boys rushing about the garden in their pyjamas. You will catch an exceedingly bad cold. You will do me two hundred lines, Latin and English. Exceedingly so. I will not have it. Did you not hear me call to you?"

"Please, sir, so excited," said Mike, standing outside with his hands on the sill.

"You have no business to be excited. I will not have it. It is exceedingly impertinent of you."

"Please, sir, may I come in?"

"Come in! Of course, come in. Have you no sense, boy? You are laying the seeds of a bad cold. Come in at once."

Mike clambered through the window.

"I couldn't find him, sir. He must have got out of the garden."

"Undoubtedly," said Mr. Wain. "Undoubtedly so. It was very wrong of you to search for him. You have been seriously injured. Exceedingly so."

He was about to say more on the subject when Wyatt strolled into the room. Wyatt wore the rather dazed expression of one who has been aroused from deep sleep. He yawned before he spoke.

"I thought I heard a noise, sir," he said.

He called Mr. Wain "father" in private, "sir" in public. The presence of Mike made this a public occasion.

"Has there been a burglary?"

"Yes," said Mike, "only he has got away."

"Shall I go out into the garden, and have a look round, sir?" asked Wyatt helpfully.

The question stung Mr. Wain into active eruption once more.

"Under no circumstances whatever," he said excitedly. "Stay where you are, James. I will not have boys running about my garden at night. It is preposterous. Inordinately so. Both of you go to bed immediately. I shall not speak to you again on this subject. I must be obeyed instantly. You hear me, Jackson? James, you understand me? To bed at once. And, if I find you outside your dormitory again to-night, you will both be punished with extreme severity. I will not have this lax and reckless behaviour."

"But the burglar, sir?" said Wyatt.

"We might catch him, sir," said Mike.

Mr. Wain's manner changed to a slow and stately sarcasm, in much the same way as a motor-car changes from the top speed to its first.

"I was under the impression," he said, in the heavy way almost invariably affected by weak masters in their dealings with the obstreperous, "I was distinctly under the impression that I had ordered you to retire immediately to your dormitory. It is possible that you mistook my meaning. In that case I shall be happy to repeat what I said. It is also in my mind that I threatened to punish you with the utmost severity if you did not retire at once. In these circumstances, James—and you, Jackson—you will doubtless see the necessity of complying with my wishes."

They made it so.

CHAPTER VII

IN WHICH MIKE IS DISCUSSED

Trevor and Clowes, of Donaldson's, were sitting in their study a week after the gramophone incident, preparatory to going on the river. At least Trevor was in the study, getting tea ready. Clowes was on the window-sill, one leg in the room, the other outside, hanging over space. He loved to sit in this attitude, watching some one else work, and giving his views on life to whoever would listen to them. Clowes was tall, and looked sad, which he was not. Trevor was shorter, and very much in earnest over all that he did. On the present occasion he was measuring out tea with a concentration worthy of a general planning a campaign.

"One for the pot," said Clowes.

"All right," breathed Trevor. "Come and help, you slacker."

"Too busy."

"You aren't doing a stroke."

"My lad, I'm thinking of Life. That's a thing you couldn't do. I often say to people, 'Good chap, Trevor, but can't think of Life. Give

26

him a tea-pot and half a pound of butter to mess about with,' I say, 'and he's all right. But when it comes to deep thought, where is he? Among the also-rans.' That's what I say."

"Silly ass," said Trevor, slicing bread. "What particular rot were you thinking about just then? What fun it was sitting back and watching other fellows work, I should think."

"My mind at the moment," said Clowes, "was tensely occupied with the problem of brothers at school. Have you got any brothers, Trevor?"

"One. Couple of years younger than me. I say, we shall want some more jam to-morrow. Better order it to-day."

"See it done, Tigellinus, as our old pal Nero used to remark. Where is he? Your brother, I mean."

"Marlborough."

"That shows your sense. I have always had a high opinion of your sense, Trevor. If you'd been a silly ass, you'd have let your people send him here."

"Why not? Shouldn't have minded."

"I withdraw what I said about your sense. Consider it unsaid. I have a brother myself. Aged fifteen. Not a bad chap in his way. Like the heroes of the school stories. 'Big blue eyes literally bubbling over with fun.' At least, I suppose it's fun to him. Cheek's what I call it. My people wanted to send him here. I lodged a protest. I said, 'One Clowes is ample for any public school.'"

"You were right there," said Trevor.

"I said, 'One Clowes is luxury, two excess.' I pointed out that I was just on the verge of becoming rather a blood at Wrykyn, and that I didn't want the work of years spoiled by a brother who would think it a rag to tell fellows who respected and admired me—"

"Such as who?"

"—Anecdotes of a chequered infancy. There are stories about me which only my brother knows. Did I want them spread about the school? No, laddie, I did not. Hence, we see my brother two terms ago, packing up his little box, and tooling off to Rugby. And here am I at Wrykyn, with an unstained reputation, loved by all who know me, revered by all who don't; courted by boys, fawned upon by masters. People's faces brighten when I throw them a nod. If I frown—"

"Oh, come on," said Trevor.

Bread and jam and cake monopolised Clowes's attention for the next quarter of an hour. At the end of that period, however, he returned to his subject.

"After the serious business of the meal was concluded, and a simple hymn had been sung by those present," he said, "Mr. Clowes resumed his very interesting remarks. We were on the subject of brothers at school. Now, take the melancholy case of Jackson Brothers. My heart bleeds for Bob."

"Jackson's all right. What's wrong with him? Besides, naturally, young Jackson came to Wrykyn when all his brothers had been here."

"What a rotten argument. It's just the one used by chaps' people, too. They think how nice it will be for all the sons to have been at the same school. It may be all right after they're left, but while they're there, it's the limit. You say Jackson's all right. At present, perhaps, he is. But the term's hardly started yet."

"Well?"

"Look here, what's at the bottom of this sending young brothers to the same school as elder brothers?"

"Elder brother can keep an eye on him, I suppose."

"That's just it. For once in your life you've touched the spot. In other words, Bob Jackson is practically responsible for the kid. That's where the whole rotten trouble starts."

"Why?"

"Well, what happens? He either lets the kid rip, in which case he may find himself any morning in the pleasant position of having to explain to his people exactly why it is that little Willie has just received the boot, and why he didn't look after him better: or he spends all his spare time shadowing him to see that he doesn't get into trouble. He feels that his reputation hangs on the kid's conduct, so he broods over him like a policeman, which is pretty rotten for him and maddens the kid, who looks on him as no sportsman. Bob seems to be trying the first way, which is what I should do myself. It's all right, so far, but, as I said, the term's only just started."

"Young Jackson seems all right. What's wrong with him? He doesn't stick on side any way, which he might easily do, considering his cricket."

"There's nothing wrong with him in that way. I've talked to him several times at the nets, and he's very decent. But his getting into trouble hasn't anything to do with us. It's the masters you've got to consider."

"What's up? Does he rag?"

"From what I gather from fellows in his form he's got a genius for ragging. Thinks of things that don't occur to anybody else, and does them, too."

"He never seems to be in extra. One always sees him about on half-holidays."

"That's always the way with that sort of chap. He keeps on wriggling out of small rows till he thinks he can do anything he likes without being dropped on, and then all of a sudden he finds himself up to the eyebrows in a record smash. I don't say young Jackson will land himself like that. All I say is that he's just the sort who does. He's asking for trouble. Besides, who do you see him about with all the time?"

"He's generally with Wyatt when I meet him."

28

"Yes. Well, then!"

"What's wrong with Wyatt? He's one of the decentest men in the school."

"I know. But he's working up for a tremendous row one of these days, unless he leaves before it comes off. The odds are, if Jackson's so thick with him, that he'll be roped into it too. Wyatt wouldn't land him if he could help it, but he probably wouldn't realise what he was letting the kid in for. For instance, I happen to know that Wyatt breaks out of his dorm. every other night. I don't know if he takes Jackson with him. I shouldn't think so. But there's nothing to prevent Jackson following him on his own. And if you're caught at that game, it's the boot every time."

Trevor looked disturbed.

"Somebody ought to speak to Bob."

"What's the good? Why worry him? Bob couldn't do anything. You'd only make him do the policeman business, which he hasn't time for, and which is bound to make rows between them. Better leave him alone."

"I don't know. It would be a beastly thing for Bob if the kid did get into a really bad row."

"If you must tell anybody, tell the Gazeka. He's head of Wain's, and has got far more chance of keeping an eye on Jackson than Bob has."

"The Gazeka is a fool."

"All front teeth and side. Still, he's on the spot. But what's the good of worrying. It's nothing to do with us, anyhow. Let's stagger out, shall we?"

Trevor's conscientious nature, however, made it impossible for him to drop the matter. It disturbed him all the time that he and Clowes were on the river; and, walking back to the house, he resolved to see Bob about it during preparation.

He found him in his study, oiling a bat.

"I say, Bob," he said, "look here. Are you busy?"

"No. Why?"

"It's this way. Clowes and I were talking—"

"If Clowes was there he was probably talking. Well?"

"About your brother."

"Oh, by Jove," said Bob, sitting up. "That reminds me. I forgot to get the evening paper. Did he get his century all right?"

"Who?" asked Trevor, bewildered.

"My brother, J. W. He'd made sixty-three not out against Kent in this morning's paper. What happened?"

"I didn't get a paper either. I didn't mean that brother. I meant the one here."

"Oh, Mike? What's Mike been up to?"

29

"Nothing as yet, that I know of; but, I say, you know, he seems a great pal of Wyatt's."

"I know. I spoke to him about it."

"Oh, you did? That's all right, then."

"Not that there's anything wrong with Wyatt."

"Not a bit. Only he is rather mucking about this term, I hear. It's his last, so I suppose he wants to have a rag."

"Don't blame him."

"Nor do I. Rather rot, though, if he lugged your brother into a row by accident."

"I should get blamed. I think I'll speak to him again."

"I should, I think."

"I hope he isn't idiot enough to go out at night with Wyatt. If Wyatt likes to risk it, all right. That's his look out. But it won't do for Mike to go playing the goat too."

"Clowes suggested putting Firby-Smith on to him. He'd have more chance, being in the same house, of seeing that he didn't come a mucker than you would."

"I've done that. Smith said he'd speak to him."

"That's all right then. Is that a new bat?"

"Got it to-day. Smashed my other yesterday—against the school house."

Donaldson's had played a friendly with the school house during the last two days, and had beaten them.

"I thought I heard it go. You were rather in form."

"Better than at the beginning of the term, anyhow. I simply couldn't do a thing then. But my last three innings have been 33 not out, 18, and 51.

"I should think you're bound to get your first all right."

"Hope so. I see Mike's playing for the second against the O.W.s."

"Yes. Pretty good for his first term. You have a pro. to coach you in the holidays, don't you?"

"Yes. I didn't go to him much this last time. I was away a lot. But Mike fairly lived inside the net."

"Well, it's not been chucked away. I suppose he'll get his first next year. There'll be a big clearing-out of colours at the end of this term. Nearly all the first are leaving. Henfrey'll be captain, I expect."

"Saunders, the pro. at home, always says that Mike's going to be the star cricketer of the family. Better than J. W. even, he thinks. I asked him what he thought of me, and he said, 'You'll be making a lot of runs some day, Mr. Bob.' There's a subtle difference, isn't there? I shall have Mike cutting me out before I leave school if I'm not careful."

"Sort of infant prodigy," said Trevor. "Don't think he's quite up to it yet, though."

He went back to his study, and Bob, having finished his oiling and washed his hands, started on his Thucydides. And, in the stress of

30

wrestling with the speech of an apparently delirious Athenian general, whose remarks seemed to contain nothing even remotely resembling sense and coherence, he allowed the question of Mike's welfare to fade from his mind like a dissolving view.

CHAPTER VIII

A ROW WITH THE TOWN

The beginning of a big row, one of those rows which turn a school upside down like a volcanic eruption and provide old boys with something to talk about, when they meet, for years, is not unlike the beginning of a thunderstorm.

You are walking along one seemingly fine day, when suddenly there is a hush, and there falls on you from space one big drop. The next moment the thing has begun, and you are standing in a shower-bath. It is just the same with a row. Some trivial episode occurs, and in an instant the place is in a ferment. It was so with the great picnic at Wrykyn.

The bare outlines of the beginning of this affair are included in a letter which Mike wrote to his father on the Sunday following the Old Wrykynian matches.

This was the letter:

"DEAR FATHER,—Thanks awfully for your letter. I hope you are quite well. I have been getting on all right at cricket lately. My scores since I wrote last have been 0 in a scratch game (the sun got in my eyes just as I played, and I got bowled); 15 for the third against an eleven of masters (without G. B. Jones, the Surrey man, and Spence); 28 not out in the Under Sixteen game; and 30 in a form match. Rather decent. Yesterday one of the men put down for the second against the O.W.'s second couldn't play because his father was very ill, so I played. Wasn't it luck? It's the first time I've played for the second. I didn't do much, because I didn't get an innings. They stop the cricket on O.W. matches day because they have a lot of rotten Greek plays and things which take up a frightful time, and half the chaps are acting, so we stop from lunch to four. Rot I call it. So I didn't go in, because they won the toss and made 215, and by the time we'd made 140 for 6 it was close of play. They'd stuck me in eighth wicket. Rather rot. Still, I may get another shot. And I made rather a decent catch at mid-on. Low down.

31

I had to dive for it. Bob played for the first, but didn't do much. He was run out after he'd got ten. I believe he's rather sick about it.

"Rather a rummy thing happened after lock-up. I wasn't in it, but a fellow called Wyatt (awfully decent chap. He's Wain's step-son, only they bar one another) told me about it. He was in it all right. There's a dinner after the matches on O.W. day, and some of the chaps were going back to their houses after it when they got into a row with a lot of brickies from the town, and there was rather a row. There was a policeman mixed up in it somehow, only I don't quite know where he comes in. I'll find out and tell you next time I write. Love to everybody. Tell Marjory I'll write to her in a day or two.

"Your loving son,
"MIKE.

"P.S.—I say, I suppose you couldn't send me five bob, could you? I'm rather broke.
"P.P.S.—Half-a-crown would do, only I'd rather it was five bob."

And, on the back of the envelope, these words: "Or a bob would be better than nothing."

The outline of the case was as Mike had stated. But there were certain details of some importance which had not come to his notice when he sent the letter. On the Monday they were public property.

The thing had happened after this fashion. At the conclusion of the day's cricket, all those who had been playing in the four elevens which the school put into the field against the old boys, together with the school choir, were entertained by the headmaster to supper in the Great Hall. The banquet, lengthened by speeches, songs, and recitations which the reciters imagined to be songs, lasted, as a rule, till about ten o'clock, when the revellers were supposed to go back to their houses by the nearest route, and turn in. This was the official programme. The school usually performed it with certain modifications and improvements.

About midway between Wrykyn, the school, and Wrykyn, the town, there stands on an island in the centre of the road a solitary lamp-post. It was the custom, and had been the custom for generations back, for the diners to trudge off to this lamp-post, dance round it for some minutes singing the school song or whatever happened to be the popular song of the moment, and then race back to their houses. Antiquity had given the custom a sort of sanctity, and the authorities, if they knew—which they must have done—never interfered.

But there were others.

Wrykyn, the town, was peculiarly rich in "gangs of youths." Like the vast majority of the inhabitants of the place, they seemed to have no work of any kind whatsoever to occupy their time, which they used,

32

accordingly, to spend prowling about and indulging in a mild, brainless, rural type of hooliganism. They seldom proceeded to practical rowdyism and never except with the school. As a rule, they amused themselves by shouting rude chaff. The school regarded them with a lofty contempt, much as an Oxford man regards the townee. The school was always anxious for a row, but it was the unwritten law that only in special circumstances should they proceed to active measures. A curious dislike for school-and-town rows and most misplaced severity in dealing with the offenders when they took place, were among the few flaws in the otherwise admirable character of the headmaster of Wrykyn. It was understood that one scragged bargees at one's own risk, and, as a rule, it was not considered worth it.

But after an excellent supper and much singing and joviality, one's views are apt to alter. Risks which before supper seemed great, show a tendency to dwindle.

When, therefore, the twenty or so Wrykynians who were dancing round the lamp-post were aware, in the midst of their festivities, that they were being observed and criticised by an equal number of townees, and that the criticisms were, as usual, essentially candid and personal, they found themselves forgetting the headmaster's prejudices and feeling only that these outsiders must be put to the sword as speedily as possible, for the honour of the school.

Possibly, if the town brigade had stuck to a purely verbal form of attack, all might yet have been peace. Words can be overlooked.

But tomatoes cannot.

No man of spirit can bear to be pelted with over-ripe tomatoes for any length of time without feeling that if the thing goes on much longer he will be reluctantly compelled to take steps.

In the present crisis, the first tomato was enough to set matters moving.

As the two armies stood facing each other in silence under the dim and mysterious rays of the lamp, it suddenly whizzed out from the enemy's ranks, and hit Wyatt on the right ear.

There was a moment of suspense. Wyatt took out his handkerchief and wiped his face, over which the succulent vegetable had spread itself.

"I don't know how you fellows are going to pass the evening," he said quietly. "My idea of a good after-dinner game is to try and find the chap who threw that. Anybody coming?"

For the first five minutes it was as even a fight as one could have wished to see. It raged up and down the road without a pause, now in a solid mass, now splitting up into little groups. The science was on the side of the school. Most Wrykynians knew how to box to a certain extent. But, at any rate at first, it was no time for science. To be scientific one must have an opponent who observes at least the more important rules of the ring. It is impossible to do the latest ducks and

33

hooks taught you by the instructor if your antagonist butts you in the chest, and then kicks your shins, while some dear friend of his, of whose presence you had no idea, hits you at the same time on the back of the head. The greatest expert would lose his science in such circumstances.

Probably what gave the school the victory in the end was the righteousness of their cause. They were smarting under a sense of injury, and there is nothing that adds a force to one's blows and a recklessness to one's style of delivering them more than a sense of injury.

Wyatt, one side of his face still showing traces of the tomato, led the school with a vigour that could not be resisted. He very seldom lost his temper, but he did draw the line at bad tomatoes.

Presently the school noticed that the enemy were vanishing little by little into the darkness which concealed the town. Barely a dozen remained. And their lonely condition seemed to be borne in upon these by a simultaneous brain-wave, for they suddenly gave the fight up, and stampeded as one man.

The leaders were beyond recall, but two remained, tackled low by Wyatt and Clowes after the fashion of the football-field.

The school gathered round its prisoners, panting. The scene of the conflict had shifted little by little to a spot some fifty yards from where it had started. By the side of the road at this point was a green, depressed looking pond. Gloomy in the daytime, it looked unspeakable at night. It struck Wyatt, whose finer feelings had been entirely blotted out by tomato, as an ideal place in which to bestow the captives.

"Let's chuck 'em in there," he said.

The idea was welcomed gladly by all, except the prisoners. A move was made towards the pond, and the procession had halted on the brink, when a new voice made itself heard.

"Now then," it said, "what's all this?"

A stout figure in policeman's uniform was standing surveying them with the aid of a small bull's-eye lantern.

"What's all this?"

"It's all right," said Wyatt.

"All right, is it? What's on?"

One of the prisoners spoke.

"Make 'em leave hold of us, Mr. Butt. They're a-going to chuck us in the pond."

"Ho!" said the policeman, with a change in his voice. "Ho, are they? Come now, young gentleman, a lark's a lark, but you ought to know where to stop."

"It's anything but a lark," said Wyatt in the creamy voice he used when feeling particularly savage. "We're the Strong Right Arm of Justice. That's what we are. This isn't a lark, it's an execution."

34

"I don't want none of your lip, whoever you are," said Mr. Butt, understanding but dimly, and suspecting impudence by instinct.

"This is quite a private matter," said Wyatt. "You run along on your beat. You can't do anything here."

"Ho!"

"Shove 'em in, you chaps."

"Stop!" From Mr. Butt.

"Oo-er!" From prisoner number one.

There was a sounding splash as willing hands urged the first of the captives into the depths. He ploughed his way to the bank, scrambled out, and vanished.

Wyatt turned to the other prisoner.

"You'll have the worst of it, going in second. He'll have churned up the mud a bit. Don't swallow more than you can help, or you'll go getting typhoid. I expect there are leeches and things there, but if you nip out quick they may not get on to you. Carry on, you chaps."

It was here that the regrettable incident occurred. Just as the second prisoner was being launched, Constable Butt, determined to assert himself even at the eleventh hour, sprang forward, and seized the captive by the arm. A drowning man will clutch at a straw. A man about to be hurled into an excessively dirty pond will clutch at a stout policeman. The prisoner did.

Constable Butt represented his one link with dry land. As he came within reach he attached himself to his tunic with the vigour and concentration of a limpet.

At the same moment the executioners gave their man the final heave. The policeman realised his peril too late. A medley of noises made the peaceful night hideous. A howl from the townee, a yell from the policeman, a cheer from the launching party, a frightened squawk from some birds in a neighbouring tree, and a splash compared with which the first had been as nothing, and all was over.

The dark waters were lashed into a maelstrom; and then two streaming figures squelched up the further bank.

The school stood in silent consternation. It was no occasion for light apologies.

"Do you know," said Wyatt, as he watched the Law shaking the water from itself on the other side of the pond, "I'm not half sure that we hadn't better be moving!"

35

CHAPTER IX

BEFORE THE STORM

Your real, devastating row has many points of resemblance with a prairie fire. A man on a prairie lights his pipe, and throws away the match. The flame catches a bunch of dry grass, and, before any one can realise what is happening, sheets of fire are racing over the country; and the interested neighbours are following their example. (I have already compared a row with a thunderstorm; but both comparisons may stand. In dealing with so vast a matter as a row there must be no stint.)

The tomato which hit Wyatt in the face was the thrown-away match. But for the unerring aim of the town marksman great events would never have happened. A tomato is a trivial thing (though it is possible that the man whom it hits may not think so), but in the present case, it was the direct cause of epoch-making trouble.

The tomato hit Wyatt. Wyatt, with others, went to look for the thrower. The remnants of the thrower's friends were placed in the pond, and "with them," as they say in the courts of law, Police Constable Alfred Butt.

Following the chain of events, we find Mr. Butt, having prudently changed his clothes, calling upon the headmaster.

The headmaster was grave and sympathetic; Mr. Butt fierce and revengeful.

The imagination of the force is proverbial. Nurtured on motor-cars and fed with stop-watches, it has become world-famous. Mr. Butt gave free rein to it.

"Threw me in, they did, sir. Yes, sir."

"Threw you in!"

"Yes, sir. Plop!" said Mr. Butt, with a certain sad relish.

"Really, really!" said the headmaster. "Indeed! This is—dear me! I shall certainly—They threw you in!—Yes, I shall—certainly—"

Encouraged by this appreciative reception of his story, Mr. Butt started it again, right from the beginning.

"I was on my beat, sir, and I thought I heard a disturbance. I says to myself, ''Allo,' I says, 'a frakkus. Lots of them all gathered together, and fighting.' I says, beginning to suspect something, 'Wot's this all about, I wonder?' I says. 'Blow me if I don't think it's a frakkus.' And," concluded Mr. Butt, with the air of one confiding a secret, "and it was a frakkus!"

"And these boys actually threw you into the pond?"

"Plop, sir! Mrs. Butt is drying my uniform at home at this very moment as we sit talking here, sir. She says to me, 'Why, whatever 'ave you been a-doing? You're all wet.' And," he added, again with the confidential air, "I was wet, too. Wringin' wet."

The headmaster's frown deepened.

"And you are certain that your assailants were boys from the school?"

"Sure as I am that I'm sitting here, sir. They all 'ad their caps on their heads, sir."

"I have never heard of such a thing. I can hardly believe that it is possible. They actually seized you, and threw you into the water—"

"Splish, sir!" said the policeman, with a vividness of imagery both surprising and gratifying.

The headmaster tapped restlessly on the floor with his foot.

"How many boys were there?" he asked.

"Couple of 'undred, sir," said Mr. Butt promptly.

"Two hundred!"

"It was dark, sir, and I couldn't see not to say properly; but if you ask me my frank and private opinion I should say couple of 'undred."

"H'm—Well, I will look into the matter at once. They shall be punished."

"Yes, sir."

"Ye-e-s—H'm—Yes—Most severely."

"Yes, sir."

"Yes—Thank you, constable. Good-night."

"Good-night, sir."

The headmaster of Wrykyn was not a motorist. Owing to this disadvantage he made a mistake. Had he been a motorist, he would have known that statements by the police in the matter of figures must be divided by any number from two to ten, according to discretion. As it was, he accepted Constable Butt's report almost as it stood. He thought that he might possibly have been mistaken as to the exact numbers of those concerned in his immersion; but he accepted the statement in so far as it indicated that the thing had been the work of a considerable section of the school, and not of only one or two individuals. And this made all the difference to his method of dealing with the affair. Had he known how few were the numbers of those responsible for the cold in the head which subsequently attacked Constable Butt, he would have asked for their names, and an extra lesson would have settled the entire matter.

As it was, however, he got the impression that the school, as a whole, was culpable, and he proceeded to punish the school as a whole.

It happened that, about a week before the pond episode, a certain member of the Royal Family had recovered from a dangerous illness, which at one time had looked like being fatal. No official holiday had been given to the schools in honour of the recovery, but Eton and Harrow had set the example, which was followed throughout the kingdom, and Wrykyn had come into line with the rest. Only two days

37

before the O.W.'s matches the headmaster had given out a notice in the hall that the following Friday would be a whole holiday; and the school, always ready to stop work, had approved of the announcement exceedingly.

The step which the headmaster decided to take by way of avenging Mr. Butt's wrongs was to stop this holiday.

He gave out a notice to that effect on the Monday.

The school was thunderstruck. It could not understand it. The pond affair had, of course, become public property; and those who had had nothing to do with it had been much amused. "There'll be a frightful row about it," they had said, thrilled with the pleasant excitement of those who see trouble approaching and themselves looking on from a comfortable distance without risk or uneasiness. They were not malicious. They did not want to see their friends in difficulties. But there is no denying that a row does break the monotony of a school term. The thrilling feeling that something is going to happen is the salt of life....

And here they were, right in it after all. The blow had fallen, and crushed guilty and innocent alike.

The school's attitude can be summed up in three words. It was one vast, blank, astounded "Here, I say!"

Everybody was saying it, though not always in those words. When condensed, everybody's comment on the situation came to that.

There is something rather pathetic in the indignation of a school. It must always, or nearly always, expend itself in words, and in private at that. Even the consolation of getting on to platforms and shouting at itself is denied to it. A public school has no Hyde Park.

There is every probability—in fact, it is certain—that, but for one malcontent, the school's indignation would have been allowed to simmer down in the usual way, and finally become a mere vague memory.

The malcontent was Wyatt. He had been responsible for the starting of the matter, and he proceeded now to carry it on till it blazed up into the biggest thing of its kind ever known at Wrykyn—the Great Picnic.

Any one who knows the public schools, their ironbound conservatism, and, as a whole, intense respect for order and authority, will appreciate the magnitude of his feat, even though he may not approve of it. Leaders of men are rare. Leaders of boys are almost unknown. It requires genius to sway a school.

It would be an absorbing task for a psychologist to trace the various stages by which an impossibility was changed into a reality. Wyatt's coolness and matter-of-fact determination were his chief weapons. His popularity and reputation for lawlessness helped him. A conversation which he had with Neville-Smith, a day-boy, is typical of the way in which he forced his point of view on the school.

Neville-Smith was thoroughly representative of the average Wrykynian. He could play his part in any minor "rag" which interested him, and probably considered himself, on the whole, a daring sort of person. But at heart he had an enormous respect for authority. Before he came to Wyatt, he would not have dreamed of proceeding beyond words in his revolt. Wyatt acted on him like some drug.

Neville-Smith came upon Wyatt on his way to the nets. The notice concerning the holiday had only been given out that morning, and he was full of it. He expressed his opinion of the headmaster freely and in well-chosen words. He said it was a swindle, that it was all rot, and that it was a beastly shame. He added that something ought to be done about it.

"What are you going to do?" asked Wyatt.

"Well," said Neville-Smith a little awkwardly, guiltily conscious that he had been frothing, and scenting sarcasm, "I don't suppose one can actually do anything."

"Why not?" said Wyatt.

"What do you mean?"

"Why don't you take the holiday?"

"What? Not turn up on Friday!"

"Yes. I'm not going to."

Neville-Smith stopped and stared. Wyatt was unmoved.

"You're what?"

"I simply sha'n't go to school."

"You're rotting."

"All right."

"No, but, I say, ragging barred. Are you just going to cut off, though the holiday's been stopped?"

"That's the idea."

"You'll get sacked."

"I suppose so. But only because I shall be the only one to do it. If the whole school took Friday off, they couldn't do much. They couldn't sack the whole school."

"By Jove, nor could they! I say!"

They walked on, Neville-Smith's mind in a whirl, Wyatt whistling.

"I say," said Neville-Smith after a pause. "It would be a bit of a rag."

"Not bad."

"Do you think the chaps would do it?"

"If they understood they wouldn't be alone."

Another pause.

"Shall I ask some of them?" said Neville-Smith.

"Do."

"I could get quite a lot, I believe."

"That would be a start, wouldn't it? I could get a couple of dozen from Wain's. We should be forty or fifty strong to start with."

"I say, what a score, wouldn't it be?"

"Yes."

"I'll speak to the chaps to-night, and let you know."

"All right," said Wyatt. "Tell them that I shall be going anyhow. I should be glad of a little company."

The school turned in on the Thursday night in a restless, excited way. There were mysterious whisperings and gigglings. Groups kept forming in corners apart, to disperse casually and innocently on the approach of some person in authority.

An air of expectancy permeated each of the houses.

CHAPTER X

THE GREAT PICNIC

Morning school at Wrykyn started at nine o'clock. At that hour there was a call-over in each of the form-rooms. After call-over the forms proceeded to the Great Hall for prayers.

A strangely desolate feeling was in the air at nine o'clock on the Friday morning. Sit in the grounds of a public school any afternoon in the summer holidays, and you will get exactly the same sensation of being alone in the world as came to the dozen or so day-boys who bicycled through the gates that morning. Wrykyn was a boarding-school for the most part, but it had its leaven of day-boys. The majority of these lived in the town, and walked to school. A few, however, whose homes were farther away, came on bicycles. One plutocrat did the journey in a motor-car, rather to the scandal of the authorities, who, though unable to interfere, looked askance when compelled by the warning toot of the horn to skip from road to pavement. A form-master has the strongest objection to being made to skip like a young ram by a boy to whom he has only the day before given a hundred lines for shuffling his feet in form.

It seemed curious to these cyclists that there should be nobody about. Punctuality is the politeness of princes, but it was not a leading characteristic of the school; and at three minutes to nine, as a general rule, you might see the gravel in front of the buildings freely dotted with sprinters, trying to get in in time to answer their names.

It was curious that there should be nobody about to-day. A wave of reform could scarcely have swept through the houses during the night.

And yet—where was everybody?

Time only deepened the mystery. The form-rooms, like the gravel, were empty.

The cyclists looked at one another in astonishment. What could it mean?

It was an occasion on which sane people wonder if their brains are not playing them some unaccountable trick.

"I say," said Willoughby, of the Lower Fifth, to Brown, the only other occupant of the form-room, "the old man did stop the holiday to-day, didn't he?"

"Just what I was going to ask you," said Brown. "It's jolly rum. I distinctly remember him giving it out in hall that it was going to be stopped because of the O.W.'s day row."

"So do I. I can't make it out. Where is everybody?"

"They can't all be late."

"Somebody would have turned up by now. Why, it's just striking."

"Perhaps he sent another notice round the houses late last night, saying it was on again all right. I say, what a swindle if he did. Some one might have let us know. I should have got up an hour later."

"So should I."

"Hullo, here is somebody."

It was the master of the Lower Fifth, Mr. Spence. He walked briskly into the room, as was his habit. Seeing the obvious void, he stopped in his stride, and looked puzzled.

"Willoughby. Brown. Are you the only two here? Where is everybody?"

"Please, sir, we don't know. We were just wondering."

"Have you seen nobody?"

"No, sir."

"We were just wondering, sir, if the holiday had been put on again, after all."

"I've heard nothing about it. I should have received some sort of intimation if it had been."

"Yes, sir."

"Do you mean to say that you have seen nobody, Brown?"

"Only about a dozen fellows, sir. The usual lot who come on bikes, sir."

"None of the boarders?"

"No, sir. Not a single one."

"This is extraordinary."

Mr. Spence pondered.

"Well," he said, "you two fellows had better go along up to Hall. I

41

shall go to the Common Room and make inquiries. Perhaps, as you say, there is a holiday to-day, and the notice was not brought to me."

Mr. Spence told himself, as he walked to the Common Room, that this might be a possible solution of the difficulty. He was not a house-master, and lived by himself in rooms in the town. It was just conceivable that they might have forgotten to tell him of the change in the arrangements.

But in the Common Room the same perplexity reigned. Half a dozen masters were seated round the room, and a few more were standing. And they were all very puzzled.

A brisk conversation was going on. Several voices hailed Mr. Spence as he entered.

"Hullo, Spence. Are you alone in the world too?"

"Any of your boys turned up, Spence?"

"You in the same condition as we are, Spence?"

Mr. Spence seated himself on the table.

"Haven't any of your fellows turned up, either?" he said.

"When I accepted the honourable post of Lower Fourth master in this abode of sin," said Mr. Seymour, "it was on the distinct understanding that there was going to be a Lower Fourth. Yet I go into my form-room this morning, and what do I find? Simply Emptiness, and Pickersgill II. whistling 'The Church Parade,' all flat. I consider I have been hardly treated."

"I have no complaint to make against Brown and Willoughby, as individuals," said Mr. Spence; "but, considered as a form, I call them short measure."

"I confess that I am entirely at a loss," said Mr. Shields precisely. "I have never been confronted with a situation like this since I became a schoolmaster."

"It is most mysterious," agreed Mr. Wain, plucking at his beard. "Exceedingly so."

The younger masters, notably Mr. Spence and Mr. Seymour, had begun to look on the thing as a huge jest.

"We had better teach ourselves," said Mr. Seymour. "Spence, do a hundred lines for laughing in form."

The door burst open.

"Hullo, here's another scholastic Little Bo-Peep," said Mr. Seymour. "Well, Appleby, have you lost your sheep, too?"

"You don't mean to tell me—" began Mr. Appleby.

"I do," said Mr. Seymour. "Here we are, fifteen of us, all good men and true, graduates of our Universities, and, as far as I can see, if we divide up the boys who have come to school this morning on fair share-and-share-alike lines, it will work out at about two-thirds of a boy each. Spence, will you take a third of Pickersgill II.?"

"I want none of your charity," said Mr. Spence loftily. "You don't seem to realise that I'm the best off of you all. I've got two in my form.

It's no good offering me your Pickersgills. I simply haven't room for them."

"What does it all mean?" exclaimed Mr. Appleby.

"If you ask me," said Mr. Seymour, "I should say that it meant that the school, holding the sensible view that first thoughts are best, have ignored the head's change of mind, and are taking their holiday as per original programme."

"They surely cannot—!"

"Well, where are they then?"

"Do you seriously mean that the entire school has—has rebelled?"

"'Nay, sire,'" quoted Mr. Spence, "'a revolution!'"

"I never heard of such a thing!"

"We're making history," said Mr. Seymour.

"It will be rather interesting," said Mr. Spence, "to see how the head will deal with a situation like this. One can rely on him to do the statesman-like thing, but I'm bound to say I shouldn't care to be in his place. It seems to me these boys hold all the cards. You can't expel a whole school. There's safety in numbers. The thing is colossal."

"It is deplorable," said Mr. Wain, with austerity. "Exceedingly so."

"I try to think so," said Mr. Spence, "but it's a struggle. There's a Napoleonic touch about the business that appeals to one. Disorder on a small scale is bad, but this is immense. I've never heard of anything like it at any public school. When I was at Winchester, my last year there, there was pretty nearly a revolution because the captain of cricket was expelled on the eve of the Eton match. I remember making inflammatory speeches myself on that occasion. But we stopped on the right side of the line. We were satisfied with growling. But this—!"

Mr. Seymour got up.

"It's an ill wind," he said. "With any luck we ought to get the day off, and it's ideal weather for a holiday. The head can hardly ask us to sit indoors, teaching nobody. If I have to stew in my form-room all day, instructing Pickersgill II., I shall make things exceedingly sultry for that youth. He will wish that the Pickersgill progeny had stopped short at his elder brother. He will not value life. In the meantime, as it's already ten past, hadn't we better be going up to Hall to see what the orders of the day are?"

"Look at Shields," said Mr. Spence. "He might be posing for a statue to be called 'Despair!' He reminds me of Macduff. Macbeth, Act iv., somewhere near the end. 'What, all my pretty chickens, at one fell swoop?' That's what Shields is saying to himself."

"It's all very well to make a joke of it, Spence," said Mr. Shields querulously, "but it is most disturbing. Most."

"Exceedingly," agreed Mr. Wain.

The bereaved company of masters walked on up the stairs that led to the Great Hall.

43

CHAPTER XI

THE CONCLUSION OF THE PICNIC

If the form-rooms had been lonely, the Great Hall was doubly, trebly, so. It was a vast room, stretching from side to side of the middle block, and its ceiling soared up into a distant dome. At one end was a dais and an organ, and at intervals down the room stood long tables. The panels were covered with the names of Wrykynians who had won scholarships at Oxford and Cambridge, and of Old Wrykynians who had taken first in Mods or Greats, or achieved any other recognised success, such as a place in the Indian Civil Service list. A silent testimony, these panels, to the work the school had done in the world.

Nobody knew exactly how many the Hall could hold, when packed to its fullest capacity. The six hundred odd boys at the school seemed to leave large gaps unfilled.

This morning there was a mere handful, and the place looked worse than empty.

The Sixth Form were there, and the school prefects. The Great Picnic had not affected their numbers. The Sixth stood by their table in a solid group. The other tables were occupied by ones and twos. A buzz of conversation was going on, which did not cease when the masters filed into the room and took their places. Every one realised by this time that the biggest row in Wrykyn history was well under way; and the thing had to be discussed.

In the Masters' library Mr. Wain and Mr. Shields, the spokesmen of the Common Room, were breaking the news to the headmaster.

The headmaster was a man who rarely betrayed emotion in his public capacity. He heard Mr. Shields's rambling remarks, punctuated by Mr. Wain's "Exceedinglys," to an end. Then he gathered up his cap and gown.

"You say that the whole school is absent?" he remarked quietly.

Mr. Shields, in a long-winded flow of words, replied that that was what he did say.

"Ah!" said the headmaster.

There was a silence.

"'M!" said the headmaster.

There was another silence.

"Ye—e—s!" said the headmaster.

He then led the way into the Hall.

Conversation ceased abruptly as he entered. The school, like an audience at a theatre when the hero has just appeared on the stage, felt that the serious interest of the drama had begun. There was a dead silence at every table as he strode up the room and on to the dais.

There was something Titanic in his calmness. Every eye was on his face as he passed up the Hall, but not a sign of perturbation could the school read. To judge from his expression, he might have been unaware of the emptiness around him.

The master who looked after the music of the school, and incidentally accompanied the hymn with which prayers at Wrykyn opened, was waiting, puzzled, at the foot of the dais. It seemed improbable that things would go on as usual, and he did not know whether he was expected to be at the organ, or not. The headmaster's placid face reassured him. He went to his post.

The hymn began. It was a long hymn, and one which the school liked for its swing and noise. As a rule, when it was sung, the Hall re-echoed. To-day, the thin sound of the voices had quite an uncanny effect. The organ boomed through the deserted room.

The school, or the remnants of it, waited impatiently while the prefect whose turn it was to read stammered nervously through the lesson. They were anxious to get on to what the Head was going to say at the end of prayers. At last it was over. The school waited, all ears.

The headmaster bent down from the dais and called to Firby-Smith, who was standing in his place with the Sixth.

The Gazeka, blushing warmly, stepped forward.

"Bring me a school list, Firby-Smith," said the headmaster.

The Gazeka was wearing a pair of very squeaky boots that morning. They sounded deafening as he walked out of the room.

The school waited.

Presently a distant squeaking was heard, and Firby-Smith returned, bearing a large sheet of paper.

The headmaster thanked him, and spread it out on the reading-desk.

Then, calmly, as if it were an occurrence of every day, he began to call the roll.

"Abney."

No answer.

"Adams."

No answer.

"Allenby."

"Here, sir," from a table at the end of the room. Allenby was a prefect, in the Science Sixth.

The headmaster made a mark against his name with a pencil.

"Arkwright."

No answer.

He began to call the names more rapidly.

"Arlington. Arthur. Ashe. Aston."

"Here, sir," in a shrill treble from the rider in motorcars.

The headmaster made another tick.

The list came to an end after what seemed to the school an

45

unconscionable time, and he rolled up the paper again, and stepped to the edge of the dais.

"All boys not in the Sixth Form," he said, "will go to their form-rooms and get their books and writing-materials, and return to the Hall."

("Good work," murmured Mr. Seymour to himself. "Looks as if we should get that holiday after all.")

"The Sixth Form will go to their form-room as usual. I should like to speak to the masters for a moment."

He nodded dismissal to the school.

The masters collected on the daïs.

"I find that I shall not require your services to-day," said the headmaster. "If you will kindly set the boys in your forms some work that will keep them occupied, I will look after them here. It is a lovely day," he added, with a smile, "and I am sure you will all enjoy yourselves a great deal more in the open air."

"That," said Mr. Seymour to Mr. Spence, as they went downstairs, "is what I call a genuine sportsman."

"My opinion neatly expressed," said Mr. Spence. "Come on the river. Or shall we put up a net, and have a knock?"

"River, I think. Meet you at the boat-house."

"All right. Don't be long."

"If every day were run on these lines, school-mastering wouldn't be such a bad profession. I wonder if one could persuade one's form to run amuck as a regular thing."

"Pity one can't. It seems to me the ideal state of things. Ensures the greatest happiness of the greatest number."

"I say! Suppose the school has gone up the river, too, and we meet them! What shall we do?"

"Thank them," said Mr. Spence, "most kindly. They've done us well."

The school had not gone up the river. They had marched in a solid body, with the school band at their head playing Sousa, in the direction of Worfield, a market town of some importance, distant about five miles. Of what they did and what the natives thought of it all, no very distinct records remain. The thing is a tradition on the countryside now, an event colossal and heroic, to be talked about in the tap-room of the village inn during the long winter evenings. The papers got hold of it, but were curiously misled as to the nature of the demonstration. This was the fault of the reporter on the staff of the Worfield Intelligencer and Farmers' Guide, who saw in the thing a legitimate "march-out," and, questioning a straggler as to the reason for the expedition and gathering foggily that the restoration to health of the Eminent Person was at the bottom of it, said so in his paper. And two days later, at about the time when Retribution had got seriously to work, the Daily Mail reprinted the account, with comments and

46

elaborations, and headed it "Loyal Schoolboys." The writer said that great credit was due to the headmaster of Wrykyn for his ingenuity in devising and organising so novel a thanksgiving celebration. And there was the usual conversation between "a rosy-cheeked lad of some sixteen summers" and "our representative," in which the rosy-cheeked one spoke most kindly of the head-master, who seemed to be a warm personal friend of his.

The remarkable thing about the Great Picnic was its orderliness. Considering that five hundred and fifty boys were ranging the country in a compact mass, there was wonderfully little damage done to property. Wyatt's genius did not stop short at organising the march. In addition, he arranged a system of officers which effectually controlled the animal spirits of the rank and file. The prompt and decisive way in which rioters were dealt with during the earlier stages of the business proved a wholesome lesson to others who would have wished to have gone and done likewise. A spirit of martial law reigned over the Great Picnic. And towards the end of the day fatigue kept the rowdy-minded quiet.

At Worfield the expedition lunched. It was not a market-day, fortunately, or the confusion in the narrow streets would have been hopeless. On ordinary days Worfield was more or less deserted. It is astonishing that the resources of the little town were equal to satisfying the needs of the picnickers. They descended on the place like an army of locusts.

Wyatt, as generalissimo of the expedition, walked into the "Grasshopper and Ant," the leading inn of the town.

"Anything I can do for you, sir?" inquired the landlord politely.

"Yes, please," said Wyatt, "I want lunch for five hundred and fifty."

That was the supreme moment in mine host's life. It was his big subject of conversation ever afterwards. He always told that as his best story, and he always ended with the words, "You could ha' knocked me down with a feather!"

The first shock over, the staff of the "Grasshopper and Ant" bustled about. Other inns were called upon for help. Private citizens rallied round with bread, jam, and apples. And the army lunched sumptuously.

In the early afternoon they rested, and as evening began to fall, the march home was started.

At the school, net practice was just coming to an end when, faintly, as the garrison of Lucknow heard the first skirl of the pipes of the relieving force, those on the grounds heard the strains of the school band and a murmur of many voices. Presently the sounds grew more distinct, and up the Wrykyn road came marching the vanguard of the column, singing the school song. They looked weary but cheerful.

As the army drew near to the school, it melted away little by little, each house claiming its representatives. At the school gates only a handful were left.

Bob Jackson, walking back to Donaldson's, met Wyatt at the gate, and gazed at him, speechless.

"Hullo," said Wyatt, "been to the nets? I wonder if there's time for a ginger-beer before the shop shuts."

CHAPTER XII

MIKE GETS HIS CHANCE

The headmaster was quite bland and business-like about it all. There were no impassioned addresses from the dais. He did not tell the school that it ought to be ashamed of itself. Nor did he say that he should never have thought it of them. Prayers on the Saturday morning were marked by no unusual features. There was, indeed, a stir of excitement when he came to the edge of the dais, and cleared his throat as a preliminary to making an announcement. Now for it, thought the school.

This was the announcement.

"There has been an outbreak of chicken-pox in the town. All streets except the High Street will in consequence be out of bounds till further notice."

He then gave the nod of dismissal.

The school streamed downstairs, marvelling.

The less astute of the picnickers, unmindful of the homely proverb about hallooing before leaving the wood, were openly exulting. It seemed plain to them that the headmaster, baffled by the magnitude of the thing, had resolved to pursue the safe course of ignoring it altogether. To lie low is always a shrewd piece of tactics, and there seemed no reason why the Head should not have decided on it in the present instance.

Neville-Smith was among these premature rejoicers.

"I say," he chuckled, overtaking Wyatt in the cloisters, "this is all right, isn't it! He's funked it. I thought he would. Finds the job too big to tackle."

Wyatt was damping.

"My dear chap," he said, "it's not over yet by a long chalk. It hasn't started yet."

48

"What do you mean? Why didn't he say anything about it in Hall, then?"

"Why should he? Have you ever had tick at a shop?"

"Of course I have. What do you mean? Why?"

"Well, they didn't send in the bill right away. But it came all right."

"Do you think he's going to do something, then?"

"Rather. You wait."

Wyatt was right.

Between ten and eleven on Wednesdays and Saturdays old Bates, the school sergeant, used to copy out the names of those who were in extra lesson, and post them outside the school shop. The school inspected the list during the quarter to eleven interval.

To-day, rushing to the shop for its midday bun, the school was aware of a vast sheet of paper where usually there was but a small one. They surged round it. Buns were forgotten. What was it?

Then the meaning of the notice flashed upon them. The headmaster had acted. This bloated document was the extra lesson list, swollen with names as a stream swells with rain. It was a comprehensive document. It left out little.

"The following boys will go in to extra lesson this afternoon and next Wednesday," it began. And "the following boys" numbered four hundred.

"Bates must have got writer's cramp," said Clowes, as he read the huge scroll.

Wyatt met Mike after school, as they went back to the house.

"Seen the 'extra' list?" he remarked. "None of the kids are in it, I notice. Only the bigger fellows. Rather a good thing. I'm glad you got off."

"Thanks," said Mike, who was walking a little stiffly. "I don't know what you call getting off. It seems to me you're the chaps who got off."

"How do you mean?"

"We got tanned," said Mike ruefully.

"What!"

"Yes. Everybody below the Upper Fourth."

Wyatt roared with laughter.

"By Gad," he said, "he is an old sportsman. I never saw such a man. He lowers all records."

"Glad you think it funny. You wouldn't have if you'd been me. I was one of the first to get it. He was quite fresh."

"Sting?"

"Should think it did."

"Well, buck up. Don't break down."

"I'm not breaking down," said Mike indignantly.

49

"All right, I thought you weren't. Anyhow, you're better off than I am."

"An extra's nothing much," said Mike.

"It is when it happens to come on the same day as the M.C.C. match."

"Oh, by Jove! I forgot. That's next Wednesday, isn't it? You won't be able to play!"

"No."

"I say, what rot!"

"It is, rather. Still, nobody can say I didn't ask for it. If one goes out of one's way to beg and beseech the Old Man to put one in extra, it would be a little rough on him to curse him when he does it."

"I should be awfully sick, if it were me."

"Well, it isn't you, so you're all right. You'll probably get my place in the team."

Mike smiled dutifully at what he supposed to be a humorous sally.

"Or, rather, one of the places," continued Wyatt, who seemed to be sufficiently in earnest. "They'll put a bowler in instead of me. Probably Druce. But there'll be several vacancies. Let's see. Me. Adams. Ashe. Any more? No, that's the lot. I should think they'd give you a chance."

"You needn't rot," said Mike uncomfortably. He had his day-dreams, like everybody else, and they always took the form of playing for the first eleven (and, incidentally, making a century in record time). To have to listen while the subject was talked about lightly made him hot and prickly all over.

"I'm not rotting," said Wyatt seriously, "I'll suggest it to Burgess to-night."

"You don't think there's any chance of it, really, do you?" said Mike awkwardly.

"I don't see why not? Buck up in the scratch game this afternoon. Fielding especially. Burgess is simply mad on fielding. I don't blame him either, especially as he's a bowler himself. He'd shove a man into the team like a shot, whatever his batting was like, if his fielding was something extra special. So you field like a demon this afternoon, and I'll carry on the good work in the evening."

"I say," said Mike, overcome, "it's awfully decent of you, Wyatt."

Billy Burgess, captain of Wrykyn cricket, was a genial giant, who seldom allowed himself to be ruffled. The present was one of the rare occasions on which he permitted himself that luxury. Wyatt found him in his study, shortly before lock-up, full of strange oaths, like the soldier in Shakespeare.

"You rotter! You rotter! You worm!" he observed crisply, as Wyatt appeared.

50

"Dear old Billy!" said Wyatt. "Come on, give me a kiss, and let's be friends."

"You—!"

"William! William!"

"If it wasn't illegal, I'd like to tie you and Ashe and that blackguard Adams up in a big sack, and drop you into the river. And I'd jump on the sack first. What do you mean by letting the team down like this? I know you were at the bottom of it all."

He struggled into his shirt—he was changing after a bath—and his face popped wrathfully out at the other end.

"I'm awfully sorry, Bill," said Wyatt. "The fact is, in the excitement of the moment the M.C.C. match went clean out of my mind."

"You haven't got a mind," grumbled Burgess. "You've got a cheap brown paper substitute. That's your trouble."

Wyatt turned the conversation tactfully.

"How many wickets did you get to-day?" he asked.

"Eight. For a hundred and three. I was on the spot. Young Jackson caught a hot one off me at third man. That kid's good."

"Why don't you play him against the M.C.C. on Wednesday?" said Wyatt, jumping at his opportunity.

"What? Are you sitting on my left shoe?"

"No. There it is in the corner."

"Right ho!... What were you saying?"

"Why not play young Jackson for the first?"

"Too small."

"Rot. What does size matter? Cricket isn't footer. Besides, he isn't small. He's as tall as I am."

"I suppose he is. Dash, I've dropped my stud."

Wyatt waited patiently till he had retrieved it. Then he returned to the attack.

"He's as good a bat as his brother, and a better field."

"Old Bob can't field for toffee. I will say that for him. Dropped a sitter off me to-day. Why the deuce fellows can't hold catches when they drop slowly into their mouths I'm hanged if I can see."

"You play him," said Wyatt. "Just give him a trial. That kid's a genius at cricket. He's going to be better than any of his brothers, even Joe. Give him a shot."

Burgess hesitated.

"You know, it's a bit risky," he said. "With you three lunatics out of the team we can't afford to try many experiments. Better stick to the men at the top of the second."

Wyatt got up, and kicked the wall as a vent for his feelings.

"You rotter," he said. "Can't you see when you've got a good man? Here's this kid waiting for you ready made with a style like Trumper's, and you rave about top men in the second, chaps who play

51

forward at everything, and pat half-volleys back to the bowler! Do you realise that your only chance of being known to Posterity is as the man who gave M. Jackson his colours at Wrykyn? In a few years he'll be playing for England, and you'll think it a favour if he nods to you in the pav. at Lord's. When you're a white-haired old man you'll go doddering about, gassing to your grandchildren, poor kids, how you 'discovered' M. Jackson. It'll be the only thing they'll respect you for."

Wyatt stopped for breath.

"All right," said Burgess, "I'll think it over. Frightful gift of the gab you've got, Wyatt."

"Good," said Wyatt. "Think it over. And don't forget what I said about the grandchildren. You would like little Wyatt Burgess and the other little Burgesses to respect you in your old age, wouldn't you? Very well, then. So long. The bell went ages ago. I shall be locked out."

On the Monday morning Mike passed the notice-board just as Burgess turned away from pinning up the list of the team to play the M.C.C. He read it, and his heart missed a beat. For, bottom but one, just above the W. B. Burgess, was a name that leaped from the paper at him. His own name.

CHAPTER XIII

THE M.C.C. MATCH

If the day happens to be fine, there is a curious, dream-like atmosphere about the opening stages of a first eleven match. Everything seems hushed and expectant. The rest of the school have gone in after the interval at eleven o'clock, and you are alone on the grounds with a cricket-bag. The only signs of life are a few pedestrians on the road beyond the railings and one or two blazer and flannel-clad forms in the pavilion. The sense of isolation is trying to the nerves, and a school team usually bats 25 per cent. better after lunch, when the strangeness has worn off.

Mike walked across from Wain's, where he had changed, feeling quite hollow. He could almost have cried with pure fright. Bob had shouted after him from a window as he passed Donaldson's, to wait, so that they could walk over together; but conversation was the last thing Mike desired at that moment.

He had almost reached the pavilion when one of the M.C.C. team came down the steps, saw him, and stopped dead.

"By Jove, Saunders!" cried Mike.

"Why, Master Mike!"

The professional beamed, and quite suddenly, the lost, hopeless feeling left Mike. He felt as cheerful as if he and Saunders had met in the meadow at home, and were just going to begin a little quiet net-practice.

"Why, Master Mike, you don't mean to say you're playing for the school already?"

Mike nodded happily.

"Isn't it ripping," he said.

Saunders slapped his leg in a sort of ecstasy.

"Didn't I always say it, sir," he chuckled. "Wasn't I right? I used to say to myself it 'ud be a pretty good school team that 'ud leave you out."

"Of course, I'm only playing as a sub., you know. Three chaps are in extra, and I got one of the places."

"Well, you'll make a hundred to-day, Master Mike, and then they'll have to put you in."

"Wish I could!"

"Master Joe's come down with the Club," said Saunders.

"Joe! Has he really? How ripping! Hullo, here he is. Hullo, Joe?"

The greatest of all the Jacksons was descending the pavilion steps with the gravity befitting an All England batsman. He stopped short, as Saunders had done.

"Mike! You aren't playing!"

"Yes."

"Well, I'm hanged! Young marvel, isn't he, Saunders?"

"He is, sir," said Saunders. "Got all the strokes. I always said it, Master Joe. Only wants the strength."

Joe took Mike by the shoulder, and walked him off in the direction of a man in a Zingari blazer who was bowling slows to another of the M.C.C. team. Mike recognised him with awe as one of the three best amateur wicket-keepers in the country.

"What do you think of this?" said Joe, exhibiting Mike, who grinned bashfully. "Aged ten last birthday, and playing for the school. You are only ten, aren't you, Mike?"

"Brother of yours?" asked the wicket-keeper.

"Probably too proud to own the relationship, but he is."

"Isn't there any end to you Jacksons?" demanded the wicket-keeper in an aggrieved tone. "I never saw such a family."

"This is our star. You wait till he gets at us to-day. Saunders is our only bowler, and Mike's been brought up on Saunders. You'd better win the toss if you want a chance of getting a knock and lifting your average out of the minuses."

53

"I have won the toss," said the other with dignity. "Do you think I don't know the elementary duties of a captain?"

The school went out to field with mixed feelings. The wicket was hard and true, which would have made it pleasant to be going in first. On the other hand, they would feel decidedly better and fitter for centuries after the game had been in progress an hour or so. Burgess was glad as a private individual, sorry as a captain. For himself, the sooner he got hold of the ball and began to bowl the better he liked it. As a captain, he realised that a side with Joe Jackson on it, not to mention the other first-class men, was not a side to which he would have preferred to give away an advantage. Mike was feeling that by no possibility could he hold the simplest catch, and hoping that nothing would come his way. Bob, conscious of being an uncertain field, was feeling just the same.

The M.C.C. opened with Joe and a man in an Oxford Authentic cap. The beginning of the game was quiet. Burgess's yorker was nearly too much for the latter in the first over, but he contrived to chop it away, and the pair gradually settled down. At twenty, Joe began to open his shoulders. Twenty became forty with disturbing swiftness, and Burgess tried a change of bowling.

It seemed for one instant as if the move had been a success, for Joe, still taking risks, tried to late-cut a rising ball, and snicked it straight into Bob's hands at second slip. It was the easiest of slip-catches, but Bob fumbled it, dropped it, almost held it a second time, and finally let it fall miserably to the ground. It was a moment too painful for words. He rolled the ball back to the bowler in silence.

One of those weary periods followed when the batsman's defence seems to the fieldsmen absolutely impregnable. There was a sickening inevitableness in the way in which every ball was played with the very centre of the bat. And, as usual, just when things seemed most hopeless, relief came. The Authentic, getting in front of his wicket, to pull one of the simplest long-hops ever seen on a cricket field, missed it, and was l.b.w. And the next ball upset the newcomer's leg stump.

The school revived. Bowlers and field were infused with a new life. Another wicket—two stumps knocked out of the ground by Burgess—helped the thing on. When the bell rang for the end of morning school, five wickets were down for a hundred and thirteen.

But from the end of school till lunch things went very wrong indeed. Joe was still in at one end, invincible; and at the other was the great wicket-keeper. And the pair of them suddenly began to force the pace till the bowling was in a tangled knot. Four after four, all round the wicket, with never a chance or a mishit to vary the monotony. Two hundred went up, and two hundred and fifty. Then Joe reached his century, and was stumped next ball. Then came lunch.

The rest of the innings was like the gentle rain after the thunderstorm. Runs came with fair regularity, but wickets fell at intervals, and when the wicket-keeper was run out at length for a lively sixty-three, the end was very near. Saunders, coming in last, hit two boundaries, and was then caught by Mike. His second hit had just lifted the M.C.C. total over the three hundred.

Three hundred is a score that takes some making on any ground, but on a fine day it was not an unusual total for the Wrykyn eleven. Some years before, against Ripton, they had run up four hundred and sixteen; and only last season had massacred a very weak team of Old Wrykynians with a score that only just missed the fourth hundred.

Unfortunately, on the present occasion, there was scarcely time, unless the bowling happened to get completely collared, to make the runs. It was a quarter to four when the innings began, and stumps were to be drawn at a quarter to seven. A hundred an hour is quick work.

Burgess, however, was optimistic, as usual. "Better have a go for them," he said to Berridge and Marsh, the school first pair.

Following out this courageous advice, Berridge, after hitting three boundaries in his first two overs, was stumped half-way through the third.

After this, things settled down. Morris, the first-wicket man, was a thoroughly sound bat, a little on the slow side, but exceedingly hard to shift. He and Marsh proceeded to play themselves in, until it looked as if they were likely to stay till the drawing of stumps.

A comfortable, rather somnolent feeling settled upon the school. A long stand at cricket is a soothing sight to watch. There was an absence of hurry about the batsmen which harmonised well with the drowsy summer afternoon. And yet runs were coming at a fair pace. The hundred went up at five o'clock, the hundred and fifty at half-past. Both batsmen were completely at home, and the M.C.C. third-change bowlers had been put on.

Then the great wicket-keeper took off the pads and gloves, and the fieldsmen retired to posts at the extreme edge of the ground.

"Lobs," said Burgess. "By Jove, I wish I was in."

It seemed to be the general opinion among the members of the Wrykyn eleven on the pavilion balcony that Morris and Marsh were in luck. The team did not grudge them their good fortune, because they had earned it; but they were distinctly envious.

Lobs are the most dangerous, insinuating things in the world. Everybody knows in theory the right way to treat them. Everybody knows that the man who is content not to try to score more than a single cannot get out to them. Yet nearly everybody does get out to them.

It was the same story to-day. The first over yielded six runs, all through gentle taps along the ground. In the second, Marsh hit an over-pitched one along the ground to the terrace bank. The next ball he swept round to the leg boundary. And that was the end of Marsh.

55

He saw himself scoring at the rate of twenty-four an over. Off the last ball he was stumped by several feet, having done himself credit by scoring seventy.

The long stand was followed, as usual, by a series of disasters. Marsh's wicket had fallen at a hundred and eighty. Ellerby left at a hundred and eighty-six. By the time the scoring-board registered two hundred, five wickets were down, three of them victims to the lobs. Morris was still in at one end. He had refused to be tempted. He was jogging on steadily to his century.

Bob Jackson went in next, with instructions to keep his eye on the lob-man.

For a time things went well. Saunders, who had gone on to bowl again after a rest, seemed to give Morris no trouble, and Bob put him through the slips with apparent ease. Twenty runs were added, when the lob-bowler once more got in his deadly work. Bob, letting alone a ball wide of the off-stump under the impression that it was going to break away, was disagreeably surprised to find it break in instead, and hit the wicket. The bowler smiled sadly, as if he hated to have to do these things.

Mike's heart jumped as he saw the bails go. It was his turn next.

"Two hundred and twenty-nine," said Burgess, "and it's ten past six. No good trying for the runs now. Stick in," he added to Mike. "That's all you've got to do."

All!... Mike felt as if he was being strangled. His heart was racing like the engines of a motor. He knew his teeth were chattering. He wished he could stop them. What a time Bob was taking to get back to the pavilion! He wanted to rush out, and get the thing over.

At last he arrived, and Mike, fumbling at a glove, tottered out into the sunshine. He heard miles and miles away a sound of clapping, and a thin, shrill noise as if somebody were screaming in the distance. As a matter of fact, several members of his form and of the junior day-room at Wain's nearly burst themselves at that moment.

At the wickets, he felt better. Bob had fallen to the last ball of the over, and Morris, standing ready for Saunders's delivery, looked so calm and certain of himself that it was impossible to feel entirely without hope and self-confidence. Mike knew that Morris had made ninety-eight, and he supposed that Morris knew that he was very near his century; yet he seemed to be absolutely undisturbed. Mike drew courage from his attitude.

Morris pushed the first ball away to leg. Mike would have liked to have run two, but short leg had retrieved the ball as he reached the crease.

The moment had come, the moment which he had experienced only in dreams. And in the dreams he was always full of confidence, and invariably hit a boundary. Sometimes a drive, sometimes a cut, but always a boundary.

56

"To leg, sir," said the umpire.

"Don't be in a funk," said a voice. "Play straight, and you can't get out."

It was Joe, who had taken the gloves when the wicket-keeper went on to bowl.

Mike grinned, wryly but gratefully.

Saunders was beginning his run. It was all so home-like that for a moment Mike felt himself again. How often he had seen those two little skips and the jump. It was like being in the paddock again, with Marjory and the dogs waiting by the railings to fetch the ball if he made a drive.

Saunders ran to the crease, and bowled.

Now, Saunders was a conscientious man, and, doubtless, bowled the very best ball that he possibly could. On the other hand, it was Mike's first appearance for the school, and Saunders, besides being conscientious, was undoubtedly kind-hearted. It is useless to speculate as to whether he was trying to bowl his best that ball. If so, he failed signally. It was a half-volley, just the right distance away from the off-stump; the sort of ball Mike was wont to send nearly through the net at home....

The next moment the dreams had come true. The umpire was signalling to the scoring-box, the school was shouting, extra-cover was trotting to the boundary to fetch the ball, and Mike was blushing and wondering whether it was bad form to grin.

From that ball onwards all was for the best in this best of all possible worlds. Saunders bowled no more half-volleys; but Mike played everything that he did bowl. He met the lobs with a bat like a barn-door. Even the departure of Morris, caught in the slips off Saunders's next over for a chanceless hundred and five, did not disturb him. All nervousness had left him. He felt equal to the situation. Burgess came in, and began to hit out as if he meant to knock off the runs. The bowling became a shade loose. Twice he was given full tosses to leg, which he hit to the terrace bank. Half-past six chimed, and two hundred and fifty went up on the telegraph board. Burgess continued to hit. Mike's whole soul was concentrated on keeping up his wicket. There was only Reeves to follow him, and Reeves was a victim to the first straight ball. Burgess had to hit because it was the only game he knew; but he himself must simply stay in.

The hands of the clock seemed to have stopped. Then suddenly he heard the umpire say "Last over," and he settled down to keep those six balls out of his wicket.

The lob bowler had taken himself off, and the Oxford Authentic had gone on, fast left-hand.

The first ball was short and wide of the off-stump. Mike let it alone. Number two: yorker. Got him! Three: straight half-volley. Mike played it back to the bowler. Four: beat him, and missed the

57

wicket by an inch. Five: another yorker. Down on it again in the old familiar way.

All was well. The match was a draw now whatever happened to him. He hit out, almost at a venture, at the last ball, and mid-off, jumping, just failed to reach it. It hummed over his head, and ran like a streak along the turf and up the bank, and a great howl of delight went up from the school as the umpire took off the bails.

Mike walked away from the wickets with Joe and the wicket-keeper.

"I'm sorry about your nose, Joe," said the wicket-keeper in tones of grave solicitude.

"What's wrong with it?"

"At present," said the wicket-keeper, "nothing. But in a few years I'm afraid it's going to be put badly out of joint."

CHAPTER XIV

A SLIGHT IMBROGLIO

Mike got his third eleven colours after the M.C.C. match. As he had made twenty-three not out in a crisis in a first eleven match, this may not seem an excessive reward. But it was all that he expected. One had to take the rungs of the ladder singly at Wrykyn. First one was given one's third eleven cap. That meant, "You are a promising man, and we have our eye on you." Then came the second colours. They might mean anything from "Well, here you are. You won't get any higher, so you may as well have the thing now," to "This is just to show that we still have our eye on you."

Mike was a certainty now for the second. But it needed more than one performance to secure the first cap.

"I told you so," said Wyatt, naturally, to Burgess after the match.

"He's not bad," said Burgess. "I'll give him another shot."

But Burgess, as has been pointed out, was not a person who ever became gushing with enthusiasm.

So Wilkins, of the School House, who had played twice for the first eleven, dropped down into the second, as many a good man had done before him, and Mike got his place in the next match, against the Gentlemen of the County. Unfortunately for him, the visiting team, however gentlemanly, were not brilliant cricketers, at any rate as far as bowling was concerned. The school won the toss, went in first, and

58

made three hundred and sixteen for five wickets, Morris making another placid century. The innings was declared closed before Mike had a chance of distinguishing himself. In an innings which lasted for one over he made two runs, not out; and had to console himself for the cutting short of his performance by the fact that his average for the school was still infinity. Bob, who was one of those lucky enough to have an unabridged innings, did better in this match, making twenty-five. But with Morris making a hundred and seventeen, and Berridge, Ellerby, and Marsh all passing the half-century, this score did not show up excessively.

We now come to what was practically a turning-point in Mike's career at Wrykyn. There is no doubt that his meteor-like flights at cricket had an unsettling effect on him. He was enjoying life amazingly, and, as is not uncommon with the prosperous, he waxed fat and kicked. Fortunately for him—though he did not look upon it in that light at the time—he kicked the one person it was most imprudent to kick. The person he selected was Firby-Smith. With anybody else the thing might have blown over, to the detriment of Mike's character; but Firby-Smith, having the most tender affection for his dignity, made a fuss.

It happened in this way. The immediate cause of the disturbance was a remark of Mike's, but the indirect cause was the unbearably patronising manner which the head of Wain's chose to adopt towards him. The fact that he was playing for the school seemed to make no difference at all. Firby-Smith continued to address Mike merely as the small boy.

The following, verbatim, was the tactful speech which he addressed to him on the evening of the M.C.C. match, having summoned him to his study for the purpose.

"Well," he said, "you played a very decent innings this afternoon, and I suppose you're frightfully pleased with yourself, eh? Well, mind you don't go getting swelled head. See? That's all. Run along."

Mike departed, bursting with fury.

The next link in the chain was forged a week after the Gentlemen of the County match. House matches had begun, and Wain's were playing Appleby's. Appleby's made a hundred and fifty odd, shaping badly for the most part against Wyatt's slows. Then Wain's opened their innings. The Gazeka, as head of the house, was captain of the side, and he and Wyatt went in first. Wyatt made a few mighty hits, and was then caught at cover. Mike went in first wicket.

For some ten minutes all was peace. Firby-Smith scratched away at his end, getting here and there a single and now and then a two, and Mike settled down at once to play what he felt was going to be the innings of a lifetime. Appleby's bowling was on the feeble side, with Raikes, of the third eleven, as the star, supported by some small change. Mike pounded it vigorously. To one who had been brought up

59

on Saunders, Raikes possessed few subtleties. He had made seventeen, and was thoroughly set, when the Gazeka, who had the bowling, hit one in the direction of cover-point. With a certain type of batsman a single is a thing to take big risks for. And the Gazeka badly wanted that single.

"Come on," he shouted, prancing down the pitch.

Mike, who had remained in his crease with the idea that nobody even moderately sane would attempt a run for a hit like that, moved forward in a startled and irresolute manner. Firby-Smith arrived, shouting "Run!" and, cover having thrown the ball in, the wicket-keeper removed the bails.

These are solemn moments.

The only possible way of smoothing over an episode of this kind is for the guilty man to grovel.

Firby-Smith did not grovel.

"Easy run there, you know," he said reprovingly.

The world swam before Mike's eyes. Through the red mist he could see Firby-Smith's face. The sun glinted on his rather prominent teeth. To Mike's distorted vision it seemed that the criminal was amused.

"Don't laugh, you grinning ape!" he cried. "It isn't funny."

He then made for the trees where the rest of the team were sitting.

Now Firby-Smith not only possessed rather prominent teeth; he was also sensitive on the subject. Mike's shaft sank in deeply. The fact that emotion caused him to swipe at a straight half-volley, miss it, and be bowled next ball made the wound rankle.

He avoided Mike on his return to the trees. And Mike, feeling now a little apprehensive, avoided him.

The Gazeka brooded apart for the rest of the afternoon, chewing the insult. At close of play he sought Burgess.

Burgess, besides being captain of the eleven, was also head of the school. He was the man who arranged prefects' meetings. And only a prefects' meeting, thought Firby-Smith, could adequately avenge his lacerated dignity.

"I want to speak to you, Burgess," he said.

"What's up?" said Burgess.

"You know young Jackson in our house."

"What about him?"

"He's been frightfully insolent."

"Cheeked you?" said Burgess, a man of simple speech.

"I want you to call a prefects' meeting, and lick him."

Burgess looked incredulous.

"Rather a large order, a prefects' meeting," he said. "It has to be a pretty serious sort of thing for that."

"Frightful cheek to a school prefect is a serious thing," said Firby-Smith, with the air of one uttering an epigram.

"Well, I suppose—What did he say to you?"

Firby-Smith related the painful details.

Burgess started to laugh, but turned the laugh into a cough.

"Yes," he said meditatively. "Rather thick. Still, I mean—A prefects' meeting. Rather like crushing a thingummy with a what-d'you-call-it. Besides, he's a decent kid."

"He's frightfully conceited."

"Oh, well—Well, anyhow, look here, I'll think it over, and let you know to-morrow. It's not the sort of thing to rush through without thinking about it."

And the matter was left temporarily at that.

CHAPTER XV

MIKE CREATES A VACANCY

Burgess walked off the ground feeling that fate was not using him well.

Here was he, a well-meaning youth who wanted to be on good terms with all the world, being jockeyed into slaughtering a kid whose batting he admired and whom personally he liked. And the worst of it was that he sympathised with Mike. He knew what it felt like to be run out just when one had got set, and he knew exactly how maddening the Gazeka's manner would be on such an occasion. On the other hand, officially he was bound to support the head of Wain's. Prefects must stand together or chaos will come.

He thought he would talk it over with somebody. Bob occurred to him. It was only fair that Bob should be told, as the nearest of kin.

And here was another grievance against fate. Bob was a person he did not particularly wish to see just then. For that morning he had posted up the list of the team to play for the school against Geddington, one of the four schools which Wrykyn met at cricket; and Bob's name did not appear on that list. Several things had contributed to that melancholy omission. In the first place, Geddington, to judge from the weekly reports in the Sportsman and Field, were strong this year at batting. In the second place, the results of the last few matches, and particularly the M.C.C. match, had given Burgess the idea that Wrykyn was weak at bowling. It became necessary, therefore, to drop a batsman out of the team in favour of a bowler. And either Mike or Bob must be the man.

Burgess was as rigidly conscientious as the captain of a school eleven should be. Bob was one of his best friends, and he would have given much to be able to put him in the team; but he thought the thing over, and put the temptation sturdily behind him. At batting there was not much to choose between the two, but in fielding there was a great deal. Mike was good. Bob was bad. So out Bob had gone, and Neville-Smith, a fair fast bowler at all times and on his day dangerous, took his place.

These clashings of public duty with private inclination are the drawbacks to the despotic position of captain of cricket at a public school. It is awkward having to meet your best friend after you have dropped him from the team, and it is difficult to talk to him as if nothing had happened.

Burgess felt very self-conscious as he entered Bob's study, and was rather glad that he had a topic of conversation ready to hand.

"Busy, Bob?" he asked.

"Hullo," said Bob, with a cheerfulness rather over-done in his anxiety to show Burgess, the man, that he did not hold him responsible in any way for the distressing acts of Burgess, the captain. "Take a pew. Don't these studies get beastly hot this weather. There's some ginger-beer in the cupboard. Have some?"

"No, thanks. I say, Bob, look here, I want to see you."

"Well, you can, can't you? This is me, sitting over here. The tall, dark, handsome chap."

"It's awfully awkward, you know," continued Burgess gloomily; "that ass of a young brother of yours—Sorry, but he is an ass, though he's your brother—"

"Thanks for the 'though,' Billy. You know how to put a thing nicely. What's Mike been up to?"

"It's that old fool the Gazeka. He came to me frothing with rage, and wanted me to call a prefects' meeting and touch young Mike up."

Bob displayed interest and excitement for the first time.

"Prefects' meeting! What the dickens is up? What's he been doing? Smith must be drunk. What's all the row about?"

Burgess repeated the main facts of the case as he had them from Firby-Smith.

"Personally, I sympathise with the kid," he added, "Still, the Gazeka is a prefect—"

Bob gnawed a pen-holder morosely.

"Silly young idiot," he said.

"Sickening thing being run out," suggested Burgess.

"Still—"

"I know. It's rather hard to see what to do. I suppose if the Gazeka insists, one's bound to support him."

62

"I suppose so."

"Awful rot. Prefects' lickings aren't meant for that sort of thing. They're supposed to be for kids who steal buns at the shop or muck about generally. Not for a chap who curses a fellow who runs him out. I tell you what, there's just a chance Firby-Smith won't press the thing. He hadn't had time to get over it when he saw me. By now he'll have simmered down a bit. Look here, you're a pal of his, aren't you? Well, go and ask him to drop the business. Say you'll curse your brother and make him apologise, and that I'll kick him out of the team for the Geddington match."

It was a difficult moment for Bob. One cannot help one's thoughts, and for an instant the idea of going to Geddington with the team, as he would certainly do if Mike did not play, made him waver. But he recovered himself.

"Don't do that," he said. "I don't see there's a need for anything of that sort. You must play the best side you've got. I can easily talk the old Gazeka over. He gets all right in a second if he's treated the right way. I'll go and do it now."

Burgess looked miserable.

"I say, Bob," he said.

"Yes?"

"Oh, nothing—I mean, you're not a bad sort." With which glowing eulogy he dashed out of the room, thanking his stars that he had won through a confoundedly awkward business.

Bob went across to Wain's to interview and soothe Firby-Smith.

He found that outraged hero sitting moodily in his study like Achilles in his tent.

Seeing Bob, he became all animation.

"Look here," he said, "I wanted to see you. You know, that frightful young brother of yours—"

"I know, I know," said Bob. "Burgess was telling me. He wants kicking."

"He wants a frightful licking from the prefects," emended the aggrieved party.

"Well, I don't know, you know. Not much good lugging the prefects into it, is there? I mean, apart from everything else, not much of a catch for me, would it be, having to sit there and look on. I'm a prefect, too, you know."

Firby-Smith looked a little blank at this. He had a great admiration for Bob.

"I didn't think of you," he said.

"I thought you hadn't," said Bob. "You see it now, though, don't you?"

Firby-Smith returned to the original grievance.

"Well, you know, it was frightful cheek."

"Of course it was. Still, I think if I saw him and cursed him, and sent him up to you to apologise—How would that do?"

"All right. After all, I did run him out."

"Yes, there's that, of course. Mike's all right, really. It isn't as if he did that sort of thing as a habit."

"No. All right then."

"Thanks," said Bob, and went to find Mike.

The lecture on deportment which he read that future All-England batsman in a secluded passage near the junior day-room left the latter rather limp and exceedingly meek. For the moment all the jauntiness and exuberance had been drained out of him. He was a punctured balloon. Reflection, and the distinctly discouraging replies of those experts in school law to whom he had put the question, "What d'you think he'll do?" had induced a very chastened frame of mind.

He perceived that he had walked very nearly into a hornets' nest, and the realisation of his escape made him agree readily to all the conditions imposed. The apology to the Gazeka was made without reserve, and the offensively forgiving, say-no-more-about-it-but-take-care-in-future air of the head of the house roused no spark of resentment in him, so subdued was his fighting spirit. All he wanted was to get the thing done with. He was not inclined to be critical.

And, most of all, he felt grateful to Bob. Firby-Smith, in the course of his address, had not omitted to lay stress on the importance of Bob's intervention. But for Bob, he gave him to understand, he, Mike, would have been prosecuted with the utmost rigour of the law. Mike came away with a confused picture in his mind of a horde of furious prefects bent on his slaughter, after the manner of a stage "excited crowd," and Bob waving them back. He realised that Bob had done him a good turn. He wished he could find some way of repaying him.

Curiously enough, it was an enemy of Bob's who suggested the way—Burton, of Donaldson's. Burton was a slippery young gentleman, fourteen years of age, who had frequently come into contact with Bob in the house, and owed him many grudges. With Mike he had always tried to form an alliance, though without success.

He happened to meet Mike going to school next morning, and unburdened his soul to him. It chanced that Bob and he had had another small encounter immediately after breakfast, and Burton felt revengeful.

"I say," said Burton, "I'm jolly glad you're playing for the first against Geddington."

"Thanks," said Mike.

"I'm specially glad for one reason."

"What's that?" inquired Mike, without interest.

"Because your beast of a brother has been chucked out. He'd have been playing but for you."

At any other time Mike would have heard Bob called a beast without active protest. He would have felt that it was no business of his to fight his brother's battles for him. But on this occasion he deviated from his rule.

He kicked Burton. Not once or twice, but several times, so that Burton, retiring hurriedly, came to the conclusion that it must be something in the Jackson blood, some taint, as it were. They were all beasts.

Mike walked on, weighing this remark, and gradually made up his mind. It must be remembered that he was in a confused mental condition, and that the only thing he realised clearly was that Bob had pulled him out of an uncommonly nasty hole. It seemed to him that it was necessary to repay Bob. He thought the thing over more fully during school, and his decision remained unaltered.

On the evening before the Geddington match, just before lock-up, Mike tapped at Burgess's study door. He tapped with his right hand, for his left was in a sling.

"Come in!" yelled the captain. "Hullo!"

"I'm awfully sorry, Burgess," said Mike. "I've crocked my wrist a bit."

"How did you do that? You were all right at the nets?"

"Slipped as I was changing," said Mike stolidly.

"Is it bad?"

"Nothing much. I'm afraid I shan't be able to play to-morrow."

"I say, that's bad luck. Beastly bad luck. We wanted your batting, too. Be all right, though, in a day or two, I suppose?"

"Oh, yes, rather."

"Hope so, anyway."

"Thanks. Good-night."

"Good-night."

And Burgess, with the comfortable feeling that he had managed to combine duty and pleasure after all, wrote a note to Bob at Donaldson's, telling him to be ready to start with the team for Geddington by the 8.54 next morning.

CHAPTER XVI

AN EXPERT EXAMINATION

Mike's Uncle John was a wanderer on the face of the earth. He had been an army surgeon in the days of his youth, and, after an adventurous career, mainly in Afghanistan, had inherited enough

65

money to keep him in comfort for the rest of his life. He had thereupon left the service, and now spent most of his time flitting from one spot of Europe to another. He had been dashing up to Scotland on the day when Mike first became a Wrykynian, but a few weeks in an uncomfortable hotel in Skye and a few days in a comfortable one in Edinburgh had left him with the impression that he had now seen all that there was to be seen in North Britain and might reasonably shift his camp again.

Coming south, he had looked in on Mike's people for a brief space, and, at the request of Mike's mother, took the early express to Wrykyn in order to pay a visit of inspection.

His telegram arrived during morning school. Mike went down to the station to meet him after lunch.

Uncle John took command of the situation at once.

"School playing anybody to-day, Mike? I want to see a match."

"They're playing Geddington. Only it's away. There's a second match on."

"Why aren't you—Hullo, I didn't see. What have you been doing to yourself?"

"Crocked my wrist a bit. It's nothing much."

"How did you do that?"

"Slipped while I was changing after cricket."

"Hurt?"

"Not much, thanks."

"Doctor seen it?"

"No. But it's really nothing. Be all right by Monday."

"H'm. Somebody ought to look at it. I'll have a look later on."

Mike did not appear to relish this prospect.

"It isn't anything, Uncle John, really. It doesn't matter a bit."

"Never mind. It won't do any harm having somebody examine it who knows a bit about these things. Now, what shall we do. Go on the river?"

"I shouldn't be able to steer."

"I could manage about that. Still, I think I should like to see the place first. Your mother's sure to ask me if you showed me round. It's like going over the stables when you're stopping at a country-house. Got to be done, and better do it as soon as possible."

It is never very interesting playing the part of showman at school. Both Mike and his uncle were inclined to scamp the business. Mike pointed out the various landmarks without much enthusiasm—it is only after one has left a few years that the school buildings take to themselves romance—and Uncle John said, "Ah yes, I see. Very nice," two or three times in an absent voice; and they passed on to the cricket field, where the second eleven were playing a neighbouring engineering school. It was a glorious day. The sun had never seemed to Mike so bright or the grass so green. It was one of those days when the ball

66

looks like a large vermilion-coloured football as it leaves the bowler's hand. If ever there was a day when it seemed to Mike that a century would have been a certainty, it was this Saturday. A sudden, bitter realisation of all he had given up swept over him, but he choked the feeling down. The thing was done, and it was no good brooding over the might-have-beens now. Still—And the Geddington ground was supposed to be one of the easiest scoring grounds of all the public schools!

"Well hit, by George!" remarked Uncle John, as Trevor, who had gone in first wicket for the second eleven, swept a half-volley to leg round to the bank where they were sitting.

"That's Trevor," said Mike. "Chap in Donaldson's. The fellow at the other end is Wilkins. He's in the School House. They look as if they were getting set. By Jove," he said enviously, "pretty good fun batting on a day like this."

Uncle John detected the envious note.

"I suppose you would have been playing here but for your wrist?"

"No, I was playing for the first."

"For the first? For the school! My word, Mike, I didn't know that. No wonder you're feeling badly treated. Of course, I remember your father saying you had played once for the school, and done well; but I thought that was only as a substitute. I didn't know you were a regular member of the team. What bad luck. Will you get another chance?"

"Depends on Bob."

"Has Bob got your place?"

Mike nodded.

"If he does well to-day, they'll probably keep him in."

"Isn't there room for both of you?"

"Such a lot of old colours. There are only three vacancies, and Henfrey got one of those a week ago. I expect they'll give one of the other two to a bowler, Neville-Smith, I should think, if he does well against Geddington. Then there'll be only the last place left."

"Rather awkward, that."

"Still, it's Bob's last year. I've got plenty of time. But I wish I could get in this year."

After they had watched the match for an hour, Uncle John's restless nature asserted itself.

"Suppose we go for a pull on the river now?" he suggested.

They got up.

"Let's just call at the shop," said Mike. "There ought to be a telegram from Geddington by this time. I wonder how Bob's got on."

Apparently Bob had not had a chance yet of distinguishing himself. The telegram read, "Geddington 151 for four. Lunch."

"Not bad that," said Mike. "But I believe they're weak in bowling."

67

They walked down the road towards the school landing-stage.

"The worst of a school," said Uncle John, as he pulled up-stream with strong, unskilful stroke, "is that one isn't allowed to smoke on the grounds. I badly want a pipe. The next piece of shade that you see, sing out, and we'll put in there."

"Pull your left," said Mike. "That willow's what you want."

Uncle John looked over his shoulder, caught a crab, recovered himself, and steered the boat in under the shade of the branches.

"Put the rope over that stump. Can you manage with one hand? Here, let me—Done it? Good. A-ah!"

He blew a great cloud of smoke into the air, and sighed contentedly.

"I hope you don't smoke, Mike?"

"No."

"Rotten trick for a boy. When you get to my age you need it. Boys ought to be thinking about keeping themselves fit and being good at games. Which reminds me. Let's have a look at the wrist."

A hunted expression came into Mike's eyes.

"It's really nothing," he began, but his uncle had already removed the sling, and was examining the arm with the neat rapidity of one who has been brought up to such things.

To Mike it seemed as if everything in the world was standing still and waiting. He could hear nothing but his own breathing.

His uncle pressed the wrist gingerly once or twice, then gave it a little twist.

"That hurt?" he asked.

"Ye—no," stammered Mike.

Uncle John looked up sharply. Mike was crimson.

"What's the game?" inquired Uncle John.

Mike said nothing.

There was a twinkle in his uncle's eyes.

"May as well tell me. I won't give you away. Why this wounded warrior business when you've no more the matter with you than I have?"

Mike hesitated.

"I only wanted to get out of having to write this morning. There was an exam. on."

The idea had occurred to him just before he spoke. It had struck him as neat and plausible.

To Uncle John it did not appear in the same light.

"Do you always write with your left hand? And if you had gone with the first eleven to Geddington, wouldn't that have got you out of your exam? Try again."

When in doubt, one may as well tell the truth. Mike told it.

"I know. It wasn't that, really. Only—"

"Well?"

68

"Oh, well, dash it all then. Old Bob got me out of an awful row the day before yesterday, and he seemed a bit sick at not playing for the first, so I thought I might as well let him. That's how it was. Look here, swear you won't tell him."

Uncle John was silent. Inwardly he was deciding that the five shillings which he had intended to bestow on Mike on his departure should become a sovereign. (This, it may be mentioned as an interesting biographical fact, was the only occasion in his life on which Mike earned money at the rate of fifteen shillings a half-minute.)

"Swear you won't tell him. He'd be most frightfully sick if he knew."

"I won't tell him."

Conversation dwindled to vanishing-point. Uncle John smoked on in weighty silence, while Mike, staring up at the blue sky through the branches of the willow, let his mind wander to Geddington, where his fate was even now being sealed. How had the school got on? What had Bob done? If he made about twenty, would they give him his cap? Supposing....

A faint snore from Uncle John broke in on his meditations. Then there was a clatter as a briar pipe dropped on to the floor of the boat, and his uncle sat up, gaping.

"Jove, I was nearly asleep. What's the time? Just on six? Didn't know it was so late."

"I ought to be getting back soon, I think. Lock-up's at half-past."

"Up with the anchor, then. You can tackle that rope with two hands now, eh? We are not observed. Don't fall overboard. I'm going to shove her off."

"There'll be another telegram, I should think," said Mike, as they reached the school gates.

"Shall we go and look?"

They walked to the shop.

A second piece of grey paper had been pinned up under the first. Mike pushed his way through the crowd. It was a longer message this time.

It ran as follows:

"Geddington 247 (Burgess six wickets, Neville-Smith four).

Wrykyn 270 for nine (Berridge 86, Marsh 58, Jackson 48)."

Mike worked his way back through the throng, and rejoined his uncle.

"Well?" said Uncle John.

"We won."

He paused for a moment.

"Bob made forty-eight," he added carelessly.

Uncle John felt in his pocket, and silently slid a sovereign into Mike's hand.

It was the only possible reply.

69

CHAPTER XVII

ANOTHER VACANCY

Wyatt got back late that night, arriving at the dormitory as Mike was going to bed.

"By Jove, I'm done," he said. "It was simply baking at Geddington. And I came back in a carriage with Neville-Smith and Ellerby, and they ragged the whole time. I wanted to go to sleep, only they wouldn't let me. Old Smith was awfully bucked because he'd taken four wickets. I should think he'd go off his nut if he took eight ever. He was singing comic songs when he wasn't trying to put Ellerby under the seat. How's your wrist?"

"Oh, better, thanks."

Wyatt began to undress.

"Any colours?" asked Mike after a pause. First eleven colours were generally given in the pavilion after a match or on the journey home.

"No. Only one or two thirds. Jenkins and Clephane, and another chap, can't remember who. No first, though."

"What was Bob's innings like?"

"Not bad. A bit lucky. He ought to have been out before he'd scored, and he was out when he'd made about sixteen, only the umpire didn't seem to know that it's l-b-w when you get your leg right in front of the wicket and the ball hits it. Never saw a clearer case in my life. I was in at the other end. Bit rotten for the Geddington chaps. Just lost them the match. Their umpire, too. Bit of luck for Bob. He didn't give the ghost of a chance after that."

"I should have thought they'd have given him his colours."

"Most captains would have done, only Burgess is so keen on fielding that he rather keeps off it."

"Why, did he field badly?"

"Rottenly. And the man always will choose Billy's bowling to drop catches off. And Billy would cut his rich uncle from Australia if he kept on dropping them off him. Bob's fielding's perfectly sinful. He was pretty bad at the beginning of the season, but now he's got so nervous that he's a dozen times worse. He turns a delicate green when he sees a catch coming. He let their best man off twice in one over, off Billy, to-day; and the chap went on and made a hundred odd. Ripping innings bar those two chances. I hear he's got an average of eighty in school matches this season. Beastly man to bowl to. Knocked me off in half a dozen overs. And, when he does give a couple of easy chances, Bob puts them both on the floor. Billy wouldn't have given him his cap after the match if he'd made a hundred. Bob's the sort of man who wouldn't catch a ball if you handed it to him on a plate, with watercress round it."

Burgess, reviewing the match that night, as he lay awake in his cubicle, had come to much the same conclusion. He was very fond of Bob, but two missed catches in one over was straining the bonds of human affection too far. There would have been serious trouble between David and Jonathan if either had persisted in dropping catches off the other's bowling. He writhed in bed as he remembered the second of the two chances which the wretched Bob had refused. The scene was indelibly printed on his mind. Chap had got a late cut which he fancied rather. With great guile he had fed this late cut. Sent down a couple which he put to the boundary. Then fired a third much faster and a bit shorter. Chap had a go at it, just as he had expected: and he felt that life was a good thing after all when the ball just touched the corner of the bat and flew into Bob's hands. And Bob dropped it!

The memory was too bitter. If he dwelt on it, he felt, he would get insomnia. So he turned to pleasanter reflections: the yorker which had shattered the second-wicket man, and the slow head-ball which had led to a big hitter being caught on the boundary. Soothed by these memories, he fell asleep.

Next morning he found himself in a softened frame of mind. He thought of Bob's iniquities with sorrow rather than wrath. He felt towards him much as a father feels towards a prodigal son whom there is still a chance of reforming. He overtook Bob on his way to chapel.

Directness was always one of Burgess's leading qualities.

"Look here, Bob. About your fielding. It's simply awful."

Bob was all remorse.

"It's those beastly slip catches. I can't time them."

"That one yesterday was right into your hands. Both of them were."

"I know. I'm frightfully sorry."

"Well, but I mean, why can't you hold them? It's no good being a good bat—you're that all right—if you're going to give away runs in the field."

"Do you know, I believe I should do better in the deep. I could get time to watch them there. I wish you'd give me a shot in the deep—for the second."

"Second be blowed! I want your batting in the first. Do you think you'd really do better in the deep?"

"I'm almost certain I should. I'll practise like mad. Trevor'll hit me up catches. I hate the slips. I get in the dickens of a funk directly the bowler starts his run now. I know that if a catch does come, I shall miss it. I'm certain the deep would be much better."

"All right then. Try it."

The conversation turned to less pressing topics.

In the next two matches, accordingly, Bob figured on the

boundary, where he had not much to do except throw the ball back to the bowler, and stop an occasional drive along the carpet. The beauty of fielding in the deep is that no unpleasant surprises can be sprung upon one. There is just that moment or two for collecting one's thoughts which makes the whole difference. Bob, as he stood regarding the game from afar, found his self-confidence returning slowly, drop by drop.

As for Mike, he played for the second, and hoped for the day.

His opportunity came at last. It will be remembered that on the morning after the Great Picnic the headmaster made an announcement in Hall to the effect that, owing to an outbreak of chicken-pox in the town, all streets except the High Street would be out of bounds. This did not affect the bulk of the school, for most of the shops to which any one ever thought of going were in the High Street. But there were certain inquiring minds who liked to ferret about in odd corners.

Among these was one Leather-Twigg, of Seymour's, better known in criminal circles as Shoeblossom.

Shoeblossom was a curious mixture of the Energetic Ragger and the Quiet Student. On a Monday evening you would hear a hideous uproar proceeding from Seymour's junior day-room; and, going down with a swagger-stick to investigate, you would find a tangled heap of squealing humanity on the floor, and at the bottom of the heap, squealing louder than any two others, would be Shoeblossom, his collar burst and blackened and his face apoplectically crimson. On the Tuesday afternoon, strolling in some shady corner of the grounds you would come upon him lying on his chest, deep in some work of fiction and resentful of interruption. On the Wednesday morning he would be in receipt of four hundred lines from his housemaster for breaking three windows and a gas-globe. Essentially a man of moods, Shoeblossom.

It happened about the date of the Geddington match that he took out from the school library a copy of "The Iron Pirate," and for the next day or two he wandered about like a lost spirit trying to find a sequestered spot in which to read it. His inability to hit on such a spot was rendered more irritating by the fact that, to judge from the first few chapters (which he had managed to get through during prep. one night under the eye of a short-sighted master), the book was obviously the last word in hot stuff. He tried the junior day-room, but people threw cushions at him. He tried out of doors, and a ball hit from a neighbouring net nearly scalped him. Anything in the nature of concentration became impossible in these circumstances.

Then he recollected that in a quiet backwater off the High Street there was a little confectioner's shop, where tea might be had at a reasonable sum, and also, what was more important, peace.

He made his way there, and in the dingy back shop, all amongst

72

the dust and bluebottles, settled down to a thoughtful perusal of chapter six.

Upstairs, at the same moment, the doctor was recommending that Master John George, the son of the house, be kept warm and out of draughts and not permitted to scratch himself, however necessary such an action might seem to him. In brief, he was attending J. G. for chicken-pox.

Shoeblossom came away, entering the High Street furtively, lest Authority should see him out of bounds, and returned to the school, where he went about his lawful occasions as if there were no such thing as chicken-pox in the world.

But all the while the microbe was getting in some unostentatious but clever work. A week later Shoeblossom began to feel queer. He had occasional headaches, and found himself oppressed by a queer distaste for food. The professional advice of Dr. Oakes, the school doctor, was called for, and Shoeblossom took up his abode in the Infirmary, where he read Punch, sucked oranges, and thought of Life.

Two days later Barry felt queer. He, too, disappeared from Society.

Chicken-pox is no respecter of persons. The next victim was Marsh, of the first eleven. Marsh, who was top of the school averages. Where were his drives now, his late cuts that were wont to set the pavilion in a roar. Wrapped in a blanket, and looking like the spotted marvel of a travelling circus, he was driven across to the Infirmary in a four-wheeler, and it became incumbent upon Burgess to select a substitute for him.

And so it came about that Mike soared once again into the ranks of the elect, and found his name down in the team to play against the Incogniti.

CHAPTER XVIII

BOB HAS NEWS TO IMPART

Wrykyn went down badly before the Incogs. It generally happens at least once in a school cricket season that the team collapses hopelessly, for no apparent reason. Some schools do it in nearly every match, but Wrykyn so far had been particularly fortunate this year. They had only been beaten once, and that by a mere twenty odd runs in a hard-fought game. But on this particular day, against a not overwhelmingly strong side, they failed miserably. The weather may have had something to do with it, for rain fell early in the morning, and the school, batting first on the drying wicket, found themselves considerably puzzled by a slow left-hander. Morris and Berridge left with the score still short of ten, and after that the rout began. Bob, going in fourth wicket, made a dozen, and Mike kept his end up, and was not out eleven; but nobody except Wyatt, who hit out at everything and knocked up thirty before he was stumped, did anything to distinguish himself. The total was a hundred and seven, and the Incogniti, batting when the wicket was easier, doubled this.

The general opinion of the school after this match was that either Mike or Bob would have to stand down from the team when it was definitely filled up, for Neville-Smith, by showing up well with the ball against the Incogniti when the others failed with the bat, made it practically certain that he would get one of the two vacancies.

"If I do" he said to Wyatt, "there will be the biggest bust of modern times at my place. My pater is away for a holiday in Norway, and I'm alone, bar the servants. And I can square them. Will you come?"

"Tea?"

"Tea!" said Neville-Smith scornfully.

"Well, what then?"

"Don't you ever have feeds in the dorms. after lights-out in the houses?"

"Used to when I was a kid. Too old now. Have to look after my digestion. I remember, three years ago, when Wain's won the footer cup, we got up and fed at about two in the morning. All sorts of luxuries. Sardines on sugar-biscuits. I've got the taste in my mouth still. Do you remember Macpherson? Left a couple of years ago. His food ran out, so he spread brown-boot polish on bread, and ate that. Got through a slice, too. Wonderful chap! But what about this thing of yours? What time's it going to be?"

"Eleven suit you?"

"All right."

"How about getting out?"

"I'll do it as quickly as the team did to-day. I can't say more than that."

"You were all right."

"I'm an exceptional sort of chap."

"What about the Jacksons?"

"It's going to be a close thing. If Bob's fielding were to improve suddenly, he would just do it. But young Mike's all over him as a bat. In a year or two that kid'll be a marvel. He's bound to get in next year, of course, so perhaps it would be better if Bob got the place as it's his last season. Still, one wants the best man, of course."

Mike avoided Bob as much as possible during this anxious

period; and he privately thought it rather tactless of the latter when, meeting him one day outside Donaldson's, he insisted on his coming in and having some tea.

Mike shuffled uncomfortably as his brother filled the kettle and lit the Etna. It required more tact than he had at his disposal to carry off a situation like this.

Bob, being older, was more at his ease. He got tea ready, making desultory conversation the while, as if there were no particular reason why either of them should feel uncomfortable in the other's presence. When he had finished, he poured Mike out a cup, passed him the bread, and sat down.

"Not seen much of each other lately, Mike, what?"

Mike murmured unintelligibly through a mouthful of bread-and-jam.

"It's no good pretending it isn't an awkward situation," continued Bob, "because it is. Beastly awkward."

"Awful rot the pater sending us to the same school."

"Oh, I don't know. We've all been at Wrykyn. Pity to spoil the record. It's your fault for being such a young Infant Prodigy, and mine for not being able to field like an ordinary human being."

"You get on much better in the deep."

"Bit better, yes. Liable at any moment to miss a sitter, though. Not that it matters much really whether I do now."

Mike stared.

"What! Why?"

"That's what I wanted to see you about. Has Burgess said anything to you yet?"

"No. Why? What about?"

"Well, I've a sort of idea our little race is over. I fancy you've won."

"I've not heard a word—"

"I have. I'll tell you what makes me think the thing's settled. I was in the pav. just now, in the First room, trying to find a batting-glove I'd mislaid. There was a copy of the Wrykynian lying on the mantelpiece, and I picked it up and started reading it. So there wasn't any noise to show anybody outside that there was some one in the room. And then I heard Burgess and Spence jawing on the steps. They thought the place was empty, of course. I couldn't help hearing what they said. The pav.'s like a sounding-board. I heard every word. Spence said, 'Well, it's about as difficult a problem as any captain of cricket at Wrykyn has ever had to tackle.' I had a sort of idea that old Billy liked to boss things all on his own, but apparently he does consult Spence sometimes. After all, he's cricket-master, and that's what he's there for. Well, Billy said, 'I don't know what to do. What do you think, sir?' Spence said, 'Well, I'll give you my opinion, Burgess, but don't feel bound to act on it. I'm simply saying what I think.' 'Yes, sir,' said old Bill, doing a big Young Disciple with Wise Master act. 'I think M.,' said Spence. 'Decidedly M. He's a shade better than R. now, and in a year or two, of course, there'll be no comparison.'"

"Oh, rot," muttered Mike, wiping the sweat off his forehead. This was one of the most harrowing interviews he had ever been through.

"Not at all. Billy agreed with him. 'That's just what I think, sir,' he said. 'It's rough on Bob, but still—' And then they walked down the steps. I waited a bit to give them a good start, and then sheered off myself. And so home."

Mike looked at the floor, and said nothing.

There was nothing much to be said.

"Well, what I wanted to see you about was this," resumed Bob. "I don't propose to kiss you or anything; but, on the other hand, don't let's go to the other extreme. I'm not saying that it isn't a bit of a brick just missing my cap like this, but it would have been just as bad for you if you'd been the one dropped. It's the fortune of war. I don't want you to go about feeling that you've blighted my life, and so on, and dashing up side-streets to avoid me because you think the sight of you will be painful. As it isn't me, I'm jolly glad it's you; and I shall càdge a seat in the pavilion from you when you're playing for England at the Oval. Congratulate you."

It was the custom at Wrykyn, when you congratulated a man on getting colours, to shake his hand. They shook hands.

"Thanks, awfully, Bob," said Mike. And after that there seemed to be nothing much to talk about. So Mike edged out of the room, and tore across to Wain's.

He was sorry for Bob, but he would not have been human (which he certainly was) if the triumph of having won through at last into the first eleven had not dwarfed commiseration. It had been his one ambition, and now he had achieved it.

The annoying part of the thing was that he had nobody to talk to about it. Until the news was official he could not mention it to the common herd. It wouldn't do. The only possible confidant was Wyatt. And Wyatt was at Bisley, shooting with the School Eight for the Ashburton. For bull's-eyes as well as cats came within Wyatt's range as a marksman. Cricket took up too much of his time for him to be captain of the Eight and the man chosen to shoot for the Spencer, as he would otherwise almost certainly have been; but even though short of practice he was well up in the team.

Until he returned, Mike could tell nobody. And by the time he returned the notice would probably be up in the Senior Block with the other cricket notices.

In this fermenting state Mike went into the house.

The list of the team to play for Wain's v. Seymour's on the following Monday was on the board. As he passed it, a few words scrawled in pencil at the bottom caught his eye.

"All the above will turn out for house-fielding at 6.30 to-morrow morning.—W. F.-S."

"Oh, dash it," said Mike, "what rot! Why on earth can't he leave us alone!"

For getting up an hour before his customary time for rising was not among Mike's favourite pastimes. Still, orders were orders, he felt. It would have to be done.

CHAPTER XIX

MIKE GOES TO SLEEP AGAIN

Mike was a stout supporter of the view that sleep in large quantities is good for one. He belonged to the school of thought which holds that a man becomes plain and pasty if deprived of his full spell in bed. He aimed at the peach-bloom complexion.

To be routed out of bed a clear hour before the proper time, even on a summer morning, was not, therefore, a prospect that appealed to him.

When he woke it seemed even less attractive than it had done when he went to sleep. He had banged his head on the pillow six times over-night, and this silent alarm proved effective, as it always does. Reaching out a hand for his watch, he found that it was five minutes past six.

This was to the good. He could manage another quarter of an hour between the sheets. It would only take him ten minutes to wash and get into his flannels.

He took his quarter of an hour, and a little more. He woke from a sort of doze to find that it was twenty-five past.

Man's inability to get out of bed in the morning is a curious thing. One may reason with oneself clearly and forcibly without the slightest effect. One knows that delay means inconvenience. Perhaps it may spoil one's whole day. And one also knows that a single resolute heave will do the trick. But logic is of no use. One simply lies there.

Mike thought he would take another minute.

And during that minute there floated into his mind the question, Who was Firby-Smith? That was the point. Who was he, after all?

This started quite a new train of thought. Previously Mike had firmly intended to get up—some time. Now he began to waver.

The more he considered the Gazeka's insignificance and futility

77

and his own magnificence, the more outrageous did it seem that he should be dragged out of bed to please Firby-Smith's vapid mind. Here was he, about to receive his first eleven colours on this very day probably, being ordered about, inconvenienced—in short, put upon by a worm who had only just scraped into the third.

Was this right, he asked himself. Was this proper?

And the hands of the watch moved round to twenty to.

What was the matter with his fielding? It was all right. Make the rest of the team fag about, yes. But not a chap who, dash it all, had got his first for fielding!

It was with almost a feeling of self-righteousness that Mike turned over on his side and went to sleep again.

And outside in the cricket-field, the massive mind of the Gazeka was filled with rage, as it was gradually borne in upon him that this was not a question of mere lateness—which, he felt, would be bad enough, for when he said six-thirty he meant six-thirty—but of actual desertion. It was time, he said to himself, that the foot of Authority was set firmly down, and the strong right hand of Justice allowed to put in some energetic work. His comments on the team's fielding that morning were bitter and sarcastic. His eyes gleamed behind their pince-nez.

The painful interview took place after breakfast. The head of the house despatched his fag in search of Mike, and waited. He paced up and down the room like a hungry lion, adjusting his pince-nez (a thing, by the way, which lions seldom do) and behaving in other respects like a monarch of the desert. One would have felt, looking at him, that Mike, in coming to his den, was doing a deed which would make the achievement of Daniel seem in comparison like the tentative effort of some timid novice.

And certainly Mike was not without qualms as he knocked at the door, and went in in response to the hoarse roar from the other side of it.

Firby-Smith straightened his tie, and glared.

"Young Jackson," he said, "look here, I want to know what it all means, and jolly quick. You weren't at house-fielding this morning. Didn't you see the notice?"

Mike admitted that he had seen the notice.

"Then you frightful kid, what do you mean by it? What?"

Mike hesitated. Awfully embarrassing, this. His real reason for not turning up to house-fielding was that he considered himself above such things, and Firby-Smith a toothy weed. Could he give this excuse? He had not his Book of Etiquette by him at the moment, but he rather fancied not. There was no arguing against the fact that the head of the house was a toothy weed; but he felt a firm conviction that it would not be politic to say so.

Happy thought: over-slept himself.

He mentioned this.

"Over-slept yourself! You must jolly well not over-sleep yourself. What do you mean by over-sleeping yourself?"

Very trying this sort of thing.

"What time did you wake up?"

"Six," said Mike.

It was not according to his complicated, yet intelligible code of morality to tell lies to save himself. When others were concerned he could suppress the true and suggest the false with a face of brass.

"Six!"

"Five past."

"Why didn't you get up then?"

"I went to sleep again."

"Oh, you went to sleep again, did you? Well, just listen to me. I've had my eye on you for some time, and I've seen it coming on. You've got swelled head, young man. That's what you've got. Frightful swelled head. You think the place belongs to you."

"I don't," said Mike indignantly.

"Yes, you do," said the Gazeka shrilly. "You think the whole frightful place belongs to you. You go siding about as if you'd bought it. Just because you've got your second, you think you can do what you like; turn up or not, as you please. It doesn't matter whether I'm only in the third and you're in the first. That's got nothing to do with it. The point is that you're one of the house team, and I'm captain of it, so you've jolly well got to turn out for fielding with the others when I think it necessary. See?"

Mike said nothing.

"Do—you—see, you frightful kid?"

Mike remained stonily silent. The rather large grain of truth in what Firby-Smith had said had gone home, as the unpleasant truth about ourselves is apt to do; and his feelings were hurt. He was determined not to give in and say that he saw even if the head of the house invoked all the majesty of the prefects' room to help him, as he had nearly done once before. He set his teeth, and stared at a photograph on the wall.

Firby-Smith's manner became ominously calm. He produced a swagger-stick from a corner.

"Do you see?" he asked again.

Mike's jaw set more tightly.

What one really wants here is a row of stars.

*****

Mike was still full of his injuries when Wyatt came back. Wyatt was worn out, but cheerful. The school had finished sixth for the Ashburton, which was an improvement of eight places on their last

79

year's form, and he himself had scored thirty at the two hundred and twenty-seven at the five hundred totals, which had put him in a very good humour with the world.

"Me ancient skill has not deserted me," he said, "That's the cats. The man who can wing a cat by moonlight can put a bullet where he likes on a target. I didn't hit the bull every time, but that was to give the other fellows a chance. My fatal modesty has always been a hindrance to me in life, and I suppose it always will be. Well, well! And what of the old homestead? Anything happened since I went away? Me old father, is he well? Has the lost will been discovered, or is there a mortgage on the family estates? By Jove, I could do with a stoup of Malvoisie. I wonder if the moke's gone to bed yet. I'll go down and look. A jug of water drawn from the well in the old courtyard where my ancestors have played as children for centuries back would just about save my life."

He left the dormitory, and Mike began to brood over his wrongs once more.

Wyatt came back, brandishing a jug of water and a glass.

"Oh, for a beaker full of the warm south, full of the true, the blushful Hippocrene! Have you ever tasted Hippocrene, young Jackson? Rather like ginger-beer, with a dash of raspberry-vinegar. Very heady. Failing that, water will do. A-ah!"

He put down the glass, and surveyed Mike, who had maintained a moody silence throughout this speech.

"What's your trouble?" he asked. "For pains in the back try Ju-jar. If it's a broken heart, Zam-buk's what you want. Who's been quarrelling with you?"

"It's only that ass Firby-Smith."

"Again! I never saw such chaps as you two. Always at it. What was the trouble this time? Call him a grinning ape again? Your passion for the truth'll be getting you into trouble one of these days."

"He said I stuck on side."

"Why?"

"I don't know."

"I mean, did he buttonhole you on your way to school, and say, 'Jackson, a word in your ear. You stick on side.' Or did he lead up to it in any way? Did he say, 'Talking of side, you stick it on.' What had you been doing to him?"

"It was the house-fielding."

"But you can't stick on side at house-fielding. I defy any one to. It's too early in the morning."

"I didn't turn up."

"What! Why?"

"Oh, I don't know."

"No, but, look here, really. Did you simply bunk it?"

"Yes."

80

Wyatt leaned on the end of Mike's bed, and, having observed its occupant thoughtfully for a moment, proceeded to speak wisdom for the good of his soul.

"I say, I don't want to jaw—I'm one of those quiet chaps with strong, silent natures; you may have noticed it—but I must put in a well-chosen word at this juncture. Don't pretend to be dropping off to sleep. Sit up and listen to what your kind old uncle's got to say to you about manners and deportment. Otherwise, blood as you are at cricket, you'll have a rotten time here. There are some things you simply can't do; and one of them is bunking a thing when you're put down for it. It doesn't matter who it is puts you down. If he's captain, you've got to obey him. That's discipline, that 'ere is. The speaker then paused, and took a sip of water from the carafe which stood at his elbow. Cheers from the audience, and a voice 'Hear! Hear!'"

Mike rolled over in bed and glared up at the orator. Most of his face was covered by the water-jug, but his eyes stared fixedly from above it. He winked in a friendly way, and, putting down the jug, drew a deep breath.

"Nothing like this old '87 water," he said. "Such body."

"I like you jawing about discipline," said Mike morosely.

"And why, my gentle che-ild, should I not talk about discipline?"

"Considering you break out of the house nearly every night."

"In passing, rather rum when you think that a burglar would get it hot for breaking in, while I get dropped on if I break out. Why should there be one law for the burglar and one for me? But you were saying— just so. I thank you. About my breaking out. When you're a white-haired old man like me, young Jackson, you'll see that there are two sorts of discipline at school. One you can break if you feel like taking the risks; the other you mustn't ever break. I don't know why, but it isn't done. Until you learn that, you can never hope to become the Perfect Wrykynian like," he concluded modestly, "me."

Mike made no reply. He would have perished rather than admit it, but Wyatt's words had sunk in. That moment marked a distinct epoch in his career. His feelings were curiously mixed. He was still furious with Firby-Smith, yet at the same time he could not help acknowledging to himself that the latter had had the right on his side. He saw and approved of Wyatt's point of view, which was the more impressive to him from his knowledge of his friend's contempt for, or, rather, cheerful disregard of, most forms of law and order. If Wyatt, reckless though he was as regarded written school rules, held so rigid a respect for those that were unwritten, these last must be things which could not be treated lightly. That night, for the first time in his life, Mike went to sleep with a clear idea of what the public school spirit, of which so much is talked and written, really meant.

CHAPTER XX

THE TEAM IS FILLED UP

When Burgess, at the end of the conversation in the pavilion with Mr. Spence which Bob Jackson had overheard, accompanied the cricket-master across the field to the boarding-houses, he had distinctly made up his mind to give Mike his first eleven colours next day. There was only one more match to be played before the school fixture-list was finished. That was the match with Ripton. Both at cricket and football Ripton was the school that mattered most. Wrykyn did not always win its other school matches; but it generally did. The public schools of England divide themselves naturally into little groups, as far as games are concerned. Harrow, Eton, and Winchester are one group: Westminster and Charterhouse another: Bedford, Tonbridge, Dulwich, Haileybury, and St. Paul's are a third. In this way, Wrykyn, Ripton, Geddington, and Wilborough formed a group. There was no actual championship competition, but each played each, and by the end of the season it was easy to see which was entitled to first place. This nearly always lay between Ripton and Wrykyn. Sometimes an exceptional Geddington team would sweep the board, or Wrykyn, having beaten Ripton, would go down before Wilborough. But this did not happen often. Usually Wilborough and Geddington were left to scramble for the wooden spoon.

Secretaries of cricket at Ripton and Wrykyn always liked to arrange the date of the match towards the end of the term, so that they might take the field with representative and not experimental teams. By July the weeding-out process had generally finished. Besides which the members of the teams had had time to get into form.

At Wrykyn it was the custom to fill up the team, if possible, before the Ripton match. A player is likely to show better form if he has got his colours than if his fate depends on what he does in that particular match.

Burgess, accordingly, had resolved to fill up the first eleven just a week before Ripton visited Wrykyn. There were two vacancies. One gave him no trouble. Neville-Smith was not a great bowler, but he was steady, and he had done well in the earlier matches. He had fairly earned his place. But the choice between Bob and Mike had kept him awake into the small hours two nights in succession. Finally he had consulted Mr. Spence, and Mr. Spence had voted for Mike.

Burgess was glad the thing was settled. The temptation to allow sentiment to interfere with business might have become too strong if he had waited much longer. He knew that it would be a wrench definitely excluding Bob from the team, and he hated to have to do it.

The more he thought of it, the sorrier he was for him. If he could have pleased himself, he would have kept Bob In. But, as the poet has it, "Pleasure is pleasure, and biz is biz, and kep' in a sepyrit jug." The first duty of a captain is to have no friends.

From small causes great events do spring. If Burgess had not picked up a particularly interesting novel after breakfast on the morning of Mike's interview with Firby-Smith in the study, the list would have gone up on the notice-board after prayers. As it was, engrossed in his book, he let the moments go by till the sound on the bell startled him into movement. And then there was only time to gather up his cap, and sprint. The paper on which he had intended to write the list and the pen he had laid out to write it with lay untouched on the table.

And, as it was not his habit to put up notices except during the morning, he postponed the thing. He could write it after tea. After all, there was a week before the match.

When school was over, he went across to the Infirmary to inquire about Marsh. The report was more than favourable. Marsh had better not see any one just yet, In case of accident, but he was certain to be out in time to play against Ripton.

"Doctor Oakes thinks he will be back in school on Tuesday."

"Banzai!" said Burgess, feeling that life was good. To take the field against Ripton without Marsh would have been to court disaster. Marsh's fielding alone was worth the money. With him at short slip, Burgess felt safe when he bowled.

The uncomfortable burden of the knowledge that he was about temporarily to sour Bob Jackson's life ceased for the moment to trouble him. He crooned extracts from musical comedy as he walked towards the nets.

Recollection of Bob's hard case was brought to him by the sight of that about-to-be-soured sportsman tearing across the ground in the middle distance in an effort to get to a high catch which Trevor had hit up to him. It was a difficult catch, and Burgess waited to see if he would bring it off.

Bob got to it with one hand, and held it. His impetus carried him on almost to where Burgess was standing.

"Well held," said Burgess.

"Hullo," said Bob awkwardly. A gruesome thought had flashed across his mind that the captain might think that this gallery-work was an organised advertisement.

"I couldn't get both hands to it," he explained.

"You're hot stuff in the deep."

"Easy when you're only practising."

"I've just been to the Infirmary."

"Oh. How's Marsh?"

"They wouldn't let me see him, but it's all right. He'll be able to play on Saturday."

"Good," said Bob, hoping he had said it as if he meant it. It was decidedly a blow. He was glad for the sake of the school, of course, but one has one's personal ambitions. To the fact that Mike and not himself was the eleventh cap he had become partially resigned: but he had wanted rather badly to play against Ripton.

Burgess passed on, his mind full of Bob once more. What hard luck it was! There was he, dashing about in the sun to improve his fielding, and all the time the team was filled up. He felt as if he were playing some low trick on a pal.

Then the Jekyll and Hyde business completed itself. He suppressed his personal feelings, and became the cricket captain again.

It was the cricket captain who, towards the end of the evening, came upon Firby-Smith and Mike parting at the conclusion of a conversation. That it had not been a friendly conversation would have been evident to the most casual observer from the manner in which Mike stumped off, swinging his cricket-bag as if it were a weapon of offence. There are many kinds of walk. Mike's was the walk of the Overwrought Soul.

"What's up?" inquired Burgess.

"Young Jackson, do you mean? Oh, nothing. I was only telling him that there was going to be house-fielding to-morrow before breakfast."

"Didn't he like the idea?"

"He's jolly well got to like it," said the Gazeka, as who should say, "This way for Iron Wills." "The frightful kid cut it this morning. There'll be worse trouble if he does it again."

There was, it may be mentioned, not an ounce of malice in the head of Wain's house. That by telling the captain of cricket that Mike had shirked fielding-practice he might injure the latter's prospects of a first eleven cap simply did not occur to him. That Burgess would feel, on being told of Mike's slackness, much as a bishop might feel if he heard that a favourite curate had become a Mahometan or a Mumbo-Jumboist, did not enter his mind. All he considered was that the story of his dealings with Mike showed him, Firby-Smith, in the favourable and dashing character of the fellow-who-will-stand-no-nonsense, a sort of Captain Kettle on dry land, in fact; and so he proceeded to tell it in detail.

Burgess parted with him with the firm conviction that Mike was a young slacker. Keenness in fielding was a fetish with him; and to cut practice struck him as a crime.

He felt that he had been deceived in Mike.

When, therefore, one takes into consideration his private bias in favour of Bob, and adds to it the reaction caused by this sudden unmasking of Mike, it is not surprising that the list Burgess made out that night before he went to bed differed in an important respect from the one he had intended to write before school.

Mike happened to be near the notice-board when he pinned it up. It was only the pleasure of seeing his name down in black-and-white that made him trouble to look at the list. Bob's news of the day before yesterday had made it clear how that list would run.

The crowd that collected the moment Burgess had walked off carried him right up to the board.

He looked at the paper.

"Hard luck!" said somebody.

Mike scarcely heard him.

He felt physically sick with the shock of the disappointment. For the initial before the name Jackson was R.

There was no possibility of mistake. Since writing was invented, there had never been an R. that looked less like an M. than the one on that list.

Bob had beaten him on the tape.

CHAPTER XXI

MARJORY THE FRANK

At the door of the senior block Burgess, going out, met Bob coming in, hurrying, as he was rather late.

"Congratulate you, Bob," he said; and passed on.

Bob stared after him. As he stared, Trevor came out of the block.

"Congratulate you, Bob."

"What's the matter now?"

"Haven't you seen?"

"Seen what?"

"Why the list. You've got your first."

"My—what? you're rotting."

"No, I'm not. Go and look."

The thing seemed incredible. Had he dreamed that conversation between Spence and Burgess on the pavilion steps? Had he mixed up the names? He was certain that he had heard Spence give his verdict for Mike, and Burgess agree with him.

Just then, Mike, feeling very ill, came down the steps. He caught sight of Bob and was passing with a feeble grin, when something told him that this was one of those occasions on which one has to show a Red Indian fortitude and stifle one's private feelings.

"Congratulate you, Bob," he said awkwardly.

"Thanks awfully," said Bob, with equal awkwardness. Trevor moved on, delicately. This was no place for him. Bob's face was looking like a stuffed frog's, which was Bob's way of trying to appear unconcerned and at his ease, while Mike seemed as if at any moment he might burst into tears. Spectators are not wanted at these awkward interviews.

There was a short silence.

"Jolly glad you've got it," said Mike.

"I believe there's a mistake. I swear I heard Burgess say to Spence—"

"He changed his mind probably. No reason why he shouldn't."

"Well, it's jolly rummy."

Bob endeavoured to find consolation.

"Anyhow, you'll have three years in the first. You're a cert. for next year."

"Hope so," said Mike, with such manifest lack of enthusiasm that Bob abandoned this line of argument. When one has missed one's colours, next year seems a very, very long way off.

They moved slowly through the cloisters, neither speaking, and up the stairs that led to the Great Hall. Each was gratefully conscious of the fact that prayers would be beginning in another minute, putting an end to an uncomfortable situation.

"Heard from home lately?" inquired Mike.

Bob snatched gladly at the subject.

"Got a letter from mother this morning. I showed you the last one, didn't I? I've only just had time to skim through this one, as the post was late, and I only got it just as I was going to dash across to school. Not much in it. Here it is, if you want to read it."

"Thanks. It'll be something to do during Math."

"Marjory wrote, too, for the first time in her life. Haven't had time to look at it yet."

"After you. Sure it isn't meant for me? She owes me a letter."

"No, it's for me all right. I'll give it you in the interval."

The arrival of the headmaster put an end to the conversation.

By a quarter to eleven Mike had begun to grow reconciled to his fate. The disappointment was still there, but it was lessened. These things are like kicks on the shin. A brief spell of agony, and then a dull pain of which we are not always conscious unless our attention is directed to it, and which in time disappears altogether. When the bell rang for the interval that morning, Mike was, as it were, sitting up and taking nourishment.

He was doing this in a literal as well as in a figurative sense when Bob entered the school shop.

Bob appeared curiously agitated. He looked round, and, seeing Mike, pushed his way towards him through the crowd. Most of those present congratulated him as he passed; and Mike noticed, with some surprise, that, in place of the blushful grin which custom demands from the man who is being congratulated on receipt of colours, there appeared on his face a worried, even an irritated look. He seemed to have something on his mind.

"Hullo," said Mike amiably. "Got that letter?"

"Yes. I'll show it you outside."

"Why not here?"

"Come on."

Mike resented the tone, but followed. Evidently something had happened to upset Bob seriously. As they went out on the gravel, somebody congratulated Bob again, and again Bob hardly seemed to appreciate it.'

Bob led the way across the gravel and on to the first terrace. When they had left the crowd behind, he stopped.

"What's up?" asked Mike.

"I want you to read—"

"Jackson!"

They both turned. The headmaster was standing on the edge of the gravel.

Bob pushed the letter into Mike's hands.

"Read that," he said, and went up to the headmaster. Mike heard the words "English Essay," and, seeing that the conversation was apparently going to be one of some length, capped the headmaster and walked off. He was just going to read the letter when the bell rang. He put the missive in his pocket, and went to his form-room wondering what Marjory could have found to say to Bob to touch him on the raw to such an extent. She was a breezy correspondent, with a style of her own, but usually she entertained rather than upset people. No suspicion of the actual contents of the letter crossed his mind.

He read it during school, under the desk; and ceased to wonder. Bob had had cause to look worried. For the thousand and first time in her career of crime Marjory had been and done it! With a strong hand she had shaken the cat out of the bag, and exhibited it plainly to all whom it might concern.

There was a curious absence of construction about the letter. Most authors of sensational matter nurse their bomb-shell, lead up to it, and display it to the best advantage. Marjory dropped hers into the body of the letter, and let it take its chance with the other news-items.

"DEAR BOB" (the letter ran),—

"I hope you are quite well. I am quite well. Phyllis has a cold, Ella cheeked Mademoiselle yesterday, and had to write out 'Little Girls must be polite and obedient' a hundred times in French. She was jolly sick about it. I told her it served her right. Joe made eighty-three against Lancashire. Reggie made a duck. Have you got your first? If you have, it will be all through Mike. Uncle John told Father that Mike pretended to hurt his wrist so that you could play instead of him for the school, and Father said it was very sporting of Mike but nobody must tell you because it wouldn't be fair if you got your first for you to know that you owed it to Mike and I wasn't supposed to hear but I did because I was in the room only they didn't know I was (we were playing hide-and-seek and I was hiding) so I'm writing to tell you,

"From your affectionate sister
"Marjory"

There followed a P.S.
"I'll tell you what you ought to do. I've been reading a jolly good book called 'The Boys of Dormitory Two,' and the hero's an awfully nice boy named Lionel Tremayne, and his friend Jack Langdale saves his life when a beast of a boatman who's really employed by Lionel's cousin who wants the money that Lionel's going to have when he grows up stuns him and leaves him on the beach to drown. Well, Lionel is going to play for the school against Loamshire, and it's the match of the season, but he goes to the headmaster and says he wants Jack to play instead of him. Why don't you do that?
"M.
"P.P.S.—This has been a frightful fag to write."
For the life of him Mike could not help giggling as he pictured what Bob's expression must have been when his brother read this document. But the humorous side of the thing did not appeal to him for long. What should he say to Bob? What would Bob say to him? Dash it all, it made him look such an awful ass! Anyhow, Bob couldn't do much. In fact he didn't see that he could do anything. The team was filled up, and Burgess was not likely to alter it. Besides, why should he alter it? Probably he would have given Bob his colours anyhow. Still, it was beastly awkward. Marjory meant well, but she had put her foot right in it. Girls oughtn't to meddle with these things. No girl ought to be taught to write till she came of age. And Uncle John had behaved in many respects like the Complete Rotter. If he was going to let out things like that, he might at least have whispered them, or looked behind the curtains to see that the place wasn't chock-full of female kids. Confound Uncle John!
Throughout the dinner-hour Mike kept out of Bob's way. But in a small community like a school it is impossible to avoid a man for ever. They met at the nets.
"Well?" said Bob.
"How do you mean?" said Mike.
"Did you read it?"
"Yes."

"Well, is it all rot, or did you—you know what I mean—sham a crocked wrist?"

"Yes," said Mike, "I did."

Bob stared gloomily at his toes.

"I mean," he said at last, apparently putting the finishing-touch to some train of thought, "I know I ought to be grateful, and all that. I suppose I am. I mean it was jolly good of you—Dash it all," he broke off hotly, as if the putting his position into words had suddenly showed him how inglorious it was, "what did you want to do it for? What was the idea? What right have you got to go about playing Providence over me? Dash it all, it's like giving a fellow money without consulting him."

"I didn't think you'd ever know. You wouldn't have if only that ass Uncle John hadn't let it out."

"How did he get to know? Why did you tell him?"

"He got it out of me. I couldn't choke him off. He came down when you were away at Geddington, and would insist on having a look at my arm, and naturally he spotted right away there was nothing the matter with it. So it came out; that's how it was."

Bob scratched thoughtfully at the turf with a spike of his boot.

"Of course, it was awfully decent—"

Then again the monstrous nature of the affair came home to him.

"But what did you do it for? Why should you rot up your own chances to give me a look in?"

"Oh, I don't know.... You know, you did me a jolly good turn."

"I don't remember. When?"

"That Firby-Smith business."

"What about it?"

"Well, you got me out of a jolly bad hole."

"Oh, rot! And do you mean to tell me it was simply because of that—?"

Mike appeared to him in a totally new light. He stared at him as if he were some strange creature hitherto unknown to the human race. Mike shuffled uneasily beneath the scrutiny.

"Anyhow, it's all over now," Mike said, "so I don't see what's the point of talking about it."

"I'm hanged if it is. You don't think I'm going to sit tight and take my first as if nothing had happened?"

"What can you do? The list's up. Are you going to the Old Man to ask him if I can play, like Lionel Tremayne?"

The hopelessness of the situation came over Bob like a wave. He looked helplessly at Mike.

"Besides," added Mike, "I shall get in next year all right. Half a second, I just want to speak to Wyatt about something."

He sidled off.

"Well, anyhow," said Bob to himself, "I must see Burgess about it."

89

CHAPTER XXII

WYATT IS REMINDED OF AN ENGAGEMENT

There are situations in life which are beyond one. The sensible man realises this, and slides out of such situations, admitting himself beaten. Others try to grapple with them, but it never does any good. When affairs get into a real tangle, it is best to sit still and let them straighten themselves out. Or, if one does not do that, simply to think no more about them. This is Philosophy. The true philosopher is the man who says "All right," and goes to sleep in his arm-chair. One's attitude towards Life's Little Difficulties should be that of the gentleman in the fable, who sat down on an acorn one day, and happened to doze. The warmth of his body caused the acorn to germinate, and it grew so rapidly that, when he awoke, he found himself sitting in the fork of an oak, sixty feet from the ground. He thought he would go home, but, finding this impossible, he altered his plans. "Well, well," he said, "if I cannot compel circumstances to my will, I can at least adapt my will to circumstances. I decide to remain here." Which he did, and had a not unpleasant time. The oak lacked some of the comforts of home, but the air was splendid and the view excellent.

To-day's Great Thought for Young Readers. Imitate this man.

Bob should have done so, but he had not the necessary amount of philosophy. He still clung to the idea that he and Burgess, in council, might find some way of making things right for everybody. Though, at the moment, he did not see how eleven caps were to be divided amongst twelve candidates in such a way that each should have one.

And Burgess, consulted on the point, confessed to the same inability to solve the problem. It took Bob at least a quarter of an hour to get the facts of the case into the captain's head, but at last Burgess grasped the idea of the thing. At which period he remarked that it was a rum business.

"Very rum," Bob agreed. "Still, what you say doesn't help us out much, seeing that the point is, what's to be done?"

"Why do anything?"

Burgess was a philosopher, and took the line of least resistance, like the man in the oak-tree.

"But I must do something," said Bob. "Can't you see how rotten it is for me?"

"I don't see why. It's not your fault. Very sporting of your brother and all that, of course, though I'm blowed if I'd have done it

90

myself; but why should you do anything? You're all right. Your brother stood out of the team to let you in it, and here you are, in it. What's he got to grumble about?"

"He's not grumbling. It's me."

"What's the matter with you? Don't you want your first?"

"Not like this. Can't you see what a rotten position it is for me?"

"Don't you worry. You simply keep on saying you're all right. Besides, what do you want me to do? Alter the list?"

But for the thought of those unspeakable outsiders, Lionel Tremayne and his headmaster, Bob might have answered this question in the affirmative; but he had the public-school boy's terror of seeming to pose or do anything theatrical. He would have done a good deal to put matters right, but he could not do the self-sacrificing young hero business. It would not be in the picture. These things, if they are to be done at school, have to be carried through stealthily, after Mike's fashion.

"I suppose you can't very well, now it's up. Tell you what, though, I don't see why I shouldn't stand out of the team for the Ripton match. I could easily fake up some excuse."

"I do. I don't know if it's occurred to you, but the idea is rather to win the Ripton match, if possible. So that I'm a lot keen on putting the best team into the field. Sorry if it upsets your arrangements in any way."

"You know perfectly well Mike's every bit as good as me."

"He isn't so keen."

"What do you mean?"

"Fielding. He's a young slacker."

When Burgess had once labelled a man as that, he did not readily let the idea out of his mind.

"Slacker? What rot! He's as keen as anything."

"Anyhow, his keenness isn't enough to make him turn out for house-fielding. If you really want to know, that's why you've got your first instead of him. You sweated away, and improved your fielding twenty per cent.; and I happened to be talking to Firby-Smith and found that young Mike had been shirking his, so out he went. A bad field's bad enough, but a slack field wants skinning."

"Smith oughtn't to have told you."

"Well, he did tell me. So you see how it is. There won't be any changes from the team I've put up on the board."

"Oh, all right," said Bob. "I was afraid you mightn't be able to do anything. So long."

"Mind the step," said Burgess.

At about the time when this conversation was in progress, Wyatt, crossing the cricket-field towards the school shop in search of something fizzy that might correct a burning thirst acquired at the nets, espied on the horizon a suit of cricket flannels surmounted by a huge, expansive grin. As the distance between them lessened, he discovered that inside the flannels was Neville-Smith's body and behind the grin the rest of Neville-Smith's face. Their visit to the nets not having coincided in point of time, as the Greek exercise books say, Wyatt had not seen his friend since the list of the team had been posted on the board, so he proceeded to congratulate him on his colours.

"Thanks," said Neville-Smith, with a brilliant display of front teeth.

"Feeling good?"

"Not the word for it. I feel like—I don't know what."

"I'll tell you what you look like, if that's any good to you. That slight smile of yours will meet behind, if you don't look out, and then the top of your head'll come off."

"I don't care. I've got my first, whatever happens. Little Willie's going to buy a nice new cap and a pretty striped jacket all for his own self! I say, thanks for reminding me. Not that you did, but supposing you had. At any rate, I remember what it was I wanted to say to you. You know what I was saying to you about the bust I meant to have at home in honour of my getting my first, if I did, which I have—well, anyhow it's to-night. You can roll up, can't you?"

"Delighted. Anything for a free feed in these hard times. What time did you say it was?"

"Eleven. Make it a bit earlier, if you like."

"No, eleven'll do me all right."

"How are you going to get out?"

"'Stone walls do not a prison make, nor iron bars a cage.' That's what the man said who wrote the libretto for the last set of Latin Verses we had to do. I shall manage it."

"They ought to allow you a latch-key."

"Yes, I've often thought of asking my pater for one. Still, I get on very well. Who are coming besides me?"

"No boarders. They all funked it."

"The race is degenerating."

"Said it wasn't good enough."

"The school is going to the dogs. Who did you ask?"

"Clowes was one. Said he didn't want to miss his beauty-sleep. And Henfrey backed out because he thought the risk of being sacked wasn't good enough."

"That's an aspect of the thing that might occur to some people. I don't blame him—I might feel like that myself if I'd got another couple of years at school."

"But one or two day-boys are coming. Clephane is, for one. And Beverley. We shall have rather a rag. I'm going to get the things now."

"When I get to your place—I don't believe I know the way, now I come to think of it—what do I do? Ring the bell and send in my card? or smash the nearest window and climb in?"

"Don't make too much row, for goodness sake. All the servants'll have gone to bed. You'll see the window of my room. It's just above the porch. It'll be the only one lighted up. Heave a pebble at it, and I'll come down."

"So will the glass—with a run, I expect. Still, I'll try to do as little damage as possible. After all, I needn't throw a brick."

"You will turn up, won't you?"

"Nothing shall stop me."

"Good man."

As Wyatt was turning away, a sudden compunction seized upon Neville-Smith. He called him back.

"I say, you don't think it's too risky, do you? I mean, you always are breaking out at night, aren't you? I don't want to get you into a row."

"Oh, that's all right," said Wyatt. "Don't you worry about me. I should have gone out anyhow to-night."

CHAPTER XXIII

A SURPRISE FOR MR. APPLEBY

"You may not know it," said Wyatt to Mike in the dormitory that night, "but this is the maddest, merriest day of all the glad New Year."

Mike could not help thinking that for himself it was the very reverse, but he did not state his view of the case.

"What's up?" he asked.

"Neville-Smith's giving a meal at his place in honour of his getting his first. I understand the preparations are on a scale of the utmost magnificence. No expense has been spared. Ginger-beer will flow like water. The oldest cask of lemonade has been broached; and a sardine is roasting whole in the market-place."

"Are you going?"

"If I can tear myself away from your delightful society. The kick-off is fixed for eleven sharp. I am to stand underneath his window and heave bricks till something happens. I don't know if he keeps a dog. If so, I shall probably get bitten to the bone."

"When are you going to start?"

"About five minutes after Wain has been round the dormitories to see that all's well. That ought to be somewhere about half-past ten."

"Don't go getting caught."

"I shall do my little best not to be. Rather tricky work, though, getting back. I've got to climb two garden walls, and I shall probably be so full of Malvoisie that you'll be able to hear it swishing about inside me. No catch steeple-chasing if you're like that. They've no thought for people's convenience here. Now at Bradford they've got studies on the ground floor, the windows looking out over the boundless prairie. No climbing or steeple-chasing needed at all. All you have to do is to open the window and step out. Still, we must make the best of things. Push us over a pinch of that tooth-powder of yours. I've used all mine."

Wyatt very seldom penetrated further than his own garden on the occasions when he roamed abroad at night. For cat-shooting the Wain spinneys were unsurpassed. There was one particular dustbin where one might be certain of flushing a covey any night; and the wall by the potting-shed was a feline club-house.

But when he did wish to get out into the open country he had a special route which he always took. He climbed down from the wall that ran beneath the dormitory window into the garden belonging to Mr. Appleby, the master who had the house next to Mr. Wain's. Crossing this, he climbed another wall, and dropped from it into a small lane which ended in the main road leading to Wrykyn town.

This was the route which he took to-night. It was a glorious July night, and the scent of the flowers came to him with a curious distinctness as he let himself down from the dormitory window. At any other time he might have made a lengthy halt, and enjoyed the scents and small summer noises, but now he felt that it would be better not to delay. There was a full moon, and where he stood he could be seen distinctly from the windows of both houses. They were all dark, it is true, but on these occasions it was best to take no risks.

He dropped cautiously into Appleby's garden, ran lightly across it, and was in the lane within a minute.

There he paused, dusted his trousers, which had suffered on the two walls, and strolled meditatively in the direction of the town. Half-past ten had just chimed from the school clock. He was in plenty of time.

"What a night!" he said to himself, sniffing as he walked.

Now it happened that he was not alone in admiring the beauty of that particular night. At ten-fifteen it had struck Mr. Appleby, looking out of his study into the moonlit school grounds, that a pipe in the open would make an excellent break in his night's work. He had acquired a slight headache as the result of correcting a batch of examination papers, and he thought that an interval of an hour in the open air before approaching the half-dozen or so papers which still remained to be looked at might do him good. The window of his study was open, but the room had got hot and stuffy. Nothing like a little fresh air for putting him right.

For a few moments he debated the rival claims of a stroll in the

94

cricket-field and a seat in the garden. Then he decided on the latter. The little gate in the railings opposite his house might not be open, and it was a long way round to the main entrance. So he took a deck-chair which leaned against the wall, and let himself out of the back door.

He took up his position in the shadow of a fir-tree with his back to the house. From here he could see the long garden. He was fond of his garden, and spent what few moments he could spare from work and games pottering about it. He had his views as to what the ideal garden should be, and he hoped in time to tinker his own three acres up to the desired standard. At present there remained much to be done. Why not, for instance, take away those laurels at the end of the lawn, and have a flower-bed there instead? Laurels lasted all the year round, true, whereas flowers died and left an empty brown bed in the winter, but then laurels were nothing much to look at at any time, and a garden always had a beastly appearance in winter, whatever you did to it. Much better have flowers, and get a decent show for one's money in summer at any rate.

The problem of the bed at the end of the lawn occupied his complete attention for more than a quarter of an hour, at the end of which period he discovered that his pipe had gone out.

He was just feeling for his matches to relight it when Wyatt dropped with a slight thud into his favourite herbaceous border.

The surprise, and the agony of feeling that large boots were trampling among his treasures kept him transfixed for just the length of time necessary for Wyatt to cross the garden and climb the opposite wall. As he dropped into the lane, Mr. Appleby recovered himself sufficiently to emit a sort of strangled croak, but the sound was too slight to reach Wyatt. That reveller was walking down the Wrykyn road before Mr. Appleby had left his chair.

It is an interesting point that it was the gardener rather than the schoolmaster in Mr. Appleby that first awoke to action. It was not the idea of a boy breaking out of his house at night that occurred to him first as particularly heinous; it was the fact that the boy had broken out via his herbaceous border. In four strides he was on the scene of the outrage, examining, on hands and knees, with the aid of the moonlight, the extent of the damage done.

As far as he could see, it was not serious. By a happy accident Wyatt's boots had gone home to right and left of precious plants but not on them. With a sigh of relief Mr. Appleby smoothed over the cavities, and rose to his feet.

At this point it began to strike him that the episode affected him as a schoolmaster also.

In that startled moment when Wyatt had suddenly crossed his line of vision, he had recognised him. The moon had shone full on his face as he left the flowerbed. There was no doubt in his mind as to the identity of the intruder.

He paused, wondering how he should act. It was not an easy question. There was nothing of the spy about Mr. Appleby. He went his way openly, liked and respected by boys and masters. He always played the game. The difficulty here was to say exactly what the game was. Sentiment, of course, bade him forget the episode, treat it as if it had never happened. That was the simple way out of the difficulty. There was nothing unsporting about Mr. Appleby. He knew that there were times when a master might, without blame, close his eyes or look the other way. If he had met Wyatt out of bounds in the day-time, and it had been possible to convey the impression that he had not seen him, he would have done so. To be out of bounds is not a particularly deadly sin. A master must check it if it occurs too frequently, but he may use his discretion.

Breaking out at night, however, was a different thing altogether. It was on another plane. There are times when a master must waive sentiment, and remember that he is in a position of trust, and owes a duty directly to his headmaster, and indirectly, through the headmaster, to the parents. He receives a salary for doing this duty, and, if he feels that sentiment is too strong for him, he should resign in favour of some one of tougher fibre.

This was the conclusion to which Mr. Appleby came over his relighted pipe. He could not let the matter rest where it was.

In ordinary circumstances it would have been his duty to report the affair to the headmaster but in the present case he thought that a slightly different course might be pursued. He would lay the whole thing before Mr. Wain, and leave him to deal with it as he thought best. It was one of the few cases where it was possible for an assistant master to fulfil his duty to a parent directly, instead of through the agency of the headmaster.

Knocking out the ashes of his pipe against a tree, he folded his deck-chair and went into the house. The examination papers were spread invitingly on the table, but they would have to wait. He turned down his lamp, and walked round to Wain's.

There was a light in one of the ground-floor windows. He tapped on the window, and the sound of a chair being pushed back told him that he had been heard. The blind shot up, and he had a view of a room littered with books and papers, in the middle of which stood Mr. Wain, like a sea-beast among rocks.

Mr. Wain recognised his visitor and opened the window. Mr. Appleby could not help feeling how like Wain it was to work on a warm summer's night in a hermetically sealed room. There was always something queer and eccentric about Wyatt's step-father.

"Can I have a word with you, Wain?" he said.

"Appleby! Is there anything the matter? I was startled when you tapped. Exceedingly so."

"Sorry," said Mr. Appleby. "Wouldn't have disturbed you, only it's something important. I'll climb in through here, shall I? No need to unlock the door." And, greatly to Mr. Wain's surprise and rather to his disapproval, Mr. Appleby vaulted on to the window-sill, and squeezed through into the room.

CHAPTER XXIV

CAUGHT

"Got some rather bad news for you, I'm afraid," began Mr. Appleby. "I'll smoke, if you don't mind. About Wyatt."

"James!"

"I was sitting in my garden a few minutes ago, having a pipe before finishing the rest of my papers, and Wyatt dropped from the wall on to my herbaceous border."

Mr. Appleby said this with a tinge of bitterness. The thing still rankled.

"James! In your garden! Impossible. Why, it is not a quarter of an hour since I left him in his dormitory."

"He's not there now."

"You astound me, Appleby. I am astonished."

"So was I."

"How is such a thing possible? His window is heavily barred."

"Bars can be removed."

"You must have been mistaken."

"Possibly," said Mr. Appleby, a little nettled. Gaping astonishment is always apt to be irritating. "Let's leave it at that, then. Sorry to have disturbed you."

"No, sit down, Appleby. Dear me, this is most extraordinary. Exceedingly so. You are certain it was James?"

"Perfectly. It's like daylight out of doors."

Mr. Wain drummed on the table with his fingers.

"What shall I do?"

Mr. Appleby offered no suggestion.

"I ought to report it to the headmaster. That is certainly the course I should pursue."

"I don't see why. It isn't like an ordinary case. You're the parent. You can deal with the thing directly. If you come to think of it, a headmaster's only a sort of middleman between boys and parents. He plays substitute for the parent in his absence. I don't see why you should drag in the master at all here."

"There is certainly something in what you say," said Mr. Wain on reflection.

"A good deal. Tackle the boy when he comes in, and have it out with him. Remember that it must mean expulsion if you report him to the headmaster. He would have no choice. Everybody who has ever broken out of his house here and been caught has been expelled. I should strongly advise you to deal with the thing yourself."

"I will. Yes. You are quite right, Appleby. That is a very good idea of yours. You are not going?"

"Must. Got a pile of examination papers to look over. Good-night."

"Good-night."

Mr. Appleby made his way out of the window and through the gate into his own territory in a pensive frame of mind. He was wondering what would happen. He had taken the only possible course, and, if only Wain kept his head and did not let the matter get through officially to the headmaster, things might not be so bad for Wyatt after all. He hoped they would not. He liked Wyatt. It would be a thousand pities, he felt, if he were to be expelled. What would Wain do? What would he do in a similar case? It was difficult to say. Probably talk violently for as long as he could keep it up, and then consider the episode closed. He doubted whether Wain would have the common sense to do this. Altogether it was very painful and disturbing, and he was taking a rather gloomy view of the assistant master's lot as he sat down to finish off the rest of his examination papers. It was not all roses, the life of an assistant master at a public school. He had continually to be sinking his own individual sympathies in the claims of his duty. Mr. Appleby was the last man who would willingly have reported a boy for enjoying a midnight ramble. But he was the last man to shirk the duty of reporting him, merely because it was one decidedly not to his taste.

Mr. Wain sat on for some minutes after his companion had left, pondering over the news he had heard. Even now he clung to the idea that Appleby had made some extraordinary mistake. Gradually he began to convince himself of this. He had seen Wyatt actually in bed a quarter of an hour before—not asleep, it was true, but apparently on the verge of dropping off. And the bars across the window had looked so solid.... Could Appleby have been dreaming? Something of the kind might easily have happened. He had been working hard, and the night was warm....

Then it occurred to him that he could easily prove or disprove the truth of his colleague's statement by going to the dormitory and seeing if Wyatt were there or not. If he had gone out, he would hardly have returned yet.

He took a candle, and walked quietly upstairs.

Arrived at his step-son's dormitory, he turned the door-handle softly and went in. The light of the candle fell on both beds. Mike was there, asleep. He grunted, and turned over with his face to the wall as the light shone on his eyes. But the other bed was empty. Appleby had been right.

If further proof had been needed, one of the bars was missing from the window. The moon shone in through the empty space.

The house-master sat down quietly on the vacant bed. He blew the candle out, and waited there in the semi-darkness, thinking. For years he and Wyatt had lived in a state of armed neutrality, broken by various small encounters. Lately, by silent but mutual agreement, they had kept out of each other's way as much as possible, and it had become rare for the house-master to have to find fault officially with his step-son. But there had never been anything even remotely approaching friendship between them. Mr. Wain was not a man who inspired affection readily, least of all in those many years younger than himself. Nor did he easily grow fond of others. Wyatt he had regarded, from the moment when the threads of their lives became entangled, as a complete nuisance.

It was not, therefore, a sorrowful, so much as an exasperated, vigil that he kept in the dormitory. There was nothing of the sorrowing father about his frame of mind. He was the house-master about to deal with a mutineer, and nothing else.

This breaking-out, he reflected wrathfully, was the last straw. Wyatt's presence had been a nervous inconvenience to him for years. The time had come to put an end to it. It was with a comfortable feeling of magnanimity that he resolved not to report the breach of discipline to the headmaster. Wyatt should not be expelled. But he should leave, and that immediately. He would write to the bank before he went to bed, asking them to receive his step-son at once; and the letter should go by the first post next day. The discipline of the bank would be salutary and steadying. And—this was a particularly grateful reflection—a fortnight annually was the limit of the holiday allowed by the management to its junior employees.

Mr. Wain had arrived at this conclusion, and was beginning to feel a little cramped, when Mike Jackson suddenly sat up.

"Hullo!" said Mike.

"Go to sleep, Jackson, immediately," snapped the house-master.

Mike had often heard and read of people's hearts leaping to their mouths, but he had never before experienced that sensation of something hot and dry springing in the throat, which is what really happens to us on receipt of a bad shock. A sickening feeling that the game was up beyond all hope of salvation came to him. He lay down again without a word.

What a frightful thing to happen! How on earth had this come

99

about? What in the world had brought Wain to the dormitory at that hour? Poor old Wyatt! If it had upset him (Mike) to see the house-master in the room, what would be the effect of such a sight on Wyatt, returning from the revels at Neville-Smith's!

And what could he do? Nothing. There was literally no way out. His mind went back to the night when he had saved Wyatt by a brilliant coup. The most brilliant of coups could effect nothing now. Absolutely and entirely the game was up.

Every minute that passed seemed like an hour to Mike. Dead silence reigned in the dormitory, broken every now and then by the creak of the other bed, as the house-master shifted his position. Twelve boomed across the field from the school clock. Mike could not help thinking what a perfect night it must be for him to be able to hear the strokes so plainly. He strained his ears for any indication of Wyatt's approach, but could hear nothing. Then a very faint scraping noise broke the stillness, and presently the patch of moonlight on the floor was darkened.

At that moment Mr. Wain relit his candle.

The unexpected glare took Wyatt momentarily aback. Mike saw him start. Then he seemed to recover himself. In a calm and leisurely manner he climbed into the room.

"James!" said Mr. Wain. His voice sounded ominously hollow.

Wyatt dusted his knees, and rubbed his hands together. "Hullo, is that you, father!" he said pleasantly.

CHAPTER XXV

MARCHING ORDERS

A silence followed. To Mike, lying in bed, holding his breath, it seemed a long silence. As a matter of fact it lasted for perhaps ten seconds. Then Mr. Wain spoke.

"You have been out, James?"

It is curious how in the more dramatic moments of life the inane remark is the first that comes to us.

"Yes, sir," said Wyatt.

"I am astonished. Exceedingly astonished."

"I got a bit of a start myself," said Wyatt.

"I shall talk to you in my study. Follow me there."

"Yes, sir."

He left the room, and Wyatt suddenly began to chuckle.

"I say, Wyatt!" said Mike, completely thrown off his balance by the events of the night.

Wyatt continued to giggle helplessly. He flung himself down on his bed, rolling with laughter. Mike began to get alarmed.

"It's all right," said Wyatt at last, speaking with difficulty. "But, I say, how long had he been sitting there?"

"It seemed hours. About an hour, I suppose, really."

"It's the funniest thing I've ever struck. Me sweating to get in quietly, and all the time him camping out on my bed!"

"But look here, what'll happen?"

Wyatt sat up.

"That reminds me. Suppose I'd better go down."

"What'll he do, do you think?"

"Ah, now, what!"

"But, I say, it's awful. What'll happen?"

"That's for him to decide. Speaking at a venture, I should say—"

"You don't think—?"

"The boot. The swift and sudden boot. I shall be sorry to part with you, but I'm afraid it's a case of 'Au revoir, my little Hyacinth.' We shall meet at Philippi. This is my Moscow. To-morrow I shall go out into the night with one long, choking sob. Years hence a white-haired bank-clerk will tap at your door when you're a prosperous professional cricketer with your photograph in Wisden. That'll be me. Well, I suppose I'd better go down. We'd better all get to bed some time to-night. Don't go to sleep."

"Not likely."

"I'll tell you all the latest news when I come back. Where are me slippers? Ha, 'tis well! Lead on, then, minions. I follow."

In the study Mr. Wain was fumbling restlessly with his papers when Wyatt appeared.

"Sit down, James," he said.

Wyatt sat down. One of his slippers fell off with a clatter. Mr. Wain jumped nervously.

"Only my slipper," explained Wyatt. "It slipped."

Mr. Wain took up a pen, and began to tap the table.

"Well, James?"

Wyatt said nothing.

"I should be glad to hear your explanation of this disgraceful matter."

"The fact is—" said Wyatt.

"Well?"

"I haven't one, sir."

"What were you doing out of your dormitory, out of the house, at that hour?"

"I went for a walk, sir."

101

"And, may I inquire, are you in the habit of violating the strictest school rules by absenting yourself from the house during the night?"

"Yes, sir."

"What?"

"Yes, sir."

"This is an exceedingly serious matter."

Wyatt nodded agreement with this view.

"Exceedingly."

The pen rose and fell with the rapidity of the cylinder of a motor-car. Wyatt, watching it, became suddenly aware that the thing was hypnotising him. In a minute or two he would be asleep.

"I wish you wouldn't do that, father. Tap like that, I mean. It's sending me to sleep."

"James!"

"It's like a woodpecker."

"Studied impertinence—"

"I'm very sorry. Only it was sending me off."

Mr. Wain suspended tapping operations, and resumed the thread of his discourse.

"I am sorry, exceedingly, to see this attitude in you, James. It is not fitting. It is in keeping with your behaviour throughout. Your conduct has been lax and reckless in the extreme. It is possible that you imagine that the peculiar circumstances of our relationship secure you from the penalties to which the ordinary boy—"

"No, sir."

"I need hardly say," continued Mr. Wain, ignoring the interruption, "that I shall treat you exactly as I should treat any other member of my house whom I had detected in the same misdemeanour."

"Of course," said Wyatt, approvingly.

"I must ask you not to interrupt me when I am speaking to you, James. I say that your punishment will be no whit less severe than would be that of any other boy. You have repeatedly proved yourself lacking in ballast and a respect for discipline in smaller ways, but this is a far more serious matter. Exceedingly so. It is impossible for me to overlook it, even were I disposed to do so. You are aware of the penalty for such an action as yours?"

"The sack," said Wyatt laconically.

"It is expulsion. You must leave the school. At once."

Wyatt nodded.

"As you know, I have already secured a nomination for you in the London and Oriental Bank. I shall write to-morrow to the manager asking him to receive you at once—"

"After all, they only gain an extra fortnight of me."

"You will leave directly I receive his letter. I shall arrange with the headmaster that you are withdrawn privately—"

"Not the sack?"

"Withdrawn privately. You will not go to school to-morrow. Do you understand? That is all. Have you anything to say?"

Wyatt reflected.

"No, I don't think—"

His eye fell on a tray bearing a decanter and a syphon.

"Oh, yes," he said. "Can't I mix you a whisky and soda, father, before I go off to bed?"

"Well?" said Mike.

Wyatt kicked off his slippers, and began to undress.

"What happened?"

"We chatted."

"Has he let you off?"

"Like a gun. I shoot off almost immediately. To-morrow I take a well-earned rest away from school, and the day after I become the gay young bank-clerk, all amongst the ink and ledgers."

Mike was miserably silent.

"Buck up," said Wyatt cheerfully. "It would have happened anyhow in another fortnight. So why worry?"

Mike was still silent. The reflection was doubtless philosophic, but it failed to comfort him.

CHAPTER XXVI

THE AFTERMATH

Bad news spreads quickly. By the quarter to eleven interval next day the facts concerning Wyatt and Mr. Wain were public property. Mike, as an actual spectator of the drama, was in great request as an informant. As he told the story to a group of sympathisers outside the school shop, Burgess came up, his eyes rolling in a fine frenzy.

"Anybody seen young—oh, here you are. What's all this about Jimmy Wyatt? They're saying he's been sacked, or some rot."

"So he has—at least, he's got to leave."

"What? When?"

"He's left already. He isn't coming to school again."

Burgess's first thought, as befitted a good cricket captain, was for his team.

"And the Ripton match on Saturday!"

Nobody seemed to have anything except silent sympathy at his command.

"Dash the man! Silly ass! What did he want to do it for! Poor old Jimmy, though!" he added after a pause. "What rot for him!"

"Beastly," agreed Mike.

"All the same," continued Burgess, with a return to the austere manner of the captain of cricket, "he might have chucked playing the goat till after the Ripton match. Look here, young Jackson, you'll turn out for fielding with the first this afternoon. You'll play on Saturday."

"All right," said Mike, without enthusiasm. The Wyatt disaster was too recent for him to feel much pleasure at playing against Ripton vice his friend, withdrawn.

Bob was the next to interview him. They met in the cloisters.

"Hullo, Mike!" said Bob. "I say, what's all this about Wyatt?"

"Wain caught him getting back into the dorm. last night after Neville-Smith's, and he's taken him away from the school."

"What's he going to do? Going into that bank straight away?"

"Yes. You know, that's the part he bars most. He'd have been leaving anyhow in a fortnight, you see; only it's awful rot for a chap like Wyatt to have to go and froust in a bank for the rest of his life."

"He'll find it rather a change, I expect. I suppose you won't be seeing him before he goes?"

"I shouldn't think so. Not unless he comes to the dorm. during the night. He's sleeping over in Wain's part of the house, but I shouldn't be surprised if he nipped out after Wain has gone to bed. Hope he does, anyway."

"I should like to say good-bye. But I don't suppose it'll be possible."

They separated in the direction of their respective form-rooms. Mike felt bitter and disappointed at the way the news had been received. Wyatt was his best friend, his pal; and it offended him that the school should take the tidings of his departure as they had done. Most of them who had come to him for information had expressed a sort of sympathy with the absent hero of his story, but the chief sensation seemed to be one of pleasurable excitement at the fact that something big had happened to break the monotony of school routine. They treated the thing much as they would have treated the announcement that a record score had been made in first-class cricket. The school was not so much regretful as comfortably thrilled. And Burgess had actually cursed before sympathising. Mike felt resentful towards Burgess. As a matter of fact, the cricket captain wrote a letter to Wyatt during preparation that night which would have satisfied even Mike's sense of what was fit. But Mike had no opportunity of learning this.

There was, however, one exception to the general rule, one member of the school who did not treat the episode as if it were merely

104

an interesting and impersonal item of sensational news. Neville-Smith heard of what had happened towards the end of the interval, and rushed off instantly in search of Mike. He was too late to catch him before he went to his form-room, so he waited for him at half-past twelve, when the bell rang for the end of morning school.

"I say, Jackson, is this true about old Wyatt?"

Mike nodded.

"What happened?"

Mike related the story for the sixteenth time. It was a melancholy pleasure to have found a listener who heard the tale in the right spirit. There was no doubt about Neville-Smith's interest and sympathy. He was silent for a moment after Mike had finished.

"It was all my fault," he said at length. "If it hadn't been for me, this wouldn't have happened. What a fool I was to ask him to my place! I might have known he would be caught."

"Oh, I don't know," said Mike.

"It was absolutely my fault."

Mike was not equal to the task of soothing Neville-Smith's wounded conscience. He did not attempt it. They walked on without further conversation till they reached Wain's gate, where Mike left him. Neville-Smith proceeded on his way, plunged in meditation.

The result of which meditation was that Burgess got a second shock before the day was out. Bob, going over to the nets rather late in the afternoon, came upon the captain of cricket standing apart from his fellow men with an expression on his face that spoke of mental upheavals on a vast scale.

"What's up?" asked Bob.

"Nothing much," said Burgess, with a forced and grisly calm. "Only that, as far as I can see, we shall play Ripton on Saturday with a sort of second eleven. You don't happen to have got sacked or anything, by the way, do you?"

"What's happened now?"

"Neville-Smith. In extra on Saturday. That's all. Only our first- and second-change bowlers out of the team for the Ripton match in one day. I suppose by to-morrow half the others'll have gone, and we shall take the field on Saturday with a scratch side of kids from the Junior School."

"Neville-Smith! Why, what's he been doing?"

"Apparently he gave a sort of supper to celebrate his getting his first, and it was while coming back from that that Wyatt got collared. Well, I'm blowed if Neville-Smith doesn't toddle off to the Old Man after school to-day and tell him the whole yarn! Said it was all his fault. What rot! Sort of thing that might have happened to any one. If Wyatt hadn't gone to him, he'd probably have gone out somewhere else."

"And the Old Man shoved him in extra?"

"Next two Saturdays."

105

"Are Ripton strong this year?" asked Bob, for lack of anything better to say.

"Very, from all accounts. They whacked the M.C.C. Jolly hot team of M.C.C. too. Stronger than the one we drew with."

"Oh, well, you never know what's going to happen at cricket. I may hold a catch for a change."

Burgess grunted.

Bob went on his way to the nets. Mike was just putting on his pads.

"I say, Mike," said Bob. "I wanted to see you. It's about Wyatt. I've thought of something."

"What's that?"

"A way of getting him out of that bank. If it comes off, that's to say."

"By Jove, he'd jump at anything. What's the idea?"

"Why shouldn't he get a job of sorts out in the Argentine? There ought to be heaps of sound jobs going there for a chap like Wyatt. He's a jolly good shot, to start with. I shouldn't wonder if it wasn't rather a score to be able to shoot out there. And he can ride, I know."

"By Jove, I'll write to father to-night. He must be able to work it, I should think. He never chucked the show altogether, did he?"

Mike, as most other boys of his age would have been, was profoundly ignorant as to the details by which his father's money had been, or was being, made. He only knew vaguely that the source of revenue had something to do with the Argentine. His brother Joe had been born in Buenos Ayres; and once, three years ago, his father had gone over there for a visit, presumably on business. All these things seemed to show that Mr. Jackson senior was a useful man to have about if you wanted a job in that Eldorado, the Argentine Republic.

As a matter of fact, Mike's father owned vast tracts of land up country, where countless sheep lived and had their being. He had long retired from active superintendence of his estate. Like Mr. Spenlow, he had a partner, a stout fellow with the work-taint highly developed, who asked nothing better than to be left in charge. So Mr. Jackson had returned to the home of his fathers, glad to be there again. But he still had a decided voice in the ordering of affairs on the ranches, and Mike was going to the fountain-head of things when he wrote to his father that night, putting forward Wyatt's claims to attention and ability to perform any sort of job with which he might be presented.

The reflection that he had done all that could be done tended to console him for the non-appearance of Wyatt either that night or next morning—a non-appearance which was due to the simple fact that he passed that night in a bed in Mr. Wain's dressing-room, the door of which that cautious pedagogue, who believed in taking no chances, locked from the outside on retiring to rest.

CHAPTER XXVII

THE RIPTON MATCH

Mike got an answer from his father on the morning of the Ripton match. A letter from Wyatt also lay on his plate when he came down to breakfast.

Mr. Jackson's letter was short, but to the point. He said he would go and see Wyatt early in the next week. He added that being expelled from a public school was not the only qualification for success as a sheep-farmer, but that, if Mike's friend added to this a general intelligence and amiability, and a skill for picking off cats with an air-pistol and bull's-eyes with a Lee-Enfield, there was no reason why something should not be done for him. In any case he would buy him a lunch, so that Wyatt would extract at least some profit from his visit. He said that he hoped something could be managed. It was a pity that a boy accustomed to shoot cats should be condemned for the rest of his life to shoot nothing more exciting than his cuffs.

Wyatt's letter was longer. It might have been published under the title "My First Day in a Bank, by a Beginner." His advent had apparently caused little sensation. He had first had a brief conversation with the manager, which had run as follows:

"Mr. Wyatt?"

"Yes, sir."

"H'm ... Sportsman?"

"Yes, sir."

"Cricketer?"

"Yes, sir."

"Play football?"

"Yes, sir."

"H'm ... Racquets?"

"Yes, sir."

"Everything?"

"Yes, sir."

"H'm ... Well, you won't get any more of it now."

After which a Mr. Blenkinsop had led him up to a vast ledger, in which he was to inscribe the addresses of all out-going letters. These letters he would then stamp, and subsequently take in bundles to the post office. Once a week he would be required to buy stamps. "If I were one of those Napoleons of Finance," wrote Wyatt, "I should cook the accounts, I suppose, and embezzle stamps to an incredible amount. But it doesn't seem in my line. I'm afraid I wasn't cut out for a business career. Still, I have stamped this letter at the expense of the office, and entered it up under the heading 'Sundries,' which is a sort of start.

Look out for an article in the Wrykynian, 'Hints for Young Criminals, by J. Wyatt, champion catch-as-catch-can stamp-stealer of the British Isles.' So long. I suppose you are playing against Ripton, now that the world of commerce has found that it can't get on without me. Mind you make a century, and then perhaps Burgess'll give you your first after all. There were twelve colours given three years ago, because one chap left at half-term and the man who played instead of him came off against Ripton."

This had occurred to Mike independently. The Ripton match was a special event, and the man who performed any outstanding feat against that school was treated as a sort of Horatius. Honours were heaped upon him. If he could only make a century! or even fifty. Even twenty, if it got the school out of a tight place. He was as nervous on the Saturday morning as he had been on the morning of the M.C.C. match. It was Victory or Westminster Abbey now. To do only averagely well, to be among the ruck, would be as useless as not playing at all, as far as his chance of his first was concerned.

It was evident to those who woke early on the Saturday morning that this Ripton match was not likely to end in a draw. During the Friday rain had fallen almost incessantly in a steady drizzle. It had stopped late at night; and at six in the morning there was every prospect of another hot day. There was that feeling in the air which shows that the sun is trying to get through the clouds. The sky was a dull grey at breakfast time, except where a flush of deeper colour gave a hint of the sun. It was a day on which to win the toss, and go in first. At eleven-thirty, when the match was timed to begin, the wicket would be too wet to be difficult. Runs would come easily till the sun came out and began to dry the ground. When that happened there would be trouble for the side that was batting.

Burgess, inspecting the wicket with Mr. Spence during the quarter to eleven interval, was not slow to recognise this fact.

"I should win the toss to-day, if I were you, Burgess," said Mr. Spence.

"Just what I was thinking, sir."

"That wicket's going to get nasty after lunch, if the sun comes out. A regular Rhodes wicket it's going to be."

"I wish we had Rhodes," said Burgess. "Or even Wyatt. It would just suit him, this."

Mr. Spence, as a member of the staff, was not going to be drawn into discussing Wyatt and his premature departure, so he diverted the conversation on to the subject of the general aspect of the school's attack.

"Who will go on first with you, Burgess?"

"Who do you think, sir? Ellerby? It might be his wicket."

Ellerby bowled medium inclining to slow. On a pitch that suited

108

him he was apt to turn from leg and get people out caught at the wicket or short slip.

"Certainly, Ellerby. This end, I think. The other's yours, though I'm afraid you'll have a poor time bowling fast to-day. Even with plenty of sawdust I doubt if it will be possible to get a decent foothold till after lunch."

"I must win the toss," said Burgess. "It's a nuisance too, about our batting. Marsh will probably be dead out of form after being in the Infirmary so long. If he'd had a chance of getting a bit of practice yesterday, it might have been all right."

"That rain will have a lot to answer for if we lose. On a dry, hard wicket I'm certain we should beat them four times out of six. I was talking to a man who played against them for the Nomads. He said that on a true wicket there was not a great deal of sting in their bowling, but that they've got a slow leg-break man who might be dangerous on a day like this. A boy called de Freece. I don't know of him. He wasn't in the team last year."

"I know the chap. He played wing three for them at footer against us this year on their ground. He was crocked when they came here. He's a pretty useful chap all round, I believe. Plays racquets for them too."

"Well, my friend said he had one very dangerous ball, of the Bosanquet type. Looks as if it were going away, and comes in instead."

"I don't think a lot of that," said Burgess ruefully. "One consolation is, though, that that sort of ball is easier to watch on a slow wicket. I must tell the fellows to look out for it."

"I should. And, above all, win the toss."

Burgess and Maclaine, the Ripton captain, were old acquaintances. They had been at the same private school, and they had played against one another at football and cricket for two years now.

"We'll go in first, Mac," said Burgess, as they met on the pavilion steps after they had changed.

"It's awfully good of you to suggest it," said Maclaine. "but I think we'll toss. It's a hobby of mine. You call."

"Heads."

"Tails it is. I ought to have warned you that you hadn't a chance. I've lost the toss five times running, so I was bound to win to-day."

"You'll put us in, I suppose?"

"Yes—after us."

"Oh, well, we sha'n't have long to wait for our knock, that's a comfort. Buck up and send some one in, and let's get at you."

And Burgess went off to tell the ground-man to have plenty of sawdust ready, as he would want the field paved with it.

The policy of the Ripton team was obvious from the first over. They meant to force the game. Already the sun was beginning to peep through the haze. For about an hour run-getting ought to be a tolerably simple process; but after that hour singles would be as valuable as threes and boundaries an almost unheard-of luxury.

So Ripton went in to hit.

The policy proved successful for a time, as it generally does. Burgess, who relied on a run that was a series of tiger-like leaps culminating in a spring that suggested that he meant to lower the long jump record, found himself badly handicapped by the state of the ground. In spite of frequent libations of sawdust, he was compelled to tread cautiously, and this robbed his bowling of much of its pace. The score mounted rapidly. Twenty came in ten minutes. At thirty-five the first wicket fell, run out.

At sixty Ellerby, who had found the pitch too soft for him and had been expensive, gave place to Grant. Grant bowled what were supposed to be slow leg-breaks, but which did not always break. The change worked.

Maclaine, after hitting the first two balls to the boundary, skied the third to Bob Jackson in the deep, and Bob, for whom constant practice had robbed this sort of catch of its terrors, held it.

A yorker from Burgess disposed of the next man before he could settle down; but the score, seventy-four for three wickets, was large enough in view of the fact that the pitch was already becoming more difficult, and was certain to get worse, to make Ripton feel that the advantage was with them. Another hour of play remained before lunch. The deterioration of the wicket would be slow during that period. The sun, which was now shining brightly, would put in its deadliest work from two o'clock onwards. Maclaine's instructions to his men were to go on hitting.

A too liberal interpretation of the meaning of the verb "to hit" led to the departure of two more Riptonians in the course of the next two overs. There is a certain type of school batsman who considers that to force the game means to swipe blindly at every ball on the chance of taking it half-volley. This policy sometimes leads to a boundary or two, as it did on this occasion, but it means that wickets will fall, as also happened now. Seventy-four for three became eighty-six for five. Burgess began to look happier.

His contentment increased when he got the next man leg-before-wicket with the total unaltered. At this rate Ripton would be out before lunch for under a hundred.

But the rot stopped with the fall of that wicket. Dashing tactics were laid aside. The pitch had begun to play tricks, and the pair now in settled down to watch the ball. They plodded on, scoring slowly and jerkily till the hands of the clock stood at half-past one. Then Ellerby, who had gone on again instead of Grant, beat the less steady of the pair with a ball that pitched on the middle stump and shot into the base of the off. A hundred and twenty had gone up on the board at the beginning of the over.

That period which is always so dangerous, when the wicket is bad, the ten minutes before lunch, proved fatal to two more of the enemy. The last man had just gone to the wickets, with the score at a hundred and thirty-one, when a quarter to two arrived, and with it the luncheon interval.

So far it was anybody's game.

CHAPTER XXVIII

MIKE WINS HOME

The Ripton last-wicket man was de Freece, the slow bowler. He was apparently a young gentleman wholly free from the curse of nervousness. He wore a cheerful smile as he took guard before receiving the first ball after lunch, and Wrykyn had plenty of opportunity of seeing that that was his normal expression when at the wickets. There is often a certain looseness about the attack after lunch, and the bowler of googlies took advantage of it now. He seemed to be a batsman with only one hit; but he had also a very accurate eye, and his one hit, a semicircular stroke, which suggested the golf links rather than the cricket field, came off with distressing frequency. He mowed Burgess's first ball to the square-leg boundary, missed his second, and snicked the third for three over long-slip's head. The other batsman played out the over, and de Freece proceeded to treat Ellerby's bowling with equal familiarity. The scoring-board showed an increase of twenty as the result of three overs. Every run was invaluable now, and the Ripton contingent made the pavilion re-echo as a fluky shot over mid-on's head sent up the hundred and fifty.

There are few things more exasperating to the fielding side than a last-wicket stand. It resembles in its effect the dragging-out of a book or play after the dénouement has been reached. At the fall of the ninth wicket the fieldsmen nearly always look on their outing as finished. Just a ball or two to the last man, and it will be their turn to bat. If the last man insists on keeping them out in the field, they resent it.

What made it especially irritating now was the knowledge that a straight yorker would solve the whole thing. But when Burgess bowled a yorker, it was not straight. And when he bowled a straight ball, it was not a yorker. A four and a three to de Freece, and a four bye sent up a hundred and sixty.

It was beginning to look as if this might go on for ever, when

Ellerby, who had been missing the stumps by fractions of an inch, for the last ten minutes, did what Burgess had failed to do. He bowled a straight, medium-paced yorker, and de Freece, swiping at it with a bright smile, found his leg-stump knocked back. He had made twenty-eight. His record score, he explained to Mike, as they walked to the pavilion, for this or any ground.

The Ripton total was a hundred and sixty-six.

With the ground in its usual true, hard condition, Wrykyn would have gone in against a score of a hundred and sixty-six with the cheery intention of knocking off the runs for the loss of two or three wickets. It would have been a gentle canter for them.

But ordinary standards would not apply here. On a good wicket Wrykyn that season were a two hundred and fifty to three hundred side. On a bad wicket—well, they had met the Incogniti on a bad wicket, and their total—with Wyatt playing and making top score—had worked out at a hundred and seven.

A grim determination to do their best, rather than confidence that their best, when done, would be anything record-breaking, was the spirit which animated the team when they opened their innings.

And in five minutes this had changed to a dull gloom.

The tragedy started with the very first ball. It hardly seemed that the innings had begun, when Morris was seen to leave the crease, and make for the pavilion.

"It's that googly man," said Burgess blankly.

"What's happened?" shouted a voice from the interior of the first eleven room.

"Morris is out."

"Good gracious! How?" asked Ellerby, emerging from the room with one pad on his leg and the other in his hand.

"L.-b.-w. First ball."

"My aunt! Who's in next? Not me?"

"No. Berridge. For goodness sake, Berry, stick a bat in the way, and not your legs. Watch that de Freece man like a hawk. He breaks like sin all over the shop. Hullo, Morris! Bad luck! Were you out, do you think?" A batsman who has been given l.-b.-w. is always asked this question on his return to the pavilion, and he answers it in nine cases out of ten in the negative. Morris was the tenth case. He thought it was all right, he said.

"Thought the thing was going to break, but it didn't."

"Hear that, Berry? He doesn't always break. You must look out for that," said Burgess helpfully. Morris sat down and began to take off his pads.

"That chap'll have Berry, if he doesn't look out," he said.

But Berridge survived the ordeal. He turned his first ball to leg for a single.

112

This brought Marsh to the batting end; and the second tragedy occurred.

It was evident from the way he shaped that Marsh was short of practice. His visit to the Infirmary had taken the edge off his batting. He scratched awkwardly at three balls without hitting them. The last of the over had him in two minds. He started to play forward, changed his stroke suddenly and tried to step back, and the next moment the bails had shot up like the débris of a small explosion, and the wicket-keeper was clapping his gloved hands gently and slowly in the introspective, dreamy way wicket-keepers have on these occasions.

A silence that could be felt brooded over the pavilion.

The voice of the scorer, addressing from his little wooden hut the melancholy youth who was working the telegraph-board, broke it.

"One for two. Last man duck."

Ellerby echoed the remark. He got up, and took off his blazer.

"This is all right," he said, "isn't it! I wonder if the man at the other end is a sort of young Rhodes too!"

Fortunately he was not. The star of the Ripton attack was evidently de Freece. The bowler at the other end looked fairly plain. He sent them down medium-pace, and on a good wicket would probably have been simple. But to-day there was danger in the most guileless-looking deliveries.

Berridge relieved the tension a little by playing safely through the over, and scoring a couple of twos off it. And when Ellerby not only survived the destructive de Freece's second over, but actually lifted a loose ball on to the roof of the scoring-hut, the cloud began perceptibly to lift. A no-ball in the same over sent up the first ten. Ten for two was not good; but it was considerably better than one for two.

With the score at thirty, Ellerby was missed in the slips off de Freece. He had been playing with slowly increasing confidence till then, but this seemed to throw him out of his stride. He played inside the next ball, and was all but bowled: and then, jumping out to drive, he was smartly stumped. The cloud began to settle again.

Bob was the next man in.

Ellerby took off his pads, and dropped into the chair next to Mike's. Mike was silent and thoughtful. He was in after Bob, and to be on the eve of batting does not make one conversational.

"You in next?" asked Ellerby.

Mike nodded.

"It's getting trickier every minute," said Ellerby. "The only thing is, if we can only stay in, we might have a chance. The wicket'll get better, and I don't believe they've any bowling at all bar de Freece. By George, Bob's out!... No, he isn't."

Bob had jumped out at one of de Freece's slows, as Ellerby had done, and had nearly met the same fate. The wicket-keeper, however, had fumbled the ball.

113

"That's the way I was had," said Ellerby. "That man's keeping such a jolly good length that you don't know whether to stay in your ground or go out at them. If only somebody would knock him off his length, I believe we might win yet."

The same idea apparently occurred to Burgess. He came to where Mike was sitting.

"I'm going to shove you down one, Jackson," he said. "I shall go in next myself and swipe, and try and knock that man de Freece off."

"All right," said Mike. He was not quite sure whether he was glad or sorry at the respite.

"It's a pity old Wyatt isn't here," said Ellerby. "This is just the sort of time when he might have come off."

"Bob's broken his egg," said Mike.

"Good man. Every little helps.... Oh, you silly ass, get back!"

Berridge had called Bob for a short run that was obviously no run. Third man was returning the ball as the batsmen crossed. The next moment the wicket-keeper had the bails off. Berridge was out by a yard.

"Forty-one for four," said Ellerby. "Help!"

Burgess began his campaign against de Freece by skying his first ball over cover's head to the boundary. A howl of delight went up from the school, which was repeated, fortissimo, when, more by accident than by accurate timing, the captain put on two more fours past extra-cover. The bowler's cheerful smile never varied.

Whether Burgess would have knocked de Freece off his length or not was a question that was destined to remain unsolved, for in the middle of the other bowler's over Bob hit a single; the batsmen crossed; and Burgess had his leg-stump uprooted while trying a gigantic pull-stroke.

The melancholy youth put up the figures, 54, 5, 12, on the board.

Mike, as he walked out of the pavilion to join Bob, was not conscious of any particular nervousness. It had been an ordeal having to wait and look on while wickets fell, but now that the time of inaction was at an end he felt curiously composed. When he had gone out to bat against the M.C.C. on the occasion of his first appearance for the school, he experienced a quaint sensation of unreality. He seemed to be watching his body walking to the wickets, as if it were some one else's. There was no sense of individuality.

But now his feelings were different. He was cool. He noticed small things—mid-off chewing bits of grass, the bowler re-tying the scarf round his waist, little patches of brown where the turf had been worn away. He took guard with a clear picture of the positions of the fieldsmen photographed on his brain.

Fitness, which in a batsman exhibits itself mainly in an increased power of seeing the ball, is one of the most inexplicable things connected with cricket. It has nothing, or very little, to do with actual

114

health. A man may come out of a sick-room with just that extra quickness in sighting the ball that makes all the difference; or he may be in perfect training and play inside straight half-volleys. Mike would not have said that he felt more than ordinarily well that day. Indeed, he was rather painfully conscious of having bolted his food at lunch. But something seemed to whisper to him, as he settled himself to face the bowler, that he was at the top of his batting form. A difficult wicket always brought out his latent powers as a bat. It was a standing mystery with the sporting Press how Joe Jackson managed to collect fifties and sixties on wickets that completely upset men who were, apparently, finer players. On days when the Olympians of the cricket world were bringing their averages down with ducks and singles, Joe would be in his element, watching the ball and pushing it through the slips as if there were no such thing as a tricky wicket. And Mike took after Joe.

A single off the fifth ball of the over opened his score and brought him to the opposite end. Bob played ball number six back to the bowler, and Mike took guard preparatory to facing de Freece.

The Ripton slow bowler took a long run, considering his pace. In the early part of an innings he often trapped the batsmen in this way, by leading them to expect a faster ball than he actually sent down. A queer little jump in the middle of the run increased the difficulty of watching him.

The smiting he had received from Burgess in the previous over had not had the effect of knocking de Freece off his length. The ball was too short to reach with comfort, and not short enough to take liberties with. It pitched slightly to leg, and whipped in quickly. Mike had faced half-left, and stepped back. The increased speed of the ball after it had touched the ground beat him. The ball hit his right pad.

"'S that?" shouted mid-on. Mid-on has a habit of appealing for l.-b.-w. in school matches.

De Freece said nothing. The Ripton bowler was as conscientious in the matter of appeals as a good bowler should be. He had seen that the ball had pitched off the leg-stump.

The umpire shook his head. Mid-on tried to look as if he had not spoken.

Mike prepared himself for the next ball with a glow of confidence. He felt that he knew where he was now. Till then he had not thought the wicket was so fast. The two balls he had played at the other end had told him nothing. They had been well pitched up, and he had smothered them. He knew what to do now. He had played on wickets of this pace at home against Saunders's bowling, and Saunders had shown him the right way to cope with them.

The next ball was of the same length, but this time off the off-stump. Mike jumped out, and hit it before it had time to break. It flew along the ground through the gap between cover and extra-cover, a comfortable three.

Bob played out the over with elaborate care.

Off the second ball of the other man's over Mike scored his first boundary. It was a long-hop on the off. He banged it behind point to the terrace-bank. The last ball of the over, a half-volley to leg, he lifted over the other boundary.

"Sixty up," said Ellerby, in the pavilion, as the umpire signalled another no-ball. "By George! I believe these chaps are going to knock off the runs. Young Jackson looks as if he was in for a century."

"You ass," said Berridge. "Don't say that, or he's certain to get out."

Berridge was one of those who are skilled in cricket superstitions.

But Mike did not get out. He took seven off de Freece's next over by means of two cuts and a drive. And, with Bob still exhibiting a stolid and rock-like defence, the score mounted to eighty, thence to ninety, and so, mainly by singles, to a hundred.

At a hundred and four, when the wicket had put on exactly fifty, Bob fell to a combination of de Freece and extra-cover. He had stuck like a limpet for an hour and a quarter, and made twenty-one.

Mike watched him go with much the same feelings as those of a man who turns away from the platform after seeing a friend off on a long railway journey. His departure upset the scheme of things. For himself he had no fear now. He might possibly get out off his next ball, but he felt set enough to stay at the wickets till nightfall. He had had narrow escapes from de Freece, but he was full of that conviction, which comes to all batsmen on occasion, that this was his day. He had made twenty-six, and the wicket was getting easier. He could feel the sting going out of the bowling every over.

Henfrey, the next man in, was a promising rather than an effective bat. He had an excellent style, but he was uncertain. (Two years later, when he captained the Wrykyn teams, he made a lot of runs.) But this season his batting had been spasmodic.

To-day he never looked like settling down. He survived an over from de Freece, and hit a fast change bowler who had been put on at the other end for a couple of fluky fours. Then Mike got the bowling for three consecutive overs, and raised the score to a hundred and twenty-six. A bye brought Henfrey to the batting end again, and de Freece's pet googly, which had not been much in evidence hitherto, led to his snicking an easy catch into short-slip's hands.

A hundred and twenty-seven for seven against a total of a hundred and sixty-six gives the impression that the batting side has the advantage. In the present case, however, it was Ripton who were really in the better position. Apparently, Wrykyn had three more wickets to fall. Practically they had only one, for neither Ashe, nor Grant, nor Devenish had any pretensions to be considered batsmen. Ashe was the

116

school wicket-keeper. Grant and Devenish were bowlers. Between them the three could not be relied on for a dozen in a decent match.

Mike watched Ashe shape with a sinking heart. The wicket-keeper looked like a man who feels that his hour has come. Mike could see him licking his lips. There was nervousness written all over him.

He was not kept long in suspense. De Freece's first ball made a hideous wreck of his wicket.

"Over," said the umpire.

Mike felt that the school's one chance now lay in his keeping the bowling. But how was he to do this? It suddenly occurred to him that it was a delicate position that he was in. It was not often that he was troubled by an inconvenient modesty, but this happened now. Grant was a fellow he hardly knew, and a school prefect to boot. Could he go up to him and explain that he, Jackson, did not consider him competent to bat in this crisis? Would not this get about and be accounted to him for side? He had made forty, but even so....

Fortunately Grant solved the problem on his own account. He came up to Mike and spoke with an earnestness born of nerves. "For goodness sake," he whispered, "collar the bowling all you know, or we're done. I shall get outed first ball."

"All right," said Mike, and set his teeth. Forty to win! A large order. But it was going to be done. His whole existence seemed to concentrate itself on those forty runs.

The fast bowler, who was the last of several changes that had been tried at the other end, was well-meaning but erratic. The wicket was almost true again now, and it was possible to take liberties.

Mike took them.

A distant clapping from the pavilion, taken up a moment later all round the ground, and echoed by the Ripton fieldsmen, announced that he had reached his fifty.

The last ball of the over he mishit. It rolled in the direction of third man.

"Come on," shouted Grant.

Mike and the ball arrived at the opposite wicket almost simultaneously. Another fraction of a second, and he would have been run out.

The last balls of the next two overs provided repetitions of this performance. But each time luck was with him, and his bat was across the crease before the bails were off. The telegraph-board showed a hundred and fifty.

The next over was doubly sensational. The original medium-paced bowler had gone on again in place of the fast man, and for the first five balls he could not find his length. During those five balls Mike raised the score to a hundred and sixty.

But the sixth was of a different kind. Faster than the rest and of a perfect length, it all but got through Mike's defence. As it was, he stopped it. But he did not score. The umpire called "Over!" and there was Grant at the batting end, with de Freece smiling pleasantly as he walked back to begin his run with the comfortable reflection that at last he had got somebody except Mike to bowl at.

That over was an experience Mike never forgot.

Grant pursued the Fabian policy of keeping his bat almost immovable and trusting to luck. Point and the slips crowded round. Mid-off and mid-on moved half-way down the pitch. Grant looked embarrassed, but determined. For four balls he baffled the attack, though once nearly caught by point a yard from the wicket. The fifth curled round his bat, and touched the off-stump. A bail fell silently to the ground.

Devenish came in to take the last ball of the over.

It was an awe-inspiring moment. A great stillness was over all the ground. Mike's knees trembled. Devenish's face was a delicate grey.

The only person unmoved seemed to be de Freece. His smile was even more amiable than usual as he began his run.

The next moment the crisis was past. The ball hit the very centre of Devenish's bat, and rolled back down the pitch.

The school broke into one great howl of joy. There were still seven runs between them and victory, but nobody appeared to recognise this fact as important. Mike had got the bowling, and the bowling was not de Freece's.

It seemed almost an anti-climax when a four to leg and two two's through the slips settled the thing.

Devenish was caught and bowled in de Freece's next over; but the Wrykyn total was one hundred and seventy-two.

"Good game," said Maclaine, meeting Burgess in the pavilion. "Who was the man who made all the runs? How many, by the way?"

"Eighty-three. It was young Jackson. Brother of the other one."

"That family! How many more of them are you going to have here?"

"He's the last. I say, rough luck on de Freece. He bowled rippingly."

Politeness to a beaten foe caused Burgess to change his usual "not bad."

"The funny part of it is," continued he, "that young Jackson was only playing as a sub."

"You've got a rum idea of what's funny," said Maclaine.

118

CHAPTER XXIX

WYATT AGAIN

It was a morning in the middle of September. The Jacksons were breakfasting. Mr. Jackson was reading letters. The rest, including Gladys Maud, whose finely chiselled features were gradually disappearing behind a mask of bread-and-milk, had settled down to serious work. The usual catch-as-catch-can contest between Marjory and Phyllis for the jam (referee and time-keeper, Mrs. Jackson) had resulted, after both combatants had been cautioned by the referee, in a victory for Marjory, who had duly secured the stakes. The hour being nine-fifteen, and the official time for breakfast nine o'clock, Mike's place was still empty.

"I've had a letter from MacPherson," said Mr. Jackson.

MacPherson was the vigorous and persevering gentleman, referred to in a previous chapter, who kept a fatherly eye on the Buenos Ayres sheep.

"He seems very satisfied with Mike's friend Wyatt. At the moment of writing Wyatt is apparently incapacitated owing to a bullet in the shoulder, but expects to be fit again shortly. That young man seems to make things fairly lively wherever he is. I don't wonder he found a public school too restricted a sphere for his energies."

"Has he been fighting a duel?" asked Marjory, interested.

"Bushrangers," said Phyllis.

"There aren't any bushrangers in Buenos Ayres," said Ella.

"How do you know?" said Phyllis clinchingly.

"Bush-ray, bush-ray, bush-ray," began Gladys Maud, conversationally, through the bread-and-milk; but was headed off.

"He gives no details. Perhaps that letter on Mike's plate supplies them. I see it comes from Buenos Ayres."

"I wish Mike would come and open it," said Marjory. "Shall I go and hurry him up?"

The missing member of the family entered as she spoke.

"Buck up, Mike," she shouted. "There's a letter from Wyatt. He's been wounded in a duel."

"With a bushranger," added Phyllis.

"Bush-ray," explained Gladys Maud.

"Is there?" said Mike. "Sorry I'm late."

He opened the letter and began to read.

"What does he say?" inquired Marjory. "Who was the duel with?"

"How many bushrangers were there?" asked Phyllis.

Mike read on.

"Good old Wyatt! He's shot a man."

"Killed him?" asked Marjory excitedly.

"No. Only potted him in the leg. This is what he says. First page is mostly about the Ripton match and so on. Here you are. 'I'm dictating this to a sportsman of the name of Danvers, a good chap who can't help being ugly, so excuse bad writing. The fact is we've been having a bust-up here, and I've come out of it with a bullet in the shoulder, which has crocked me for the time being. It happened like this. An ass of a Gaucho had gone into the town and got jolly tight, and coming back, he wanted to ride through our place. The old woman who keeps the lodge wouldn't have it at any price. Gave him the absolute miss-in-baulk. So this rotter, instead of shifting off, proceeded to cut the fence, and go through that way. All the farms out here have their boundaries marked by wire fences, and it is supposed to be a deadly sin to cut these. Well, the lodge-keeper's son dashed off in search of help. A chap called Chester, an Old Wykehamist, and I were dipping sheep close by, so he came to us and told us what had happened. We nipped on to a couple of horses, pulled out our revolvers, and tooled after him. After a bit we overtook him, and that's when the trouble began. The johnny had dismounted when we arrived. I thought he was simply tightening his horse's girths. What he was really doing was getting a steady aim at us with his revolver. He fired as we came up, and dropped poor old Chester. I thought he was killed at first, but it turned out it was only his leg. I got going then. I emptied all the six chambers of my revolver, and missed him clean every time. In the meantime he got me in the right shoulder. Hurt like sin afterwards, though it was only a sort of dull shock at the moment. The next item of the programme was a forward move in force on the part of the enemy. The man had got his knife out now—why he didn't shoot again I don't know—and toddled over in our direction to finish us off. Chester was unconscious, and it was any money on the Gaucho, when I happened to catch sight of Chester's pistol, which had fallen just by where I came down. I picked it up, and loosed off. Missed the first shot, but got him with the second in the ankle at about two yards; and his day's work was done. That's the painful story. Danvers says he's getting writer's cramp, so I shall have to stop....'"

"By Jove!" said Mike.

"What a dreadful thing!" said Mrs. Jackson.

"Anyhow, it was practically a bushranger," said Phyllis.

"I told you it was a duel, and so it was," said Marjory.

"What a terrible experience for the poor boy!" said Mrs. Jackson.

"Much better than being in a beastly bank," said Mike, summing up. "I'm glad he's having such a ripping time. It must be almost as decent as Wrykyn out there.... I say, what's under that dish?"

120

CHAPTER XXX

MR. JACKSON MAKES UP HIS MIND

Two years have elapsed and Mike is home again for the Easter holidays.

If Mike had been in time for breakfast that morning he might have gathered from the expression on his father's face, as Mr. Jackson opened the envelope containing his school report and read the contents, that the document in question was not exactly a paean of praise from beginning to end. But he was late, as usual. Mike always was late for breakfast in the holidays.

When he came down on this particular morning, the meal was nearly over. Mr. Jackson had disappeared, taking his correspondence with him; Mrs. Jackson had gone into the kitchen, and when Mike appeared the thing had resolved itself into a mere vulgar brawl between Phyllis and Ella for the jam, while Marjory, who had put her hair up a fortnight before, looked on in a detached sort of way, as if these juvenile gambols distressed her.

"Hullo, Mike," she said, jumping up as he entered; "here you are—I've been keeping everything hot for you."

"Have you? Thanks awfully. I say—" his eye wandered in mild surprise round the table. "I'm a bit late."

Marjory was bustling about, fetching and carrying for Mike, as she always did. She had adopted him at an early age, and did the thing thoroughly. She was fond of her other brothers, especially when they made centuries in first-class cricket, but Mike was her favourite. She would field out in the deep as a natural thing when Mike was batting at the net in the paddock, though for the others, even for Joe, who had played in all five Test Matches in the previous summer, she would do it only as a favour.

Phyllis and Ella finished their dispute and went out. Marjory sat on the table and watched Mike eat.

"Your report came this morning, Mike," she said.

The kidneys failed to retain Mike's undivided attention. He looked up interested. "What did it say?"

"I didn't see—I only caught sight of the Wrykyn crest on the envelope. Father didn't say anything."

Mike seemed concerned. "I say, that looks rather rotten! I wonder if it was awfully bad. It's the first I've had from Appleby."

"It can't be any worse than the horrid ones Mr. Blake used to write when you were in his form."

"No, that's a comfort," said Mike philosophically. "Think there's any more tea in that pot?"

"I call it a shame," said Marjory; "they ought to be jolly glad to have you at Wrykyn just for cricket, instead of writing beastly reports that make father angry and don't do any good to anybody."

"Last summer he said he'd take me away if I got another one."

"He didn't mean it really, I know he didn't! He couldn't! You're the best bat Wrykyn's ever had."

"What ho!" interpolated Mike.

"You are. Everybody says you are. Why, you got your first the very first term you were there—even Joe didn't do anything nearly so good as that. Saunders says you're simply bound to play for England in another year or two."

"Saunders is a jolly good chap. He bowled me a half-volley on the off the first ball I had in a school match. By the way, I wonder if he's out at the net now. Let's go and see."

Saunders was setting up the net when they arrived. Mike put on his pads and went to the wickets, while Marjory and the dogs retired as usual to the far hedge to retrieve.

She was kept busy. Saunders was a good sound bowler of the M.C.C. minor match type, and there had been a time when he had worried Mike considerably, but Mike had been in the Wrykyn team for three seasons now, and each season he had advanced tremendously in his batting. He had filled out in three years. He had always had the style, and now he had the strength as well. Saunders's bowling on a true wicket seemed simple to him. It was early in the Easter holidays, but already he was beginning to find his form. Saunders, who looked on Mike as his own special invention, was delighted.

"If you don't be worried by being too anxious now that you're captain, Master Mike," he said, "you'll make a century every match next term."

"I wish I wasn't; it's a beastly responsibility."

Henfrey, the Wrykyn cricket captain of the previous season, was not returning next term, and Mike was to reign in his stead. He liked the prospect, but it certainly carried with it a rather awe-inspiring responsibility. At night sometimes he would lie awake, appalled by the fear of losing his form, or making a hash of things by choosing the wrong men to play for the school and leaving the right men out. It is no light thing to captain a public school at cricket.

As he was walking towards the house, Phyllis met him. "Oh, I've been hunting for you, Mike; father wants you."

"What for?"

"I don't know."

"Where?"

"He's in the study. He seems—" added Phyllis, throwing in the information by way of a make-weight, "in a beastly wax."

Mike's jaw fell slightly. "I hope the dickens it's nothing to do with that bally report," was his muttered exclamation.

122

Mike's dealings with his father were as a rule of a most pleasant nature. Mr. Jackson was an understanding sort of man, who treated his sons as companions. From time to time, however, breezes were apt to ruffle the placid sea of good-fellowship. Mike's end-of-term report was an unfailing wind-raiser; indeed, on the arrival of Mr. Blake's sarcastic résumé of Mike's short-comings at the end of the previous term, there had been something not unlike a typhoon. It was on this occasion that Mr. Jackson had solemnly declared his intention of removing Mike from Wrykyn unless the critics became more flattering; and Mr. Jackson was a man of his word.

It was with a certain amount of apprehension, therefore, that Jackson entered the study.

"Come in, Mike," said his father, kicking the waste-paper basket; "I want to speak to you."

Mike, skilled in omens, scented a row in the offing. Only in moments of emotion was Mr. Jackson in the habit of booting the basket.

There followed an awkward silence, which Mike broke by remarking that he had carted a half-volley from Saunders over the on-side hedge that morning.

"It was just a bit short and off the leg stump, so I stepped out— may I bag the paper-knife for a jiffy? I'll just show—"

"Never mind about cricket now," said Mr. Jackson; "I want you to listen to this report."

"Oh, is that my report, father?" said Mike, with a sort of sickly interest, much as a dog about to be washed might evince in his tub.

"It is," replied Mr. Jackson in measured tones, "your report; what is more, it is without exception the worst report you have ever had."

"Oh, I say!" groaned the record-breaker.

"'His conduct,'" quoted Mr. Jackson, "'has been unsatisfactory in the extreme, both in and out of school.'"

"It wasn't anything really. I only happened—"

Remembering suddenly that what he had happened to do was to drop a cannon-ball (the school weight) on the form-room floor, not once, but on several occasions, he paused.

"'French bad; conduct disgraceful—'"

"Everybody rags in French."

"'Mathematics bad. Inattentive and idle.'"

"Nobody does much work in Math."

"'Latin poor. Greek, very poor.'"

"We were doing Thucydides, Book Two, last term—all speeches and doubtful readings, and cruxes and things—beastly hard! Everybody says so."

"Here are Mr. Appleby's remarks: 'The boy has genuine ability, which he declines to use in the smallest degree.'"

Mike moaned a moan of righteous indignation.

123

"'An abnormal proficiency at games has apparently destroyed all desire in him to realise the more serious issues of life.' There is more to the same effect."

Mr. Appleby was a master with very definite ideas as to what constituted a public-school master's duties. As a man he was distinctly pro-Mike. He understood cricket, and some of Mike's shots on the off gave him thrills of pure aesthetic joy; but as a master he always made it his habit to regard the manners and customs of the boys in his form with an unbiased eye, and to an unbiased eye Mike in a form-room was about as near the extreme edge as a boy could be, and Mr. Appleby said as much in a clear firm hand.

"You remember what I said to you about your report at Christmas, Mike?" said Mr. Jackson, folding the lethal document and replacing it in its envelope.

Mike said nothing; there was a sinking feeling in his interior.

"I shall abide by what I said."

Mike's heart thumped.

"You will not go back to Wrykyn next term."

Somewhere in the world the sun was shining, birds were twittering; somewhere in the world lambkins frisked and peasants sang blithely at their toil (flat, perhaps, but still blithely), but to Mike at that moment the sky was black, and an icy wind blew over the face of the earth.

The tragedy had happened, and there was an end of it. He made no attempt to appeal against the sentence. He knew it would be useless, his father, when he made up his mind, having all the unbending tenacity of the normally easy-going man.

Mr. Jackson was sorry for Mike. He understood him, and for that reason he said very little now.

"I am sending you to Sedleigh," was his next remark.

Sedleigh! Mike sat up with a jerk. He knew Sedleigh by name—one of those schools with about a hundred fellows which you never hear of except when they send up their gymnasium pair to Aldershot, or their Eight to Bisley. Mike's outlook on life was that of a cricketer, pure and simple. What had Sedleigh ever done? What were they ever likely to do? Whom did they play? What Old Sedleighan had ever done anything at cricket? Perhaps they didn't even play cricket!

"But it's an awful hole," he said blankly.

Mr. Jackson could read Mike's mind like a book. Mike's point of view was plain to him. He did not approve of it, but he knew that in Mike's place and at Mike's age he would have felt the same. He spoke drily to hide his sympathy.

"It is not a large school," he said, "and I don't suppose it could play Wrykyn at cricket, but it has one merit—boys work there. Young Barlitt won a Balliol scholarship from Sedleigh last year." Barlitt was the vicar's son, a silent, spectacled youth who did not enter very largely

124

into Mike's world. They had met occasionally at tennis-parties, but not much conversation had ensued. Barlitt's mind was massive, but his topics of conversation were not Mike's.

"Mr. Barlitt speaks very highly of Sedleigh," added Mr. Jackson.

Mike said nothing, which was a good deal better than saying what he would have liked to have said.

CHAPTER XXXI

SEDLEIGH

The train, which had been stopping everywhere for the last half-hour, pulled up again, and Mike, seeing the name of the station, got up, opened the door, and hurled a Gladstone bag out on to the platform in an emphatic and vindictive manner. Then he got out himself and looked about him.

"For the school, sir?" inquired the solitary porter, bustling up, as if he hoped by sheer energy to deceive the traveller into thinking that Sedleigh station was staffed by a great army of porters.

Mike nodded. A sombre nod. The nod Napoleon might have given if somebody had met him in 1812, and said, "So you're back from Moscow, eh?" Mike was feeling thoroughly jaundiced. The future seemed wholly gloomy. And, so far from attempting to make the best of things, he had set himself deliberately to look on the dark side. He thought, for instance, that he had never seen a more repulsive porter, or one more obviously incompetent than the man who had attached himself with a firm grasp to the handle of the bag as he strode off in the direction of the luggage-van. He disliked his voice, his appearance, and the colour of his hair. Also the boots he wore. He hated the station, and the man who took his ticket.

"Young gents at the school, sir," said the porter, perceiving from Mike's distrait air that the boy was a stranger to the place, "goes up in the 'bus mostly. It's waiting here, sir. Hi, George!"

"I'll walk, thanks," said Mike frigidly.

"It's a goodish step, sir."

"Here you are."

"Thank you, sir. I'll send up your luggage by the 'bus, sir. Which 'ouse was it you was going to?"

"Outwood's."

"Right, sir. It's straight on up this road to the school. You can't miss it, sir."

"Worse luck," said Mike.

He walked off up the road, sorrier for himself than ever. It was such absolutely rotten luck. About now, instead of being on his way to a place where they probably ran a diabolo team instead of a cricket eleven, and played hunt-the-slipper in winter, he would be on the point of arriving at Wrykyn. And as captain of cricket, at that. Which was the bitter part of it. He had never been in command. For the last two seasons he had been the star man, going in first, and heading the averages easily at the end of the season; and the three captains under whom he had played during his career as a Wrykynian, Burgess, Enderby, and Henfrey had always been sportsmen to him. But it was not the same thing. He had meant to do such a lot for Wrykyn cricket this term. He had had an entirely new system of coaching in his mind. Now it might never be used. He had handed it on in a letter to Strachan, who would be captain in his place; but probably Strachan would have some scheme of his own. There is nobody who could not edit a paper in the ideal way; and there is nobody who has not a theory of his own about cricket-coaching at school.

Wrykyn, too, would be weak this year, now that he was no longer there. Strachan was a good, free bat on his day, and, if he survived a few overs, might make a century in an hour, but he was not to be depended upon. There was no doubt that Mike's sudden withdrawal meant that Wrykyn would have a bad time that season. And it had been such a wretched athletic year for the school. The football fifteen had been hopeless, and had lost both the Ripton matches, the return by over sixty points. Sheen's victory in the light-weights at Aldershot had been their one success. And now, on top of all this, the captain of cricket was removed during the Easter holidays. Mike's heart bled for Wrykyn, and he found himself loathing Sedleigh and all its works with a great loathing.

The only thing he could find in its favour was the fact that it was set in a very pretty country. Of a different type from the Wrykyn country, but almost as good. For three miles Mike made his way through woods and past fields. Once he crossed a river. It was soon after this that he caught sight, from the top of a hill, of a group of buildings that wore an unmistakably school-like look.

This must be Sedleigh.

Ten minutes' walk brought him to the school gates, and a baker's boy directed him to Mr. Outwood's.

There were three houses in a row, separated from the school buildings by a cricket-field. Outwood's was the middle one of these.

Mike went to the front door, and knocked. At Wrykyn he had always charged in at the beginning of term at the boys' entrance, but this formal reporting of himself at Sedleigh suited his mood.

He inquired for Mr. Outwood, and was shown into a room lined with books. Presently the door opened, and the house-master appeared.

There was something pleasant and homely about Mr. Outwood. In appearance he reminded Mike of Smee in "Peter Pan." He had the same eyebrows and pince-nez and the same motherly look.

"Jackson?" he said mildly.

"Yes, sir."

"I am very glad to see you, very glad indeed. Perhaps you would like a cup of tea after your journey. I think you might like a cup of tea. You come from Crofton, in Shropshire, I understand, Jackson, near Brindleford? It is a part of the country which I have always wished to visit. I daresay you have frequently seen the Cluniac Priory of St. Ambrose at Brindleford?"

Mike, who would not have recognised a Cluniac Priory if you had handed him one on a tray, said he had not.

"Dear me! You have missed an opportunity which I should have been glad to have. I am preparing a book on Ruined Abbeys and Priories of England, and it has always been my wish to see the Cluniac Priory of St. Ambrose. A deeply interesting relic of the sixteenth century. Bishop Geoffrey, 1133-40—"

"Shall I go across to the boys' part, sir?"

"What? Yes. Oh, yes. Quite so. And perhaps you would like a cup of tea after your journey? No? Quite so. Quite so. You should make a point of visiting the remains of the Cluniac Priory in the summer holidays, Jackson. You will find the matron in her room. In many respects it is unique. The northern altar is in a state of really wonderful preservation. It consists of a solid block of masonry five feet long and two and a half wide, with chamfered plinth, standing quite free from the apse wall. It will well repay a visit. Good-bye for the present, Jackson, good-bye."

Mike wandered across to the other side of the house, his gloom visibly deepened. All alone in a strange school, where they probably played hopscotch, with a house-master who offered one cups of tea after one's journey and talked about chamfered plinths and apses. It was a little hard.

He strayed about, finding his bearings, and finally came to a room which he took to be the equivalent of the senior day-room at a Wrykyn house. Everywhere else he had found nothing but emptiness. Evidently he had come by an earlier train than was usual. But this room was occupied.

A very long, thin youth, with a solemn face and immaculate clothes, was leaning against the mantelpiece. As Mike entered, he fumbled in his top left waistcoat pocket, produced an eyeglass attached to a cord, and fixed it in his right eye. With the help of this aid to vision he inspected Mike in silence for a while, then, having flicked an invisible speck of dust from the left sleeve of his coat, he spoke.

127

"Hullo," he said.

He spoke in a tired voice.

"Hullo," said Mike.

"Take a seat," said the immaculate one. "If you don't mind dirtying your bags, that's to say. Personally, I don't see any prospect of ever sitting down in this place. It looks to me as if they meant to use these chairs as mustard-and-cress beds. A Nursery Garden in the Home. That sort of idea. My name," he added pensively, "is Smith. What's yours?"

CHAPTER XXXII

PSMITH

"Jackson," said Mike.

"Are you the Bully, the Pride of the School, or the Boy who is Led Astray and takes to Drink in Chapter Sixteen?"

"The last, for choice," said Mike, "but I've only just arrived, so I don't know."

"The boy—what will he become? Are you new here, too, then?"

"Yes! Why, are you new?"

"Do I look as if I belonged here? I'm the latest import. Sit down on yonder settee, and I will tell you the painful story of my life. By the way, before I start, there's just one thing. If you ever have occasion to write to me, would you mind sticking a P at the beginning of my name? P-s-m-i-t-h. See? There are too many Smiths, and I don't care for Smythe. My father's content to worry along in the old-fashioned way, but I've decided to strike out a fresh line. I shall found a new dynasty. The resolve came to me unexpectedly this morning, as I was buying a simple penn'orth of butterscotch out of the automatic machine at Paddington. I jotted it down on the back of an envelope. In conversation you may address me as Rupert (though I hope you won't), or simply Smith, the P not being sounded. Cp. the name Zbysco, in which the Z is given a similar miss-in-baulk. See?"

Mike said he saw. Psmith thanked him with a certain stately old-world courtesy.

"Let us start at the beginning," he resumed. "My infancy. When I was but a babe, my eldest sister was bribed with a shilling an hour by my nurse to keep an eye on me, and see that I did not raise Cain. At the end of the first day she struck for one-and-six, and got it. We now pass to my boyhood. At an early age, I was sent to Eton, everybody predicting a bright career for me. But," said Psmith solemnly, fixing an owl-like gaze on Mike through the eye-glass, "it was not to be."

"No?" said Mike.

"No. I was superannuated last term."

"Bad luck."

"For Eton, yes. But what Eton loses, Sedleigh gains."

"But why Sedleigh, of all places?"

"This is the most painful part of my narrative. It seems that a certain scug in the next village to ours happened last year to collar a Balliol—"

"Not Barlitt!" exclaimed Mike.

"That was the man. The son of the vicar. The vicar told the curate, who told our curate, who told our vicar, who told my father, who sent me off here to get a Balliol too. Do you know Barlitt?"

"His pater's vicar of our village. It was because his son got a Balliol that I was sent here."

"Do you come from Crofton?"

"Yes."

"I've lived at Lower Benford all my life. We are practically long-lost brothers. Cheer a little, will you?"

Mike felt as Robinson Crusoe felt when he met Friday. Here was a fellow human being in this desert place. He could almost have embraced Psmith. The very sound of the name Lower Benford was heartening. His dislike for his new school was not diminished, but now he felt that life there might at least be tolerable.

"Where were you before you came here?" asked Psmith. "You have heard my painful story. Now tell me yours."

"Wrykyn. My pater took me away because I got such a lot of bad reports."

"My reports from Eton were simply scurrilous. There's a libel action in every sentence. How do you like this place from what you've seen of it?"

"Rotten."

"I am with you, Comrade Jackson. You won't mind my calling you Comrade, will you? I've just become a Socialist. It's a great scheme. You ought to be one. You work for the equal distribution of property, and start by collaring all you can and sitting on it. We must stick together. We are companions in misfortune. Lost lambs. Sheep that have gone astray. Divided, we fall, together we may worry through. Have you seen Professor Radium yet? I should say Mr. Outwood. What do you think of him?"

"He doesn't seem a bad sort of chap. Bit off his nut. Jawed about apses and things."

"And thereby," said Psmith, "hangs a tale. I've been making inquiries of a stout sportsman in a sort of Salvation Army uniform, whom I met in the grounds—he's the school sergeant or something, quite a solid man—and I hear that Comrade Outwood's an archaeological cove. Goes about the country beating up old ruins and fossils and things. There's an Archaeological Society in the school, run by him. It goes out on half-holidays, prowling about, and is allowed to break bounds and generally steep itself to the eyebrows in reckless devilry. And, mark you, laddie, if you belong to the Archaeological Society you get off cricket. To get off cricket," said Psmith, dusting his right trouser-leg, "was the dream of my youth and the aspiration of my riper years. A noble game, but a bit too thick for me. At Eton I used to have to field out at the nets till the soles of my boots wore through. I suppose you are a blood at the game? Play for the school against Loamshire, and so on."

"I'm not going to play here, at any rate," said Mike.

He had made up his mind on this point in the train. There is a certain fascination about making the very worst of a bad job. Achilles knew his business when he sat in his tent. The determination not to play cricket for Sedleigh as he could not play for Wrykyn gave Mike a sort of pleasure. To stand by with folded arms and a sombre frown, as it were, was one way of treating the situation, and one not without its meed of comfort.

Psmith approved the resolve.

"Stout fellow," he said. "'Tis well. You and I, hand in hand, will search the countryside for ruined abbeys. We will snare the elusive fossil together. Above all, we will go out of bounds. We shall thus improve our minds, and have a jolly good time as well. I shouldn't wonder if one mightn't borrow a gun from some friendly native, and do a bit of rabbit-shooting here and there. From what I saw of Comrade Outwood during our brief interview, I shouldn't think he was one of the lynx-eyed contingent. With tact we ought to be able to slip away from the merry throng of fossil-chasers, and do a bit on our own account."

"Good idea," said Mike. "We will. A chap at Wrykyn, called Wyatt, used to break out at night and shoot at cats with an air-pistol."

"It would take a lot to make me do that. I am all against anything that interferes with my sleep. But rabbits in the daytime is a scheme. We'll nose about for a gun at the earliest opp. Meanwhile we'd better go up to Comrade Outwood, and get our names shoved down for the Society."

"I vote we get some tea first somewhere."

"Then let's beat up a study. I suppose they have studies here. Let's go and look."

They went upstairs. On the first floor there was a passage with doors on either side. Psmith opened the first of these.

"This'll do us well," he said.

It was a biggish room, looking out over the school grounds.

130

There were a couple of deal tables, two empty bookcases, and a looking-glass, hung on a nail.

"Might have been made for us," said Psmith approvingly.

"I suppose it belongs to some rotter."

"Not now."

"You aren't going to collar it!"

"That," said Psmith, looking at himself earnestly in the mirror, and straightening his tie, "is the exact programme. We must stake out our claims. This is practical Socialism."

"But the real owner's bound to turn up some time or other."

"His misfortune, not ours. You can't expect two master-minds like us to pig it in that room downstairs. There are moments when one wants to be alone. It is imperative that we have a place to retire to after a fatiguing day. And now, if you want to be really useful, come and help me fetch up my box from downstairs. It's got an Etna and various things in it."

CHAPTER XXXIII

STAKING OUT A CLAIM

Psmith, in the matter of decorating a study and preparing tea in it, was rather a critic than an executant. He was full of ideas, but he preferred to allow Mike to carry them out. It was he who suggested that the wooden bar which ran across the window was unnecessary, but it was Mike who wrenched it from its place. Similarly, it was Mike who abstracted the key from the door of the next study, though the idea was Psmith's.

"Privacy," said Psmith, as he watched Mike light the Etna, "is what we chiefly need in this age of publicity. If you leave a study door unlocked in these strenuous times, the first thing you know is, somebody comes right in, sits down, and begins to talk about himself. I think with a little care we ought to be able to make this room quite decently comfortable. That putrid calendar must come down, though. Do you think you could make a long arm, and haul it off the parent tin-tack? Thanks. We make progress. We make progress."

"We shall jolly well make it out of the window," said Mike, spooning up tea from a paper bag with a postcard, "if a sort of young Hackenschmidt turns up and claims the study. What are you going to do about it?"

131

"Don't let us worry about it. I have a presentiment that he will be an insignificant-looking little weed. How are you getting on with the evening meal?"

"Just ready. What would you give to be at Eton now? I'd give something to be at Wrykyn."

"These school reports," said Psmith sympathetically, "are the very dickens. Many a bright young lad has been soured by them. Hullo. What's this, I wonder."

A heavy body had plunged against the door, evidently without a suspicion that there would be any resistance. A rattling at the handle followed, and a voice outside said, "Dash the door!"

"Hackenschmidt!" said Mike.

"The weed," said Psmith. "You couldn't make a long arm, could you, and turn the key? We had better give this merchant audience. Remind me later to go on with my remarks on school reports. I had several bright things to say on the subject."

Mike unlocked the door, and flung it open. Framed in the entrance was a smallish, freckled boy, wearing a bowler hat and carrying a bag. On his face was an expression of mingled wrath and astonishment.

Psmith rose courteously from his chair, and moved forward with slow stateliness to do the honours.

"What the dickens," inquired the newcomer, "are you doing here?"

"We were having a little tea," said Psmith, "to restore our tissues after our journey. Come in and join us. We keep open house, we Psmiths. Let me introduce you to Comrade Jackson. A stout fellow. Homely in appearance, perhaps, but one of us. I am Psmith. Your own name will doubtless come up in the course of general chit-chat over the tea-cups."

"My name's Spiller, and this is my study."

Psmith leaned against the mantelpiece, put up his eyeglass, and harangued Spiller in a philosophical vein.

"Of all sad words of tongue or pen," said he, "the saddest are these: 'It might have been.' Too late! That is the bitter cry. If you had torn yourself from the bosom of the Spiller family by an earlier train, all might have been well. But no. Your father held your hand and said huskily, 'Edwin, don't leave us!' Your mother clung to you weeping, and said, 'Edwin, stay!' Your sisters—"

"I want to know what—"

"Your sisters froze on to your knees like little octopuses (or octopi), and screamed, 'Don't go, Edwin!' And so," said Psmith, deeply affected by his recital, "you stayed on till the later train; and, on arrival, you find strange faces in the familiar room, a people that know not Spiller." Psmith went to the table, and cheered himself with a sip of tea. Spiller's sad case had moved him greatly.

The victim of Fate seemed in no way consoled.

"It's beastly cheek, that's what I call it. Are you new chaps?"

"The very latest thing," said Psmith.

"Well, it's beastly cheek."

Mike's outlook on life was of the solid, practical order. He went straight to the root of the matter.

"What are you going to do about it?" he asked.

Spiller evaded the question.

"It's beastly cheek," he repeated. "You can't go about the place bagging studies."

"But we do," said Psmith. "In this life, Comrade Spiller, we must be prepared for every emergency. We must distinguish between the unusual and the impossible. It is unusual for people to go about the place bagging studies, so you have rashly ordered your life on the assumption that it is impossible. Error! Ah, Spiller, Spiller, let this be a lesson to you."

"Look here, I tell you what it—"

"I was in a motor with a man once. I said to him: 'What would happen if you trod on that pedal thing instead of that other pedal thing?' He said, 'I couldn't. One's the foot-brake, and the other's the accelerator.' 'But suppose you did?' I said. 'I wouldn't,' he said. 'Now we'll let her rip.' So he stamped on the accelerator. Only it turned out to be the foot-brake after all, and we stopped dead, and skidded into a ditch. The advice I give to every young man starting life is: 'Never confuse the unusual and the impossible.' Take the present case. If you had only realised the possibility of somebody some day collaring your study, you might have thought out dozens of sound schemes for dealing with the matter. As it is, you are unprepared. The thing comes on you as a surprise. The cry goes round: 'Spiller has been taken unawares. He cannot cope with the situation.'"

"Can't I! I'll—"

"What are you going to do about it?" said Mike.

"All I know is, I'm going to have it. It was Simpson's last term, and Simpson's left, and I'm next on the house list, so, of course, it's my study."

"But what steps," said Psmith, "are you going to take? Spiller, the man of Logic, we know. But what of Spiller, the Man of Action? How do you intend to set about it? Force is useless. I was saying to Comrade Jackson before you came in, that I didn't mind betting you were an insignificant-looking little weed. And you are an insignificant-looking little weed."

"We'll see what Outwood says about it."

"Not an unsound scheme. By no means a scaly project. Comrade Jackson and myself were about to interview him upon another point. We may as well all go together."

The trio made their way to the Presence, Spiller pink and

determined, Mike sullen, Psmith particularly debonair. He hummed lightly as he walked, and now and then pointed out to Spiller objects of interest by the wayside.

Mr. Outwood received them with the motherly warmth which was evidently the leading characteristic of his normal manner.

"Ah, Spiller," he said. "And Smith, and Jackson. I am glad to see that you have already made friends."

"Spiller's, sir," said Psmith, laying a hand patronisingly on the study-claimer's shoulder—a proceeding violently resented by Spiller—"is a character one cannot help but respect. His nature expands before one like some beautiful flower."

Mr. Outwood received this eulogy with rather a startled expression, and gazed at the object of the tribute in a surprised way.

"Er—quite so, Smith, quite so," he said at last. "I like to see boys in my house friendly towards one another."

"There is no vice in Spiller," pursued Psmith earnestly. "His heart is the heart of a little child."

"Please, sir," burst out this paragon of all the virtues, "I—"

"But it was not entirely with regard to Spiller that I wished to speak to you, sir, if you were not too busy."

"Not at all, Smith, not at all. Is there anything—"

"Please, sir—" began Spiller.

"I understand, sir," said Psmith, "that there is an Archaeological Society in the school."

Mr. Outwood's eyes sparkled behind their pince-nez. It was a disappointment to him that so few boys seemed to wish to belong to his chosen band. Cricket and football, games that left him cold, appeared to be the main interest in their lives. It was but rarely that he could induce new boys to join. His colleague, Mr. Downing, who presided over the School Fire Brigade, never had any difficulty in finding support. Boys came readily at his call. Mr. Outwood pondered wistfully on this at times, not knowing that the Fire Brigade owed its support to the fact that it provided its light-hearted members with perfectly unparalleled opportunities for ragging, while his own band, though small, were in the main earnest.

"Yes, Smith." he said. "Yes. We have a small Archaeological Society. I—er—in a measure look after it. Perhaps you would care to become a member?"

"Please, sir—" said Spiller.

"One moment, Spiller. Do you want to join, Smith?"

"Intensely, sir. Archaeology fascinates me. A grand pursuit, sir."

"Undoubtedly, Smith. I am very pleased, very pleased indeed. I will put down your name at once."

"And Jackson's, sir."

"Jackson, too!" Mr. Outwood beamed. "I am delighted. Most delighted. This is capital. This enthusiasm is most capital."

"Spiller, sir," said Psmith sadly, "I have been unable to induce to join."

"Oh, he is one of our oldest members."

"Ah," said Psmith, tolerantly, "that accounts for it."

"Please, sir—" said Spiller.

"One moment, Spiller. We shall have the first outing of the term on Saturday. We intend to inspect the Roman Camp at Embury Hill, two miles from the school."

"We shall be there, sir."

"Capital!"

"Please, sir—" said Spiller.

"One moment, Spiller," said Psmith. "There is just one other matter, if you could spare the time, sir."

"Certainly, Smith. What is that?"

"Would there be any objection to Jackson and myself taking Simpson's old study?"

"By all means, Smith. A very good idea."

"Yes, sir. It would give us a place where we could work quietly in the evenings."

"Quite so. Quite so."

"Thank you very much, sir. We will move our things in."

"Thank you very much, sir," said Mike.

"Please, sir," shouted Spiller, "aren't I to have it? I'm next on the list, sir. I come next after Simpson. Can't I have it?"

"I'm afraid I have already promised it to Smith, Spiller. You should have spoken before."

"But, sir—"

Psmith eyed the speaker pityingly.

"This tendency to delay, Spiller," he said, "is your besetting fault. Correct it, Edwin. Fight against it."

He turned to Mr. Outwood.

"We should, of course, sir, always be glad to see Spiller in our study. He would always find a cheery welcome waiting there for him. There is no formality between ourselves and Spiller."

"Quite so. An excellent arrangement, Smith. I like this spirit of comradeship in my house. Then you will be with us on Saturday?"

"On Saturday, sir."

"All this sort of thing, Spiller," said Psmith, as they closed the door, "is very, very trying for a man of culture. Look us up in our study one of these afternoons."

135

CHAPTER XXXIV

GUERRILLA WARFARE

"There are few pleasures," said Psmith, as he resumed his favourite position against the mantelpiece and surveyed the commandeered study with the pride of a householder, "keener to the reflective mind than sitting under one's own roof-tree. This place would have been wasted on Spiller; he would not have appreciated it properly."

Mike was finishing his tea. "You're a jolly useful chap to have by you in a crisis, Smith," he said with approval. "We ought to have known each other before."

"The loss was mine," said Psmith courteously. "We will now, with your permission, face the future for awhile. I suppose you realise that we are now to a certain extent up against it. Spiller's hot Spanish blood is not going to sit tight and do nothing under a blow like this."

"What can he do? Outwood's given us the study."

"What would you have done if somebody had bagged your study?"

"Made it jolly hot for them!"

"So will Comrade Spiller. I take it that he will collect a gang and make an offensive movement against us directly he can. To all appearances we are in a fairly tight place. It all depends on how big Comrade Spiller's gang will be. I don't like rows, but I'm prepared to take on a reasonable number of bravoes in defence of the home."

Mike intimated that he was with him on the point. "The difficulty is, though," he said, "about when we leave this room. I mean, we're all right while we stick here, but we can't stay all night."

"That's just what I was about to point out when you put it with such admirable clearness. Here we are in a stronghold, they can only get at us through the door, and we can lock that."

"And jam a chair against it."

"And, as you rightly remark, jam a chair against it. But what of the nightfall? What of the time when we retire to our dormitory?"

"Or dormitories. I say, if we're in separate rooms we shall be in the cart."

Psmith eyed Mike with approval. "He thinks of everything! You're the man, Comrade Jackson, to conduct an affair of this kind— such foresight! such resource! We must see to this at once; if they put us in different rooms we're done—we shall be destroyed singly in the watches of the night."

"We'd better nip down to the matron right off."

"Not the matron—Comrade Outwood is the man. We are as sons

136

to him; there is nothing he can deny us. I'm afraid we are quite spoiling his afternoon by these interruptions, but we must rout him out once more."

As they got up, the door handle rattled again, and this time there followed a knocking.

"This must be an emissary of Comrade Spiller's," said Psmith. "Let us parley with the man."

Mike unlocked the door. A light-haired youth with a cheerful, rather vacant face and a receding chin strolled into the room, and stood giggling with his hands in his pockets.

"I just came up to have a look at you," he explained.

"If you move a little to the left," said Psmith, "you will catch the light and shade effects on Jackson's face better."

The new-comer giggled with renewed vigour. "Are you the chap with the eyeglass who jaws all the time?"

"I do wear an eyeglass," said Psmith; "as to the rest of the description—"

"My name's Jellicoe."

"Mine is Psmith—P-s-m-i-t-h—one of the Shropshire Psmiths. The object on the skyline is Comrade Jackson."

"Old Spiller," giggled Jellicoe, "is cursing you like anything downstairs. You are chaps! Do you mean to say you simply bagged his study? He's making no end of a row about it."

"Spiller's fiery nature is a byword," said Psmith.

"What's he going to do?" asked Mike, in his practical way.

"He's going to get the chaps to turn you out."

"As I suspected," sighed Psmith, as one mourning over the frailty of human nature. "About how many horny-handed assistants should you say that he would be likely to bring? Will you, for instance, join the glad throng?"

"Me? No fear! I think Spiller's an ass."

"There's nothing like a common thought for binding people together. I think Spiller's an ass."

"How many will there be, then?" asked Mike.

"He might get about half a dozen, not more, because most of the chaps don't see why they should sweat themselves just because Spiller's study has been bagged."

"Sturdy common sense," said Psmith approvingly, "seems to be the chief virtue of the Sedleigh character."

"We shall be able to tackle a crowd like that," said Mike. "The only thing is we must get into the same dormitory."

"This is where Comrade Jellicoe's knowledge of the local geography will come in useful. Do you happen to know of any snug little room, with, say, about four beds in it? How many dormitories are there?"

"Five—there's one with three beds in it, only it belongs to three chaps."

"I believe in the equal distribution of property. We will go to Comrade Outwood and stake out another claim."

Mr. Outwood received them even more beamingly than before. "Yes, Smith?" he said.

"We must apologise for disturbing you, sir—"

"Not at all, Smith, not at all! I like the boys in my house to come to me when they wish for my advice or help."

"We were wondering, sir, if you would have any objection to Jackson, Jellicoe and myself sharing the dormitory with the three beds in it. A very warm friendship—" explained Psmith, patting the gurgling Jellicoe kindly on the shoulder, "has sprung up between Jackson, Jellicoe and myself."

"You make friends easily, Smith. I like to see it—I like to see it."

"And we can have the room, sir?"

"Certainly—certainly! Tell the matron as you go down."

"And now," said Psmith, as they returned to the study, "we may say that we are in a fairly winning position. A vote of thanks to Comrade Jellicoe for his valuable assistance."

"You are a chap!" said Jellicoe.

The handle began to revolve again.

"That door," said Psmith, "is getting a perfect incubus! It cuts into one's leisure cruelly."

This time it was a small boy. "They told me to come up and tell you to come down," he said.

Psmith looked at him searchingly through his eyeglass.

"Who?"

"The senior day-room chaps."

"Spiller?"

"Spiller and Robinson and Stone, and some other chaps."

"They want us to speak to them?"

"They told me to come up and tell you to come down."

"Go and give Comrade Spiller our compliments and say that we can't come down, but shall be delighted to see him up here. Things," he said, as the messenger departed, "are beginning to move. Better leave the door open, I think; it will save trouble. Ah, come in, Comrade Spiller, what can we do for you?"

Spiller advanced into the study; the others waited outside, crowding in the doorway.

"Look here," said Spiller, "are you going to clear out of here or not?"

"After Mr. Outwood's kindly thought in giving us the room? You suggest a black and ungrateful action, Comrade Spiller."

"You'll get it hot, if you don't."

"We'll risk it," said Mike.

138

Jellicoe giggled in the background; the drama in the atmosphere appealed to him. His was a simple and appreciative mind.

"Come on, you chaps," cried Spiller suddenly.

There was an inward rush on the enemy's part, but Mike had been watching. He grabbed Spiller by the shoulders and ran him back against the advancing crowd. For a moment the doorway was blocked, then the weight and impetus of Mike and Spiller prevailed, the enemy gave back, and Mike, stepping into the room again, slammed the door and locked it.

"A neat piece of work," said Psmith approvingly, adjusting his tie at the looking-glass. "The preliminaries may now be considered over, the first shot has been fired. The dogs of war are now loose."

A heavy body crashed against the door.

"They'll have it down," said Jellicoe.

"We must act, Comrade Jackson! Might I trouble you just to turn that key quietly, and the handle, and then to stand by for the next attack."

There was a scrambling of feet in the passage outside, and then a repetition of the onslaught on the door. This time, however, the door, instead of resisting, swung open, and the human battering-ram staggered through into the study. Mike, turning after re-locking the door, was just in time to see Psmith, with a display of energy of which one would not have believed him capable, grip the invader scientifically by an arm and a leg.

Mike jumped to help, but it was needless; the captive was already on the window-sill. As Mike arrived, Psmith dropped him on to the flower-bed below.

Psmith closed the window gently and turned to Jellicoe. "Who was our guest?" he asked, dusting the knees of his trousers where they had pressed against the wall.

"Robinson. I say, you are a chap!"

"Robinson, was it? Well, we are always glad to see Comrade Robinson, always. I wonder if anybody else is thinking of calling?"

Apparently frontal attack had been abandoned. Whisperings could be heard in the corridor.

Somebody hammered on the door.

"Yes?" called Psmith patiently.

"You'd better come out, you know; you'll only get it hotter if you don't."

"Leave us, Spiller; we would be alone."

A bell rang in the distance.

"Tea," said Jellicoe; "we shall have to go now."

"They won't do anything till after tea, I shouldn't think," said Mike. "There's no harm in going out."

The passage was empty when they opened the door; the call to food was evidently a thing not to be treated lightly by the enemy.

139

In the dining-room the beleaguered garrison were the object of general attention. Everybody turned to look at them as they came in. It was plain that the study episode had been a topic of conversation. Spiller's face was crimson, and Robinson's coat-sleeve still bore traces of garden mould.

Mike felt rather conscious of the eyes, but Psmith was in his element. His demeanour throughout the meal was that of some whimsical monarch condescending for a freak to revel with his humble subjects.

Towards the end of the meal Psmith scribbled a note and passed it to Mike. It read: "Directly this is over, nip upstairs as quickly as you can."

Mike followed the advice; they were first out of the room. When they had been in the study a few moments, Jellicoe knocked at the door. "Lucky you two cut away so quick," he said. "They were going to try and get you into the senior day-room and scrag you there."

"This," said Psmith, leaning against the mantelpiece, "is exciting, but it can't go on. We have got for our sins to be in this place for a whole term, and if we are going to do the Hunted Fawn business all the time, life in the true sense of the word will become an impossibility. My nerves are so delicately attuned that the strain would simply reduce them to hash. We are not prepared to carry on a long campaign—the thing must be settled at once."

"Shall we go down to the senior day-room, and have it out?" said Mike.

"No, we will play the fixture on our own ground. I think we may take it as tolerably certain that Comrade Spiller and his hired ruffians will try to corner us in the dormitory to-night. Well, of course, we could fake up some sort of barricade for the door, but then we should have all the trouble over again to-morrow and the day after that. Personally I don't propose to be chivvied about indefinitely like this, so I propose that we let them come into the dormitory, and see what happens. Is this meeting with me?"

"I think that's sound," said Mike. "We needn't drag Jellicoe into it."

"As a matter of fact—if you don't mind—" began that man of peace.

"Quite right," said Psmith; "this is not Comrade Jellicoe's scene at all; he has got to spend the term in the senior day-room, whereas we have our little wooden châlet to retire to in times of stress. Comrade Jellicoe must stand out of the game altogether. We shall be glad of his moral support, but otherwise, ne pas. And now, as there won't be anything doing till bedtime, I think I'll collar this table and write home and tell my people that all is well with their Rupert."

140

CHAPTER XXXV

UNPLEASANTNESS IN THE SMALL HOURS

Jellicoe, that human encyclopaedia, consulted on the probable movements of the enemy, deposed that Spiller, retiring at ten, would make for Dormitory One in the same passage, where Robinson also had a bed. The rest of the opposing forces were distributed among other and more distant rooms. It was probable, therefore, that Dormitory One would be the rendezvous. As to the time when an attack might be expected, it was unlikely that it would occur before half-past eleven. Mr. Outwood went the round of the dormitories at eleven.

"And touching," said Psmith, "the matter of noise, must this business be conducted in a subdued and sotto voce manner, or may we let ourselves go a bit here and there?"

"I shouldn't think old Outwood's likely to hear you—he sleeps miles away on the other side of the house. He never hears anything. We often rag half the night and nothing happens."

"This appears to be a thoroughly nice, well-conducted establishment. What would my mother say if she could see her Rupert in the midst of these reckless youths!"

"All the better," said Mike; "we don't want anybody butting in and stopping the show before it's half started."

"Comrade Jackson's Berserk blood is up—I can hear it sizzling. I quite agree these things are all very disturbing and painful, but it's as well to do them thoroughly when one's once in for them. Is there nobody else who might interfere with our gambols?"

"Barnes might," said Jellicoe, "only he won't."

"Who is Barnes?"

"Head of the house—a rotter. He's in a funk of Stone and Robinson; they rag him; he'll simply sit tight."

"Then I think," said Psmith placidly, "we may look forward to a very pleasant evening. Shall we be moving?"

Mr. Outwood paid his visit at eleven, as predicted by Jellicoe, beaming vaguely into the darkness over a candle, and disappeared again, closing the door.

"How about that door?" said Mike. "Shall we leave it open for them?"

"Not so, but far otherwise. If it's shut we shall hear them at it when they come. Subject to your approval, Comrade Jackson, I have evolved the following plan of action. I always ask myself on these occasions, 'What would Napoleon have done?' I think Napoleon would have sat in a chair by his washhand-stand, which is close to the door; he would have posted you by your washhand-stand, and he would have instructed Comrade Jellicoe, directly he heard the door-handle turned,

141

to give his celebrated imitation of a dormitory breathing heavily in its sleep. He would then—"

"I tell you what," said Mike, "how about tying a string at the top of the steps?"

"Yes, Napoleon would have done that, too. Hats off to Comrade Jackson, the man with the big brain!"

The floor of the dormitory was below the level of the door. There were three steps leading down to it. Psmith lit a candle and they examined the ground. The leg of a wardrobe and the leg of Jellicoe's bed made it possible for the string to be fastened in a satisfactory manner across the lower step. Psmith surveyed the result with approval.

"Dashed neat!" he said. "Practically the sunken road which dished the Cuirassiers at Waterloo. I seem to see Comrade Spiller coming one of the finest purlers in the world's history."

"If they've got a candle—"

"They won't have. If they have, stand by with your water-jug and douse it at once; then they'll charge forward and all will be well. If they have no candle, fling the water at a venture—fire into the brown! Lest we forget, I'll collar Comrade Jellicoe's jug now and keep it handy. A couple of sheets would also not be amiss—we will enmesh the enemy!"

"Right ho!" said Mike.

"These humane preparations being concluded," said Psmith, "we will retire to our posts and wait. Comrade Jellicoe, don't forget to breathe like an asthmatic sheep when you hear the door opened; they may wait at the top of the steps, listening."

"You are a chap!" said Jellicoe.

Waiting in the dark for something to happen is always a trying experience, especially if, as on this occasion, silence is essential. Mike found his thoughts wandering back to the vigil he had kept with Mr. Wain at Wrykyn on the night when Wyatt had come in through the window and found authority sitting on his bed, waiting for him. Mike was tired after his journey, and he had begun to doze when he was jerked back to wakefulness by the stealthy turning of the door-handle; the faintest rustle from Psmith's direction followed, and a slight giggle, succeeded by a series of deep breaths, showed that Jellicoe, too, had heard the noise.

There was a creaking sound.

It was pitch-dark in the dormitory, but Mike could follow the invaders' movements as clearly as if it had been broad daylight. They had opened the door and were listening. Jellicoe's breathing grew more asthmatic; he was flinging himself into his part with the whole-heartedness of the true artist.

The creak was followed by a sound of whispering, then another creak. The enemy had advanced to the top step.... Another creak.... The vanguard had reached the second step.... In another moment—

CRASH!

And at that point the proceedings may be said to have formally opened.

A struggling mass bumped against Mike's shins as he rose from his chair; he emptied his jug on to this mass, and a yell of anguish showed that the contents had got to the right address.

Then a hand grabbed his ankle and he went down, a million sparks dancing before his eyes as a fist, flying out at a venture, caught him on the nose.

Mike had not been well-disposed towards the invaders before, but now he ran amok, hitting out right and left at random. His right missed, but his left went home hard on some portion of somebody's anatomy. A kick freed his ankle and he staggered to his feet. At the same moment a sudden increase in the general volume of noise spoke eloquently of good work that was being put in by Psmith.

Even at that crisis, Mike could not help feeling that if a row of this calibre did not draw Mr. Outwood from his bed, he must be an unusual kind of house-master.

He plunged forward again with outstretched arms, and stumbled and fell over one of the on-the-floor section of the opposing force. They seized each other earnestly and rolled across the room till Mike, contriving to secure his adversary's head, bumped it on the floor with such abandon that, with a muffled yell, the other let go, and for the second time he rose. As he did so he was conscious of a curious thudding sound that made itself heard through the other assorted noises of the battle.

All this time the fight had gone on in the blackest darkness, but now a light shone on the proceedings. Interested occupants of other dormitories, roused from their slumbers, had come to observe the sport. They were crowding in the doorway with a candle.

By the light of this Mike got a swift view of the theatre of war. The enemy appeared to number five. The warrior whose head Mike had bumped on the floor was Robinson, who was sitting up feeling his skull in a gingerly fashion. To Mike's right, almost touching him, was Stone. In the direction of the door, Psmith, wielding in his right hand the cord of a dressing-gown, was engaging the remaining three with a patient smile. They were clad in pyjamas, and appeared to be feeling the dressing-gown cord acutely.

The sudden light dazed both sides momentarily. The defence was the first to recover, Mike, with a swing, upsetting Stone, and Psmith, having seized and emptied Jellicoe's jug over Spiller, getting to work again with the cord in a manner that roused the utmost enthusiasm of the spectators.

Agility seemed to be the leading feature of Psmith's tactics. He was everywhere—on Mike's bed, on his own, on Jellicoe's (drawing a passionate complaint from that non-combatant, on whose face he inadvertently trod), on the floor—he ranged the room, sowing destruction.

The enemy were disheartened; they had started with the idea that this was to be a surprise attack, and it was disconcerting to find the garrison armed at all points. Gradually they edged to the door, and a final rush sent them through.

"Hold the door for a second," cried Psmith, and vanished. Mike was alone in the doorway.

It was a situation which exactly suited his frame of mind; he stood alone in direct opposition to the community into which Fate had pitchforked him so abruptly. He liked the feeling; for the first time since his father had given him his views upon school reports that morning in the Easter holidays, he felt satisfied with life. He hoped, outnumbered as he was, that the enemy would come on again and not give the thing up in disgust; he wanted more.

On an occasion like this there is rarely anything approaching concerted action on the part of the aggressors. When the attack came, it was not a combined attack; Stone, who was nearest to the door, made a sudden dash forward, and Mike hit him under the chin.

Stone drew back, and there was another interval for rest and reflection.

It was interrupted by the reappearance of Psmith, who strolled back along the passage swinging his dressing-gown cord as if it were some clouded cane.

"Sorry to keep you waiting, Comrade Jackson," he said politely. "Duty called me elsewhere. With the kindly aid of a guide who knows the lie of the land, I have been making a short tour of the dormitories. I have poured divers jugfuls of water over Comrade Spiller's bed, Comrade Robinson's bed, Comrade Stone's—Spiller, Spiller, these are harsh words; where you pick them up I can't think—not from me. Well, well, I suppose there must be an end to the pleasantest of functions. Good-night, good-night."

The door closed behind Mike and himself. For ten minutes shufflings and whisperings went on in the corridor, but nobody touched the handle.

Then there was a sound of retreating footsteps, and silence reigned.

On the following morning there was a notice on the house-board. It ran:

INDOOR GAMES

Dormitory-raiders are informed that in future neither Mr. Psmith nor Mr. Jackson will be at home to visitors. This nuisance must now cease.

R. PSMITH.
M. JACKSON.

CHAPTER XXXVI

ADAIR

On the same morning Mike met Adair for the first time.

He was going across to school with Psmith and Jellicoe, when a group of three came out of the gate of the house next door.

"That's Adair," said Jellicoe, "in the middle."

His voice had assumed a tone almost of awe.

"Who's Adair?" asked Mike.

"Captain of cricket, and lots of other things."

Mike could only see the celebrity's back. He had broad shoulders and wiry, light hair, almost white. He walked well, as if he were used to running. Altogether a fit-looking sort of man. Even Mike's jaundiced eye saw that.

As a matter of fact, Adair deserved more than a casual glance. He was that rare type, the natural leader. Many boys and men, if accident, or the passage of time, places them in a position where they are expected to lead, can handle the job without disaster; but that is a very different thing from being a born leader. Adair was of the sort that comes to the top by sheer force of character and determination. He was not naturally clever at work, but he had gone at it with a dogged resolution which had carried him up the school, and landed him high in the Sixth. As a cricketer he was almost entirely self-taught. Nature had given him a good eye, and left the thing at that. Adair's doggedness had triumphed over her failure to do her work thoroughly. At the cost of more trouble than most people give to their life-work he had made himself into a bowler. He read the authorities, and watched first-class players, and thought the thing out on his own account, and he divided the art of bowling into three sections. First, and most important—pitch. Second on the list—break. Third—pace. He set himself to acquire pitch. He acquired it. Bowling at his own pace and without any attempt at break, he could now drop the ball on an envelope seven times out of ten.

Break was a more uncertain quantity. Sometimes he could get it at the expense of pitch, sometimes at the expense of pace. Some days he could get all three, and then he was an uncommonly bad man to face on anything but a plumb wicket.

Running he had acquired in a similar manner. He had nothing approaching style, but he had twice won the mile and half-mile at the Sports off elegant runners, who knew all about stride and the correct timing of the sprints and all the rest of it.

Briefly, he was a worker. He had heart.

A boy of Adair's type is always a force in a school. In a big public

145

school of six or seven hundred, his influence is felt less; but in a small school like Sedleigh he is like a tidal wave, sweeping all before him. There were two hundred boys at Sedleigh, and there was not one of them in all probability who had not, directly or indirectly, been influenced by Adair. As a small boy his sphere was not large, but the effects of his work began to be apparent even then. It is human nature to want to get something which somebody else obviously values very much; and when it was observed by members of his form that Adair was going to great trouble and inconvenience to secure a place in the form eleven or fifteen, they naturally began to think, too, that it was worth being in those teams. The consequence was that his form always played hard. This made other forms play hard. And the net result was that, when Adair succeeded to the captaincy of football and cricket in the same year, Sedleigh, as Mr. Downing, Adair's house-master and the nearest approach to a cricket-master that Sedleigh possessed, had a fondness for saying, was a keen school. As a whole, it both worked and played with energy.

All it wanted now was opportunity.

This Adair was determined to give it. He had that passionate fondness for his school which every boy is popularly supposed to have, but which really is implanted in about one in every thousand. The average public-school boy likes his school. He hopes it will lick Bedford at footer and Malvern at cricket, but he rather bets it won't. He is sorry to leave, and he likes going back at the end of the holidays, but as for any passionate, deep-seated love of the place, he would think it rather bad form than otherwise. If anybody came up to him, slapped him on the back, and cried, "Come along, Jenkins, my boy! Play up for the old school, Jenkins! The dear old school! The old place you love so!" he would feel seriously ill.

Adair was the exception.

To Adair, Sedleigh was almost a religion. Both his parents were dead; his guardian, with whom he spent the holidays, was a man with neuralgia at one end of him and gout at the other; and the only really pleasant times Adair had had, as far back as he could remember, he owed to Sedleigh. The place had grown on him, absorbed him. Where Mike, violently transplanted from Wrykyn, saw only a wretched little hole not to be mentioned in the same breath with Wrykyn, Adair, dreaming of the future, saw a colossal establishment, a public school among public schools, a lump of human radium, shooting out Blues and Balliol Scholars year after year without ceasing.

It would not be so till long after he was gone and forgotten, but he did not mind that. His devotion to Sedleigh was purely unselfish. He did not want fame. All he worked for was that the school should grow and grow, keener and better at games and more prosperous year by year, till it should take its rank among the schools, and to be an Old Sedleighan should be a badge passing its owner everywhere.

146

"He's captain of cricket and footer," said Jellicoe impressively. "He's in the shooting eight. He's won the mile and half two years running. He would have boxed at Aldershot last term, only he sprained his wrist. And he plays fives jolly well!"

"Sort of little tin god," said Mike, taking a violent dislike to Adair from that moment.

Mike's actual acquaintance with this all-round man dated from the dinner-hour that day. Mike was walking to the house with Psmith. Psmith was a little ruffled on account of a slight passage-of-arms he had had with his form-master during morning school.

"'There's a P before the Smith,' I said to him. 'Ah, P. Smith, I see,' replied the goat. 'Not Peasmith,' I replied, exercising wonderful self-restraint, 'just Psmith.' It took me ten minutes to drive the thing into the man's head; and when I had driven it in, he sent me out of the room for looking at him through my eye-glass. Comrade Jackson, I fear me we have fallen among bad men. I suspect that we are going to be much persecuted by scoundrels."

"Both you chaps play cricket, I suppose?"

They turned. It was Adair. Seeing him face to face, Mike was aware of a pair of very bright blue eyes and a square jaw. In any other place and mood he would have liked Adair at sight. His prejudice, however, against all things Sedleighan was too much for him. "I don't," he said shortly.

"Haven't you ever played?"

"My little sister and I sometimes play with a soft ball at home."

Adair looked sharply at him. A temper was evidently one of his numerous qualities.

"Oh," he said. "Well, perhaps you wouldn't mind turning out this afternoon and seeing what you can do with a hard ball—if you can manage without your little sister."

"I should think the form at this place would be about on a level with hers. But I don't happen to be playing cricket, as I think I told you."

Adair's jaw grew squarer than ever. Mike was wearing a gloomy scowl.

Psmith joined suavely in the dialogue.

"My dear old comrades," he said, "don't let us brawl over this matter. This is a time for the honeyed word, the kindly eye, and the pleasant smile. Let me explain to Comrade Adair. Speaking for Comrade Jackson and myself, we should both be delighted to join in the mimic warfare of our National Game, as you suggest, only the fact is, we happen to be the Young Archaeologists. We gave in our names last night. When you are being carried back to the pavilion after your century against Loamshire—do you play Loamshire?—we shall be grubbing in the hard ground for ruined abbeys. The old choice between Pleasure and Duty, Comrade Adair. A Boy's Cross-Roads."

"Then you won't play?"

"No," said Mike.

"Archaeology," said Psmith, with a deprecatory wave of the hand, "will brook no divided allegiance from her devotees."

Adair turned, and walked on.

Scarcely had he gone, when another voice hailed them with precisely the same question.

"Both you fellows are going to play cricket, eh?"

It was a master. A short, wiry little man with a sharp nose and a general resemblance, both in manner and appearance, to an excitable bullfinch.

"I saw Adair speaking to you. I suppose you will both play. I like every new boy to begin at once. The more new blood we have, the better. We want keenness here. We are, above all, a keen school. I want every boy to be keen."

"We are, sir," said Psmith, with fervour.

"Excellent."

"On archaeology."

Mr. Downing—for it was no less a celebrity—started, as one who perceives a loathly caterpillar in his salad.

"Archaeology!"

"We gave in our names to Mr. Outwood last night, sir. Archaeology is a passion with us, sir. When we heard that there was a society here, we went singing about the house."

"I call it an unnatural pursuit for boys," said Mr. Downing vehemently. "I don't like it. I tell you I don't like it. It is not for me to interfere with one of my colleagues on the staff, but I tell you frankly that in my opinion it is an abominable waste of time for a boy. It gets him into idle, loafing habits."

"I never loaf, sir," said Psmith.

"I was not alluding to you in particular. I was referring to the principle of the thing. A boy ought to be playing cricket with other boys, not wandering at large about the country, probably smoking and going into low public-houses."

"A very wild lot, sir, I fear, the Archaeological Society here," sighed Psmith, shaking his head.

"If you choose to waste your time, I suppose I can't hinder you. But in my opinion it is foolery, nothing else."

He stumped off.

"Now he's cross," said Psmith, looking after him. "I'm afraid we're getting ourselves disliked here."

"Good job, too."

"At any rate, Comrade Outwood loves us. Let's go on and see what sort of a lunch that large-hearted fossil-fancier is going to give us."

148

CHAPTER XXXVII

MIKE FINDS OCCUPATION

There was more than one moment during the first fortnight of term when Mike found himself regretting the attitude he had imposed upon himself with regard to Sedleighan cricket. He began to realise the eternal truth of the proverb about half a loaf and no bread. In the first flush of his resentment against his new surroundings he had refused to play cricket. And now he positively ached for a game. Any sort of a game. An innings for a Kindergarten v. the Second Eleven of a Home of Rest for Centenarians would have soothed him. There were times, when the sun shone, and he caught sight of white flannels on a green ground, and heard the "plonk" of bat striking ball, when he felt like rushing to Adair and shouting, "I will be good. I was in the Wrykyn team three years, and had an average of over fifty the last two seasons. Lead me to the nearest net, and let me feel a bat in my hands again."

But every time he shrank from such a climb down. It couldn't be done.

What made it worse was that he saw, after watching behind the nets once or twice, that Sedleigh cricket was not the childish burlesque of the game which he had been rash enough to assume that it must be. Numbers do not make good cricket. They only make the presence of good cricketers more likely, by the law of averages.

Mike soon saw that cricket was by no means an unknown art at Sedleigh. Adair, to begin with, was a very good bowler indeed. He was not a Burgess, but Burgess was the only Wrykyn bowler whom, in his three years' experience of the school, Mike would have placed above him. He was a long way better than Neville-Smith, and Wyatt, and Milton, and the others who had taken wickets for Wrykyn.

The batting was not so good, but there were some quite capable men. Barnes, the head of Outwood's, he who preferred not to interfere with Stone and Robinson, was a mild, rather timid-looking youth—not unlike what Mr. Outwood must have been as a boy—but he knew how to keep balls out of his wicket. He was a good bat of the old plodding type.

Stone and Robinson themselves, that swash-buckling pair, who now treated Mike and Psmith with cold but consistent politeness, were both fair batsmen, and Stone was a good slow bowler.

There were other exponents of the game, mostly in Downing's house.

Altogether, quite worthy colleagues even for a man who had been a star at Wrykyn.

One solitary overture Mike made during that first fortnight. He

149

did not repeat the experiment. It was on a Thursday afternoon, after school. The day was warm, but freshened by an almost imperceptible breeze. The air was full of the scent of the cut grass which lay in little heaps behind the nets. This is the real cricket scent, which calls to one like the very voice of the game.

Mike, as he sat there watching, could stand it no longer.

He went up to Adair.

"May I have an innings at this net?" he asked. He was embarrassed and nervous, and was trying not to show it. The natural result was that his manner was offensively abrupt.

Adair was taking off his pads after his innings. He looked up. "This net," it may be observed, was the first eleven net.

"What?" he said.

Mike repeated his request. More abruptly this time, from increased embarrassment.

"This is the first eleven net," said Adair coldly. "Go in after Lodge over there."

"Over there" was the end net, where frenzied novices were bowling on a corrugated pitch to a red-haired youth with enormous feet, who looked as if he were taking his first lesson at the game.

Mike walked away without a word.

The Archaeological Society expeditions, even though they carried with them the privilege of listening to Psmith's views on life, proved but a poor substitute for cricket. Psmith, who had no counter-attraction shouting to him that he ought to be elsewhere, seemed to enjoy them hugely, but Mike almost cried sometimes from boredom. It was not always possible to slip away from the throng, for Mr. Outwood evidently looked upon them as among the very faithful, and kept them by his aide.

Mike on these occasions was silent and jumpy, his brow "sicklied o'er with the pale cast of care." But Psmith followed his leader with the pleased and indulgent air of a father whose infant son is showing him round the garden. Psmith's attitude towards archaeological research struck a new note in the history of that neglected science. He was amiable, but patronising. He patronised fossils, and he patronised ruins. If he had been confronted with the Great Pyramid, he would have patronised that.

He seemed to be consumed by a thirst for knowledge.

That this was not altogether a genuine thirst was proved on the third expedition. Mr. Outwood and his band were pecking away at the site of an old Roman camp. Psmith approached Mike.

"Having inspired confidence," he said, "by the docility of our demeanour, let us slip away, and brood apart for awhile. Roman camps, to be absolutely accurate, give me the pip. And I never want to see another putrid fossil in my life. Let us find some shady nook where a man may lie on his back for a bit."

150

Mike, over whom the proceedings connected with the Roman camp had long since begun to shed a blue depression, offered no opposition, and they strolled away down the hill.

Looking back, they saw that the archaeologists were still hard at it. Their departure had passed unnoticed.

"A fatiguing pursuit, this grubbing for mementoes of the past," said Psmith. "And, above all, dashed bad for the knees of the trousers. Mine are like some furrowed field. It's a great grief to a man of refinement, I can tell you, Comrade Jackson. Ah, this looks a likely spot."

They had passed through a gate into the field beyond. At the further end there was a brook, shaded by trees and running with a pleasant sound over pebbles.

"Thus far," said Psmith, hitching up the knees of his trousers, and sitting down, "and no farther. We will rest here awhile, and listen to the music of the brook. In fact, unless you have anything important to say, I rather think I'll go to sleep. In this busy life of ours these naps by the wayside are invaluable. Call me in about an hour." And Psmith, heaving the comfortable sigh of the worker who by toil has earned rest, lay down, with his head against a mossy tree-stump, and closed his eyes.

Mike sat on for a few minutes, listening to the water and making centuries in his mind, and then, finding this a little dull, he got up, jumped the brook, and began to explore the wood on the other side.

He had not gone many yards when a dog emerged suddenly from the undergrowth, and began to bark vigorously at him.

Mike liked dogs, and, on acquaintance, they always liked him. But when you meet a dog in some one else's wood, it is as well not to stop in order that you may get to understand each other. Mike began to thread his way back through the trees.

He was too late.

"Stop! What the dickens are you doing here?" shouted a voice behind him.

In the same situation a few years before, Mike would have carried on, and trusted to speed to save him. But now there seemed a lack of dignity in the action. He came back to where the man was standing.

"I'm sorry if I'm trespassing," he said. "I was just having a look round."

"The dickens you—Why, you're Jackson!"

Mike looked at him. He was a short, broad young man with a fair moustache. Mike knew that he had seen him before somewhere, but he could not place him.

"I played against you, for the Free Foresters last summer. In passing, you seem to be a bit of a free forester yourself, dancing in among my nesting pheasants."

151

"I'm frightfully sorry."

"That's all right. Where do you spring from?"

"Of course—I remember you now. You're Prendergast. You made fifty-eight not out."

"Thanks. I was afraid the only thing you would remember about me was that you took a century mostly off my bowling."

"You ought to have had me second ball, only cover dropped it."

"Don't rake up forgotten tragedies. How is it you're not at Wrykyn? What are you doing down here?"

"I've left Wrykyn."

Prendergast suddenly changed the conversation. When a fellow tells you that he has left school unexpectedly, it is not always tactful to inquire the reason. He began to talk about himself.

"I hang out down here. I do a little farming and a good deal of pottering about."

"Get any cricket?" asked Mike, turning to the subject next his heart.

"Only village. Very keen, but no great shakes. By the way, how are you off for cricket now? Have you ever got a spare afternoon?"

Mike's heart leaped.

"Any Wednesday or Saturday. Look here, I'll tell you how it is."

And he told how matters stood with him.

"So, you see," he concluded, "I'm supposed to be hunting for ruins and things"—Mike's ideas on the subject of archaeology were vague—"but I could always slip away. We all start out together, but I could nip back, get on to my bike—I've got it down here—and meet you anywhere you liked. By Jove, I'm simply dying for a game. I can hardly keep my hands off a bat."

"I'll give you all you want. What you'd better do is to ride straight to Lower Borlock—that's the name of the place—and I'll meet you on the ground. Any one will tell you where Lower Borlock is. It's just off the London road. There's a sign-post where you turn off. Can you come next Saturday?"

"Rather. I suppose you can fix me up with a bat and pads? I don't want to bring mine."

"I'll lend you everything. I say, you know, we can't give you a Wrykyn wicket. The Lower Borlock pitch isn't a shirt-front."

"I'll play on a rockery, if you want me to," said Mike.

"You're going to what?" asked Psmith, sleepily, on being awakened and told the news.

"I'm going to play cricket, for a village near here. I say, don't tell a soul, will you? I don't want it to get about, or I may get lugged in to play for the school."

"My lips are sealed. I think I'll come and watch you. Cricket I dislike, but watching cricket is one of the finest of Britain's manly sports. I'll borrow Jellicoe's bicycle."

152

That Saturday, Lower Borlock smote the men of Chidford hip and thigh. Their victory was due to a hurricane innings of seventy-five by a new-comer to the team, M. Jackson.

CHAPTER XXXVIII

THE FIRE BRIGADE MEETING

Cricket is the great safety-valve. If you like the game, and are in a position to play it at least twice a week, life can never be entirely grey. As time went on, and his average for Lower Borlock reached the fifties and stayed there, Mike began, though he would not have admitted it, to enjoy himself. It was not Wrykyn, but it was a very decent substitute.

The only really considerable element making for discomfort now was Mr. Downing. By bad luck it was in his form that Mike had been placed on arrival; and Mr. Downing, never an easy form-master to get on with, proved more than usually difficult in his dealings with Mike.

They had taken a dislike to each other at their first meeting; and it grew with further acquaintance. To Mike, Mr. Downing was all that a master ought not to be, fussy, pompous, and openly influenced in his official dealings with his form by his own private likes and dislikes. To Mr. Downing, Mike was simply an unamiable loafer, who did nothing for the school and apparently had none of the instincts which should be implanted in the healthy boy. Mr. Downing was rather strong on the healthy boy.

The two lived in a state of simmering hostility, punctuated at intervals by crises, which usually resulted in Lower Borlock having to play some unskilled labourer in place of their star batsman, employed doing "over-time."

One of the most acute of these crises, and the most important, in that it was the direct cause of Mike's appearance in Sedleigh cricket, had to do with the third weekly meeting of the School Fire Brigade.

It may be remembered that this well-supported institution was under Mr. Downing's special care. It was, indeed, his pet hobby and the apple of his eye.

Just as you had to join the Archaeological Society to secure the esteem of Mr. Outwood, so to become a member of the Fire Brigade was a safe passport to the regard of Mr. Downing. To show a keenness for cricket was good, but to join the Fire Brigade was best of all. The Brigade was carefully organised. At its head was Mr. Downing, a sort of high priest; under him was a captain, and under the captain a vice-captain. These two officials were those sportive allies, Stone and Robinson, of Outwood's house, who, having perceived at a very early date the gorgeous opportunities for ragging which the Brigade offered to its members, had joined young and worked their way up.

Under them were the rank and file, about thirty in all, of whom perhaps seven were earnest workers, who looked on the Brigade in the right, or Downing, spirit. The rest were entirely frivolous.

The weekly meetings were always full of life and excitement.

At this point it is as well to introduce Sammy to the reader.

Sammy, short for Sampson, was a young bull-terrier belonging to Mr. Downing. If it is possible for a man to have two apples of his eye, Sammy was the other. He was a large, light-hearted dog with a white coat, an engaging expression, the tongue of an ant-eater, and a manner which was a happy blend of hurricane and circular saw. He had long legs, a tenor voice, and was apparently made of india-rubber.

Sammy was a great favourite in the school, and a particular friend of Mike's, the Wrykynian being always a firm ally of every dog he met after two minutes' acquaintance.

In passing, Jellicoe owned a clock-work rat, much in request during French lessons.

We will now proceed to the painful details.

The meetings of the Fire Brigade were held after school in Mr. Downing's form-room. The proceedings always began in the same way, by the reading of the minutes of the last meeting. After that the entertainment varied according to whether the members happened to be fertile or not in ideas for the disturbing of the peace.

To-day they were in very fair form.

As soon as Mr. Downing had closed the minute-book, Wilson, of the School House, held up his hand.

"Well, Wilson?"

"Please, sir, couldn't we have a uniform for the Brigade?"

"A uniform?" Mr. Downing pondered

"Red, with green stripes, sir,"

Red, with a thin green stripe, was the Sedleigh colour.

"Shall I put it to the vote, sir?" asked Stone.

"One moment, Stone."

"Those in favour of the motion move to the left, those against it to the right."

A scuffling of feet, a slamming of desk-lids and an upset blackboard, and the meeting had divided.

Mr. Downing rapped irritably on his desk.

"Sit down!" he said, "sit down! I won't have this noise and disturbance. Stone, sit down—Wilson, get back to your place."

"Please, sir, the motion is carried by twenty-five votes to six."

"Please, sir, may I go and get measured this evening?"

"Please, sir—"

"Si-lence! The idea of a uniform is, of course, out of the question."

"Oo-oo-oo-oo, sir-r-r!"

"Be quiet! Entirely out of the question. We cannot plunge into needless expense. Stone, listen to me. I cannot have this noise and disturbance! Another time when a point arises it must be settled by a show of hands. Well, Wilson?"

"Please, sir, may we have helmets?"

"Very useful as a protection against falling timbers, sir," said Robinson.

"I don't think my people would be pleased, sir, if they knew I was going out to fires without a helmet," said Stone.

The whole strength of the company: "Please, sir, may we have helmets?"

"Those in favour—" began Stone.

Mr. Downing banged on his desk. "Silence! Silence!! Silence!!! Helmets are, of course, perfectly preposterous."

"Oo-oo-oo-oo, sir-r-r!"

"But, sir, the danger!"

"Please, sir, the falling timbers!"

The Fire Brigade had been in action once and once only in the memory of man, and that time it was a haystack which had burnt itself out just as the rescuers had succeeded in fastening the hose to the hydrant.

"Silence!"

"Then, please, sir, couldn't we have an honour cap? It wouldn't be expensive, and it would be just as good as a helmet for all the timbers that are likely to fall on our heads."

Mr. Downing smiled a wry smile.

"Our Wilson is facetious," he remarked frostily.

"Sir, no, sir! I wasn't facetious! Or couldn't we have footer-tops, like the first fifteen have? They—"

"Wilson, leave the room!"

"Sir, please, sir!"

"This moment, Wilson. And," as he reached the door, "do me one hundred lines."

A pained "OO-oo-oo, sir-r-r," was cut off by the closing door.

Mr. Downing proceeded to improve the occasion. "I deplore this growing spirit of flippancy," he said. "I tell you I deplore it! It is not right! If this Fire Brigade is to be of solid use, there must be less of this flippancy. We must have keenness. I want you boys above all to be keen. I—What is that noise?"

From the other side of the door proceeded a sound like water gurgling from a bottle, mingled with cries half-suppressed, as if somebody were being prevented from uttering them by a hand laid over his mouth. The sufferer appeared to have a high voice.

There was a tap at the door and Mike walked in. He was not alone. Those near enough to see, saw that he was accompanied by Jellicoe's clock-work rat, which moved rapidly over the floor in the direction of the opposite wall.

"May I fetch a book from my desk, sir?" asked Mike.

"Very well—be quick, Jackson; we are busy."

Being interrupted in one of his addresses to the Brigade irritated Mr. Downing.

The muffled cries grew more distinct.

"What—is—that—noise?" shrilled Mr. Downing.

"Noise, sir?" asked Mike, puzzled.

"I think it's something outside the window, sir," said Stone helpfully.

"A bird, I think, sir," said Robinson.

"Don't be absurd!" snapped Mr. Downing. "It's outside the door. Wilson!"

"Yes, sir?" said a voice "off."

"Are you making that whining noise?"

"Whining noise, sir? No, sir, I'm not making a whining noise."

"What sort of noise, sir?" inquired Mike, as many Wrykynians had asked before him. It was a question invented by Wrykyn for use in just such a case as this.

"I do not propose," said Mr. Downing acidly, "to imitate the noise; you can all hear it perfectly plainly. It is a curious whining noise."

"They are mowing the cricket field, sir," said the invisible Wilson. "Perhaps that's it."

"It may be one of the desks squeaking, sir," put in Stone. "They do sometimes."

"Or somebody's boots, sir," added Robinson.

"Silence! Wilson?"

"Yes, sir?" bellowed the unseen one.

"Don't shout at me from the corridor like that. Come in."

"Yes, sir!"

As he spoke the muffled whining changed suddenly to a series of tenor shrieks, and the india-rubber form of Sammy bounded into the room like an excited kangaroo.

Willing hands had by this time deflected the clockwork rat from the wall to which it had been steering, and pointed it up the alley-way between the two rows of desks. Mr. Downing, rising from his place, was just in time to see Sammy with a last leap spring on his prey and begin worrying it.

Chaos reigned.

"A rat!" shouted Robinson.

The twenty-three members of the Brigade who were not earnest instantly dealt with the situation, each in the manner that seemed proper to him. Some leaped on to forms, others flung books, all shouted. It was a stirring, bustling scene.

Sammy had by this time disposed of the clock-work rat, and was now standing, like Marius, among the ruins barking triumphantly.

The banging on Mr. Downing's desk resembled thunder. It rose above all the other noises till in time they gave up the competition and died away.

Mr. Downing shot out orders, threats, and penalties with the rapidity of a Maxim gun.

"Stone, sit down! Donovan, if you do not sit down, you will be severely punished. Henderson, one hundred lines for gross disorder! Windham, the same! Go to your seat, Vincent. What are you doing, Broughton-Knight? I will not have this disgraceful noise and disorder! The meeting is at an end; go quietly from the room, all of you. Jackson and Wilson, remain. Quietly, I said, Durand! Don't shuffle your feet in that abominable way."

Crash!

"Wolferstan, I distinctly saw you upset that black-board with a movement of your hand—one hundred lines. Go quietly from the room, everybody."

The meeting dispersed.

"Jackson and Wilson, come here. What's the meaning of this disgraceful conduct? Put that dog out of the room, Jackson."

Mike removed the yelling Sammy and shut the door on him.

"Well, Wilson?"

"Please, sir, I was playing with a clock-work rat—"

"What business have you to be playing with clock-work rats?"

"Then I remembered," said Mike, "that I had left my Horace in my desk, so I came in—"

"And by a fluke, sir," said Wilson, as one who tells of strange things, "the rat happened to be pointing in the same direction, so he came in, too."

"I met Sammy on the gravel outside and he followed me."

"I tried to collar him, but when you told me to come in, sir, I had to let him go, and he came in after the rat."

It was plain to Mr. Downing that the burden of sin was shared equally by both culprits. Wilson had supplied the rat, Mike the dog; but Mr. Downing liked Wilson and disliked Mike. Wilson was in the Fire Brigade, frivolous at times, it was true, but nevertheless a member. Also he kept wicket for the school. Mike was a member of the Archaeological Society, and had refused to play cricket.

Mr. Downing allowed these facts to influence him in passing sentence.

"One hundred lines, Wilson," he said. "You may go."

Wilson departed with the air of a man who has had a great deal of fun, and paid very little for it.

Mr. Downing turned to Mike. "You will stay in on Saturday afternoon, Jackson; it will interfere with your Archaeological studies, I fear, but it may teach you that we have no room at Sedleigh for boys who spend their time loafing about and making themselves a nuisance. We are a keen school; this is no place for boys who do nothing but waste their time. That will do, Jackson."

And Mr. Downing walked out of the room. In affairs of this kind a master has a habit of getting the last word.

CHAPTER XXXIX

ACHILLES LEAVES HIS TENT

They say misfortunes never come singly. As Mike sat brooding over his wrongs in his study, after the Sammy incident, Jellicoe came into the room, and, without preamble, asked for the loan of a sovereign.

When one has been in the habit of confining one's lendings and borrowings to sixpences and shillings, a request for a sovereign comes as something of a blow.

"What on earth for?" asked Mike.

"I say, do you mind if I don't tell you? I don't want to tell anybody. The fact is, I'm in a beastly hole."

"Oh, sorry," said Mike. "As a matter of fact, I do happen to have a quid. You can freeze on to it, if you like. But it's about all I have got, so don't be shy about paying it back."

Jellicoe was profuse in his thanks, and disappeared in a cloud of gratitude.

Mike felt that Fate was treating him badly. Being kept in on Saturday meant that he would be unable to turn out for Little Borlock against Claythorpe, the return match. In the previous game he had scored ninety-eight, and there was a lob bowler in the Claythorpe ranks whom he was particularly anxious to meet again. Having to yield a sovereign to Jellicoe—why on earth did the man want all that?—meant that, unless a carefully worded letter to his brother Bob at Oxford had the desired effect, he would be practically penniless for weeks.

In a gloomy frame of mind he sat down to write to Bob, who was playing regularly for the 'Varsity this season, and only the previous week had made a century against Sussex, so might be expected to be in a sufficiently softened mood to advance the needful. (Which, it may be stated at once, he did, by return of post.)

Mike was struggling with the opening sentences of this letter—he was never a very ready writer—when Stone and Robinson burst into the room.

Mike put down his pen, and got up. He was in warlike mood, and welcomed the intrusion. If Stone and Robinson wanted battle, they should have it.

But the motives of the expedition were obviously friendly. Stone beamed. Robinson was laughing.

"You're a sportsman," said Robinson.

"What did he give you?" asked Stone.

They sat down, Robinson on the table, Stone in Psmith's deck-chair. Mike's heart warmed to them. The little disturbance in the dormitory was a thing of the past, done with, forgotten, contemporary with Julius Caesar. He felt that he, Stone and Robinson must learn to know and appreciate one another.

There was, as a matter of fact, nothing much wrong with Stone and Robinson. They were just ordinary raggers of the type found at every public school, small and large. They were absolutely free from brain. They had a certain amount of muscle, and a vast store of animal spirits. They looked on school life purely as a vehicle for ragging. The Stones and Robinsons are the swashbucklers of the school world. They go about, loud and boisterous, with a whole-hearted and cheerful indifference to other people's feelings, treading on the toes of their neighbour and shoving him off the pavement, and always with an eye wide open for any adventure. As to the kind of adventure, they are not particular so long as it promises excitement. Sometimes they go through their whole school career without accident. More often they run up against a snag in the shape of some serious-minded and muscular person who objects to having his toes trodden on and being shoved off the pavement, and then they usually sober down, to the mutual advantage of themselves and the rest of the community.

One's opinion of this type of youth varies according to one's point of view. Small boys whom they had occasion to kick, either from pure high spirits or as a punishment for some slip from the narrow path which the ideal small boy should tread, regarded Stone and Robinson as bullies of the genuine "Eric" and "St. Winifred's" brand. Masters were rather afraid of them. Adair had a smouldering dislike for them. They were useful at cricket, but apt not to take Sedleigh as seriously as he could have wished.

As for Mike, he now found them pleasant company, and began to get out the tea-things.

"Those Fire Brigade meetings," said Stone, "are a rag. You can do what you like, and you never get more than a hundred lines."

"Don't you!" said Mike. "I got Saturday afternoon."

"What!"

"Is Wilson in too?"

"No. He got a hundred lines."

Stone and Robinson were quite concerned.

"What a beastly swindle!"

"That's because you don't play cricket. Old Downing lets you do what you like if you join the Fire Brigade and play cricket."

"'We are, above all, a keen school,'" quoted Stone. "Don't you ever play?"

"I have played a bit," said Mike.

"Well, why don't you have a shot? We aren't such flyers here. If you know one end of a bat from the other, you could get into some sort of a team. Were you at school anywhere before you came here?"

"I was at Wrykyn."

"Why on earth did you leave?" asked Stone. "Were you sacked?"

"No. My pater took me away."

"Wrykyn?" said Robinson. "Are you any relation of the Jacksons there—J. W. and the others?"

"Brother."

"What!"

"Well, didn't you play at all there?"

"Yes," said Mike, "I did. I was in the team three years, and I should have been captain this year, if I'd stopped on."

There was a profound and gratifying sensation. Stone gaped, and Robinson nearly dropped his tea-cup.

Stone broke the silence.

"But I mean to say—look here! What I mean is, why aren't you playing? Why don't you play now?"

"I do. I play for a village near here. Place called Little Borlock. A man who played against Wrykyn for the Free Foresters captains them. He asked me if I'd like some games for them."

"But why not for the school?"

"Why should I? It's much better fun for the village. You don't get ordered about by Adair, for a start."

"Adair sticks on side," said Stone.

"Enough for six," agreed Robinson.

"By Jove," said Stone, "I've got an idea. My word, what a rag!"

"What's wrong now?" inquired Mike politely.

"Why, look here. To-morrow's Mid-term Service day. It's nowhere near the middle of the term, but they always have it in the fourth week. There's chapel at half-past nine till half-past ten. Then the rest of the day's a whole holiday. There are always house matches. We're playing Downing's. Why don't you play and let's smash them?"

"By Jove, yes," said Robinson. "Why don't you? They're always sticking on side because they've won the house cup three years running. I say, do you bat or bowl?"

"Bat. Why?"

Robinson rocked on the table.

"Why, old Downing fancies himself as a bowler. You must play, and knock the cover off him."

"Masters don't play in house matches, surely?"

"This isn't a real house match. Only a friendly. Downing always turns out on Mid-term Service day. I say, do play."

"Think of the rag."

"But the team's full," said Mike.

"The list isn't up yet. We'll nip across to Barnes' study, and make him alter it."

They dashed out of the room. From down the passage Mike heard yells of "Barnes!" the closing of a door, and a murmur of excited conversation. Then footsteps returning down the passage.

Barnes appeared, on his face the look of one who has seen visions.

"I say," he said, "is it true? Or is Stone rotting? About Wrykyn, I mean."

"Yes, I was in the team."

Barnes was an enthusiastic cricketer. He studied his Wisden, and he had an immense respect for Wrykyn cricket.

"Are you the M. Jackson, then, who had an average of fifty-one point nought three last year?"

"Yes."

Barnes's manner became like that of a curate talking to a bishop.

"I say," he said, "then—er—will you play against Downing's to-morrow?"

"Rather," said Mike. "Thanks awfully. Have some tea?"

CHAPTER XL

THE MATCH WITH DOWNING'S

It is the curious instinct which prompts most people to rub a thing in that makes the lot of the average convert an unhappy one. Only the very self-controlled can refrain from improving the occasion and scoring off the convert. Most leap at the opportunity.

It was so in Mike's case. Mike was not a genuine convert, but to Mr. Downing he had the outward aspect of one. When you have been impressing upon a non-cricketing boy for nearly a month that (a) the school is above all a keen school, (b) that all members of it should play cricket, and (c) that by not playing cricket he is ruining his chances in this world and imperilling them in the next; and when, quite unexpectedly, you come upon this boy dressed in cricket flannels, wearing cricket boots and carrying a cricket bag, it seems only natural to assume that you have converted him, that the seeds of your eloquence have fallen on fruitful soil and sprouted.

Mr. Downing assumed it.

He was walking to the field with Adair and another member of his team when he came upon Mike.

"What!" he cried. "Our Jackson clad in suit of mail and armed for the fray!"

This was Mr. Downing's No. 2 manner—the playful.

"This is indeed Saul among the prophets. Why this sudden enthusiasm for a game which I understood that you despised? Are our opponents so reduced?"

Psmith, who was with Mike, took charge of the affair with a languid grace which had maddened hundreds in its time, and which never failed to ruffle Mr. Downing.

"We are, above all, sir," he said, "a keen house. Drones are not welcomed by us. We are essentially versatile. Jackson, the archaeologist of yesterday, becomes the cricketer of to-day. It is the right spirit, sir," said Psmith earnestly. "I like to see it."

"Indeed, Smith? You are not playing yourself, I notice. Your enthusiasm has bounds."

"In our house, sir, competition is fierce, and the Selection Committee unfortunately passed me over."

There were a number of pitches dotted about over the field, for there was always a touch of the London Park about it on Mid-term Service day. Adair, as captain of cricket, had naturally selected the best for his own match. It was a good wicket, Mike saw. As a matter of fact the wickets at Sedleigh were nearly always good. Adair had infected the ground-man with some of his own keenness, with the result that that once-leisurely official now found himself sometimes, with a kind of mild surprise, working really hard. At the beginning of the previous season Sedleigh had played a scratch team from a neighbouring town on a wicket which, except for the creases, was absolutely undistinguishable from the surrounding turf, and behind the pavilion after the match Adair had spoken certain home truths to the ground-man. The latter's reformation had dated from that moment.

Barnes, timidly jubilant, came up to Mike with the news that he had won the toss, and the request that Mike would go in first with him.

In stories of the "Not Really a Duffer" type, where the nervous new boy, who has been found crying in the boot-room over the photograph of his sister, contrives to get an innings in a game, nobody suspects that he is really a prodigy till he hits the Bully's first ball out of the ground for six.

With Mike it was different. There was no pitying smile on Adair's face as he started his run preparatory to sending down the first ball. Mike, on the cricket field, could not have looked anything but a cricketer if he had turned out in a tweed suit and hobnail boots. Cricketer was written all over him—in his walk, in the way he took guard, in his stand at the wickets. Adair started to bowl with the feeling that this was somebody who had more than a little knowledge of how to deal with good bowling and punish bad.

Mike started cautiously. He was more than usually anxious to make runs to-day, and he meant to take no risks till he could afford to do so. He had seen Adair bowl at the nets, and he knew that he was good.

The first over was a maiden, six dangerous balls beautifully played. The fieldsmen changed over.

The general interest had now settled on the match between Outwood's and Downing's. The fact in Mike's case had gone round the field, and, as several of the other games had not yet begun, quite a large crowd had collected near the pavilion to watch. Mike's masterly treatment of the opening over had impressed the spectators, and there was a popular desire to see how he would deal with Mr. Downing's slows. It was generally anticipated that he would do something special with them.

Off the first ball of the master's over a leg-bye was run.

Mike took guard.

Mr. Downing was a bowler with a style of his own. He took two short steps, two long steps, gave a jump, took three more short steps, and ended with a combination of step and jump, during which the ball emerged from behind his back and started on its slow career to the wicket. The whole business had some of the dignity of the old-fashioned minuet, subtly blended with the careless vigour of a cake-walk. The ball, when delivered, was billed to break from leg, but the programme was subject to alterations.

If the spectators had expected Mike to begin any firework effects with the first ball, they were disappointed. He played the over through with a grace worthy of his brother Joe. The last ball he turned to leg for a single.

His treatment of Adair's next over was freer. He had got a sight of the ball now. Half-way through the over a beautiful square cut forced a passage through the crowd by the pavilion, and dashed up against the rails. He drove the sixth ball past cover for three.

The crowd was now reluctantly dispersing to its own games, but it stopped as Mr. Downing started his minuet-cake-walk, in the hope that it might see something more sensational.

This time the hope was fulfilled.

The ball was well up, slow, and off the wicket on the on-side. Perhaps if it had been allowed to pitch, it might have broken in and become quite dangerous. Mike went out at it, and hit it a couple of feet from the ground. The ball dropped with a thud and a spurting of dust in the road that ran along one side of the cricket field.

It was returned on the instalment system by helpers from other games, and the bowler began his manoeuvres again. A half-volley this time. Mike slammed it back, and mid-on, whose heart was obviously not in the thing, failed to stop it.

"Get to them, Jenkins," said Mr. Downing irritably, as the ball came back from the boundary. "Get to them."

"Sir, please, sir—"

"Don't talk in the field, Jenkins."

Having had a full-pitch hit for six and a half-volley for four, there was a strong probability that Mr. Downing would pitch his next ball short.

The expected happened. The third ball was a slow long-hop, and hit the road at about the same spot where the first had landed. A howl of untuneful applause rose from the watchers in the pavilion, and Mike, with the feeling that this sort of bowling was too good to be true, waited in position for number four.

There are moments when a sort of panic seizes a bowler. This happened now with Mr. Downing. He suddenly abandoned science and ran amok. His run lost its stateliness and increased its vigour. He charged up to the wicket as a wounded buffalo sometimes charges a gun. His whole idea now was to bowl fast.

When a slow bowler starts to bowl fast, it is usually as well to be batting, if you can manage it.

By the time the over was finished, Mike's score had been increased by sixteen, and the total of his side, in addition, by three wides.

And a shrill small voice, from the neighbourhood of the pavilion, uttered with painful distinctness the words, "Take him off!"

That was how the most sensational day's cricket began that Sedleigh had known.

A description of the details of the morning's play would be monotonous. It is enough to say that they ran on much the same lines as the third and fourth overs of the match. Mr. Downing bowled one more over, off which Mike helped himself to sixteen runs, and then retired moodily to cover-point, where, in Adair's fifth over, he missed Barnes—the first occasion since the game began on which that mild batsman had attempted to score more than a single. Scared by this escape, Outwood's captain shrank back into his shell, sat on the splice like a limpet, and, offering no more chances, was not out at lunch time with a score of eleven.

Mike had then made a hundred and three.

As Mike was taking off his pads in the pavilion, Adair came up.

"Why did you say you didn't play cricket?" he asked abruptly.

When one has been bowling the whole morning, and bowling well, without the slightest success, one is inclined to be abrupt.

Mike finished unfastening an obstinate strap. Then he looked up.

"I didn't say anything of the kind. I said I wasn't going to play here. There's a difference. As a matter of fact, I was in the Wrykyn team before I came here. Three years."

Adair was silent for a moment.

"Will you play for us against the Old Sedleighans to-morrow?" he said at length.

Mike tossed his pads into his bag and got up.

"No, thanks."

There was a silence.

"Above it, I suppose?"

"Not a bit. Not up to it. I shall want a lot of coaching at that end net of yours before I'm fit to play for Sedleigh."

There was another pause.

"Then you won't play?" asked Adair.

"I'm not keeping you, am I?" said Mike, politely.

It was remarkable what a number of members of Outwood's house appeared to cherish a personal grudge against Mr. Downing. It had been that master's somewhat injudicious practice for many years to treat his own house as a sort of Chosen People. Of all masters, the most unpopular is he who by the silent tribunal of a school is convicted of favouritism. And the dislike deepens if it is a house which he favours and not merely individuals. On occasions when boys in his own house and boys from other houses were accomplices and partners in wrong-doing, Mr. Downing distributed his thunderbolts unequally, and the school noticed it. The result was that not only he himself, but also— which was rather unfair—his house, too, had acquired a good deal of unpopularity.

The general consensus of opinion in Outwood's during the luncheon interval was that, having got Downing's up a tree, they would be fools not to make the most of the situation.

Barnes's remark that he supposed, unless anything happened and wickets began to fall a bit faster, they had better think of declaring somewhere about half-past three or four, was met with a storm of opposition.

"Declare!" said Robinson. "Great Scott, what on earth are you talking about?"

"Declare!" Stone's voice was almost a wail of indignation. "I never saw such a chump."

"They'll be rather sick if we don't, won't they?" suggested Barnes.

"Sick! I should think they would," said Stone. "That's just the

165

gay idea. Can't you see that by a miracle we've got a chance of getting a jolly good bit of our own back against those Downing's ticks? What we've got to do is to jolly well keep them in the field all day if we can, and be jolly glad it's so beastly hot. If they lose about a dozen pounds each through sweating about in the sun after Jackson's drives, perhaps they'll stick on less side about things in general in future. Besides, I want an innings against that bilge of old Downing's, if I can get it."

"So do I," said Robinson.

"If you declare, I swear I won't field. Nor will Robinson."

"Rather not."

"Well, I won't then," said Barnes unhappily. "Only you know they're rather sick already."

"Don't you worry about that," said Stone with a wide grin. "They'll be a lot sicker before we've finished."

And so it came about that that particular Mid-term Service-day match made history. Big scores had often been put up on Mid-term Service day. Games had frequently been one-sided. But it had never happened before in the annals of the school that one side, going in first early in the morning, had neither completed its innings nor declared it closed when stumps were drawn at 6.30. In no previous Sedleigh match, after a full day's play, had the pathetic words "Did not bat" been written against the whole of one of the contending teams.

These are the things which mark epochs.

Play was resumed at 2.15. For a quarter of an hour Mike was comparatively quiet. Adair, fortified by food and rest, was bowling really well, and his first half-dozen overs had to be watched carefully. But the wicket was too good to give him a chance, and Mike, playing himself in again, proceeded to get to business once more. Bowlers came and went. Adair pounded away at one end with brief intervals between the attacks. Mr. Downing took a couple more overs, in one of which a horse, passing in the road, nearly had its useful life cut suddenly short. Change-bowlers of various actions and paces, each weirder and more futile than the last, tried their luck. But still the first-wicket stand continued.

The bowling of a house team is all head and no body. The first pair probably have some idea of length and break. The first-change pair are poor. And the rest, the small change, are simply the sort of things one sees in dreams after a heavy supper, or when one is out without one's gun.

Time, mercifully, generally breaks up a big stand at cricket before the field has suffered too much, and that is what happened now. At four o'clock, when the score stood at two hundred and twenty for no wicket, Barnes, greatly daring, smote lustily at a rather wide half-volley and was caught at short-slip for thirty-three. He retired blushfully to the pavilion, amidst applause, and Stone came out.

As Mike had then made a hundred and eighty-seven, it was

166

assumed by the field, that directly he had topped his second century, the closure would be applied and their ordeal finished. There was almost a sigh of relief when frantic cheering from the crowd told that the feat had been accomplished. The fieldsmen clapped in quite an indulgent sort of way, as who should say, "Capital, capital. And now let's start our innings." Some even began to edge towards the pavilion. But the next ball was bowled, and the next over, and the next after that, and still Barnes made no sign. (The conscience-stricken captain of Outwood's was, as a matter of fact, being practically held down by Robinson and other ruffians by force.)

A grey dismay settled on the field.

The bowling had now become almost unbelievably bad. Lobs were being tried, and Stone, nearly weeping with pure joy, was playing an innings of the How-to-brighten-cricket type. He had an unorthodox style, but an excellent eye, and the road at this period of the game became absolutely unsafe for pedestrians and traffic.

Mike's pace had become slower, as was only natural, but his score, too, was mounting steadily.

"This is foolery," snapped Mr. Downing, as the three hundred and fifty went up on the board. "Barnes!" he called.

There was no reply. A committee of three was at that moment engaged in sitting on Barnes's head in the first eleven changing-room, in order to correct a more than usually feverish attack of conscience.

"Barnes!"

"Please, sir," said Stone, some species of telepathy telling him what was detaining his captain. "I think Barnes must have left the field. He has probably gone over to the house to fetch something."

"This is absurd. You must declare your innings closed. The game has become a farce."

"Declare! Sir, we can't unless Barnes does. He might be awfully annoyed if we did anything like that without consulting him."

"Absurd."

"He's very touchy, sir."

"It is perfect foolery."

"I think Jenkins is just going to bowl, sir."

Mr. Downing walked moodily to his place.

In a neat wooden frame in the senior day-room at Outwood's, just above the mantelpiece, there was on view, a week later, a slip of paper. The writing on it was as follows:

OUTWOOD'S v. DOWNING'S

Outwood's. First innings.
J. P. Barnes, c. Hammond, b. Hassall... 33
M. Jackson, not out........................ 277
W. J. Stone, not out....................... 124

Extras............................ 37

Total (for one wicket)...... 471

Downing's did not bat.

CHAPTER XLI

THE SINGULAR BEHAVIOUR OF JELLICOE

Outwood's rollicked considerably that night. Mike, if he had cared to take the part, could have been the Petted Hero. But a cordial invitation from the senior day-room to be the guest of the evening at about the biggest rag of the century had been refused on the plea of fatigue. One does not make two hundred and seventy-seven runs on a hot day without feeling the effects, even if one has scored mainly by the medium of boundaries; and Mike, as he lay back in Psmith's deck-chair, felt that all he wanted was to go to bed and stay there for a week. His hands and arms burned as if they were red-hot, and his eyes were so tired that he could not keep them open.

Psmith, leaning against the mantelpiece, discoursed in a desultory way on the day's happenings—the score off Mr. Downing, the undeniable annoyance of that battered bowler, and the probability of his venting his annoyance on Mike next day.

"In theory," said he, "the manly what-d'you-call-it of cricket and all that sort of thing ought to make him fall on your neck to-morrow and weep over you as a foeman worthy of his steel. But I am prepared to bet a reasonable sum that he will give no Jiu-jitsu exhibition of this kind. In fact, from what I have seen of our bright little friend, I should say that, in a small way, he will do his best to make it distinctly hot for you, here and there."

"I don't care," murmured Mike, shifting his aching limbs in the chair.

"In an ordinary way, I suppose, a man can put up with having his bowling hit a little. But your performance was cruelty to animals. Twenty-eight off one over, not to mention three wides, would have made Job foam at the mouth. You will probably get sacked. On the other hand, it's worth it. You have lit a candle this day which can never be blown out. You have shown the lads of the village how Comrade Downing's bowling ought to be treated. I don't suppose he'll ever take another wicket."

168

"He doesn't deserve to."

Psmith smoothed his hair at the glass and turned round again.

"The only blot on this day of mirth and good-will is," he said, "the singular conduct of our friend Jellicoe. When all the place was ringing with song and merriment, Comrade Jellicoe crept to my side, and, slipping his little hand in mine, touched me for three quid."

This interested Mike, fagged as he was.

"What! Three quid!"

"Three jingling, clinking sovereigns. He wanted four."

"But the man must be living at the rate of I don't know what. It was only yesterday that he borrowed a quid from me!"

"He must be saving money fast. There appear to be the makings of a financier about Comrade Jellicoe. Well, I hope, when he's collected enough for his needs, he'll pay me back a bit. I'm pretty well cleaned out."

"I got some from my brother at Oxford."

"Perhaps he's saving up to get married. We may be helping towards furnishing the home. There was a Siamese prince fellow at my dame's at Eton who had four wives when he arrived, and gathered in a fifth during his first summer holidays. It was done on the correspondence system. His Prime Minister fixed it up at the other end, and sent him the glad news on a picture post-card. I think an eye ought to be kept on Comrade Jellicoe."

Mike tumbled into bed that night like a log, but he could not sleep. He ached all over. Psmith chatted for a time on human affairs in general, and then dropped gently off. Jellicoe, who appeared to be wrapped in gloom, contributed nothing to the conversation.

After Psmith had gone to sleep, Mike lay for some time running over in his mind, as the best substitute for sleep, the various points of his innings that day. He felt very hot and uncomfortable.

Just as he was wondering whether it would not be a good idea to get up and have a cold bath, a voice spoke from the darkness at his side.

"Are you asleep, Jackson?"

"Who's that?"

"Me—Jellicoe. I can't get to sleep."

"Nor can I. I'm stiff all over."

"I'll come over and sit on your bed."

There was a creaking, and then a weight descended in the neighbourhood of Mike's toes.

Jellicoe was apparently not in conversational mood. He uttered no word for quite three minutes. At the end of which time he gave a sound midway between a snort and a sigh.

"I say, Jackson!" he said.

"Yes?"

"Have you—oh, nothing."

Silence again.

169

"Jackson."

"Hullo?"

"I say, what would your people say if you got sacked?"

"All sorts of things. Especially my pater. Why?"

"Oh, I don't know. So would mine."

"Everybody's would, I expect."

"Yes."

The bed creaked, as Jellicoe digested these great thoughts. Then he spoke again.

"It would be a jolly beastly thing to get sacked."

Mike was too tired to give his mind to the subject. He was not really listening. Jellicoe droned on in a depressed sort of way.

"You'd get home in the middle of the afternoon, I suppose, and you'd drive up to the house, and the servant would open the door, and you'd go in. They might all be out, and then you'd have to hang about, and wait; and presently you'd hear them come in, and you'd go out into the passage, and they'd say 'Hullo!'"

Jellicoe, in order to give verisimilitude, as it were, to an otherwise bald and unconvincing narrative, flung so much agitated surprise into the last word that it woke Mike from a troubled doze into which he had fallen.

"Hullo?" he said. "What's up?"

"Then you'd say. 'Hullo!' And then they'd say, 'What are you doing here?' And you'd say—"

"What on earth are you talking about?"

"About what would happen."

"Happen when?"

"When you got home. After being sacked, you know."

"Who's been sacked?" Mike's mind was still under a cloud.

"Nobody. But if you were, I meant. And then I suppose there'd be an awful row and general sickness, and all that. And then you'd be sent into a bank, or to Australia, or something."

Mike dozed off again.

"My pater would be frightfully sick. My mater would be sick. My sister would be jolly sick, too. Have you got any sisters, Jackson? I say, Jackson!"

"Hullo! What's the matter? Who's that?"

"Me—Jellicoe."

"What's up?"

"I asked you if you'd got any sisters."

"Any what?"

"Sisters."

"Whose sisters?"

"Yours. I asked if you'd got any."

"Any what?"

"Sisters."

"What about them?"

The conversation was becoming too intricate for Jellicoe. He changed the subject.

"I say, Jackson!"

"Well?"

"I say, you don't know any one who could lend me a pound, do you?"

"What!" cried Mike, sitting up in bed and staring through the darkness in the direction whence the numismatist's voice was proceeding. "Do what?"

"I say, look out. You'll wake Smith."

"Did you say you wanted some one to lend you a quid?"

"Yes," said Jellicoe eagerly. "Do you know any one?"

Mike's head throbbed. This thing was too much. The human brain could not be expected to cope with it. Here was a youth who had borrowed a pound from one friend the day before, and three pounds from another friend that very afternoon, already looking about him for further loans. Was it a hobby, or was he saving up to buy an aeroplane?

"What on earth do you want a pound for?"

"I don't want to tell anybody. But it's jolly serious. I shall get sacked if I don't get it."

Mike pondered.

Those who have followed Mike's career as set forth by the present historian will have realised by this time that he was a good long way from being perfect. As the Blue-Eyed Hero he would have been a rank failure. Except on the cricket field, where he was a natural genius, he was just ordinary. He resembled ninety per cent. of other members of English public schools. He had some virtues and a good many defects. He was as obstinate as a mule, though people whom he liked could do as they pleased with him. He was good-natured as a general thing, but on occasion his temper could be of the worst, and had, in his childhood, been the subject of much adverse comment among his aunts. He was rigidly truthful, where the issue concerned only himself. Where it was a case of saving a friend, he was prepared to act in a manner reminiscent of an American expert witness.

He had, in addition, one good quality without any defect to balance it. He was always ready to help people. And when he set himself to do this, he was never put off by discomfort or risk. He went at the thing with a singleness of purpose that asked no questions.

Bob's postal order, which had arrived that evening, was reposing in the breast-pocket of his coat.

It was a wrench, but, if the situation was so serious with Jellicoe, it had to be done.

Two minutes later the night was being made hideous by Jellicoe's

171

almost tearful protestations of gratitude, and the postal order had moved from one side of the dormitory to the other.

CHAPTER XLII

JELLICOE GOES ON THE SICK-LIST

Mike woke next morning with a confused memory of having listened to a great deal of incoherent conversation from Jellicoe, and a painfully vivid recollection of handing over the bulk of his worldly wealth to him. The thought depressed him, though it seemed to please Jellicoe, for the latter carolled in a gay undertone as he dressed, till Psmith, who had a sensitive ear, asked as a favour that these farm-yard imitations might cease until he was out of the room.

There were other things to make Mike low-spirited that morning. To begin with, he was in detention, which in itself is enough to spoil a day. It was a particularly fine day, which made the matter worse. In addition to this, he had never felt stiffer in his life. It seemed to him that the creaking of his joints as he walked must be audible to every one within a radius of several yards. Finally, there was the interview with Mr. Downing to come. That would probably be unpleasant. As Psmith had said, Mr. Downing was the sort of master who would be likely to make trouble. The great match had not been an ordinary match. Mr. Downing was a curious man in many ways, but he did not make a fuss on ordinary occasions when his bowling proved expensive. Yesterday's performance, however, stood in a class by itself. It stood forth without disguise as a deliberate rag. One side does not keep another in the field the whole day in a one-day match except as a grisly kind of practical joke. And Mr. Downing and his house realised this. The house's way of signifying its comprehension of the fact was to be cold and distant as far as the seniors were concerned, and abusive and pugnacious as regards the juniors. Young blood had been shed overnight, and more flowed during the eleven o'clock interval that morning to avenge the insult.

Mr. Downing's methods of retaliation would have to be, of necessity, more elusive; but Mike did not doubt that in some way or other his form-master would endeavour to get a bit of his own back.

As events turned out, he was perfectly right. When a master has got his knife into a boy, especially a master who allows himself to be influenced by his likes and dislikes, he is inclined to single him out in times of stress, and savage him as if he were the official representative of the evildoers. Just as, at sea, the skipper, when he has trouble with the crew, works it off on the boy.

Mr. Downing was in a sarcastic mood when he met Mike. That is to say, he began in a sarcastic strain. But this sort of thing is difficult to keep up. By the time he had reached his peroration, the rapier had given place to the bludgeon. For sarcasm to be effective, the user of it must be met half-way. His hearer must appear to be conscious of the sarcasm and moved by it. Mike, when masters waxed sarcastic towards him, always assumed an air of stolid stupidity, which was as a suit of mail against satire.

So Mr. Downing came down from the heights with a run, and began to express himself with a simple strength which it did his form good to listen to. Veterans who had been in the form for terms said afterwards that there had been nothing to touch it, in their experience of the orator, since the glorious day when Dunster, that prince of raggers, who had left at Christmas to go to a crammer's, had introduced three lively grass-snakes into the room during a Latin lesson.

"You are surrounded," concluded Mr. Downing, snapping his pencil in two in his emotion, "by an impenetrable mass of conceit and vanity and selfishness. It does not occur to you to admit your capabilities as a cricketer in an open, straightforward way and place them at the disposal of the school. No, that would not be dramatic enough for you. It would be too commonplace altogether. Far too commonplace!" Mr. Downing laughed bitterly. "No, you must conceal your capabilities. You must act a lie. You must—who is that shuffling his feet? I will not have it, I will have silence—you must hang back in order to make a more effective entrance, like some wretched actor who—I will not have this shuffling. I have spoken of this before. Macpherson, are you shuffling your feet?"

"Sir, no, sir."

"Please, sir."

"Well, Parsons?"

"I think it's the noise of the draught under the door, sir."

Instant departure of Parsons for the outer regions. And, in the excitement of this side-issue, the speaker lost his inspiration, and abruptly concluded his remarks by putting Mike on to translate in Cicero. Which Mike, who happened to have prepared the first half-page, did with much success.

The Old Boys' match was timed to begin shortly after eleven o'clock. During the interval most of the school walked across the field to look at the pitch. One or two of the Old Boys had already changed and were practising in front of the pavilion.

It was through one of these batsmen that an accident occurred which had a good deal of influence on Mike's affairs.

Mike had strolled out by himself. Half-way across the field Jellicoe joined him. Jellicoe was cheerful, and rather embarrassingly grateful. He was just in the middle of his harangue when the accident happened.

To their left, as they crossed the field, a long youth, with the faint beginnings of a moustache and a blazer that lit up the surrounding landscape like a glowing beacon, was lashing out recklessly at a friend's bowling. Already he had gone within an ace of slaying a small boy. As Mike and Jellicoe proceeded on their way, there was a shout of "Heads!"

The almost universal habit of batsmen of shouting "Heads!" at whatever height from the ground the ball may be, is not a little confusing. The average person, on hearing the shout, puts his hands over his skull, crouches down and trusts to luck. This is an excellent plan if the ball is falling, but is not much protection against a skimming drive along the ground.

When "Heads!" was called on the present occasion, Mike and Jellicoe instantly assumed the crouching attitude.

Jellicoe was the first to abandon it. He uttered a yell and sprang into the air. After which he sat down and began to nurse his ankle.

The bright-blazered youth walked up.

"Awfully sorry, you know, man. Hurt?"

Jellicoe was pressing the injured spot tenderly with his finger-tips, uttering sharp howls whenever, zeal outrunning discretion, he prodded himself too energetically.

"Silly ass, Dunster," he groaned, "slamming about like that."

"Awfully sorry. But I did yell."

"It's swelling up rather," said Mike. "You'd better get over to the house and have it looked at. Can you walk?"

Jellicoe tried, but sat down again with a loud "Ow!" At that moment the bell rang.

"I shall have to be going in," said Mike, "or I'd have helped you over."

"I'll give you a hand," said Dunster.

He helped the sufferer to his feet and they staggered off together, Jellicoe hopping, Dunster advancing with a sort of polka step. Mike watched them start and then turned to go in.

174

CHAPTER XLIII

MIKE RECEIVES A COMMISSION

There is only one thing to be said in favour of detention on a fine summer's afternoon, and that is that it is very pleasant to come out of. The sun never seems so bright or the turf so green as during the first five minutes after one has come out of the detention-room. One feels as if one were entering a new and very delightful world. There is also a touch of the Rip van Winkle feeling. Everything seems to have gone on and left one behind. Mike, as he walked to the cricket field, felt very much behind the times.

Arriving on the field he found the Old Boys batting. He stopped and watched an over of Adair's. The fifth ball bowled a man. Mike made his way towards the pavilion.

Before he got there he heard his name called, and turning, found Psmith seated under a tree with the bright-blazered Dunster.

"Return of the exile," said Psmith. "A joyful occasion tinged with melancholy. Have a cherry?—take one or two. These little acts of unremembered kindness are what one needs after a couple of hours in extra pupil-room. Restore your tissues, Comrade Jackson, and when you have finished those, apply again."

"Is your name Jackson?" inquired Dunster, "because Jellicoe wants to see you."

"Alas, poor Jellicoe!" said Psmith. "He is now prone on his bed in the dormitory—there a sheer hulk lies poor Tom Jellicoe, the darling of the crew, faithful below he did his duty, but Comrade Dunster has broached him to. I have just been hearing the melancholy details."

"Old Smith and I," said Dunster, "were at a private school together. I'd no idea I should find him here."

"It was a wonderfully stirring sight when we met," said Psmith; "not unlike the meeting of Ulysses and the hound Argos, of whom you have doubtless read in the course of your dabblings in the classics. I was Ulysses; Dunster gave a life-like representation of the faithful dawg."

"You still jaw as much as ever, I notice," said the animal delineator, fondling the beginnings of his moustache.

"More," sighed Psmith, "more. Is anything irritating you?" he added, eyeing the other's manoeuvres with interest.

"You needn't be a funny ass, man," said Dunster, pained; "heaps of people tell me I ought to have it waxed."

"What it really wants is top-dressing with guano. Hullo! another man out. Adair's bowling better to-day than he did yesterday."

"I heard about yesterday," said Dunster. "It must have been a

175

rag! Couldn't we work off some other rag on somebody before I go? I shall be stopping here till Monday in the village. Well hit, sir—Adair's bowling is perfectly simple if you go out to it."

"Comrade Dunster went out to it first ball," said Psmith to Mike.

"Oh! chuck it, man; the sun was in my eyes. I hear Adair's got a match on with the M.C.C. at last."

"Has he?" said Psmith; "I hadn't heard. Archaeology claims so much of my time that I have little leisure for listening to cricket chit-chat."

"What was it Jellicoe wanted?" asked Mike; "was it anything important?"

"He seemed to think so—he kept telling me to tell you to go and see him."

"I fear Comrade Jellicoe is a bit of a weak-minded blitherer—"

"Did you ever hear of a rag we worked off on Jellicoe once?" asked Dunster. "The man has absolutely no sense of humour—can't see when he's being rotted. Well it was like this—Hullo! We're all out—I shall have to be going out to field again, I suppose, dash it! I'll tell you when I see you again."

"I shall count the minutes," said Psmith.

Mike stretched himself; the sun was very soothing after his two hours in the detention-room; he felt disinclined for exertion.

"I don't suppose it's anything special about Jellicoe, do you?" he said. "I mean, it'll keep till tea-time; it's no catch having to sweat across to the house now."

"Don't dream of moving," said Psmith. "I have several rather profound observations on life to make and I can't make them without an audience. Soliloquy is a knack. Hamlet had got it, but probably only after years of patient practice. Personally, I need some one to listen when I talk. I like to feel that I am doing good. You stay where you are—don't interrupt too much."

Mike tilted his hat over his eyes and abandoned Jellicoe.

It was not until the lock-up bell rang that he remembered him. He went over to the house and made his way to the dormitory, where he found the injured one in a parlous state, not so much physical as mental. The doctor had seen his ankle and reported that it would be on the active list in a couple of days. It was Jellicoe's mind that needed attention now.

Mike found him in a condition bordering on collapse.

"I say, you might have come before!" said Jellicoe.

"What's up? I didn't know there was such a hurry about it—what did you want?"

"It's no good now," said Jellicoe gloomily; "it's too late, I shall get sacked."

"What on earth are you talking about? What's the row?"

"It's about that money."

176

"What about it?"

"I had to pay it to a man to-day, or he said he'd write to the Head—then of course I should get sacked. I was going to take the money to him this afternoon, only I got crocked, so I couldn't move. I wanted to get hold of you to ask you to take it for me—it's too late now!"

Mike's face fell. "Oh, hang it!" he said, "I'm awfully sorry. I'd no idea it was anything like that—what a fool I was! Dunster did say he thought it was something important, only like an ass I thought it would do if I came over at lock-up."

"It doesn't matter," said Jellicoe miserably; "it can't be helped."

"Yes, it can," said Mike. "I know what I'll do—it's all right. I'll get out of the house after lights-out."

Jellicoe sat up. "You can't! You'd get sacked if you were caught."

"Who would catch me? There was a chap at Wrykyn I knew who used to break out every night nearly and go and pot at cats with an air-pistol; it's as easy as anything."

The toad-under-the-harrow expression began to fade from Jellicoe's face. "I say, do you think you could, really?"

"Of course I can! It'll be rather a rag."

"I say, it's frightfully decent of you."

"What absolute rot!"

"But, look here, are you certain—"

"I shall be all right. Where do you want me to go?"

"It's a place about a mile or two from here, called Lower Borlock."

"Lower Borlock?"

"Yes, do you know it?"

"Rather! I've been playing cricket for them all the term."

"I say, have you? Do you know a man called Barley?"

"Barley? Rather—he runs the 'White Boar'."

"He's the chap I owe the money to."

"Old Barley!"

Mike knew the landlord of the "White Boar" well; he was the wag of the village team. Every village team, for some mysterious reason, has its comic man. In the Lower Borlock eleven Mr. Barley filled the post. He was a large, stout man, with a red and cheerful face, who looked exactly like the jovial inn-keeper of melodrama. He was the last man Mike would have expected to do the "money by Monday-week or I write to the headmaster" business.

But he reflected that he had only seen him in his leisure moments, when he might naturally be expected to unbend and be full of the milk of human kindness. Probably in business hours he was quite different. After all, pleasure is one thing and business another.

Besides, five pounds is a large sum of money, and if Jellicoe owed it, there was nothing strange in Mr. Barley's doing everything he could to recover it.

He wondered a little what Jellicoe could have been doing to run up a bill as big as that, but it did not occur to him to ask, which was unfortunate, as it might have saved him a good deal of inconvenience. It seemed to him that it was none of his business to inquire into Jellicoe's private affairs. He took the envelope containing the money without question.

"I shall bike there, I think," he said, "if I can get into the shed."

The school's bicycles were stored in a shed by the pavilion.

"You can manage that," said Jellicoe; "it's locked up at night, but I had a key made to fit it last summer, because I used to go out in the early morning sometimes before it was opened."

"Got it on you?"

"Smith's got it."

"I'll get it from him."

"I say!"

"Well?"

"Don't tell Smith why you want it, will you? I don't want anybody to know—if a thing once starts getting about it's all over the place in no time."

"All right, I won't tell him."

"I say, thanks most awfully! I don't know what I should have done, I—"

"Oh, chuck it!" said Mike.

CHAPTER XLIV

AND FULFILS IT

Mike started on his ride to Lower Borlock with mixed feelings. It is pleasant to be out on a fine night in summer, but the pleasure is to a certain extent modified when one feels that to be detected will mean expulsion.

Mike did not want to be expelled, for many reasons. Now that he had grown used to the place he was enjoying himself at Sedleigh to a certain extent. He still harboured a feeling of resentment against the school in general and Adair in particular, but it was pleasant in Outwood's now that he had got to know some of the members of the house, and he liked playing cricket for Lower Borlock; also, he was fairly certain that his father would not let him go to Cambridge if he were expelled from Sedleigh. Mr. Jackson was easy-going with his family, but occasionally his foot came down like a steam-hammer, as witness the Wrykyn school report affair.

So Mike pedalled along rapidly, being wishful to get the job done without delay.

Psmith had yielded up the key, but his inquiries as to why it was needed had been embarrassing. Mike's statement that he wanted to get up early and have a ride had been received by Psmith, with whom early rising was not a hobby, with honest amazement and a flood of advice and warning on the subject.

"One of the Georges," said Psmith, "I forget which, once said that a certain number of hours' sleep a day—I cannot recall for the moment how many—made a man something, which for the time being has slipped my memory. However, there you are. I've given you the main idea of the thing; and a German doctor says that early rising causes insanity. Still, if you're bent on it—" After which he had handed over the key.

Mike wished he could have taken Psmith into his confidence. Probably he would have volunteered to come, too; Mike would have been glad of a companion.

It did not take him long to reach Lower Borlock. The "White Boar" stood at the far end of the village, by the cricket field. He rode past the church—standing out black and mysterious against the light sky—and the rows of silent cottages, until he came to the inn.

The place was shut, of course, and all the lights were out—it was some time past eleven.

The advantage an inn has over a private house, from the point of view of the person who wants to get into it when it has been locked up, is that a nocturnal visit is not so unexpected in the case of the former. Preparations have been made to meet such an emergency. Where with a private house you would probably have to wander round heaving rocks and end by climbing up a water-spout, when you want to get into an inn you simply ring the night-bell, which, communicating with the boots' room, has that hard-worked menial up and doing in no time.

After Mike had waited for a few minutes there was a rattling of chains and a shooting of bolts and the door opened.

"Yes, sir?" said the boots, appearing in his shirt-sleeves. "Why, 'ullo! Mr. Jackson, sir!"

Mike was well known to all dwellers in Lower Borlock, his scores being the chief topic of conversation when the day's labours were over.

"I want to see Mr. Barley, Jack."

"He's bin in bed this half-hour back, Mr. Jackson."

"I must see him. Can you get him down?"

The boots looked doubtful. "Roust the guv'nor outer bed?" he said.

179

Mike quite admitted the gravity of the task. The landlord of the "White Boar" was one of those men who need a beauty sleep.

"I wish you would—it's a thing that can't wait. I've got some money to give to him."

"Oh, if it's that—" said the boots.

Five minutes later mine host appeared in person, looking more than usually portly in a check dressing-gown and red bedroom slippers of the Dreadnought type.

"You can pop off, Jack."

Exit boots to his slumbers once more.

"Well, Mr. Jackson, what's it all about?"

"Jellicoe asked me to come and bring you the money."

"The money? What money?"

"What he owes you; the five pounds, of course."

"The five—" Mr. Barley stared open-mouthed at Mike for a moment; then he broke into a roar of laughter which shook the sporting prints on the wall and drew barks from dogs in some distant part of the house. He staggered about laughing and coughing till Mike began to expect a fit of some kind. Then he collapsed into a chair, which creaked under him, and wiped his eyes.

"Oh dear!" he said, "oh dear! the five pounds!"

Mike was not always abreast of the rustic idea of humour, and now he felt particularly fogged. For the life of him he could not see what there was to amuse any one so much in the fact that a person who owed five pounds was ready to pay it back. It was an occasion for rejoicing, perhaps, but rather for a solemn, thankful, eyes-raised-to-heaven kind of rejoicing.

"What's up?" he asked.

"Five pounds!"

"You might tell us the joke."

Mr. Barley opened the letter, read it, and had another attack; when this was finished he handed the letter to Mike, who was waiting patiently by, hoping for light, and requested him to read it.

"Dear, dear!" chuckled Mr. Barley, "five pounds! They may teach you young gentlemen to talk Latin and Greek and what not at your school, but it 'ud do a lot more good if they'd teach you how many beans make five; it 'ud do a lot more good if they'd teach you to come in when it rained, it 'ud do—"

Mike was reading the letter.

"DEAR MR. BARLEY," it ran.—"I send the £5, which I could not get before. I hope it is in time, because I don't want you to write to the headmaster. I am sorry Jane and John ate your wife's hat and the chicken and broke the vase."

There was some more to the same effect; it was signed "T. G. Jellicoe."

180

"What on earth's it all about?" said Mike, finishing this curious document.

Mr. Barley slapped his leg. "Why, Mr. Jellicoe keeps two dogs here; I keep 'em for him till the young gentlemen go home for their holidays. Aberdeen terriers, they are, and as sharp as mustard. Mischief! I believe you, but, love us! they don't do no harm! Bite up an old shoe sometimes and such sort of things. The other day, last Wednesday it were, about 'ar parse five, Jane—she's the worst of the two, always up to it, she is—she got hold of my old hat and had it in bits before you could say knife. John upset a china vase in one of the bedrooms chasing a mouse, and they got on the coffee-room table and ate half a cold chicken what had been left there. So I says to myself, 'I'll have a game with Mr. Jellicoe over this,' and I sits down and writes off saying the little dogs have eaten a valuable hat and a chicken and what not, and the damage'll be five pounds, and will he kindly remit same by Saturday night at the latest or I write to his headmaster. Love us!" Mr. Barley slapped his thigh, "he took it all in, every word—and here's the five pounds in cash in this envelope here! I haven't had such a laugh since we got old Tom Raxley out of bed at twelve of a winter's night by telling him his house was a-fire."

It is not always easy to appreciate a joke of the practical order if one has been made even merely part victim of it. Mike, as he reflected that he had been dragged out of his house in the middle of the night, in contravention of all school rules and discipline, simply in order to satisfy Mr. Barley's sense of humour, was more inclined to be abusive than mirthful. Running risks is all very well when they are necessary, or if one chooses to run them for one's own amusement, but to be placed in a dangerous position, a position imperilling one's chance of going to the 'Varsity, is another matter altogether.

But it is impossible to abuse the Barley type of man. Barley's enjoyment of the whole thing was so honest and child-like. Probably it had given him the happiest quarter of an hour he had known for years, since, in fact, the affair of old Tom Raxley. It would have been cruel to damp the man.

So Mike laughed perfunctorily, took back the envelope with the five pounds, accepted a stone ginger beer and a plateful of biscuits, and rode off on his return journey.

Mention has been made above of the difference which exists between getting into an inn after lock-up and into a private house. Mike was to find this out for himself.

His first act on arriving at Sedleigh was to replace his bicycle in the shed. This he accomplished with success. It was pitch-dark in the shed, and as he wheeled his machine in, his foot touched something on the floor. Without waiting to discover what this might be, he leaned his bicycle against the wall, went out, and locked the door, after which he ran across to Outwood's.

Fortune had favoured his undertaking by decreeing that a stout drain-pipe should pass up the wall within a few inches of his and Psmith's study. On the first day of term, it may be remembered he had wrenched away the wooden bar which bisected the window-frame, thus rendering exit and entrance almost as simple as they had been for Wyatt during Mike's first term at Wrykyn.

He proceeded to scale this water-pipe.

He had got about half-way up when a voice from somewhere below cried, "Who's that?"

CHAPTER XLV

PURSUIT

These things are Life's Little Difficulties. One can never tell precisely how one will act in a sudden emergency. The right thing for Mike to have done at this crisis was to have ignored the voice, carried on up the water-pipe, and through the study window, and gone to bed. It was extremely unlikely that anybody could have recognised him at night against the dark background of the house. The position then would have been that somebody in Mr. Outwood's house had been seen breaking in after lights-out; but it would have been very difficult for the authorities to have narrowed the search down any further than that. There were thirty-four boys in Outwood's, of whom about fourteen were much the same size and build as Mike.

The suddenness, however, of the call caused Mike to lose his head. He made the strategic error of sliding rapidly down the pipe, and running.

There were two gates to Mr. Outwood's front garden. The carriage drive ran in a semicircle, of which the house was the centre. It was from the right-hand gate, nearest to Mr. Downing's house, that the voice had come, and, as Mike came to the ground, he saw a stout figure galloping towards him from that direction. He bolted like a rabbit for the other gate. As he did so, his pursuer again gave tongue.

"Oo-oo-oo yer!" was the exact remark.

Whereby Mike recognised him as the school sergeant.

"Oo-oo-oo yer!" was that militant gentleman's habitual way of beginning a conversation.

With this knowledge, Mike felt easier in his mind. Sergeant Collard was a man of many fine qualities, (notably a talent for what he was wont to call "spott'n," a mysterious gift which he exercised on the rifle range), but he could not run. There had been a time in his hot youth when he had sprinted like an untamed mustang in pursuit of volatile Pathans in Indian hill wars, but Time, increasing his girth, had taken from him the taste for such exercise. When he moved now it was at a stately walk. The fact that he ran to-night showed how the excitement of the chase had entered into his blood.

"Oo-oo-oo yer!" he shouted again, as Mike, passing through the gate, turned into the road that led to the school. Mike's attentive ear noted that the bright speech was a shade more puffily delivered this time. He began to feel that this was not such bad fun after all. He would have liked to be in bed, but, if that was out of the question, this was certainly the next best thing.

He ran on, taking things easily, with the sergeant panting in his wake, till he reached the entrance to the school grounds. He dashed in and took cover behind a tree.

Presently the sergeant turned the corner, going badly and evidently cured of a good deal of the fever of the chase. Mike heard him toil on for a few yards and then stop. A sound of panting was borne to him.

Then the sound of footsteps returning, this time at a walk. They passed the gate and went on down the road.

The pursuer had given the thing up.

Mike waited for several minutes behind his tree. His programme now was simple. He would give Sergeant Collard about half an hour, in case the latter took it into his head to "guard home" by waiting at the gate. Then he would trot softly back, shoot up the water-pipe once more, and so to bed. It had just struck a quarter to something—twelve, he supposed—on the school clock. He would wait till a quarter past.

Meanwhile, there was nothing to be gained from lurking behind a tree. He left his cover, and started to stroll in the direction of the pavilion. Having arrived there, he sat on the steps, looking out on to the cricket field.

His thoughts were miles away, at Wrykyn, when he was recalled to Sedleigh by the sound of somebody running. Focussing his gaze, he saw a dim figure moving rapidly across the cricket field straight for him.

His first impression, that he had been seen and followed, disappeared as the runner, instead of making for the pavilion, turned aside, and stopped at the door of the bicycle shed. Like Mike, he was evidently possessed of a key, for Mike heard it grate in the lock. At this point he left the pavilion and hailed his fellow rambler by night in a cautious undertone.

The other appeared startled.

"Who the dickens is that?" he asked. "Is that you, Jackson?"

Mike recognised Adair's voice. The last person he would have expected to meet at midnight obviously on the point of going for a bicycle ride.

"What are you doing out here, Jackson?"

"What are you, if it comes to that?"

Adair was lighting his lamp.

"I'm going for the doctor. One of the chaps in our house is bad."

"Oh!"

"What are you doing out here?"

"Just been for a stroll."

"Hadn't you better be getting back?"

"Plenty of time."

"I suppose you think you're doing something tremendously brave and dashing?"

"Hadn't you better be going to the doctor?"

"If you want to know what I think—"

"I don't. So long."

Mike turned away, whistling between his teeth. After a moment's pause, Adair rode off. Mike saw his light pass across the field and through the gate. The school clock struck the quarter.

It seemed to Mike that Sergeant Collard, even if he had started to wait for him at the house, would not keep up the vigil for more than half an hour. He would be safe now in trying for home again.

He walked in that direction.

Now it happened that Mr. Downing, aroused from his first sleep by the news, conveyed to him by Adair, that MacPhee, one of the junior members of Adair's dormitory, was groaning and exhibiting other symptoms of acute illness, was disturbed in his mind. Most housemasters feel uneasy in the event of illness in their houses, and Mr. Downing was apt to get jumpy beyond the ordinary on such occasions. All that was wrong with MacPhee, as a matter of fact, was a very fair stomach-ache, the direct and legitimate result of eating six buns, half a cocoa-nut, three doughnuts, two ices, an apple, and a pound of cherries, and washing the lot down with tea. But Mr. Downing saw in his attack the beginnings of some deadly scourge which would sweep through and decimate the house. He had despatched Adair for the doctor, and, after spending a few minutes prowling restlessly about his room, was now standing at his front gate, waiting for Adair's return.

It came about, therefore, that Mike, sprinting lightly in the direction of home and safety, had his already shaken nerves further maltreated by being hailed, at a range of about two yards, with a cry of "Is that you, Adair?" The next moment Mr. Downing emerged from his gate.

Mike stood not upon the order of his going. He was off like an arrow—a flying figure of Guilt. Mr. Downing, after the first surprise, seemed to grasp the situation. Ejaculating at intervals the words, "Who

184

is that? Stop! Who is that? Stop!" he dashed after the much-enduring Wrykynian at an extremely creditable rate of speed. Mr. Downing was by way of being a sprinter. He had won handicap events at College sports at Oxford, and, if Mike had not got such a good start, the race might have been over in the first fifty yards. As it was, that victim of Fate, going well, kept ahead. At the entrance to the school grounds he led by a dozen yards. The procession passed into the field, Mike heading as before for the pavilion.

As they raced across the soft turf, an idea occurred to Mike which he was accustomed in after years to attribute to genius, the one flash of it which had ever illumined his life.

It was this.

One of Mr. Downing's first acts, on starting the Fire Brigade at Sedleigh, had been to institute an alarm bell. It had been rubbed into the school officially—in speeches from the daïs—by the headmaster, and unofficially—in earnest private conversations—by Mr. Downing, that at the sound of this bell, at whatever hour of day or night, every member of the school must leave his house in the quickest possible way, and make for the open. The bell might mean that the school was on fire, or it might mean that one of the houses was on fire. In any case, the school had its orders—to get out into the open at once.

Nor must it be supposed that the school was without practice at this feat. Every now and then a notice would be found posted up on the board to the effect that there would be fire drill during the dinner hour that day. Sometimes the performance was bright and interesting, as on the occasion when Mr. Downing, marshalling the brigade at his front gate, had said, "My house is supposed to be on fire. Now let's do a record!" which the Brigade, headed by Stone and Robinson, obligingly did. They fastened the hose to the hydrant, smashed a window on the ground floor (Mr. Downing having retired for a moment to talk with the headmaster), and poured a stream of water into the room. When Mr. Downing was at liberty to turn his attention to the matter, he found that the room selected was his private study, most of the light furniture of which was floating on a miniature lake. That episode had rather discouraged his passion for realism, and fire drill since then had taken the form, for the most part, of "practising escaping." This was done by means of canvas shoots, kept in the dormitories. At the sound of the bell the prefect of the dormitory would heave one end of the shoot out of window, the other end being fastened to the sill. He would then go down it himself, using his elbows as a brake. Then the second man would follow his example, and these two, standing below, would hold the end of the shoot so that the rest of the dormitory could fly rapidly down it without injury, except to their digestions.

After the first novelty of the thing had worn off, the school had taken a rooted dislike to fire drill. It was a matter for self-congratulation among them that Mr. Downing had never been able to induce the headmaster to allow the alarm bell to be sounded for fire drill at night. The headmaster, a man who had his views on the amount of sleep necessary for the growing boy, had drawn the line at night operations. "Sufficient unto the day" had been the gist of his reply. If the alarm bell were to ring at night when there was no fire, the school might mistake a genuine alarm of fire for a bogus one, and refuse to hurry themselves.

So Mr. Downing had had to be content with day drill.

The alarm bell hung in the archway leading into the school grounds. The end of the rope, when not in use, was fastened to a hook half-way up the wall.

Mike, as he raced over the cricket field, made up his mind in a flash that his only chance of getting out of this tangle was to shake his pursuer off for a space of time long enough to enable him to get to the rope and tug it. Then the school would come out. He would mix with them, and in the subsequent confusion get back to bed unnoticed.

The task was easier than it would have seemed at the beginning of the chase. Mr. Downing, owing to the two facts that he was not in the strictest training, and that it is only an Alfred Shrubb who can run for any length of time at top speed shouting "Who is that? Stop! Who is that? Stop!" was beginning to feel distressed. There were bellows to mend in the Downing camp. Mike perceived this, and forced the pace. He rounded the pavilion ten yards to the good. Then, heading for the gate, he put all he knew into one last sprint. Mr. Downing was not equal to the effort. He worked gamely for a few strides, then fell behind. When Mike reached the gate, a good forty yards separated them.

As far as Mike could judge—he was not in a condition to make nice calculations—he had about four seconds in which to get busy with that bell rope.

Probably nobody has ever crammed more energetic work into four seconds than he did then.

The night was as still as only an English summer night can be, and the first clang of the clapper sounded like a million iron girders falling from a height on to a sheet of tin. He tugged away furiously, with an eye on the now rapidly advancing and loudly shouting figure of the housemaster.

And from the darkened house beyond there came a gradually swelling hum, as if a vast hive of bees had been disturbed.

The school was awake.

CHAPTER XLVI

THE DECORATION OF SAMMY

Psmith leaned against the mantelpiece in the senior day-room at Outwood's—since Mike's innings against Downing's the Lost Lambs had been received as brothers by that centre of disorder, so that even Spiller was compelled to look on the hatchet as buried—and gave his views on the events of the preceding night, or, rather, of that morning, for it was nearer one than twelve when peace had once more fallen on the school.

"Nothing that happens in this luny-bin," said Psmith, "has power to surprise me now. There was a time when I might have thought it a little unusual to have to leave the house through a canvas shoot at one o'clock in the morning, but I suppose it's quite the regular thing here. Old school tradition, &c. Men leave the school, and find that they've got so accustomed to jumping out of window that they look on it as a sort of affectation to go out by the door. I suppose none of you merchants can give me any idea when the next knockabout entertainment of this kind is likely to take place?"

"I wonder who rang that bell!" said Stone. "Jolly sporting idea."

"I believe it was Downing himself. If it was, I hope he's satisfied."

Jellicoe, who was appearing in society supported by a stick, looked meaningly at Mike, and giggled, receiving in answer a stony stare. Mike had informed Jellicoe of the details of his interview with Mr. Barley at the "White Boar," and Jellicoe, after a momentary splutter of wrath against the practical joker, was now in a particularly light-hearted mood. He hobbled about, giggling at nothing and at peace with all the world.

"It was a stirring scene," said Psmith. "The agility with which Comrade Jellicoe boosted himself down the shoot was a triumph of mind over matter. He seemed to forget his ankle. It was the nearest thing to a Boneless Acrobatic Wonder that I have ever seen."

"I was in a beastly funk, I can tell you."

Stone gurgled.

"So was I," he said, "for a bit. Then, when I saw that it was all a rag, I began to look about for ways of doing the thing really well. I emptied about six jugs of water on a gang of kids under my window."

"I rushed into Downing's, and ragged some of the beds," said Robinson.

"It was an invigorating time," said Psmith. "A sort of pageant. I was particularly struck with the way some of the bright lads caught hold of the idea. There was no skimping. Some of the kids, to my certain knowledge, went down the shoot a dozen times. There's nothing like doing a thing thoroughly. I saw them come down, rush upstairs, and be saved again, time after time. The thing became chronic with them. I should say Comrade Downing ought to be satisfied with the high state of efficiency to which he has brought us. At any rate I hope—"

There was a sound of hurried footsteps outside the door, and Sharpe, a member of the senior day-room, burst excitedly in. He seemed amused.

"I say, have you chaps seen Sammy?"

"Seen who?" said Stone. "Sammy? Why?"

"You'll know in a second. He's just outside. Here, Sammy, Sammy, Sammy! Sam! Sam!"

A bark and a patter of feet outside.

"Come on, Sammy. Good dog."

There was a moment's silence. Then a great yell of laughter burst forth. Even Psmith's massive calm was shattered. As for Jellicoe, he sobbed in a corner.

Sammy's beautiful white coat was almost entirely concealed by a thick covering of bright red paint. His head, with the exception of the ears, was untouched, and his serious, friendly eyes seemed to emphasise the weirdness of his appearance. He stood in the doorway, barking and wagging his tail, plainly puzzled at his reception. He was a popular dog, and was always well received when he visited any of the houses, but he had never before met with enthusiasm like this.

"Good old Sammy!"

"What on earth's been happening to him?"

"Who did it?"

Sharpe, the introducer, had no views on the matter.

"I found him outside Downing's, with a crowd round him. Everybody seems to have seen him. I wonder who on earth has gone and mucked him up like that!"

Mike was the first to show any sympathy for the maltreated animal.

"Poor old Sammy," he said, kneeling on the floor beside the victim, and scratching him under the ear. "What a beastly shame! It'll take hours to wash all that off him, and he'll hate it."

"It seems to me," said Psmith, regarding Sammy dispassionately through his eyeglass, "that it's not a case for mere washing. They'll either have to skin him bodily, or leave the thing to time. Time, the Great Healer. In a year or two he'll fade to a delicate pink. I don't see why you shouldn't have a pink bull-terrier. It would lend a touch of distinction to the place. Crowds would come in excursion trains to see him. By charging a small fee you might make him self-supporting. I think I'll suggest it to Comrade Downing."

"There'll be a row about this," said Stone.

"Rows are rather sport when you're not mixed up in them," said Robinson, philosophically. "There'll be another if we don't start off for chapel soon. It's a quarter to."

There was a general move. Mike was the last to leave the room. As he was going, Jellicoe stopped him. Jellicoe was staying in that Sunday, owing to his ankle.

"I say," said Jellicoe, "I just wanted to thank you again about that—"

"Oh, that's all right."

"No, but it really was awfully decent of you. You might have got into a frightful row. Were you nearly caught?"

"Jolly nearly."

"It was you who rang the bell, wasn't it?"

"Yes, it was. But for goodness sake don't go gassing about it, or somebody will get to hear who oughtn't to, and I shall be sacked."

"All right. But, I say, you are a chap!"

"What's the matter now?"

"I mean about Sammy, you know. It's a jolly good score off old Downing. He'll be frightfully sick."

"Sammy!" cried Mike. "My good man, you don't think I did that, do you? What absolute rot! I never touched the poor brute."

"Oh, all right," said Jellicoe. "But I wasn't going to tell any one, of course."

"What do you mean?"

"You are a chap!" giggled Jellicoe.

Mike walked to chapel rather thoughtfully.

CHAPTER XLVII

MR. DOWNING ON THE SCENT

There was just one moment, the moment in which, on going down to the junior day-room of his house to quell an unseemly disturbance, he was boisterously greeted by a vermilion bull terrier, when Mr. Downing was seized with a hideous fear lest he had lost his senses. Glaring down at the crimson animal that was pawing at his knees, he clutched at his reason for one second as a drowning man clutches at a lifebelt.

Then the happy laughter of the young onlookers reassured him.

"Who—" he shouted, "WHO has done this?"

"Please, sir, we don't know," shrilled the chorus.

"Please, sir, he came in like that."

"Please, sir, we were sitting here when he suddenly ran in, all red."

A voice from the crowd: "Look at old Sammy!"

The situation was impossible. There was nothing to be done. He could not find out by verbal inquiry who had painted the dog. The possibility of Sammy being painted red during the night had never occurred to Mr. Downing, and now that the thing had happened he had no scheme of action. As Psmith would have said, he had confused the unusual with the impossible, and the result was that he was taken by surprise.

While he was pondering on this the situation was rendered still more difficult by Sammy, who, taking advantage of the door being open, escaped and rushed into the road, thus publishing his condition to all and sundry. You can hush up a painted dog while it confines itself to your own premises, but once it has mixed with the great public this becomes out of the question. Sammy's state advanced from a private trouble into a row. Mr. Downing's next move was in the same direction that Sammy had taken, only, instead of running about the road, he went straight to the headmaster.

The Head, who had had to leave his house in the small hours in his pyjamas and a dressing-gown, was not in the best of tempers. He had a cold in the head, and also a rooted conviction that Mr. Downing, in spite of his strict orders, had rung the bell himself on the previous night in order to test the efficiency of the school in saving themselves in the event of fire. He received the housemaster frostily, but thawed as the latter related the events which had led up to the ringing of the bell.

"Dear me!" he said, deeply interested. "One of the boys at the school, you think?"

"I am certain of it," said Mr. Downing.

"Was he wearing a school cap?"

"He was bare-headed. A boy who breaks out of his house at night would hardly run the risk of wearing a distinguishing cap."

"No, no, I suppose not. A big boy, you say?"

"Very big."

"You did not see his face?"

"It was dark and he never looked back—he was in front of me all the time."

"Dear me!"

"There is another matter—"

"Yes?"

"This boy, whoever he was, had done something before he rang the bell—he had painted my dog Sampson red."

The headmaster's eyes protruded from their sockets. "He—he—what, Mr. Downing?"

190

"He painted my dog red—bright red." Mr. Downing was too angry to see anything humorous in the incident. Since the previous night he had been wounded in his tenderest feelings. His Fire Brigade system had been most shamefully abused by being turned into a mere instrument in the hands of a malefactor for escaping justice, and his dog had been held up to ridicule to all the world. He did not want to smile, he wanted revenge.

The headmaster, on the other hand, did want to smile. It was not his dog, he could look on the affair with an unbiased eye, and to him there was something ludicrous in a white dog suddenly appearing as a red dog.

"It is a scandalous thing!" said Mr. Downing.

"Quite so! Quite so!" said the headmaster hastily. "I shall punish the boy who did it most severely. I will speak to the school in the Hall after chapel."

Which he did, but without result. A cordial invitation to the criminal to come forward and be executed was received in wooden silence by the school, with the exception of Johnson III., of Outwood's, who, suddenly reminded of Sammy's appearance by the headmaster's words, broke into a wild screech of laughter, and was instantly awarded two hundred lines.

The school filed out of the Hall to their various lunches, and Mr. Downing was left with the conviction that, if he wanted the criminal discovered, he would have to discover him for himself.

The great thing in affairs of this kind is to get a good start, and Fate, feeling perhaps that it had been a little hard upon Mr. Downing, gave him a most magnificent start. Instead of having to hunt for a needle in a haystack, he found himself in a moment in the position of being set to find it in a mere truss of straw.

It was Mr. Outwood who helped him. Sergeant Collard had waylaid the archaeological expert on his way to chapel, and informed him that at close on twelve the night before he had observed a youth, unidentified, attempting to get into his house via the water-pipe. Mr. Outwood, whose thoughts were occupied with apses and plinths, not to mention cromlechs, at the time, thanked the sergeant with absent-minded politeness and passed on. Later he remembered the fact à propos of some reflections on the subject of burglars in mediaeval England, and passed it on to Mr. Downing as they walked back to lunch.

"Then the boy was in your house!" exclaimed Mr. Downing.

"Not actually in, as far as I understand. I gather from the sergeant that he interrupted him before—"

"I mean he must have been one of the boys in your house."

"But what was he doing out at that hour?"

"He had broken out."

"Impossible, I think. Oh yes, quite impossible! I went round the

191

dormitories as usual at eleven o'clock last night, and all the boys were asleep—all of them."

Mr. Downing was not listening. He was in a state of suppressed excitement and exultation which made it hard for him to attend to his colleague's slow utterances. He had a clue! Now that the search had narrowed itself down to Outwood's house, the rest was comparatively easy. Perhaps Sergeant Collard had actually recognised the boy. Or reflection he dismissed this as unlikely, for the sergeant would scarcely have kept a thing like that to himself; but he might very well have seen more of him than he, Downing, had seen. It was only with an effort that he could keep himself from rushing to the sergeant then and there, and leaving the house lunch to look after itself. He resolved to go the moment that meal was at an end.

Sunday lunch at a public-school house is probably one of the longest functions in existence. It drags its slow length along like a languid snake, but it finishes in time. In due course Mr. Downing, after sitting still and eyeing with acute dislike everybody who asked for a second helping, found himself at liberty.

Regardless of the claims of digestion, he rushed forth on the trail.

Sergeant Collard lived with his wife and a family of unknown dimensions in the lodge at the school front gate. Dinner was just over when Mr. Downing arrived, as a blind man could have told.

The sergeant received his visitor with dignity, ejecting the family, who were torpid after roast beef and resented having to move, in order to ensure privacy.

Having requested his host to smoke, which the latter was about to do unasked, Mr. Downing stated his case.

"Mr. Outwood," he said, "tells me that last night, sergeant, you saw a boy endeavouring to enter his house."

The sergeant blew a cloud of smoke. "Oo-oo-oo, yer," he said; "I did, sir—spotted 'im, I did. Feeflee good at spottin', I am, sir. Dook of Connaught, he used to say, ''Ere comes Sergeant Collard,' he used to say, ''e's feeflee good at spottin'.'"

"What did you do?"

"Do? Oo-oo-oo! I shouts 'Oo-oo-oo yer, yer young monkey, what yer doin' there?'"

"Yes?"

"But 'e was off in a flash, and I doubles after 'im prompt."

"But you didn't catch him?"

"No, sir," admitted the sergeant reluctantly.

"Did you catch sight of his face, sergeant?"

"No, sir, 'e was doublin' away in the opposite direction."

"Did you notice anything at all about his appearance?"

"'E was a long young chap, sir, with a pair of legs on him—feeflee fast 'e run, sir. Oo-oo-oo, feeflee!"

"You noticed nothing else?"

192

"'E wasn't wearing no cap of any sort, sir."

"Ah!"

"Bare-'eaded, sir," added the sergeant, rubbing the point in.

"It was undoubtedly the same boy, undoubtedly! I wish you could have caught a glimpse of his face, sergeant."

"So do I, sir."

"You would not be able to recognise him again if you saw him, you think?"

"Oo-oo-oo! Wouldn't go so far as to say that, sir, 'cos yer see, I'm feeflee good at spottin', but it was a dark night."

Mr. Downing rose to go.

"Well," he said, "the search is now considerably narrowed down, considerably! It is certain that the boy was one of the boys in Mr. Outwood's house."

"Young monkeys!" interjected the sergeant helpfully.

"Good-afternoon, sergeant."

"Good-afternoon to you, sir."

"Pray do not move, sergeant."

The sergeant had not shown the slightest inclination of doing anything of the kind.

"I will find my way out. Very hot to-day, is it not?"

"Feeflee warm, sir; weather's goin' to break—workin' up for thunder."

"I hope not. The school plays the M.C.C. on Wednesday, and it would be a pity if rain were to spoil our first fixture with them. Good afternoon."

And Mr. Downing went out into the baking sunlight, while Sergeant Collard, having requested Mrs. Collard to take the children out for a walk at once, and furthermore to give young Ernie a clip side of the 'ead, if he persisted in making so much noise, put a handkerchief over his face, rested his feet on the table, and slept the sleep of the just.

CHAPTER XLVIII

THE SLEUTH-HOUND

For the Doctor Watsons of this world, as opposed to the Sherlock Holmeses, success in the province of detective work must always be, to a very large extent, the result of luck. Sherlock Holmes can extract a clue from a wisp of straw or a flake of cigar-ash. But Doctor Watson

193

has got to have it taken out for him, and dusted, and exhibited clearly, with a label attached.

The average man is a Doctor Watson. We are wont to scoff in a patronising manner at that humble follower of the great investigator, but, as a matter of fact, we should have been just as dull ourselves. We should not even have risen to the modest level of a Scotland Yard Bungler. We should simply have hung around, saying:

"My dear Holmes, how—?" and all the rest of it, just as the downtrodden medico did.

It is not often that the ordinary person has any need to see what he can do in the way of detection. He gets along very comfortably in the humdrum round of life without having to measure footprints and smile quiet, tight-lipped smiles. But if ever the emergency does arise, he thinks naturally of Sherlock Holmes, and his methods.

Mr. Downing had read all the Holmes stories with great attention, and had thought many times what an incompetent ass Doctor Watson was; but, now that he had started to handle his own first case, he was compelled to admit that there was a good deal to be said in extenuation of Watson's inability to unravel tangles. It certainly was uncommonly hard, he thought, as he paced the cricket field after leaving Sergeant Collard, to detect anybody, unless you knew who had really done the crime. As he brooded over the case in hand, his sympathy for Dr. Watson increased with every minute, and he began to feel a certain resentment against Sir Arthur Conan Doyle. It was all very well for Sir Arthur to be so shrewd and infallible about tracing a mystery to its source, but he knew perfectly well who had done the thing before he started!

Now that he began really to look into this matter of the alarm bell and the painting of Sammy, the conviction was creeping over him that the problem was more difficult than a casual observer might imagine. He had got as far as finding that his quarry of the previous night was a boy in Mr. Outwood's house, but how was he to get any farther? That was the thing. There were, of course, only a limited number of boys in Mr. Outwood's house as tall as the one he had pursued; but even if there had been only one other, it would have complicated matters. If you go to a boy and say, "Either you or Jones were out of your house last night at twelve o'clock," the boy does not reply, "Sir, I cannot tell a lie—I was out of my house last night at twelve o'clock." He simply assumes the animated expression of a stuffed fish, and leaves the next move to you. It is practically Stalemate.

All these things passed through Mr. Downing's mind as he walked up and down the cricket field that afternoon.

What he wanted was a clue. But it is so hard for the novice to tell what is a clue and what isn't. Probably, if he only knew, there were clues lying all over the place, shouting to him to pick them up.

What with the oppressive heat of the day and the fatigue of hard thinking, Mr. Downing was working up for a brain-storm, when Fate once more intervened, this time in the shape of Riglett, a junior member of his house.

Riglett slunk up in the shamefaced way peculiar to some boys, even when they have done nothing wrong, and, having capped Mr. Downing with the air of one who has been caught in the act of doing something particularly shady, requested that he might be allowed to fetch his bicycle from the shed.

"Your bicycle?" snapped Mr. Downing. Much thinking had made him irritable. "What do you want with your bicycle?"

Riglett shuffled, stood first on his left foot, then on his right, blushed, and finally remarked, as if it were not so much a sound reason as a sort of feeble excuse for the low and blackguardly fact that he wanted his bicycle, that he had got leave for tea that afternoon.

Then Mr. Downing remembered. Riglett had an aunt resident about three miles from the school, whom he was accustomed to visit occasionally on Sunday afternoons during the term.

He felt for his bunch of keys, and made his way to the shed, Riglett shambling behind at an interval of two yards.

Mr. Downing unlocked the door, and there on the floor was the Clue!

A clue that even Dr. Watson could not have overlooked.

Mr. Downing saw it, but did not immediately recognise it for what it was. What he saw at first was not a Clue, but just a mess. He had a tidy soul and abhorred messes. And this was a particularly messy mess. The greater part of the flooring in the neighbourhood of the door was a sea of red paint. The tin from which it had flowed was lying on its side in the middle of the shed. The air was full of the pungent scent.

"Pah!" said Mr. Downing.

Then suddenly, beneath the disguise of the mess, he saw the clue. A foot-mark! No less. A crimson foot-mark on the grey concrete!

Riglett, who had been waiting patiently two yards away, now coughed plaintively. The sound recalled Mr. Downing to mundane matters.

"Get your bicycle, Riglett," he said, "and be careful where you tread. Somebody has upset a pot of paint on the floor."

Riglett, walking delicately through dry places, extracted his bicycle from the rack, and presently departed to gladden the heart of his aunt, leaving Mr. Downing, his brain fizzing with the enthusiasm of the detective, to lock the door and resume his perambulation of the cricket field.

Give Dr. Watson a fair start, and he is a demon at the game. Mr. Downing's brain was now working with a rapidity and clearness which a professional sleuth might have envied.

Paint. Red paint. Obviously the same paint with which Sammy

195

had been decorated. A foot-mark. Whose foot-mark? Plainly that of the criminal who had done the deed of decoration.

Yoicks!

There were two things, however, to be considered. Your careful detective must consider everything. In the first place, the paint might have been upset by the ground-man. It was the ground-man's paint. He had been giving a fresh coating to the wood-work in front of the pavilion scoring-box at the conclusion of yesterday's match. (A labour of love which was the direct outcome of the enthusiasm for work which Adair had instilled into him.) In that case the foot-mark might be his.

Note one: Interview the ground-man on this point.

In the second place Adair might have upset the tin and trodden in its contents when he went to get his bicycle in order to fetch the doctor for the suffering MacPhee. This was the more probable of the two contingencies, for it would have been dark in the shed when Adair went into it.

Note two Interview Adair as to whether he found, on returning to the house, that there was paint on his boots.

Things were moving.

He resolved to take Adair first. He could get the ground-man's address from him.

Passing by the trees under whose shade Mike and Psmith and Dunster had watched the match on the previous day, he came upon the Head of his house in a deck-chair reading a book. A summer Sunday afternoon is the time for reading in deck-chairs.

"Oh, Adair," he said. "No, don't get up. I merely wished to ask you if you found any paint on your boots when you returned to the house last night?"

"Paint, sir?" Adair was plainly puzzled. His book had been interesting, and had driven the Sammy incident out of his head.

"I see somebody has spilt some paint on the floor of the bicycle shed. You did not do that, I suppose, when you went to fetch your bicycle?"

"No, sir."

"It is spilt all over the floor. I wondered whether you had happened to tread in it. But you say you found no paint on your boots this morning?"

"No, sir, my bicycle is always quite near the door of the shed. I didn't go into the shed at all."

"I see. Quite so. Thank you, Adair. Oh, by the way, Adair, where does Markby live?"

"I forget the name of his cottage, sir, but I could show you in a second. It's one of those cottages just past the school gates, on the right as you turn out into the road. There are three in a row. His is the first you come to. There's a barn just before you get to them."

"Thank you. I shall be able to find them. I should like to speak to Markby for a moment on a small matter."

A sharp walk took him to the cottages Adair had mentioned. He rapped at the door of the first, and the ground-man came out in his shirt-sleeves, blinking as if he had just woke up, as was indeed the case.

"Oh, Markby!"

"Sir?"

"You remember that you were painting the scoring-box in the pavilion last night after the match?"

"Yes, sir. It wanted a lick of paint bad. The young gentlemen will scramble about and get through the window. Makes it look shabby, sir. So I thought I'd better give it a coating so as to look ship-shape when the Marylebone come down."

"Just so. An excellent idea. Tell me, Markby, what did you do with the pot of paint when you had finished?"

"Put it in the bicycle shed, sir."

"On the floor?"

"On the floor, sir? No. On the shelf at the far end, with the can of whitening what I use for marking out the wickets, sir."

"Of course, yes. Quite so. Just as I thought."

"Do you want it, sir?"

"No, thank you, Markby, no, thank you. The fact is, somebody who had no business to do so has moved the pot of paint from the shelf to the floor, with the result that it has been kicked over, and spilt. You had better get some more to-morrow. Thank you, Markby. That is all I wished to know."

Mr. Downing walked back to the school thoroughly excited. He was hot on the scent now. The only other possible theories had been tested and successfully exploded. The thing had become simple to a degree. All he had to do was to go to Mr. Outwood's house—the idea of searching a fellow-master's house did not appear to him at all a delicate task; somehow one grew unconsciously to feel that Mr. Outwood did not really exist as a man capable of resenting liberties—find the paint-splashed boot, ascertain its owner, and denounce him to the headmaster. Picture, Blue Fire and "God Save the King" by the full strength of the company. There could be no doubt that a paint-splashed boot must be in Mr. Outwood's house somewhere. A boy cannot tread in a pool of paint without showing some signs of having done so. It was Sunday, too, so that the boot would not yet have been cleaned. Yoicks! Also Tally-ho! This really was beginning to be something like business.

Regardless of the heat, the sleuth-hound hurried across to Outwood's as fast as he could walk.

CHAPTER XLIX

A CHECK

The only two members of the house not out in the grounds when he arrived were Mike and Psmith. They were standing on the gravel drive in front of the boys' entrance. Mike had a deck-chair in one hand and a book in the other. Psmith—for even the greatest minds will sometimes unbend—was playing diabolo. That is to say, he was trying without success to raise the spool from the ground.

"There's a kid in France," said Mike disparagingly, as the bobbin rolled off the string for the fourth time, "who can do it three thousand seven hundred and something times."

Psmith smoothed a crease out of his waistcoat and tried again. He had just succeeded in getting the thing to spin when Mr. Downing arrived. The sound of his footsteps disturbed Psmith and brought the effort to nothing.

"Enough of this spoolery," said he, flinging the sticks through the open window of the senior day-room. "I was an ass ever to try it. The philosophical mind needs complete repose in its hours of leisure. Hullo!"

He stared after the sleuth-hound, who had just entered the house.

"What the dickens," said Mike, "does he mean by barging in as if he'd bought the place?"

"Comrade Downing looks pleased with himself. What brings him round in this direction, I wonder! Still, no matter. The few articles which he may sneak from our study are of inconsiderable value. He is welcome to them. Do you feel inclined to wait awhile till I have fetched a chair and book?"

"I'll be going on. I shall be under the trees at the far end of the ground."

"'Tis well. I will be with you in about two ticks."

Mike walked on towards the field, and Psmith, strolling upstairs to fetch his novel, found Mr. Downing standing in the passage with the air of one who has lost his bearings.

"A warm afternoon, sir," murmured Psmith courteously, as he passed.

"Er—Smith!"

"Sir?"

"I—er—wish to go round the dormitories."

It was Psmith's guiding rule in life never to be surprised at anything, so he merely inclined his head gracefully, and said nothing.

"I should be glad if you would fetch the keys and show me where the rooms are."

"With acute pleasure, sir," said Psmith. "Or shall I fetch Mr. Outwood, sir?"

"Do as I tell you, Smith," snapped Mr. Downing.

Psmith said no more, but went down to the matron's room. The matron being out, he abstracted the bunch of keys from her table and rejoined the master.

"Shall I lead the way, sir?" he asked.

Mr. Downing nodded.

"Here, sir," said Psmith, opening a door, "we have Barnes' dormitory. An airy room, constructed on the soundest hygienic principles. Each boy, I understand, has quite a considerable number of cubic feet of air all to himself. It is Mr. Outwood's boast that no boy has ever asked for a cubic foot of air in vain. He argues justly—"

He broke off abruptly and began to watch the other's manoeuvres in silence. Mr. Downing was peering rapidly beneath each bed in turn.

"Are you looking for Barnes, sir?" inquired Psmith politely. "I think he's out in the field."

Mr. Downing rose, having examined the last bed, crimson in the face with the exercise.

"Show me the next dormitory, Smith," he said, panting slightly.

"This," said Psmith, opening the next door and sinking his voice to an awed whisper, "is where I sleep!"

Mr. Downing glanced swiftly beneath the three beds. "Excuse me, sir," said Psmith, "but are we chasing anything?"

"Be good enough, Smith," said Mr. Downing with asperity, "to keep your remarks to yourself."

"I was only wondering, sir. Shall I show you the next in order?"

"Certainly."

They moved on up the passage.

Drawing blank at the last dormitory, Mr. Downing paused, baffled. Psmith waited patiently by. An idea struck the master.

"The studies, Smith," he cried.

"Aha!" said Psmith. "I beg your pardon, sir. The observation escaped me unawares. The frenzy of the chase is beginning to enter into my blood. Here we have—"

Mr. Downing stopped short.

"Is this impertinence studied, Smith?"

"Ferguson's study, sir? No, sir. That's further down the passage. This is Barnes'."

Mr. Downing looked at him closely. Psmith's face was wooden in its gravity. The master snorted suspiciously, then moved on.

"Whose is this?" he asked, rapping a door.

"This, sir, is mine and Jackson's."

199

"What! Have you a study? You are low down in the school for it."

"I think, sir, that Mr. Outwood gave it us rather as a testimonial to our general worth than to our proficiency in school-work."

Mr. Downing raked the room with a keen eye. The absence of bars from the window attracted his attention.

"Have you no bars to your windows here, such as there are in my house?"

"There appears to be no bar, sir," said Psmith, putting up his eyeglass.

Mr Downing was leaning out of the window.

"A lovely view, is it not, sir?" said Psmith. "The trees, the field, the distant hills—"

Mr. Downing suddenly started. His eye had been caught by the water-pipe at the side of the window. The boy whom Sergeant Collard had seen climbing the pipe must have been making for this study.

He spun round and met Psmith's blandly inquiring gaze. He looked at Psmith carefully for a moment. No. The boy he had chased last night had not been Psmith. That exquisite's figure and general appearance were unmistakable, even in the dusk.

"Whom did you say you shared this study with, Smith?"

"Jackson, sir. The cricketer."

"Never mind about his cricket, Smith," said Mr. Downing with irritation.

"No, sir."

"He is the only other occupant of the room?"

"Yes, sir."

"Nobody else comes into it?"

"If they do, they go out extremely quickly, sir."

"Ah! Thank you, Smith."

"Not at all, sir."

Mr. Downing pondered. Jackson! The boy bore him a grudge. The boy was precisely the sort of boy to revenge himself by painting the dog Sammy. And, gadzooks! The boy whom he had pursued last night had been just about Jackson's size and build!

Mr. Downing was as firmly convinced at that moment that Mike's had been the hand to wield the paint-brush as he had ever been of anything in his life.

"Smith!" he said excitedly.

"On the spot, sir," said Psmith affably.

"Where are Jackson's boots?"

There are moments when the giddy excitement of being right on the trail causes the amateur (or Watsonian) detective to be incautious. Such a moment came to Mr. Downing then. If he had been wise, he would have achieved his object, the getting a glimpse of Mike's boots, by a devious and snaky route. As it was, he rushed straight on.

"His boots, sir? He has them on. I noticed them as he went out just now."

"Where is the pair he wore yesterday?"

"Where are the boots of yester-year?" murmured Psmith to himself. "I should say at a venture, sir, that they would be in the basket downstairs. Edmund, our genial knife-and-boot boy, collects them, I believe, at early dawn."

"Would they have been cleaned yet?"

"If I know Edmund, sir—no."

"Smith," said Mr. Downing, trembling with excitement, "go and bring that basket to me here."

Psmith's brain was working rapidly as he went downstairs. What exactly was at the back of the sleuth's mind, prompting these manoeuvres, he did not know. But that there was something, and that that something was directed in a hostile manner against Mike, probably in connection with last night's wild happenings, he was certain. Psmith had noticed, on leaving his bed at the sound of the alarm bell, that he and Jellicoe were alone in the room. That might mean that Mike had gone out through the door when the bell sounded, or it might mean that he had been out all the time. It began to look as if the latter solution were the correct one.

He staggered back with the basket, painfully conscious the while that it was creasing his waistcoat, and dumped it down on the study floor. Mr. Downing stooped eagerly over it. Psmith leaned against the wall, and straightened out the damaged garment.

"We have here, sir," he said, "a fair selection of our various bootings."

Mr. Downing looked up.

"You dropped none of the boots on your way up, Smith?"

"Not one, sir. It was a fine performance."

Mr. Downing uttered a grunt of satisfaction, and bent once more to his task. Boots flew about the room. Mr. Downing knelt on the floor beside the basket, and dug like a terrier at a rat-hole.

At last he made a dive, and, with an exclamation of triumph, rose to his feet. In his hand he held a boot.

"Put those back again, Smith," he said.

The ex-Etonian, wearing an expression such as a martyr might have worn on being told off for the stake, began to pick up the scattered footgear, whistling softly the tune of "I do all the dirty work," as he did so.

"That's the lot, sir," he said, rising.

"Ah. Now come across with me to the headmaster's house. Leave the basket here. You can carry it back when you return."

"Shall I put back that boot, sir?"

"Certainly not. I shall take this with me, of course."

"Shall I carry it, sir?"

201

Mr. Downing reflected.

"Yes, Smith," he said. "I think it would be best."

It occurred to him that the spectacle of a housemaster wandering abroad on the public highway, carrying a dirty boot, might be a trifle undignified. You never knew whom you might meet on Sunday afternoon.

Psmith took the boot, and doing so, understood what before had puzzled him.

Across the toe of the boot was a broad splash of red paint.

He knew nothing, of course, of the upset tin in the bicycle shed; but when a housemaster's dog has been painted red in the night, and when, on the following day, the housemaster goes about in search of a paint-splashed boot, one puts two and two together. Psmith looked at the name inside the boot. It was "Brown, boot-maker, Bridgnorth." Bridgnorth was only a few miles from his own home and Mike's. Undoubtedly it was Mike's boot.

"Can you tell me whose boot that is?" asked Mr. Downing.

Psmith looked at it again.

"No, sir. I can't say the little chap's familiar to me."

"Come with me, then."

Mr. Downing left the room. After a moment Psmith followed him.

The headmaster was in his garden. Thither Mr. Downing made his way, the boot-bearing Psmith in close attendance.

The Head listened to the amateur detective's statement with interest.

"Indeed?" he said, when Mr. Downing had finished.

"Indeed? Dear me! It certainly seems—It is a curiously well-connected thread of evidence. You are certain that there was red paint on this boot you discovered in Mr. Outwood's house?"

"I have it with me. I brought it on purpose to show to you. Smith!"

"Sir?"

"You have the boot?"

"Ah," said the headmaster, putting on a pair of pince-nez, "now let me look at—This, you say, is the—? Just so. Just so. Just.... But, er, Mr. Downing, it may be that I have not examined this boot with sufficient care, but—Can you point out to me exactly where this paint is that you speak of?"

Mr. Downing stood staring at the boot with a wild, fixed stare. Of any suspicion of paint, red or otherwise, it was absolutely and entirely innocent.

CHAPTER L

THE DESTROYER OF EVIDENCE

The boot became the centre of attraction, the cynosure of all eyes. Mr. Downing fixed it with the piercing stare of one who feels that his brain is tottering. The headmaster looked at it with a mildly puzzled expression. Psmith, putting up his eyeglass, gazed at it with a sort of affectionate interest, as if he were waiting for it to do a trick of some kind.

Mr. Downing was the first to break the silence.

"There was paint on this boot," he said vehemently. "I tell you there was a splash of red paint across the toe. Smith will bear me out in this. Smith, you saw the paint on this boot?"

"Paint, sir!"

"What! Do you mean to tell me that you did not see it?"

"No, sir. There was no paint on this boot."

"This is foolery. I saw it with my own eyes. It was a broad splash right across the toe."

The headmaster interposed.

"You must have made a mistake, Mr. Downing. There is certainly no trace of paint on this boot. These momentary optical delusions are, I fancy, not uncommon. Any doctor will tell you—"

"I had an aunt, sir," said Psmith chattily, "who was remarkably subject—"

"It is absurd. I cannot have been mistaken," said Mr. Downing. "I am positively certain the toe of this boot was red when I found it."

"It is undoubtedly black now, Mr. Downing."

"A sort of chameleon boot," murmured Psmith.

The goaded housemaster turned on him.

"What did you say, Smith?"

"Did I speak, sir?" said Psmith, with the start of one coming suddenly out of a trance.

Mr. Downing looked searchingly at him.

"You had better be careful, Smith."

"Yes, sir."

"I strongly suspect you of having something to do with this."

"Really, Mr. Downing," said the headmaster, "that is surely improbable. Smith could scarcely have cleaned the boot on his way to my house. On one occasion I inadvertently spilt some paint on a shoe of my own. I can assure you that it does not brush off. It needs a very systematic cleaning before all traces are removed."

"Exactly, sir," said Psmith. "My theory, if I may—?"

"Certainly, Smith."

Psmith bowed courteously and proceeded.

"My theory, sir, is that Mr. Downing was deceived by the light and shade effects on the toe of the boot. The afternoon sun, streaming in through the window, must have shone on the boot in such a manner as to give it a momentary and fictitious aspect of redness. If Mr. Downing recollects, he did not look long at the boot. The picture on the retina of the eye, consequently, had not time to fade. I remember thinking myself, at the moment, that the boot appeared to have a certain reddish tint. The mistake—"

"Bah!" said Mr. Downing shortly.

"Well, really," said the headmaster, "it seems to me that that is the only explanation that will square with the facts. A boot that is really smeared with red paint does not become black of itself in the course of a few minutes."

"You are very right, sir," said Psmith with benevolent approval. "May I go now, sir? I am in the middle of a singularly impressive passage of Cicero's speech De Senectute."

"I am sorry that you should leave your preparation till Sunday, Smith. It is a habit of which I altogether disapprove."

"I am reading it, sir," said Psmith, with simple dignity, "for pleasure. Shall I take the boot with me, sir?"

"If Mr. Downing does not want it?"

The housemaster passed the fraudulent piece of evidence to Psmith without a word, and the latter, having included both masters in a kindly smile, left the garden.

Pedestrians who had the good fortune to be passing along the road between the housemaster's house and Mr. Outwood's at that moment saw what, if they had but known it, was a most unusual sight, the spectacle of Psmith running. Psmith's usual mode of progression was a dignified walk. He believed in the contemplative style rather than the hustling.

On this occasion, however, reckless of possible injuries to the crease of his trousers, he raced down the road, and turning in at Outwood's gate, bounded upstairs like a highly trained professional athlete.

On arriving at the study, his first act was to remove a boot from the top of the pile in the basket, place it in the small cupboard under the bookshelf, and lock the cupboard. Then he flung himself into a chair and panted.

"Brain," he said to himself approvingly, "is what one chiefly needs in matters of this kind. Without brain, where are we? In the soup, every time. The next development will be when Comrade Downing thinks it over, and is struck with the brilliant idea that it's just possible that the boot he gave me to carry and the boot I did carry were not one boot but two boots. Meanwhile—"

He dragged up another chair for his feet and picked up his novel.

He had not been reading long when there was a footstep in the passage, and Mr. Downing appeared.

The possibility, in fact the probability, of Psmith having substituted another boot for the one with the incriminating splash of paint on it had occurred to him almost immediately on leaving the headmaster's garden. Psmith and Mike, he reflected, were friends. Psmith's impulse would be to do all that lay in his power to shield Mike. Feeling aggrieved with himself that he had not thought of this before, he, too, hurried over to Outwood's.

Mr. Downing was brisk and peremptory.

"I wish to look at these boots again," he said. Psmith, with a sigh, laid down his novel, and rose to assist him.

"Sit down, Smith," said the housemaster. "I can manage without your help."

Psmith sat down again, carefully tucking up the knees of his trousers, and watched him with silent interest through his eyeglass.

The scrutiny irritated Mr. Downing.

"Put that thing away, Smith," he said.

"That thing, sir?"

"Yes, that ridiculous glass. Put it away."

"Why, sir?"

"Why! Because I tell you to do so."

"I guessed that that was the reason, sir," sighed Psmith replacing the eyeglass in his waistcoat pocket. He rested his elbows on his knees, and his chin on his hands, and resumed his contemplative inspection of the boot-expert, who, after fidgeting for a few moments, lodged another complaint.

"Don't sit there staring at me, Smith."

"I was interested in what you were doing, sir."

"Never mind. Don't stare at me in that idiotic way."

"May I read, sir?" asked Psmith, patiently.

"Yes, read if you like."

"Thank you, sir."

Psmith took up his book again, and Mr. Downing, now thoroughly irritated, pursued his investigations in the boot-basket.

He went through it twice, but each time without success. After the second search, he stood up, and looked wildly round the room. He was as certain as he could be of anything that the missing piece of evidence was somewhere in the study. It was no use asking Psmith point-blank where it was, for Psmith's ability to parry dangerous questions with evasive answers was quite out of the common.

His eye roamed about the room. There was very little cover there, even for so small a fugitive as a number nine boot. The floor could be acquitted, on sight, of harbouring the quarry.

Then he caught sight of the cupboard, and something seemed to tell him that there was the place to look.

"Smith!" he said.

Psmith had been reading placidly all the while.

"Yes, sir?"

"What is in this cupboard?"

"That cupboard, sir?"

"Yes. This cupboard." Mr. Downing rapped the door irritably.

"Just a few odd trifles, sir. We do not often use it. A ball of string, perhaps. Possibly an old note-book. Nothing of value or interest."

"Open it."

"I think you will find that it is locked, sir."

"Unlock it."

"But where is the key, sir?"

"Have you not got the key?"

"If the key is not in the lock, sir, you may depend upon it that it will take a long search to find it."

"Where did you see it last?"

"It was in the lock yesterday morning. Jackson might have taken it."

"Where is Jackson?"

"Out in the field somewhere, sir."

Mr. Downing thought for a moment.

"I don't believe a word of it," he said shortly. "I have my reasons for thinking that you are deliberately keeping the contents of that cupboard from me. I shall break open the door."

Psmith got up.

"I'm afraid you mustn't do that, sir."

Mr. Downing stared, amazed.

"Are you aware whom you are talking to, Smith?" he inquired acidly.

"Yes, sir. And I know it's not Mr. Outwood, to whom that cupboard happens to belong. If you wish to break it open, you must get his permission. He is the sole lessee and proprietor of that cupboard. I am only the acting manager."

Mr. Downing paused. He also reflected. Mr. Outwood in the general rule did not count much in the scheme of things, but possibly there were limits to the treating of him as if he did not exist. To enter his house without his permission and search it to a certain extent was all very well. But when it came to breaking up his furniture, perhaps—!

On the other hand, there was the maddening thought that if he left the study in search of Mr. Outwood, in order to obtain his sanction for the house-breaking work which he proposed to carry through, Smith would be alone in the room. And he knew that, if Smith were left alone in the room, he would instantly remove the boot to some other hiding-place. He thoroughly disbelieved the story of the lost key. He was perfectly convinced that the missing boot was in the cupboard.

206

He stood chewing these thoughts for awhile, Psmith in the meantime standing in a graceful attitude in front of the cupboard, staring into vacancy.

Then he was seized with a happy idea. Why should he leave the room at all? If he sent Smith, then he himself could wait and make certain that the cupboard was not tampered with.

"Smith," he said, "go and find Mr. Outwood, and ask him to be good enough to come here for a moment."

CHAPTER LI

MAINLY ABOUT BOOTS

"Be quick, Smith," he said, as the latter stood looking at him without making any movement in the direction of the door.

"Quick, sir?" said Psmith meditatively, as if he had been asked a conundrum.

"Go and find Mr. Outwood at once."

Psmith still made no move.

"Do you intend to disobey me, Smith?" Mr. Downing's voice was steely.

"Yes, sir."

"What!"

"Yes, sir."

There was one of those you-could-have-heard-a-pin-drop silences. Psmith was staring reflectively at the ceiling. Mr. Downing was looking as if at any moment he might say, "Thwarted to me face, ha, ha! And by a very stripling!"

It was Psmith, however, who resumed the conversation. His manner was almost too respectful; which made it all the more a pity that what he said did not keep up the standard of docility.

"I take my stand," he said, "on a technical point. I say to myself, 'Mr. Downing is a man I admire as a human being and respect as a master. In—'"

"This impertinence is doing you no good, Smith."

Psmith waved a hand deprecatingly.

"If you will let me explain, sir. I was about to say that in any other place but Mr. Outwood's house, your word would be law. I would fly to do your bidding. If you pressed a button, I would do the rest. But in Mr. Outwood's house I cannot do anything except what pleases me or what is ordered by Mr. Outwood. I ought to have remembered that before. One cannot," he continued, as who should say, "Let us be reasonable," "one cannot, to take a parallel case, imagine the colonel commanding the garrison at a naval station going on board a battleship and ordering the crew to splice the jibboom spanker. It might be an admirable thing for the Empire that the jibboom spanker should be spliced at that particular juncture, but the crew would naturally decline to move in the matter until the order came from the commander of the ship. So in my case. If you will go to Mr. Outwood, and explain to him how matters stand, and come back and say to me, 'Psmith, Mr. Outwood wishes you to ask him to be good enough to come to this study,' then I shall be only too glad to go and find him. You see my difficulty, sir?"

"Go and fetch Mr. Outwood, Smith. I shall not tell you again."

Psmith flicked a speck of dust from his coat-sleeve.

"Very well, Smith."

"I can assure you, sir, at any rate, that if there is a boot in that cupboard now, there will be a boot there when you return."

Mr. Downing stalked out of the room.

"But," added Psmith pensively to himself, as the footsteps died away, "I did not promise that it would be the same boot."

He took the key from his pocket, unlocked the cupboard, and took out the boot. Then he selected from the basket a particularly battered specimen. Placing this in the cupboard, he re-locked the door.

His next act was to take from the shelf a piece of string. Attaching one end of this to the boot that he had taken from the cupboard, he went to the window. His first act was to fling the cupboard-key out into the bushes. Then he turned to the boot. On a level with the sill the water-pipe, up which Mike had started to climb the night before, was fastened to the wall by an iron band. He tied the other end of the string to this, and let the boot swing free. He noticed with approval, when it had stopped swinging, that it was hidden from above by the window-sill.

He returned to his place at the mantelpiece.

As an after-thought he took another boot from the basket, and thrust it up the chimney. A shower of soot fell into the grate, blackening his hand.

The bathroom was a few yards down the corridor. He went there, and washed off the soot.

When he returned, Mr. Downing was in the study, and with him Mr. Outwood, the latter looking dazed, as if he were not quite equal to the intellectual pressure of the situation.

"Where have you been, Smith?" asked Mr. Downing sharply.

"I have been washing my hands, sir."

"H'm!" said Mr. Downing suspiciously.

"Yes, I saw Smith go into the bathroom," said Mr. Outwood.

"Smith, I cannot quite understand what it is Mr. Downing wishes me to do."

"My dear Outwood," snapped the sleuth, "I thought I had made it perfectly clear. Where is the difficulty?"

"I cannot understand why you should suspect Smith of keeping his boots in a cupboard, and," added Mr. Outwood with spirit, catching sight of a Good-Gracious-has-the-man-no-sense look on the other's face," why he should not do so if he wishes it."

"Exactly, sir," said Psmith, approvingly. "You have touched the spot."

"If I must explain again, my dear Outwood, will you kindly give me your attention for a moment. Last night a boy broke out of your house, and painted my dog Sampson red."

"He painted—!" said Mr. Outwood, round-eyed. "Why?"

"I don't know why. At any rate, he did. During the escapade one of his boots was splashed with the paint. It is that boot which I believe Smith to be concealing in this cupboard. Now, do you understand?"

Mr. Outwood looked amazedly at Smith, and Psmith shook his head sorrowfully at Mr. Outwood. Psmith'a expression said, as plainly as if he had spoken the words, "We must humour him."

"So with your permission, as Smith declares that he has lost the key, I propose to break open the door of this cupboard. Have you any objection?"

Mr. Outwood started.

"Objection? None at all, my dear fellow, none at all. Let me see, what is it you wish to do?"

"This," said Mr. Downing shortly.

There was a pair of dumb-bells on the floor, belonging to Mike. He never used them, but they always managed to get themselves packed with the rest of his belongings on the last day of the holidays. Mr. Downing seized one of these, and delivered two rapid blows at the cupboard-door. The wood splintered. A third blow smashed the flimsy lock. The cupboard, with any skeletons it might contain, was open for all to view.

Mr. Downing uttered a cry of triumph, and tore the boot from its resting-place.

"I told you," he said. "I told you."

"I wondered where that boot had got to," said Psmith. "I've been looking for it for days."

Mr. Downing was examining his find. He looked up with an exclamation of surprise and wrath.

"This boot has no paint on it," he said, glaring at Psmith. "This is not the boot."

"It certainly appears, sir," said Psmith sympathetically, "to be free from paint. There's a sort of reddish glow just there, if you look at it sideways," he added helpfully.

209

"Did you place that boot there, Smith?"

"I must have done. Then, when I lost the key—"

"Are you satisfied now, Downing?" interrupted Mr. Outwood with asperity, "or is there any more furniture you wish to break?"

The excitement of seeing his household goods smashed with a dumb-bell had made the archaeological student quite a swashbuckler for the moment. A little more, and one could imagine him giving Mr. Downing a good, hard knock.

The sleuth-hound stood still for a moment, baffled. But his brain was working with the rapidity of a buzz-saw. A chance remark of Mr. Outwood's set him fizzing off on the trail once more. Mr. Outwood had caught sight of the little pile of soot in the grate. He bent down to inspect it.

"Dear me," he said, "I must remember to have the chimneys swept. It should have been done before."

Mr. Downing's eye, rolling in a fine frenzy from heaven to earth, from earth to heaven, also focussed itself on the pile of soot; and a thrill went through him. Soot in the fireplace! Smith washing his hands! ("You know my methods, my dear Watson. Apply them.")

Mr. Downing's mind at that moment contained one single thought; and that thought was "What ho for the chimney!"

He dived forward with a rush, nearly knocking Mr. Outwood off his feet, and thrust an arm up into the unknown. An avalanche of soot fell upon his hand and wrist, but he ignored it, for at the same instant his fingers had closed upon what he was seeking.

"Ah," he said. "I thought as much. You were not quite clever enough, after all, Smith."

"No, sir," said Psmith patiently. "We all make mistakes."

"You would have done better, Smith, not to have given me all this trouble. You have done yourself no good by it."

"It's been great fun, though, sir," argued Psmith.

"Fun!" Mr. Downing laughed grimly. "You may have reason to change your opinion of what constitutes—"

His voice failed as his eye fell on the all-black toe of the boot. He looked up, and caught Psmith's benevolent gaze. He straightened himself and brushed a bead of perspiration from his face with the back of his hand. Unfortunately, he used the sooty hand, and the result was like some gruesome burlesque of a nigger minstrel.

"Did—you—put—that—boot—there, Smith?" he asked slowly.

"Yes, sir."

"Then what did you MEAN by putting it there?" roared Mr. Downing.

"Animal spirits, sir," said Psmith.

"WHAT!"

"Animal spirits, sir."

What Mr. Downing would have replied to this one cannot tell,

210

though one can guess roughly. For, just as he was opening his mouth, Mr. Outwood, catching sight of his Chirgwin-like countenance, intervened.

"My dear Downing," he said, "your face. It is positively covered with soot, positively. You must come and wash it. You are quite black. Really, you present a most curious appearance, most. Let me show you the way to my room."

In all times of storm and tribulation there comes a breaking-point, a point where the spirit definitely refuses to battle any longer against the slings and arrows of outrageous fortune. Mr. Downing could not bear up against this crowning blow. He went down beneath it. In the language of the Ring, he took the count. It was the knock-out.

"Soot!" he murmured weakly. "Soot!"

"Your face is covered, my dear fellow, quite covered."

"It certainly has a faintly sooty aspect, sir," said Psmith.

His voice roused the sufferer to one last flicker of spirit.

"You will hear more of this, Smith," he said. "I say you will hear more of it."

Then he allowed Mr. Outwood to lead him out to a place where there were towels, soap, and sponges.

When they had gone, Psmith went to the window, and hauled in the string. He felt the calm after-glow which comes to the general after a successfully conducted battle. It had been trying, of course, for a man of refinement, and it had cut into his afternoon, but on the whole it had been worth it.

The problem now was what to do with the painted boot. It would take a lot of cleaning, he saw, even if he could get hold of the necessary implements for cleaning it. And he rather doubted if he would be able to do so. Edmund, the boot-boy, worked in some mysterious cell, far from the madding crowd, at the back of the house. In the boot-cupboard downstairs there would probably be nothing likely to be of any use.

His fears were realised. The boot-cupboard was empty. It seemed to him that, for the time being, the best thing he could do would be to place the boot in safe hiding, until he should have thought out a scheme.

Having restored the basket to its proper place, accordingly, he went up to the study again, and placed the red-toed boot in the chimney, at about the same height where Mr. Downing had found the other. Nobody would think of looking there a second time, and it was improbable that Mr. Outwood really would have the chimneys swept, as he had said. The odds were that he had forgotten about it already.

Psmith went to the bathroom to wash his hands again, with the feeling that he had done a good day's work.

CHAPTER LII

ON THE TRAIL AGAIN

The most massive minds are apt to forget things at times. The most adroit plotters make their little mistakes. Psmith was no exception to the rule. He made the mistake of not telling Mike of the afternoon's happenings.

It was not altogether forgetfulness. Psmith was one of those people who like to carry through their operations entirely by themselves. Where there is only one in a secret the secret is more liable to remain unrevealed. There was nothing, he thought, to be gained from telling Mike. He forgot what the consequences might be if he did not.

So Psmith kept his own counsel, with the result that Mike went over to school on the Monday morning in pumps.

Edmund, summoned from the hinterland of the house to give his opinion why only one of Mike's boots was to be found, had no views on the subject. He seemed to look on it as one of those things which no fellow can understand.

"'Ere's one of 'em, Mr. Jackson," he said, as if he hoped that Mike might be satisfied with a compromise.

"One? What's the good of that, Edmund, you chump? I can't go over to school in one boot."

Edmund turned this over in his mind, and then said, "No, sir," as much as to say, "I may have lost a boot, but, thank goodness, I can still understand sound reasoning."

"Well, what am I to do? Where is the other boot?"

"Don't know, Mr. Jackson," replied Edmund to both questions.

"Well, I mean—Oh, dash it, there's the bell."

And Mike sprinted off in the pumps he stood in.

It is only a deviation from those ordinary rules of school life, which one observes naturally and without thinking, that enables one to realise how strong public-school prejudices really are. At a school, for instance, where the regulations say that coats only of black or dark blue are to be worn, a boy who appears one day in even the most respectable and unostentatious brown finds himself looked on with a mixture of awe and repulsion, which would be excessive if he had sand-bagged the headmaster. So in the case of boots. School rules decree that a boy shall go to his form-room in boots, There is no real reason why, if the day is fine, he should not wear shoes, should he prefer them. But, if he does, the thing creates a perfect sensation. Boys say, "Great Scott, what have you got on?" Masters say, "Jones, what are you wearing on your feet?" In the few minutes which elapse between the assembling of the

212

form for call-over and the arrival of the form-master, some wag is sure either to stamp on the shoes, accompanying the act with some satirical remark, or else to pull one of them off, and inaugurate an impromptu game of football with it. There was once a boy who went to school one morning in elastic-sided boots....

Mike had always been coldly distant in his relations to the rest of his form, looking on them, with a few exceptions, as worms; and the form, since his innings against Downing's on the Friday, had regarded Mike with respect. So that he escaped the ragging he would have had to undergo at Wrykyn in similar circumstances. It was only Mr. Downing who gave trouble.

There is a sort of instinct which enables some masters to tell when a boy in their form is wearing shoes instead of boots, just as people who dislike cats always know when one is in a room with them. They cannot see it, but they feel it in their bones.

Mr. Downing was perhaps the most bigoted anti-shoeist in the whole list of English schoolmasters. He waged war remorselessly against shoes. Satire, abuse, lines, detention—every weapon was employed by him in dealing with their wearers. It had been the late Dunster's practice always to go over to school in shoes when, as he usually did, he felt shaky in the morning's lesson. Mr. Downing always detected him in the first five minutes, and that meant a lecture of anything from ten minutes to a quarter of an hour on Untidy Habits and Boys Who Looked like Loafers—which broke the back of the morning's work nicely. On one occasion, when a particularly tricky bit of Livy was on the bill of fare, Dunster had entered the form-room in heel-less Turkish bath-slippers, of a vivid crimson; and the subsequent proceedings, including his journey over to the house to change the heel-less atrocities, had seen him through very nearly to the quarter to eleven interval.

Mike, accordingly, had not been in his place for three minutes when Mr. Downing, stiffening like a pointer, called his name.

"Yes, sir?" said Mike.

"What are you wearing on your feet, Jackson?"

"Pumps, sir."

"You are wearing pumps? Are you not aware that PUMPS are not the proper things to come to school in? Why are you wearing PUMPS?"

The form, leaning back against the next row of desks, settled itself comfortably for the address from the throne.

"I have lost one of my boots, sir."

A kind of gulp escaped from Mr. Downing's lips. He stared at Mike for a moment in silence. Then, turning to Stone, he told him to start translating.

Stone, who had been expecting at least ten minutes' respite, was taken unawares. When he found the place in his book and began to

213

construe, he floundered hopelessly. But, to his growing surprise and satisfaction, the form-master appeared to notice nothing wrong. He said "Yes, yes," mechanically, and finally "That will do," whereupon Stone resumed his seat with the feeling that the age of miracles had returned.

Mr. Downing's mind was in a whirl. His case was complete. Mike's appearance in shoes, with the explanation that he had lost a boot, completed the chain. As Columbus must have felt when his ship ran into harbour, and the first American interviewer, jumping on board, said, "Wal, sir, and what are your impressions of our glorious country?" so did Mr. Downing feel at that moment.

When the bell rang at a quarter to eleven, he gathered up his gown, and sped to the headmaster.

CHAPTER LIII

THE KETTLE METHOD

It was during the interval that day that Stone and Robinson, discussing the subject of cricket over a bun and ginger-beer at the school shop, came to a momentous decision, to wit, that they were fed up with Adair administration and meant to strike. The immediate cause of revolt was early-morning fielding-practice, that searching test of cricket keenness. Mike himself, to whom cricket was the great and serious interest of life, had shirked early-morning fielding-practice in his first term at Wrykyn. And Stone and Robinson had but a luke-warm attachment to the game, compared with Mike's.

As a rule, Adair had contented himself with practice in the afternoon after school, which nobody objects to; and no strain, consequently, had been put upon Stone's and Robinson's allegiance. In view of the M.C.C. match on the Wednesday, however, he had now added to this an extra dose to be taken before breakfast. Stone and Robinson had left their comfortable beds that day at six o'clock, yawning and heavy-eyed, and had caught catches and fielded drives which, in the cool morning air, had stung like adders and bitten like serpents. Until the sun has really got to work, it is no joke taking a high catch. Stone's dislike of the experiment was only equalled by Robinson's. They were neither of them of the type which likes to undergo hardships for the common good. They played well enough

214

when on the field, but neither cared greatly whether the school had a good season or not. They played the game entirely for their own sakes.

The result was that they went back to the house for breakfast with a never-again feeling, and at the earliest possible moment met to debate as to what was to be done about it. At all costs another experience like to-day's must be avoided.

"It's all rot," said Stone. "What on earth's the good of sweating about before breakfast? It only makes you tired."

"I shouldn't wonder," said Robinson, "if it wasn't bad for the heart. Rushing about on an empty stomach, I mean, and all that sort of thing."

"Personally," said Stone, gnawing his bun, "I don't intend to stick it."

"Nor do I."

"I mean, it's such absolute rot. If we aren't good enough to play for the team without having to get up overnight to catch catches, he'd better find somebody else."

"Yes."

At this moment Adair came into the shop.

"Fielding-practice again to-morrow," he said briskly, "at six."

"Before breakfast?" said Robinson.

"Rather. You two must buck up, you know. You were rotten to-day." And he passed on, leaving the two malcontents speechless.

Stone was the first to recover.

"I'm hanged if I turn out to-morrow," he said, as they left the shop. "He can do what he likes about it. Besides, what can he do, after all? Only kick us out of the team. And I don't mind that."

"Nor do I."

"I don't think he will kick us out, either. He can't play the M.C.C. with a scratch team. If he does, we'll go and play for that village Jackson plays for. We'll get Jackson to shove us into the team."

"All right," said Robinson. "Let's."

Their position was a strong one. A cricket captain may seem to be an autocrat of tremendous power, but in reality he has only one weapon, the keenness of those under him. With the majority, of course, the fear of being excluded or ejected from a team is a spur that drives. The majority, consequently, are easily handled. But when a cricket captain runs up against a boy who does not much care whether he plays for the team or not, then he finds himself in a difficult position, and, unless he is a man of action, practically helpless.

Stone and Robinson felt secure. Taking it all round, they felt that they would just as soon play for Lower Borlock as for the school. The bowling of the opposition would be weaker in the former case, and the chance of making runs greater. To a certain type of cricketer runs are runs, wherever and however made.

215

The result of all this was that Adair, turning out with the team next morning for fielding-practice, found himself two short. Barnes was among those present, but of the other two representatives of Outwood's house there were no signs.

Barnes, questioned on the subject, had no information to give, beyond the fact that he had not seen them about anywhere. Which was not a great help. Adair proceeded with the fielding-practice without further delay.

At breakfast that morning he was silent and apparently wrapped in thought. Mr. Downing, who sat at the top of the table with Adair on his right, was accustomed at the morning meal to blend nourishment of the body with that of the mind. As a rule he had ten minutes with the daily paper before the bell rang, and it was his practice to hand on the results of his reading to Adair and the other house-prefects, who, not having seen the paper, usually formed an interested and appreciative audience. To-day, however, though the house-prefects expressed varying degrees of excitement at the news that Tyldesley had made a century against Gloucestershire, and that a butter famine was expected in the United States, these world-shaking news-items seemed to leave Adair cold. He champed his bread and marmalade with an abstracted air.

He was wondering what to do in this matter of Stone and Robinson.

Many captains might have passed the thing over. To take it for granted that the missing pair had overslept themselves would have been a safe and convenient way out of the difficulty. But Adair was not the sort of person who seeks for safe and convenient ways out of difficulties. He never shirked anything, physical or moral.

He resolved to interview the absentees.

It was not until after school that an opportunity offered itself. He went across to Outwood's and found the two non-starters in the senior day-room, engaged in the intellectual pursuit of kicking the wall and marking the height of each kick with chalk. Adair's entrance coincided with a record effort by Stone, which caused the kicker to overbalance and stagger backwards against the captain.

"Sorry," said Stone. "Hullo, Adair!"

"Don't mention it. Why weren't you two at fielding-practice this morning?"

Robinson, who left the lead to Stone in all matters, said nothing. Stone spoke.

"We didn't turn up," he said.

"I know you didn't. Why not?"

Stone had rehearsed this scene in his mind, and he spoke with the coolness which comes from rehearsal.

"We decided not to."

216

"Oh?"

"Yes. We came to the conclusion that we hadn't any use for early-morning fielding."

Adair's manner became ominously calm.

"You were rather fed-up, I suppose?"

"That's just the word."

"Sorry it bored you."

"It didn't. We didn't give it the chance to."

Robinson laughed appreciatively.

"What's the joke, Robinson?" asked Adair.

"There's no joke," said Robinson, with some haste. "I was only thinking of something."

"I'll give you something else to think about soon."

Stone intervened.

"It's no good making a row about it, Adair. You must see that you can't do anything. Of course, you can kick us out of the team, if you like, but we don't care if you do. Jackson will get us a game any Wednesday or Saturday for the village he plays for. So we're all right. And the school team aren't such a lot of flyers that you can afford to go chucking people out of it whenever you want to. See what I mean?"

"You and Jackson seem to have fixed it all up between you."

"What are you going to do? Kick us out?"

"No."

"Good. I thought you'd see it was no good making a beastly row. We'll play for the school all right. There's no earthly need for us to turn out for fielding-practice before breakfast."

"You don't think there is? You may be right. All the same, you're going to to-morrow morning."

"What!"

"Six sharp. Don't be late."

"Don't be an ass, Adair. We've told you we aren't going to."

"That's only your opinion. I think you are. I'll give you till five past six, as you seem to like lying in bed."

"You can turn out if you feel like it. You won't find me there."

"That'll be a disappointment. Nor Robinson?"

"No," said the junior partner in the firm; but he said it without any deep conviction. The atmosphere was growing a great deal too tense for his comfort.

"You've quite made up your minds?"

"Yes," said Stone.

"Right," said Adair quietly, and knocked him down.

He was up again in a moment. Adair had pushed the table back, and was standing in the middle of the open space.

"You cad," said Stone. "I wasn't ready."

"Well, you are now. Shall we go on?"

217

Stone dashed in without a word, and for a few moments the two might have seemed evenly matched to a not too intelligent spectator. But science tells, even in a confined space. Adair was smaller and lighter than Stone, but he was cooler and quicker, and he knew more about the game. His blow was always home a fraction of a second sooner than his opponent's. At the end of a minute Stone was on the floor again.

He got up slowly and stood leaning with one hand on the table.

"Suppose we say ten past six?" said Adair. "I'm not particular to a minute or two."

Stone made no reply.

"Will ten past six suit you for fielding-practice to-morrow?" said Adair.

"All right," said Stone.

"Thanks. How about you, Robinson?"

Robinson had been a petrified spectator of the Captain-Kettle-like manoeuvres of the cricket captain, and it did not take him long to make up his mind. He was not altogether a coward. In different circumstances he might have put up a respectable show. But it takes a more than ordinarily courageous person to embark on a fight which he knows must end in his destruction. Robinson knew that he was nothing like a match even for Stone, and Adair had disposed of Stone in a little over one minute. It seemed to Robinson that neither pleasure nor profit was likely to come from an encounter with Adair.

"All right," he said hastily, "I'll turn up."

"Good," said Adair. "I wonder if either of you chaps could tell me which is Jackson's study."

Stone was dabbing at his mouth with a handkerchief, a task which precluded anything in the shape of conversation; so Robinson replied that Mike's study was the first you came to on the right of the corridor at the top of the stairs.

"Thanks," said Adair. "You don't happen to know if he's in, I suppose?"

"He went up with Smith a quarter of an hour ago. I don't know if he's still there."

"I'll go and see," said Adair. "I should like a word with him if he isn't busy."

218

CHAPTER LIV

ADAIR HAS A WORD WITH MIKE

Mike, all unconscious of the stirring proceedings which had been going on below stairs, was peacefully reading a letter he had received that morning from Strachan at Wrykyn, in which the successor to the cricket captaincy which should have been Mike's had a good deal to say in a lugubrious strain. In Mike's absence things had been going badly with Wrykyn. A broken arm, contracted in the course of some rash experiments with a day-boy's motor-bicycle, had deprived the team of the services of Dunstable, the only man who had shown any signs of being able to bowl a side out. Since this calamity, wrote Strachan, everything had gone wrong. The M.C.C., led by Mike's brother Reggie, the least of the three first-class-cricketing Jacksons, had smashed them by a hundred and fifty runs. Geddington had wiped them off the face of the earth. The Incogs, with a team recruited exclusively from the rabbit-hutch—not a well-known man on the side except Stacey, a veteran who had been playing for the club since Fuller Pilch's time— had got home by two wickets. In fact, it was Strachan's opinion that the Wrykyn team that summer was about the most hopeless gang of dead-beats that had ever made an exhibition of itself on the school grounds. The Ripton match, fortunately, was off, owing to an outbreak of mumps at that shrine of learning and athletics—the second outbreak of the malady in two terms. Which, said Strachan, was hard lines on Ripton, but a bit of jolly good luck for Wrykyn, as it had saved them from what would probably have been a record hammering, Ripton having eight of their last year's team left, including Dixon, the fast bowler, against whom Mike alone of the Wrykyn team had been able to make runs in the previous season. Altogether, Wrykyn had struck a bad patch.

Mike mourned over his suffering school. If only he could have been there to help. It might have made all the difference. In school cricket one good batsman, to go in first and knock the bowlers off their length, may take a weak team triumphantly through a season. In school cricket the importance of a good start for the first wicket is incalculable.

As he put Strachan's letter away in his pocket, all his old bitterness against Sedleigh, which had been ebbing during the past few days, returned with a rush. He was conscious once more of that feeling of personal injury which had made him hate his new school on the first day of term.

And it was at this point, when his resentment was at its height, that Adair, the concrete representative of everything Sedleighan, entered the room.

There are moments in life's placid course when there has got to be the biggest kind of row. This was one of them.

Psmith, who was leaning against the mantelpiece, reading the serial story in a daily paper which he had abstracted from the senior day-room, made the intruder free of the study with a dignified wave of the hand, and went on reading. Mike remained in the deck-chair in which he was sitting, and contented himself with glaring at the newcomer.

Psmith was the first to speak.

"If you ask my candid opinion," he said, looking up from his paper, "I should say that young Lord Antony Trefusis was in the soup already. I seem to see the consommé splashing about his ankles. He's had a note telling him to be under the oak-tree in the Park at midnight. He's just off there at the end of this instalment. I bet Long Jack, the poacher, is waiting there with a sandbag. Care to see the paper, Comrade Adair? Or don't you take any interest in contemporary literature?"

"Thanks," said Adair. "I just wanted to speak to Jackson for a minute."

"Fate," said Psmith, "has led your footsteps to the right place. That is Comrade Jackson, the Pride of the School, sitting before you."

"What do you want?" said Mike.

He suspected that Adair had come to ask him once again to play for the school. The fact that the M.C.C. match was on the following day made this a probable solution of the reason for his visit. He could think of no other errand that was likely to have set the head of Downing's paying afternoon calls.

"I'll tell you in a minute. It won't take long."

"That," said Psmith approvingly, "is right. Speed is the key-note of the present age. Promptitude. Despatch. This is no time for loitering. We must be strenuous. We must hustle. We must Do It Now. We—"

"Buck up," said Mike.

"Certainly," said Adair. "I've just been talking to Stone and Robinson."

"An excellent way of passing an idle half-hour," said Psmith.

"We weren't exactly idle," said Adair grimly. "It didn't last long, but it was pretty lively while it did. Stone chucked it after the first round."

Mike got up out of his chair. He could not quite follow what all this was about, but there was no mistaking the truculence of Adair's manner. For some reason, which might possibly be made clear later, Adair was looking for trouble, and Mike in his present mood felt that it would be a privilege to see that he got it.

220

Psmith was regarding Adair through his eyeglass with pain and surprise.

"Surely," he said, "you do not mean us to understand that you have been brawling with Comrade Stone! This is bad hearing. I thought that you and he were like brothers. Such a bad example for Comrade Robinson, too. Leave us, Adair. We would brood. Oh, go thee, knave, I'll none of thee. Shakespeare."

Psmith turned away, and resting his elbows on the mantelpiece, gazed at himself mournfully in the looking-glass.

"I'm not the man I was," he sighed, after a prolonged inspection. "There are lines on my face, dark circles beneath my eyes. The fierce rush of life at Sedleigh is wasting me away."

"Stone and I had a discussion about early-morning fielding-practice," said Adair, turning to Mike.

Mike said nothing.

"I thought his fielding wanted working up a bit, so I told him to turn out at six to-morrow morning. He said he wouldn't, so we argued it out. He's going to all right. So is Robinson."

Mike remained silent.

"So are you," added Adair.

"I get thinner and thinner," said Psmith from the mantelpiece.

Mike looked at Adair, and Adair looked at Mike, after the manner of two dogs before they fly at one another. There was an electric silence in the study. Psmith peered with increased earnestness into the glass.

"Oh?" said Mike at last. "What makes you think that?"

"I don't think. I know."

"Any special reason for my turning out?"

"Yes."

"What's that?"

"You're going to play for the school against the M.C.C. to-morrow, and I want you to get some practice."

"I wonder how you got that idea!"

"Curious I should have done, isn't it?"

"Very. You aren't building on it much, are you?" said Mike politely.

"I am, rather," replied Adair with equal courtesy.

"I'm afraid you'll be disappointed."

"I don't think so."

"My eyes," said Psmith regretfully, "are a bit close together. However," he added philosophically, "it's too late to alter that now."

Mike drew a step closer to Adair.

"What makes you think I shall play against the M.C.C.?" he asked curiously.

"I'm going to make you."

Mike took another step forward. Adair moved to meet him.

"Would you care to try now?" said Mike.

For just one second the two drew themselves together preparatory to beginning the serious business of the interview, and in that second Psmith, turning from the glass, stepped between them.

"Get out of the light, Smith," said Mike.

Psmith waved him back with a deprecating gesture.

"My dear young friends," he said placidly, "if you will let your angry passions rise, against the direct advice of Doctor Watts, I suppose you must, But when you propose to claw each other in my study, in the midst of a hundred fragile and priceless ornaments, I lodge a protest. If you really feel that you want to scrap, for goodness sake do it where there's some room. I don't want all the study furniture smashed. I know a bank whereon the wild thyme grows, only a few yards down the road, where you can scrap all night if you want to. How would it be to move on there? Any objections? None? Then shift ho! and let's get it over."

CHAPTER LV

CLEARING THE AIR

Psmith was one of those people who lend a dignity to everything they touch. Under his auspices the most unpromising ventures became somehow enveloped in an atmosphere of measured stateliness. On the present occasion, what would have been, without his guiding hand, a mere unscientific scramble, took on something of the impressive formality of the National Sporting Club.

"The rounds," he said, producing a watch, as they passed through a gate into a field a couple of hundred yards from the house gate, "will be of three minutes' duration, with a minute rest in between. A man who is down will have ten seconds in which to rise. Are you ready, Comrades Adair and Jackson? Very well, then. Time."

After which, it was a pity that the actual fight did not quite live up to its referee's introduction. Dramatically, there should have been cautious sparring for openings and a number of tensely contested rounds, as if it had been the final of a boxing competition. But school fights, when they do occur—which is only once in a decade nowadays, unless you count junior school scuffles—are the outcome of weeks of suppressed bad blood, and are consequently brief and furious. In a boxing competition, however much one may want to win, one does not dislike one's opponent. Up to the moment when "time" was called, one was probably warmly attached to him, and at the end of the last round one expects to resume that attitude of mind. In a fight each party, as a rule, hates the other.

So it happened that there was nothing formal or cautious about the present battle. All Adair wanted was to get at Mike, and all Mike wanted was to get at Adair. Directly Psmith called "time," they rushed together as if they meant to end the thing in half a minute.

It was this that saved Mike. In an ordinary contest with the gloves, with his opponent cool and boxing in his true form, he could not have lasted three rounds against Adair. The latter was a clever boxer, while Mike had never had a lesson in his life. If Adair had kept away and used his head, nothing could have prevented him winning.

As it was, however, he threw away his advantages, much as Tom Brown did at the beginning of his fight with Slogger Williams, and the result was the same as on that historic occasion. Mike had the greater strength, and, thirty seconds from the start, knocked his man clean off his feet with an unscientific but powerful right-hander.

This finished Adair's chances. He rose full of fight, but with all the science knocked out of him. He went in at Mike with both hands. The Irish blood in him, which for the ordinary events of life made him merely energetic and dashing, now rendered him reckless. He abandoned all attempt at guarding. It was the Frontal Attack in its most futile form, and as unsuccessful as a frontal attack is apt to be. There was a swift exchange of blows, in the course of which Mike's left elbow, coming into contact with his opponent's right fist, got a shock which kept it tingling for the rest of the day; and then Adair went down in a heap.

He got up slowly and with difficulty. For a moment he stood blinking vaguely. Then he lurched forward at Mike.

In the excitement of a fight—which is, after all, about the most exciting thing that ever happens to one in the course of one's life—it is difficult for the fighters to see what the spectators see. Where the spectators see an assault on an already beaten man, the fighter himself only sees a legitimate piece of self-defence against an opponent whose chances are equal to his own. Psmith saw, as anybody looking on would have seen, that Adair was done. Mike's blow had taken him within a fraction of an inch of the point of the jaw, and he was all but knocked out. Mike could not see this. All he understood was that his man was on his feet again and coming at him, so he hit out with all his strength; and this time Adair went down and stayed down.

"Brief," said Psmith, coming forward, "but exciting. We may take that, I think, to be the conclusion of the entertainment. I will now have a dash at picking up the slain. I shouldn't stop, if I were you. He'll be sitting up and taking notice soon, and if he sees you he may want to go on with the combat, which would do him no earthly good. If it's going

223

to be continued in our next, there had better be a bit of an interval for alterations and repairs first."

"Is he hurt much, do you think?" asked Mike. He had seen knock-outs before in the ring, but this was the first time he had ever effected one on his own account, and Adair looked unpleasantly corpse-like.

"He's all right," said Psmith. "In a minute or two he'll be skipping about like a little lambkin. I'll look after him. You go away and pick flowers."

Mike put on his coat and walked back to the house. He was conscious of a perplexing whirl of new and strange emotions, chief among which was a curious feeling that he rather liked Adair. He found himself thinking that Adair was a good chap, that there was something to be said for his point of view, and that it was a pity he had knocked him about so much. At the same time, he felt an undeniable thrill of pride at having beaten him. The feat presented that interesting person, Mike Jackson, to him in a fresh and pleasing light, as one who had had a tough job to face and had carried it through. Jackson, the cricketer, he knew, but Jackson, the deliverer of knock-out blows, was strange to him, and he found this new acquaintance a man to be respected.

The fight, in fact, had the result which most fights have, if they are fought fairly and until one side has had enough. It revolutionised Mike's view of things. It shook him up, and drained the bad blood out of him. Where, before, he had seemed to himself to be acting with massive dignity, he now saw that he had simply been sulking like some wretched kid. There had appeared to him something rather fine in his policy of refusing to identify himself in any way with Sedleigh, a touch of the stone-walls-do-not-a-prison-make sort of thing. He now saw that his attitude was to be summed up in the words, "Sha'n't play."

It came upon Mike with painful clearness that he had been making an ass of himself.

He had come to this conclusion, after much earnest thought, when Psmith entered the study.

"How's Adair?" asked Mike.

"Sitting up and taking nourishment once more. We have been chatting. He's not a bad cove."

"He's all right," said Mike.

There was a pause. Psmith straightened his tie.

"Look here," he said, "I seldom interfere in terrestrial strife, but it seems to me that there's an opening here for a capable peace-maker, not afraid of work, and willing to give his services in exchange for a comfortable home. Comrade Adair's rather a stoutish fellow in his way. I'm not much on the 'Play up for the old school, Jones,' game, but every one to his taste. I shouldn't have thought anybody would get overwhelmingly attached to this abode of wrath, but Comrade Adair

224

seems to have done it. He's all for giving Sedleigh a much-needed boost-up. It's not a bad idea in its way. I don't see why one shouldn't humour him. Apparently he's been sweating since early childhood to buck the school up. And as he's leaving at the end of the term, it mightn't be a scaly scheme to give him a bit of a send-off, if possible, by making the cricket season a bit of a banger. As a start, why not drop him a line to say that you'll play against the M.C.C. to-morrow?"

Mike did not reply at once. He was feeling better disposed towards Adair and Sedleigh than he had felt, but he was not sure that he was quite prepared to go as far as a complete climb-down.

"It wouldn't be a bad idea," continued Psmith. "There's nothing like giving a man a bit in every now and then. It broadens the soul and improves the action of the skin. What seems to have fed up Comrade Adair, to a certain extent, is that Stone apparently led him to understand that you had offered to give him and Robinson places in your village team. You didn't, of course?"

"Of course not," said Mike indignantly.

"I told him he didn't know the old noblesse oblige spirit of the Jacksons. I said that you would scorn to tarnish the Jackson escutcheon by not playing the game. My eloquence convinced him. However, to return to the point under discussion, why not?"

"I don't—What I mean to say—" began Mike.

"If your trouble is," said Psmith, "that you fear that you may be in unworthy company—"

"Don't be an ass."

"—Dismiss it. I am playing."

Mike stared.

"You're what? You?"

"I," said Psmith, breathing on a coat-button, and polishing it with his handkerchief.

"Can you play cricket?"

"You have discovered," said Psmith, "my secret sorrow."

"You're rotting."

"You wrong me, Comrade Jackson."

"Then why haven't you played?"

"Why haven't you?"

"Why didn't you come and play for Lower Borlock, I mean?"

"The last time I played in a village cricket match I was caught at point by a man in braces. It would have been madness to risk another such shock to my system. My nerves are so exquisitely balanced that a thing of that sort takes years off my life."

"No, but look here, Smith, bar rotting. Are you really any good at cricket?"

"Competent judges at Eton gave me to understand so. I was told that this year I should be a certainty for Lord's. But when the cricket season came, where was I? Gone. Gone like some beautiful flower that withers in the night."

"But you told me you didn't like cricket. You said you only liked watching it."

"Quite right. I do. But at schools where cricket is compulsory you have to overcome your private prejudices. And in time the thing becomes a habit. Imagine my feelings when I found that I was degenerating, little by little, into a slow left-hand bowler with a swerve. I fought against it, but it was useless, and after a while I gave up the struggle, and drifted with the stream. Last year, in a house match"— Psmith's voice took on a deeper tone of melancholy—"I took seven for thirteen in the second innings on a hard wicket. I did think, when I came here, that I had found a haven of rest, but it was not to be. I turn out to-morrow. What Comrade Outwood will say, when he finds that his keenest archaeological disciple has deserted, I hate to think. However—"

Mike felt as if a young and powerful earthquake had passed. The whole face of his world had undergone a quick change. Here was he, the recalcitrant, wavering on the point of playing for the school, and here was Psmith, the last person whom he would have expected to be a player, stating calmly that he had been in the running for a place in the Eton eleven.

Then in a flash Mike understood. He was not by nature intuitive, but he read Psmith's mind now. Since the term began, he and Psmith had been acting on precisely similar motives. Just as he had been disappointed of the captaincy of cricket at Wrykyn, so had Psmith been disappointed of his place in the Eton team at Lord's. And they had both worked it off, each in his own way—Mike sullenly, Psmith whimsically, according to their respective natures—on Sedleigh.

If Psmith, therefore, did not consider it too much of a climb-down to renounce his resolution not to play for Sedleigh, there was nothing to stop Mike doing so, as—at the bottom of his heart—he wanted to do.

"By Jove," he said, "if you're playing, I'll play. I'll write a note to Adair now. But, I say—" he stopped—"I'm hanged if I'm going to turn out and field before breakfast to-morrow."

"That's all right. You won't have to. Adair won't be there himself. He's not playing against the M.C.C. He's sprained his wrist."

226

CHAPTER LVI

IN WHICH PEACE IS DECLARED

"Sprained his wrist?" said Mike. "How did he do that?"

"During the brawl. Apparently one of his efforts got home on your elbow instead of your expressive countenance, and whether it was that your elbow was particularly tough or his wrist particularly fragile, I don't know. Anyhow, it went. It's nothing bad, but it'll keep him out of the game to-morrow."

"I say, what beastly rough luck! I'd no idea. I'll go round."

"Not a bad scheme. Close the door gently after you, and if you see anybody downstairs who looks as if he were likely to be going over to the shop, ask him to get me a small pot of some rare old jam and tell the man to chalk it up to me. The jam Comrade Outwood supplies to us at tea is all right as a practical joke or as a food for those anxious to commit suicide, but useless to anybody who values life."

On arriving at Mr. Downing's and going to Adair's study, Mike found that his late antagonist was out. He left a note informing him of his willingness to play in the morrow's match. The lock-up bell rang as he went out of the house.

A spot of rain fell on his hand. A moment later there was a continuous patter, as the storm, which had been gathering all day, broke in earnest. Mike turned up his coat-collar, and ran back to Outwood's. "At this rate," he said to himself, "there won't be a match at all to-morrow."

When the weather decides, after behaving well for some weeks, to show what it can do in another direction, it does the thing thoroughly. When Mike woke the next morning the world was grey and dripping. Leaden-coloured clouds drifted over the sky, till there was not a trace of blue to be seen, and then the rain began again, in the gentle, determined way rain has when it means to make a day of it.

It was one of those bad days when one sits in the pavilion, damp and depressed, while figures in mackintoshes, with discoloured buckskin boots, crawl miserably about the field in couples.

Mike, shuffling across to school in a Burberry, met Adair at Downing's gate.

These moments are always difficult. Mike stopped—he could hardly walk on as if nothing had happened—and looked down at his feet.

"Coming across?" he said awkwardly.

"Right ho!" said Adair.

They walked on in silence.

"It's only about ten to, isn't it?" said Mike.

227

Adair fished out his watch, and examined it with an elaborate care born of nervousness.

"About nine to."

"Good. We've got plenty of time."

"Yes."

"I hate having to hurry over to school."

"So do I."

"I often do cut it rather fine, though."

"Yes. So do I."

"Beastly nuisance when one does."

"Beastly."

"It's only about a couple of minutes from the houses to the school, I should think, shouldn't you?"

"Not much more. Might be three."

"Yes. Three if one didn't hurry."

"Oh, yes, if one didn't hurry."

Another silence.

"Beastly day," said Adair.

"Rotten."

Silence again.

"I say," said Mike, scowling at his toes, "awfully sorry about your wrist."

"Oh, that's all right. It was my fault."

"Does it hurt?"

"Oh, no, rather not, thanks."

"I'd no idea you'd crocked yourself."

"Oh, no, that's all right. It was only right at the end. You'd have smashed me anyhow."

"Oh, rot."

"I bet you anything you like you would."

"I bet you I shouldn't.... Jolly hard luck, just before the match."

"Oh, no.... I say, thanks awfully for saying you'd play."

"Oh, rot.... Do you think we shall get a game?"

Adair inspected the sky carefully.

"I don't know. It looks pretty bad, doesn't it?"

"Rotten. I say, how long will your wrist keep you out of cricket?"

"Be all right in a week. Less, probably."

"Good."

"Now that you and Smith are going to play, we ought to have a jolly good season."

"Rummy, Smith turning out to be a cricketer."

"Yes. I should think he'd be a hot bowler, with his height."

"He must be jolly good if he was only just out of the Eton team last year."

"Yes."

"What's the time?" asked Mike.

228

Adair produced his watch once more.

"Five to."

"We've heaps of time."

"Yes, heaps."

"Let's stroll on a bit down the road, shall we?"

"Right ho!"

Mike cleared his throat.

"I say."

"Hullo?"

"I've been talking to Smith. He was telling me that you thought I'd promised to give Stone and Robinson places in the—"

"Oh, no, that's all right. It was only for a bit. Smith told me you couldn't have done, and I saw that I was an ass to think you could have. It was Stone seeming so dead certain that he could play for Lower Borlock if I chucked him from the school team that gave me the idea."

"He never even asked me to get him a place."

"No, I know."

"Of course, I wouldn't have done it, even if he had."

"Of course not."

"I didn't want to play myself, but I wasn't going to do a rotten trick like getting other fellows away from the team."

"No, I know."

"It was rotten enough, really, not playing myself."

"Oh, no. Beastly rough luck having to leave Wrykyn just when you were going to be captain, and come to a small school like this."

The excitement of the past few days must have had a stimulating effect on Mike's mind—shaken it up, as it were: for now, for the second time in two days, he displayed quite a creditable amount of intuition. He might have been misled by Adair's apparently deprecatory attitude towards Sedleigh, and blundered into a denunciation of the place. Adair had said "a small school like this" in the sort of voice which might have led his hearer to think that he was expected to say, "Yes, rotten little hole, isn't it?" or words to that effect. Mike, fortunately, perceived that the words were used purely from politeness, on the Chinese principle. When a Chinaman wishes to pay a compliment, he does so by belittling himself and his belongings.

He eluded the pitfall.

"What rot!" he said. "Sedleigh's one of the most sporting schools I've ever come across. Everybody's as keen as blazes. So they ought to be, after the way you've sweated."

Adair shuffled awkwardly.

"I've always been fairly keen on the place," he said. "But I don't suppose I've done anything much."

"You've loosened one of my front teeth," said Mike, with a grin, "if that's any comfort to you."

229

"I couldn't eat anything except porridge this morning. My jaw still aches."

For the first time during the conversation their eyes met, and the humorous side of the thing struck them simultaneously. They began to laugh.

"What fools we must have looked!" said Adair.

"You were all right. I must have looked rotten. I've never had the gloves on in my life. I'm jolly glad no one saw us except Smith, who doesn't count. Hullo, there's the bell. We'd better be moving on. What about this match? Not much chance of it from the look of the sky at present."

"It might clear before eleven. You'd better get changed, anyhow, at the interval, and hang about in case."

"All right. It's better than doing Thucydides with Downing. We've got math, till the interval, so I don't see anything of him all day; which won't hurt me."

"He isn't a bad sort of chap, when you get to know him," said Adair.

"I can't have done, then. I don't know which I'd least soon be, Downing or a black-beetle, except that if one was Downing one could tread on the black-beetle. Dash this rain. I got about half a pint down my neck just then. We sha'n't get a game to-day, of anything like it. As you're crocked, I'm not sure that I care much. You've been sweating for years to get the match on, and it would be rather rot playing it without you."

"I don't know that so much. I wish we could play, because I'm certain, with you and Smith, we'd walk into them. They probably aren't sending down much of a team, and really, now that you and Smith are turning out, we've got a jolly hot lot. There's quite decent batting all the way through, and the bowling isn't so bad. If only we could have given this M.C.C. lot a really good hammering, it might have been easier to get some good fixtures for next season. You see, it's all right for a school like Wrykyn, but with a small place like this you simply can't get the best teams to give you a match till you've done something to show that you aren't absolute rotters at the game. As for the schools, they're worse. They'd simply laugh at you. You were cricket secretary at Wrykyn last year. What would you have done if you'd had a challenge from Sedleigh? You'd either have laughed till you were sick, or else had a fit at the mere idea of the thing."

Mike stopped.

"By Jove, you've struck about the brightest scheme on record. I never thought of it before. Let's get a match on with Wrykyn."

"What! They wouldn't play us."

"Yes, they would. At least, I'm pretty sure they would. I had a letter from Strachan, the captain, yesterday, saying that the Ripton match had had to be scratched owing to illness. So they've got a vacant date. Shall I try them? I'll write to Strachan to-night, if you like. And they aren't strong this year. We'll smash them. What do you say?"

Adair was as one who has seen a vision.

"By Jove," he said at last, "if we only could!"

CHAPTER LVII

MR. DOWNING MOVES

The rain continued without a break all the morning. The two teams, after hanging about dismally, and whiling the time away with stump-cricket in the changing-rooms, lunched in the pavilion at one o'clock. After which the M.C.C. captain, approaching Adair, moved that this merry meeting be considered off and himself and his men permitted to catch the next train back to town. To which Adair, seeing that it was out of the question that there should be any cricket that afternoon, regretfully agreed, and the first Sedleigh v. M.C.C. match was accordingly scratched.

Mike and Psmith, wandering back to the house, were met by a damp junior from Downing's, with a message that Mr. Downing wished to see Mike as soon as he was changed.

"What's he want me for?" inquired Mike.

The messenger did not know. Mr. Downing, it seemed, had not confided in him. All he knew was that the housemaster was in the house, and would be glad if Mike would step across.

"A nuisance," said Psmith, "this incessant demand for you. That's the worst of being popular. If he wants you to stop to tea, edge away. A meal on rather a sumptuous scale will be prepared in the study against your return."

Mike changed quickly, and went off, leaving Psmith, who was fond of simple pleasures in his spare time, earnestly occupied with a puzzle which had been scattered through the land by a weekly paper. The prize for a solution was one thousand pounds, and Psmith had already informed Mike with some minuteness of his plans for the disposition of this sum. Meanwhile, he worked at it both in and out of school, generally with abusive comments on its inventor.

He was still fiddling away at it when Mike returned.

Mike, though Psmith was at first too absorbed to notice it, was agitated.

"I don't wish to be in any way harsh," said Psmith, without

231

looking up, "but the man who invented this thing was a blighter of the worst type. You come and have a shot. For the moment I am baffled. The whisper flies round the clubs, 'Psmith is baffled.'"

"The man's an absolute drivelling ass," said Mike warmly.

"Me, do you mean?"

"What on earth would be the point of my doing it?"

"You'd gather in a thousand of the best. Give you a nice start in life."

"I'm not talking about your rotten puzzle."

"What are you talking about?"

"That ass Downing. I believe he's off his nut."

"Then your chat with Comrade Downing was not of the old-College-chums-meeting-unexpectedly-after-years'-separation type? What has he been doing to you?"

"He's off his nut."

"I know. But what did he do? How did the brainstorm burst? Did he jump at you from behind a door and bite a piece out of your leg, or did he say he was a tea-pot?"

Mike sat down.

"You remember that painting Sammy business?"

"As if it were yesterday," said Psmith. "Which it was, pretty nearly."

"He thinks I did it."

"Why? Have you ever shown any talent in the painting line?"

"The silly ass wanted me to confess that I'd done it. He as good as asked me to. Jawed a lot of rot about my finding it to my advantage later on if I behaved sensibly."

"Then what are you worrying about? Don't you know that when a master wants you to do the confessing-act, it simply means that he hasn't enough evidence to start in on you with? You're all right. The thing's a stand-off."

"Evidence!" said Mike, "My dear man, he's got enough evidence to sink a ship. He's absolutely sweating evidence at every pore. As far as I can see, he's been crawling about, doing the Sherlock Holmes business for all he's worth ever since the thing happened, and now he's dead certain that I painted Sammy."

"Did you, by the way?" asked Psmith.

"No," said Mike shortly, "I didn't. But after listening to Downing I almost began to wonder if I hadn't. The man's got stacks of evidence to prove that I did."

"Such as what?"

"It's mostly about my boots. But, dash it, you know all about that. Why, you were with him when he came and looked for them."

"It is true," said Psmith, "that Comrade Downing and I spent a very pleasant half-hour together inspecting boots, but how does he drag you into it?"

232

"He swears one of the boots was splashed with paint."

"Yes. He babbled to some extent on that point when I was entertaining him. But what makes him think that the boot, if any, was yours?"

"He's certain that somebody in this house got one of his boots splashed, and is hiding it somewhere. And I'm the only chap in the house who hasn't got a pair of boots to show, so he thinks it's me. I don't know where the dickens my other boot has gone. Edmund swears he hasn't seen it, and it's nowhere about. Of course I've got two pairs, but one's being soled. So I had to go over to school yesterday in pumps. That's how he spotted me."

Psmith sighed.

"Comrade Jackson," he said mournfully, "all this very sad affair shows the folly of acting from the best motives. In my simple zeal, meaning to save you unpleasantness, I have landed you, with a dull, sickening thud, right in the cart. Are you particular about dirtying your hands? If you aren't, just reach up that chimney a bit?"

Mike stared, "What the dickens are you talking about?"

"Go on. Get it over. Be a man, and reach up the chimney."

"I don't know what the game is," said Mike, kneeling beside the fender and groping, "but—Hullo!"

"Ah ha!" said Psmith moodily.

Mike dropped the soot-covered object in the fender, and glared at it.

"It's my boot!" he said at last.

"It is," said Psmith, "your boot. And what is that red stain across the toe? Is it blood? No, 'tis not blood. It is red paint."

Mike seemed unable to remove his eyes from the boot.

"How on earth did—By Jove! I remember now. I kicked up against something in the dark when I was putting my bicycle back that night. It must have been the paint-pot."

"Then you were out that night?"

"Rather. That's what makes it so jolly awkward. It's too long to tell you now—"

"Your stories are never too long for me," said Psmith. "Say on!"

"Well, it was like this." And Mike related the events which had led up to his midnight excursion. Psmith listened attentively.

"This," he said, when Mike had finished, "confirms my frequently stated opinion that Comrade Jellicoe is one of Nature's blitherers. So that's why he touched us for our hard-earned, was it?"

"Yes. Of course there was no need for him to have the money at all."

"And the result is that you are in something of a tight place. You're absolutely certain you didn't paint that dog? Didn't do it, by any chance, in a moment of absent-mindedness, and forgot all about it? No? No, I suppose not. I wonder who did!"

"It's beastly awkward. You see, Downing chased me that night. That was why I rang the alarm bell. So, you see, he's certain to think that the chap he chased, which was me, and the chap who painted Sammy, are the same. I shall get landed both ways."

Psmith pondered.

"It is a tightish place," he admitted.

"I wonder if we could get this boot clean," said Mike, inspecting it with disfavour.

"Not for a pretty considerable time."

"I suppose not. I say, I am in the cart. If I can't produce this boot, they're bound to guess why."

"What exactly," asked Psmith, "was the position of affairs between you and Comrade Downing when you left him? Had you definitely parted brass-rags? Or did you simply sort of drift apart with mutual courtesies?"

"Oh, he said I was ill-advised to continue that attitude, or some rot, and I said I didn't care, I hadn't painted his bally dog, and he said very well, then, he must take steps, and—well, that was about all."

"Sufficient, too," said Psmith, "quite sufficient. I take it, then, that he is now on the war-path, collecting a gang, so to speak."

"I suppose he's gone to the Old Man about it."

"Probably. A very worrying time our headmaster is having, taking it all round, in connection with this painful affair. What do you think his move will be?"

"I suppose he'll send for me, and try to get something out of me."

"He'll want you to confess, too. Masters are all whales on confession. The worst of it is, you can't prove an alibi, because at about the time the foul act was perpetrated, you were playing Round-and-round-the-mulberry-bush with Comrade Downing. This needs thought. You had better put the case in my hands, and go out and watch the dandelions growing. I will think over the matter."

"Well, I hope you'll be able to think of something. I can't."

"Possibly. You never know."

There was a tap at the door.

"See how we have trained them," said Psmith. "They now knock before entering. There was a time when they would have tried to smash in a panel. Come in."

A small boy, carrying a straw hat adorned with the school-house ribbon, answered the invitation.

"Oh, I say, Jackson," he said, "the headmaster sent me over to tell you he wants to see you."

"I told you so," said Mike to Psmith.

"Don't go," suggested Psmith. "Tell him to write."

Mike got up.

"All this is very trying," said Psmith. "I'm seeing nothing of you

234

to-day." He turned to the small boy. "Tell Willie," he added, "that Mr. Jackson will be with him in a moment."

The emissary departed.

"You're all right," said Psmith encouragingly. "Just you keep on saying you're all right. Stout denial is the thing. Don't go in for any airy explanations. Simply stick to stout denial. You can't beat it."

With which expert advice, he allowed Mike to go on his way.

He had not been gone two minutes, when Psmith, who had leaned back in his chair, wrapped in thought, heaved himself up again. He stood for a moment straightening his tie at the looking-glass; then he picked up his hat and moved slowly out of the door and down the passage. Thence, at the same dignified rate of progress, out of the house and in at Downing's front gate.

The postman was at the door when he got there, apparently absorbed in conversation with the parlour-maid. Psmith stood by politely till the postman, who had just been told it was like his impudence, caught sight of him, and, having handed over the letters in an ultra-formal and professional manner, passed away.

"Is Mr. Downing at home?" inquired Psmith.

He was, it seemed. Psmith was shown into the dining-room on the left of the hall, and requested to wait. He was examining a portrait of Mr. Downing which hung on the wall, when the housemaster came in.

"An excellent likeness, sir," said Psmith, with a gesture of the hand towards the painting.

"Well, Smith," said Mr. Downing shortly, "what do you wish to see me about?"

"It was in connection with the regrettable painting of your dog, sir."

"Ha!" said Mr. Downing.

"I did it, sir," said Psmith, stopping and flicking a piece of fluff off his knee.

CHAPTER LVIII

THE ARTIST CLAIMS HIS WORK

The line of action which Psmith had called Stout Denial is an excellent line to adopt, especially if you really are innocent, but it does not lead to anything in the shape of a bright and snappy dialogue between accuser and accused. Both Mike and the headmaster were oppressed by a feeling that the situation was difficult. The atmosphere was heavy, and conversation showed a tendency to flag. The headmaster had opened brightly enough, with a summary of the evidence which Mr. Downing had laid before him, but after that a massive silence had been the order of the day. There is nothing in this world quite so stolid and uncommunicative as a boy who has made up his mind to be stolid and uncommunicative; and the headmaster, as he sat and looked at Mike, who sat and looked past him at the bookshelves, felt awkward. It was a scene which needed either a dramatic interruption or a neat exit speech. As it happened, what it got was the dramatic interruption.

The headmaster was just saying, "I do not think you fully realise, Jackson, the extent to which appearances—" —which was practically going back to the beginning and starting again—when there was a knock at the door. A voice without said, "Mr. Downing to see you, sir," and the chief witness for the prosecution burst in.

"I would not have interrupted you," said Mr. Downing, "but—"

"Not at all, Mr. Downing. Is there anything I can—?"

"I have discovered—I have been informed—In short, it was not Jackson, who committed the—who painted my dog."

Mike and the headmaster both looked at the speaker. Mike with a feeling of relief—for Stout Denial, unsupported by any weighty evidence, is a wearing game to play—the headmaster with astonishment.

"Not Jackson?" said the headmaster.

"No. It was a boy in the same house. Smith."

Psmith! Mike was more than surprised. He could not believe it. There is nothing which affords so clear an index to a boy's character as the type of rag which he considers humorous. Between what is a rag and what is merely a rotten trick there is a very definite line drawn. Masters, as a rule, do not realise this, but boys nearly always do. Mike could not imagine Psmith doing a rotten thing like covering a housemaster's dog with red paint, any more than he could imagine doing it himself. They had both been amused at the sight of Sammy after the operation, but anybody, except possibly the owner of the dog, would have thought it funny at first. After the first surprise, their feeling had been that it was a scuggish thing to have done and beastly rough luck on the poor brute. It was a kid's trick. As for Psmith having done it, Mike simply did not believe it.

"Smith!" said the headmaster. "What makes you think that?"

"Simply this," said Mr. Downing, with calm triumph, "that the boy himself came to me a few moments ago and confessed."

Mike was conscious of a feeling of acute depression. It did not make him in the least degree jubilant, or even thankful, to know that he himself was cleared of the charge. All he could think of was that

Psmith was done for. This was bound to mean the sack. If Psmith had painted Sammy, it meant that Psmith had broken out of his house at night: and it was not likely that the rules about nocturnal wandering were less strict at Sedleigh than at any other school in the kingdom. Mike felt, if possible, worse than he had felt when Wyatt had been caught on a similar occasion. It seemed as if Fate had a special grudge against his best friends. He did not make friends very quickly or easily, though he had always had scores of acquaintances—and with Wyatt and Psmith he had found himself at home from the first moment he had met them.

He sat there, with a curious feeling of having swallowed a heavy weight, hardly listening to what Mr. Downing was saying. Mr. Downing was talking rapidly to the headmaster, who was nodding from time to time.

Mike took advantage of a pause to get up. "May I go, sir?" he said.

"Certainly, Jackson, certainly," said the Head. "Oh, and er—, if you are going back to your house, tell Smith that I should like to see him."

"Yes, sir."

He had reached the door, when again there was a knock.

"Come in," said the headmaster.

It was Adair.

"Yes, Adair?"

Adair was breathing rather heavily, as if he had been running.

"It was about Sammy—Sampson, sir," he said, looking at Mr. Downing.

"Ah, we know—. Well, Adair, what did you wish to say?"

"It wasn't Jackson who did it, sir."

"No, no, Adair. So Mr. Downing—"

"It was Dunster, sir."

Terrific sensation! The headmaster gave a sort of strangled yelp of astonishment. Mr. Downing leaped in his chair. Mike's eyes opened to their fullest extent.

"Adair!"

There was almost a wail in the headmaster's voice. The situation had suddenly become too much for him. His brain was swimming. That Mike, despite the evidence against him, should be innocent, was curious, perhaps, but not particularly startling. But that Adair should inform him, two minutes after Mr. Downing's announcement of Psmith's confession, that Psmith, too, was guiltless, and that the real criminal was Dunster—it was this that made him feel that somebody, in the words of an American author, had played a mean trick on him, and substituted for his brain a side-order of cauliflower. Why Dunster, of all people? Dunster, who, he remembered dizzily, had left the school at Christmas. And why, if Dunster had really painted the dog, had Psmith

237

asserted that he himself was the culprit? Why—why anything? He concentrated his mind on Adair as the only person who could save him from impending brain-fever.

"Adair!"

"Yes, sir?"

"What—what do you mean?"

"It was Dunster, sir. I got a letter from him only five minutes ago, in which he said that he had painted Sammy—Sampson, the dog, sir, for a rag—for a joke, and that, as he didn't want any one here to get into a row—be punished for it, I'd better tell Mr. Downing at once. I tried to find Mr. Downing, but he wasn't in the house. Then I met Smith outside the house, and he told me that Mr. Downing had gone over to see you, sir."

"Smith told you?" said Mr. Downing.

"Yes, sir."

"Did you say anything to him about your having received this letter from Dunster?"

"I gave him the letter to read, sir."

"And what was his attitude when he had read it?"

"He laughed, sir."

"Laughed!" Mr. Downing's voice was thunderous.

"Yes, sir. He rolled about."

Mr. Downing snorted.

"But Adair," said the headmaster, "I do not understand how this thing could have been done by Dunster. He has left the school."

"He was down here for the Old Sedleighans' match, sir. He stopped the night in the village."

"And that was the night the—it happened?"

"Yes, sir."

"I see. Well, I am glad to find that the blame cannot be attached to any boy in the school. I am sorry that it is even an Old Boy. It was a foolish, discreditable thing to have done, but it is not as bad as if any boy still at the school had broken out of his house at night to do it."

"The sergeant," said Mr. Downing, "told me that the boy he saw was attempting to enter Mr. Outwood's house."

"Another freak of Dunster's, I suppose," said the headmaster. "I shall write to him."

"If it was really Dunster who painted my dog," said Mr. Downing, "I cannot understand the part played by Smith in this affair. If he did not do it, what possible motive could he have had for coming to me of his own accord and deliberately confessing?"

"To be sure," said the headmaster, pressing a bell. "It is certainly a thing that calls for explanation. Barlow," he said, as the butler appeared, "kindly go across to Mr. Outwood's house and inform Smith that I should like to see him."

"If you please, sir, Mr. Smith is waiting in the hall."

"In the hall!"

"Yes, sir. He arrived soon after Mr. Adair, sir, saying that he would wait, as you would probably wish to see him shortly."

"H'm. Ask him to step up, Barlow."

"Yes, sir."

There followed one of the tensest "stage waits" of Mike's experience. It was not long, but, while it lasted, the silence was quite solid. Nobody seemed to have anything to say, and there was not even a clock in the room to break the stillness with its ticking. A very faint drip-drip of rain could be heard outside the window.

Presently there was a sound of footsteps on the stairs. The door was opened.

"Mr. Smith, sir."

The old Etonian entered as would the guest of the evening who is a few moments late for dinner. He was cheerful, but slightly deprecating. He gave the impression of one who, though sure of his welcome, feels that some slight apology is expected from him. He advanced into the room with a gentle half-smile which suggested good-will to all men.

"It is still raining," he observed. "You wished to see me, sir?"

"Sit down, Smith."

"Thank you, sir."

He dropped into a deep arm-chair (which both Adair and Mike had avoided in favour of less luxurious seats) with the confidential cosiness of a fashionable physician calling on a patient, between whom and himself time has broken down the barriers of restraint and formality.

Mr. Downing burst out, like a reservoir that has broken its banks. "Smith."

Psmith turned his gaze politely in the housemaster's direction.

"Smith, you came to me a quarter of an hour ago and told me that it was you who had painted my dog Sampson."

"Yes, sir."

"It was absolutely untrue?"

"I am afraid so, sir."

"But, Smith—" began the headmaster.

Psmith bent forward encouragingly.

"—This is a most extraordinary affair. Have you no explanation to offer? What induced you to do such a thing?"

Psmith sighed softly.

"The craze for notoriety, sir," he replied sadly. "The curse of the present age."

"What!" cried the headmaster.

"It is remarkable," proceeded Psmith placidly, with the impersonal touch of one lecturing on generalities, "how frequently, when a murder has been committed, one finds men confessing that

239

they have done it when it is out of the question that they should have committed it. It is one of the most interesting problems with which anthropologists are confronted. Human nature—"

The headmaster interrupted.

"Smith," he said, "I should like to see you alone for a moment. Mr. Downing might I trouble—? Adair, Jackson."

He made a motion towards the door.

When he and Psmith were alone, there was silence. Psmith leaned back comfortably in his chair. The headmaster tapped nervously with his foot on the floor.

"Er—Smith."

"Sir?"

The headmaster seemed to have some difficulty in proceeding. He paused again. Then he went on.

"Er—Smith, I do not for a moment wish to pain you, but have you—er, do you remember ever having had, as a child, let us say, any—er—severe illness? Any—er—mental illness?"

"No, sir."

"There is no—forgive me if I am touching on a sad subject—there is no—none of your near relatives have ever suffered in the way I—er—have described?"

"There isn't a lunatic on the list, sir," said Psmith cheerfully.

"Of course, Smith, of course," said the headmaster hurriedly, "I did not mean to suggest—quite so, quite so.... You think, then, that you confessed to an act which you had not committed purely from some sudden impulse which you cannot explain?"

"Strictly between ourselves, sir—"

Privately, the headmaster found Psmith's man-to-man attitude somewhat disconcerting, but he said nothing.

"Well, Smith?"

"I should not like it to go any further, sir."

"I will certainly respect any confidence—"

"I don't want anybody to know, sir. This is strictly between ourselves."

"I think you are sometimes apt to forget, Smith, the proper relations existing between boy and—Well, never mind that for the present. We can return to it later. For the moment, let me hear what you wish to say. I shall, of course, tell nobody, if you do not wish it."

"Well, it was like this, sir," said Psmith. "Jackson happened to tell me that you and Mr. Downing seemed to think he had painted Mr. Downing's dog, and there seemed some danger of his being expelled, so I thought it wouldn't be an unsound scheme if I were to go and say I had done it. That was the whole thing. Of course, Dunster writing created a certain amount of confusion."

There was a pause.

240

"It was a very wrong thing to do, Smith," said the headmaster, at last, "but.... You are a curious boy, Smith. Good-night."

He held out his hand.

"Good-night, sir," said Psmith.

"Not a bad old sort," said Psmith meditatively to himself, as he walked downstairs. "By no means a bad old sort. I must drop in from time to time and cultivate him."

Mike and Adair were waiting for him outside the front door.

"Well?" said Mike.

"You are the limit," said Adair. "What's he done?"

"Nothing. We had a very pleasant chat, and then I tore myself away."

"Do you mean to say he's not going to do a thing?"

"Not a thing."

"Well, you're a marvel," said Adair.

Psmith thanked him courteously. They walked on towards the houses.

"By the way, Adair," said Mike, as the latter started to turn in at Downing's, "I'll write to Strachan to-night about that match."

"What's that?" asked Psmith.

"Jackson's going to try and get Wrykyn to give us a game," said Adair. "They've got a vacant date. I hope the dickens they'll do it."

"Oh, I should think they're certain to," said Mike. "Good-night."

"And give Comrade Downing, when you see him," said Psmith, "my very best love. It is men like him who make this Merrie England of ours what it is."

"I say, Psmith," said Mike suddenly, "what really made you tell Downing you'd done it?"

"The craving for—"

"Oh, chuck it. You aren't talking to the Old Man now. I believe it was simply to get me out of a jolly tight corner."

Psmith's expression was one of pain.

"My dear Comrade Jackson," said he, "you wrong me. You make me writhe. I'm surprised at you. I never thought to hear those words from Michael Jackson."

"Well, I believe you did, all the same," said Mike obstinately. "And it was jolly good of you, too."

Psmith moaned.

241

CHAPTER LIX

SEDLEIGH v. WRYKYN

The Wrykyn match was three-parts over, and things were going badly for Sedleigh. In a way one might have said that the game was over, and that Sedleigh had lost; for it was a one day match, and Wrykyn, who had led on the first innings, had only to play out time to make the game theirs.

Sedleigh were paying the penalty for allowing themselves to be influenced by nerves in the early part of the day. Nerves lose more school matches than good play ever won. There is a certain type of school batsman who is a gift to any bowler when he once lets his imagination run away with him. Sedleigh, with the exception of Adair, Psmith, and Mike, had entered upon this match in a state of the most azure funk. Ever since Mike had received Strachan's answer and Adair had announced on the notice-board that on Saturday, July the twentieth, Sedleigh would play Wrykyn, the team had been all on the jump. It was useless for Adair to tell them, as he did repeatedly, on Mike's authority, that Wrykyn were weak this season, and that on their present form Sedleigh ought to win easily. The team listened, but were not comforted. Wrykyn might be below their usual strength, but then Wrykyn cricket, as a rule, reached such a high standard that this probably meant little. However weak Wrykyn might be—for them— there was a very firm impression among the members of the Sedleigh first eleven that the other school was quite strong enough to knock the cover off them. Experience counts enormously in school matches. Sedleigh had never been proved. The teams they played were the sort of sides which the Wrykyn second eleven would play. Whereas Wrykyn, from time immemorial, had been beating Ripton teams and Free Foresters teams and M.C.C. teams packed with county men and sending men to Oxford and Cambridge who got their blues as freshmen.

Sedleigh had gone on to the field that morning a depressed side.

It was unfortunate that Adair had won the toss. He had had no choice but to take first innings. The weather had been bad for the last week, and the wicket was slow and treacherous. It was likely to get worse during the day, so Adair had chosen to bat first.

Taking into consideration the state of nerves the team was in, this in itself was a calamity. A school eleven are always at their worst and nerviest before lunch. Even on their own ground they find the surroundings lonely and unfamiliar. The subtlety of the bowlers becomes magnified. Unless the first pair make a really good start, a collapse almost invariably ensues.

242

To-day the start had been gruesome beyond words. Mike, the bulwark of the side, the man who had been brought up on Wrykyn bowling, and from whom, whatever might happen to the others, at least a fifty was expected—Mike, going in first with Barnes and taking first over, had played inside one from Bruce, the Wrykyn slow bowler, and had been caught at short slip off his second ball.

That put the finishing-touch on the panic. Stone, Robinson, and the others, all quite decent punishing batsmen when their nerves allowed them to play their own game, crawled to the wickets, declined to hit out at anything, and were clean bowled, several of them, playing back to half-volleys. Adair did not suffer from panic, but his batting was not equal to his bowling, and he had fallen after hitting one four. Seven wickets were down for thirty when Psmith went in.

Psmith had always disclaimed any pretensions to batting skill, but he was undoubtedly the right man for a crisis like this. He had an enormous reach, and he used it. Three consecutive balls from Bruce he turned into full-tosses and swept to the leg-boundary, and, assisted by Barnes, who had been sitting on the splice in his usual manner, he raised the total to seventy-one before being yorked, with his score at thirty-five. Ten minutes later the innings was over, with Barnes not out sixteen, for seventy-nine.

Wrykyn had then gone in, lost Strachan for twenty before lunch, and finally completed their innings at a quarter to four for a hundred and thirty-one.

This was better than Sedleigh had expected. At least eight of the team had looked forward dismally to an afternoon's leather-hunting. But Adair and Psmith, helped by the wicket, had never been easy, especially Psmith, who had taken six wickets, his slows playing havoc with the tail.

It would be too much to say that Sedleigh had any hope of pulling the game out of the fire; but it was a comfort, they felt, at any rate, having another knock. As is usual at this stage of a match, their nervousness had vanished, and they felt capable of better things than in the first innings.

It was on Mike's suggestion that Psmith and himself went in first. Mike knew the limitations of the Wrykyn bowling, and he was convinced that, if they could knock Bruce off, it might be possible to rattle up a score sufficient to give them the game, always provided that Wrykyn collapsed in the second innings. And it seemed to Mike that the wicket would be so bad then that they easily might.

So he and Psmith had gone in at four o'clock to hit. And they had hit. The deficit had been wiped off, all but a dozen runs, when Psmith was bowled, and by that time Mike was set and in his best vein. He treated all the bowlers alike. And when Stone came in, restored to his proper frame of mind, and lashed out stoutly, and after him Robinson and the rest, it looked as if Sedleigh had a chance again. The score was

243

a hundred and twenty when Mike, who had just reached his fifty, skied one to Strachan at cover. The time was twenty-five past five.

As Mike reached the pavilion, Adair declared the innings closed.

Wrykyn started batting at twenty-five minutes to six, with sixty-nine to make if they wished to make them, and an hour and ten minutes during which to keep up their wickets if they preferred to take things easy and go for a win on the first innings.

At first it looked as if they meant to knock off the runs, for Strachan forced the game from the first ball, which was Psmith's, and which he hit into the pavilion. But, at fifteen, Adair bowled him. And when, two runs later, Psmith got the next man stumped, and finished up his over with a c-and-b, Wrykyn decided that it was not good enough. Seventeen for three, with an hour all but five minutes to go, was getting too dangerous. So Drummond and Rigby, the next pair, proceeded to play with caution, and the collapse ceased.

This was the state of the game at the point at which this chapter opened. Seventeen for three had become twenty-four for three, and the hands of the clock stood at ten minutes past six. Changes of bowling had been tried, but there seemed no chance of getting past the batsmen's defence. They were playing all the good balls, and refused to hit at the bad.

A quarter past six struck, and then Psmith made a suggestion which altered the game completely.

"Why don't you have a shot this end?" he said to Adair, as they were crossing over. "There's a spot on the off which might help you a lot. You can break like blazes if only you land on it. It doesn't help my leg-breaks a bit, because they won't hit at them."

Barnes was on the point of beginning to bowl, when Adair took the ball from him. The captain of Outwood's retired to short leg with an air that suggested that he was glad to be relieved of his prominent post.

The next moment Drummond's off-stump was lying at an angle of forty-five. Adair was absolutely accurate as a bowler, and he had dropped his first ball right on the worn patch.

Two minutes later Drummond's successor was retiring to the pavilion, while the wicket-keeper straightened the stumps again.

There is nothing like a couple of unexpected wickets for altering the atmosphere of a game. Five minutes before, Sedleigh had been lethargic and without hope. Now there was a stir and buzz all round the ground. There were twenty-five minutes to go, and five wickets were down. Sedleigh was on top again.

The next man seemed to take an age coming out. As a matter of fact, he walked more rapidly than a batsman usually walks to the crease.

Adair's third ball dropped just short of the spot. The batsman, hitting out, was a shade too soon. The ball hummed through the air a couple of feet from the ground in the direction of mid-off, and Mike, diving to the right, got to it as he was falling, and chucked it up.

After that the thing was a walk-over. Psmith clean bowled a man in his next over; and the tail, demoralised by the sudden change in the game, collapsed uncompromisingly. Sedleigh won by thirty-five runs with eight minutes in hand.

Psmith and Mike sat in their study after lock-up, discussing things in general and the game in particular.

"I feel like a beastly renegade, playing against Wrykyn," said Mike. "Still, I'm glad we won. Adair's a jolly good sort, and it'll make him happy for weeks."

"When I last saw Comrade Adair," said Psmith, "he was going about in a sort of trance, beaming vaguely and wanting to stand people things at the shop."

"He bowled awfully well."

"Yes," said Psmith. "I say, I don't wish to cast a gloom over this joyful occasion in any way, but you say Wrykyn are going to give Sedleigh a fixture again next year?"

"Well?"

"Well, have you thought of the massacre which will ensue? You will have left, Adair will have left. Incidentally, I shall have left. Wrykyn will swamp them."

"I suppose they will. Still, the great thing, you see, is to get the thing started. That's what Adair was so keen on. Now Sedleigh has beaten Wrykyn, he's satisfied. They can get on fixtures with decent clubs, and work up to playing the big schools. You've got to start somehow. So it's all right, you see."

"And, besides," said Psmith, reflectively, "in an emergency they can always get Comrade Downing to bowl for them, what? Let us now sally out and see if we can't promote a rag of some sort in this abode of wrath. Comrade Outwood has gone over to dinner at the School House, and it would be a pity to waste a somewhat golden opportunity. Shall we stagger?"

They staggered.

Lightning Source UK Ltd.
Milton Keynes UK
UKHW041057201222
414211UK00001B/11